G. Raue, Johan

The Elements of Psychology

Anatiposi

G. Raue, Johan Gottlies Dressler

The Elements of Psychology

Reprint of the original, first published in 1871.

1st Edition 2023 | ISBN: 978-3-38212-662-9

Anatiposi Verlag is an imprint of Outlook Verlagsgesellschaft mbH.

Verlag (Publisher): Outlook Verlag GmbH, Zeilweg 44, 60439 Frankfurt, Deutschland
Vertretungsberechtigt (Authorized to represent): E. Roepke, Zeilweg 44, 60439 Frankfurt, Deutschland
Druck (Print): Books on Demand GmbH, In de Tarpen 42, 22848 Norderstedt, Deutschland

THE ELEMENTS OF PSYCHOLOGY

ON THE

PRINCIPLES OF BENEKE,

STATED AND ILLUSTRATED IN A SIMPLE AND POPULAR MANNER BY

DR. G. RAUE,

PROFESSOR IN THE MEDICAL COLLEGE, PHILADELPHIA;

FOURTH EDITION, CONSIDERABLY ALTERED, IMPROVED, AND ENLARGED, BY

JOHANN GOTTLIEB DRESSLER,

LATE DIRECTOR OF THE NORMAL SCHOOL AT BAUTZEN.

TRANSLATED FROM THE GERMAN.

Oxford and London:
JAMES PARKER AND CO.
1871.

NOTE BY THE TRANSLATOR.

THE translator of the present work found himself suddenly in want of a Manual of Psychology which should be at once systematic, intelligible, brief, plausible, and, above all things, suggestive. No English treatise seemed exactly to satisfy all these conditions, especially the last, and hence the *Lehrbuch der Psychologie* by Dr. Beneke was at first selected; but as it was found that there was neither time nor health to turn it into English soon enough for the purpose for which it was required, the compendium of the same author's theory by Raue and Dressler was substituted for it. The version was completed in a few weeks, and some competent judges to whom it was shewn, were pleased to express the opinion that it ought not to be confined to the narrow circle of students for whose use and benefit it was originally intended and executed: hence the publication of it.

The translator, however, desires it to be distinctly understood that he by no means identifies himself with Beneke's opinions. The determinism of the system, (for though a stout defender of what he calls Moral Freedom, Beneke is after all a determinist) —its mechanical and physical metaphors occasionally, perhaps often, taken for something more than mere figures of speech,—even its extreme simplicity, to mention no other reasons, might all be urged as objections to its truth. Still, be its defects what they may, it is well-deserving of study, and it would be difficult to mention a theory more ingenious, concatenated, and complete. That it does not solve all our puzzles, or that it fails totally to touch our gravest doubts and difficulties, is an objection which lies against it in common with all other systems whatever. It is a real advantage, however, if familiar facts, or facts supposed to be familiar, are presented to us in a new light; thought is necessarily stimulated, we get for a while out of the old groove in which we have been accustomed to move, and even if we recur to it, we feel strengthened and refreshed by the temporary change. This advantage will, it is hoped, be secured by most English readers who will take the trouble to master the psychological system, of which the present volume is a popular and faithful exposition. It was elaborated by Dr. Friedrich Eduard Beneke, (born at Berlin in 1798, where he died a Professor in the University in 1854,) and applied by him, with remarkable ingenuity, to the elucidation of Logic, Metaphysics, Ethics, Law, Politics, Mental Disease, and Education. His voluminous works appear to be but little known in this country. They are all valuable, and prove that it is possible to be even a German philosopher, and yet to write like a man of the world, simply, intelligibly, and with good temper. For Schelling, Hegel *et hoc genus omne*, and for the strange jargon which they too often affect, Dr. Beneke had a profound aversion,—an aversion, however, founded on a knowledge, and not, as is sometimes the case, on an ignorance of their productions; nor was it possible to be otherwise in one so imbued with the principles of Locke and other English philosophers of his school. But energetically opposed as he was to the magnificent absurdities of the Wissenschaftslehre of Fichte, to the Intellectual Intuition of Schelling, or the Dialectic of Hegel, Beneke had a watchful ear for the more sober utterances of German philosophy, and while steadily combating what he conceived to be their errors, he adopts much of the teaching of Kant, of Schleiermacher, of Jacobi, and especially of Herbart; yet he is no eclectic, and whether he adopts or rejects the thoughts of others, he has always a definite opinion of his own, which he never tires of presenting to us over and over again with unabated vigour, and with inexhaustible variety of expression.

Of the faithfulness of Dr. Raue's compendium as enlarged by Dressler[a], little need be said. It condenses the contents of many volumes, and puts the whole theory in such a light, that he must be blind indeed who cannot discern its outline and proportions. Like all philosophical works, it calls for some attention; but provided that is forthcoming, any one not naturally incapable of such studies will find himself able to understand the book, if he will only condescend to read it onwards from the beginning, and make free use of the cross-references with which it is studded. Those who indulge in the detestable practices of "dipping," or "skimming," need not expect to comprehend much of it.

As regards the translation, it may be observed that the speed with which it was made has left it a good deal rougher than it otherwise might have been. It is literal in almost all places, and the more important terms are represented as far as possible by the same English words, though not a few sentences have been rendered particularly clumsy in consequence. It is hoped and believed that the version is faithful, and that the author has not been made to say either more or less than he intended. It may be as well to notice that the term *Vorstellung* has been uni-

---

[a] The exact German title of the book is, Dr. F. E. Beneke's Neue Seelenlehre, für alle Freunde der Naturwahrheit in anschaulicher Weise dargestellt von Dr. G. Raue, Professor an der medicinischen Akademie in Philadelphia. Vierte Auflage. Mehrfach umgearbeitet, verbessert und vermehrt von Johann Gottlieb Dressler, Seminar-Director a. D. in Bautzen. Mainz, Verlag von F. H. Evler. (G. Faber'sche Buchhandlung.) 1865, 8vo. (pp. viii. and 263).

formly rendered by "notion." To have translated it by Sir William Hamilton's equivalent, "representation," would, it was found, have made many passages far less intelligible to an English reader than they are at present. The thing intended to be expressed is amply explained in § 10, and if any object upon principle to "notion" as a rendering of *Vorstellung*, they have merely to run their pen through the former word, wherever it occurs, and substitute any other which they prefer. The typographical peculiarities of the original have been closely adhered to: the words and notes in brackets are inserted by the translator.

OXFORD,
March, 1871.

PREFACE.

THE preface to the *fourth* edition of a book need not be lengthy. The following remarks may suffice.

The title[a] has been changed, because the treatise has completely outgrown the end for which it was originally intended, namely, to be a manual for national[b] schools. It is now a book for all who make any pretensions to education. The subject is treated with the same homely clearness as before, but the investigation into the nature of the human soul is carried further than it was in the three former editions. It is hoped that the work will on this account be deemed worthy in an increased degree of the favour which has been so abundantly shewn to it hitherto; for while the requirements of teachers have not been neglected, it may be used as a trustworthy guide to the new theory by every one who is interested in the all-important study of man's mental and spiritual nature. The book has already diffused a knowledge of that theory widely, and may now hope to spread it still further.

Professor Raue, the original compiler of the present treatise, has been kind enough to leave the preparation of a new edition of it entirely to me, and consequently I alone am responsible for the alterations and additions that have been made in it. They are so numerous, that I may venture to claim the book as wholly

---

[a] The former title ran thus: "Dr. Beneke's neue Psychologie nach methodischen Grundsätzen in einfach entwickelnder Weise für Lehrer bearbeitet von," &c. The present edition is also published by a different firm.

[b] [*Volksschulen.*]

my own. The general plan, originally sketched out by Dr. Raue, has been adhered to, because I was unable to propose a better; and the matter also, it need not be said, remains the same, for truth does not change as the fashions do. The only thing needful was greater precision and clearness of statement, and, here and there, somewhat fuller details; and in these respects all, I think, has been done that could fairly be required.

Accordingly, I again heartily commend to a candid public, the treatise of this excellent man, who has lately been appointed Professor in the Medical College, Philadelphia.

A translation of it into Flemish, by *J. Blockhuys*, Director of the Communal Schools at *Schaerbeek*, near Brussels, appeared at *Ghent*, in 1859.

DRESSLER.

BAUTZEN,
March, 1865.

CONTENTS.

PART I.

NOTIONS.

PART II.

CONATIVE POWERS.

PART III.

FEELINGS.

PART IV.

SUPPLEMENTARY REMARKS AND FURTHER DETAILS.

PART I.

NOTIONS.

§ 1. *Man's Senses.*

The sun shines; the tree is in flower; gold is yellow: this we *see.*

The bird sings; the dog barks; water murmurs: this we *hear.*

The stone is hard; down is soft; the mirror is smooth: this we feel by *touch.*

Vinegar is sour; honey is sweet; wormwood is bitter: this we *taste.*

Mould is musty; the rose fragrant; camphor pungent: this we *smell.*

(*a*) The needle pricks; the air is warm or cold; smoke makes one's eyes smart: this we *feel.*

(*b*) Hunger is painful; colic and gout are agonizing; thirst burns: this also we *feel.*

(*c*) A long walk tires the legs; protracted and rapid writing tires the arm; much talking or singing wearies our vocal organs: this too we *feel.*

Since we are able to see, hear, touch, taste, smell, and feel, man is said to have *six senses;* viz. *the sense of sight*, *of hearing*, *of touch*, *of taste*, *of smell*, and *of feeling.*

The reason why they are arranged in this order is explained below in § 8.

The note on § 46 explains why the sense of feeling is more appropriately called the *vital sense.* The other senses are called *organic*, because the powers of which they consist require the co-operation of special bodily organs, in order to be stimulated *from without.* Cf. § 75 at the end.

Can it be said that man has a *muscular sense?* See § 14 at the end.

All the senses just mentioned are *external:* the *internal senses* are treated of in § 77.

§ 2. *The Ground and Conditions of Seeing, Hearing, &c.*

A *dead* man *cannot* see, hear, touch, taste, smell, or feel, for he has no *soul;* hence whoever sees, hears, touches, tastes, smells, and feels, *must have a* soul.

Moreover, one who has fainted away, or is in profound sleep, has a soul, and yet neither sees nor hears, &c.

Again: there are persons in a morbid condition of soul, who though awake may be pricked with needles, burnt with hot iron, and yet not feel it; who do not hear the report of a pistol let off by their ears; who do not perceive the most irritating odours, notwithstanding that all their sense-organs are perfectly sound.

Many a brave soldier has been seriously wounded in the fight, and yet he has only noticed it when the battle was over.

Card-players are not unfrequently so absorbed in their game, that they neither see nor hear what is going on around them. So too, when ardently engaged in something which interests us, we do not notice what others are doing near us. A schoolboy does not hear what the master is saying, if his eyes are attracted by the tricks of a boy near him. In reading it often happens that we do not know what is on a page, which we have nevertheless read from top to bottom.

Consequently in order to see, hear, &c., it is not enough *to have a soul; that soul must direct its* attention[*] *to the things without it, if seeing, hearing, &c., is to be actual.*

Hence we deduce the following:

Because 1°. *without a soul*—when we are dead, no act of sense is possible; and

---

[*] The word 'attention' is here used in its very widest signification. Attention exists when the original powers in their as yet unconscious state meet their stimulants in such a way that a lasting union between the two is rendered possible (§ 4). In its narrower signification it is the *conscious* meeting of the homogeneous *Trace* (§ 6) already acquired and the external stimulant now operating. It is impossible, however, at this stage to go into further details on this matter; it will become self-evident by-and-by. See a note in § 71.

Because 2°. we only see, hear, &c., when our soul attends to the objects without us; or, as we may say, when it receives and appropriates external stimulants (§ 4), it follows *that the* soul *is the special* ground *of sense-acts:* i.e. those of seeing, hearing, &c.

The acts of the senses accordingly are acts of the soul itself, which however are only possible under the two following *conditions:*

(*a*) A man who becomes blind, no longer sees: one who becomes deaf, hears no longer: if one's finger is frostbitten, we no longer touch (feel): while we have a violent cold we cannot smell; and if the tongue is disordered, we either do not taste at all, or taste amiss, &c.

Therefore in order to see, hear, &c., *sound eyes, ears, &c.*—in brief, sound sense-organs, *are requisite.*

Yet it is not the eyes that see, the ears that hear, the finger that feels, &c.; *the soul* sees, *the soul* hears, &c. Eyes and ears are only instruments needful for those acts. In other words, the corporeal is not the *cause* of the so-called acts of sense—it is merely an assistant to, or help towards, sensation. Hence we may explain how it is that men occasionally, notwithstanding the soundness of their organs (cf. the examples above), do not see or hear, &c.; and conversely how the sensations thus hindered immediately return when the disordered organs of sense are cured—supposing, that is, that the soul is disposed to see, hear, &c.: on the other hand, an act of sense never takes place independently of the soul.

Therefore *sound sense-organs are the first* condition *on which the activity of the senses depends.*

Is it possible to produce the sound of a trumpet without a trumpet? or is it possible for this instrument to be deranged (stopped up or perforated), if the breath blown into it (like the soul) is to produce the intended sound? Moreover, as the foliage of a tree is caused by something very different from the branches and bark: as, however, sound branches and bark are indispensable conditions for the foliage, so there is a similar reciprocal action between body and soul.

(*b*) When it is dark I can see nothing, though my eyes may

be the best in the world, and though I may be ever so willing to do so: when nothing moves, I hear nothing, though my ear may be ever so acute, and my will ever so good: and however great my desire may be, I can neither smell, touch, nor taste the apple that hangs on the top of the tree. For

Things without us must be capable of acting on our senses, and must actually affect them if they are to be perceived by the soul: this is the second condition *for those activities of the soul which we call acts of sense, or sensation.*

The powers of sight, hearing, &c., in the soul do not reside merely in the organs of sense, but in the whole man, so that one cannot assign them any definite place. But as they reside in the sense-organs as well, they are there openly exposed as it were to impressions, and are *immediately* influenced by the latter. Cf. § 75 at the end.

§ 3. *Original Powers and Stimulants.*

As soon as it is born, a child, provided its sense-organs are sound, can at once see, hear, taste, &c.; only it is unconscious that it does so. Consequently it brings the powers of seeing, hearing, &c., along with it into the world. As yet it knows not father, mother, sister, &c.; it cannot distinguish between them: it can only do so at a later period. Still less is it able to speak, read, count, think, fancy, &c.; it is obliged to painfully learn all this as it gets older. Hence we call the soul's powers of seeing, hearing, &c., the *original powers*, i.e. the *first*, *primitive* powers innate in the soul [b], out of which all other psychical powers and forces are evolved. For in order to do any more than see, hear, &c., the child requires *special* faculties, and these it must first acquire—and they cannot be made out of nothing.

But however perfect its primitive faculties might be, the child

---

[b] Or, more correctly speaking, *of which the soul consists at birth*. The soul and what is innate in it are not two things. In like manner 'soul' and 'powers of the soul' are exactly the same thing. Man's psychical powers constitute his soul, just as the parts and atoms of the body compose and constitute his body: at the time of a child's birth these powers are less numerous than they are afterwards. See the next note.

could not perceive or apprehend if no objects from without affected them. (See § 2.) It can only *see* on condition that objects are *placed in the light*, and so operate as *visible* on the soul: it can only *hear* if there is a noise and the vibrations stimulate the faculty of hearing, &c.

All these operations of external things on the child necessary for seeing, hearing, &c., we call *stimulants*.

So that we may say that for seeing, hearing, touching, tasting, smelling, and feeling, there are required:

1°. *the original powers of the soul*, and

2°. *the stimulants of the external world*.

The latter are combined with the former so long as we are in the body, invariably through the medium of healthy *organs of sense*.

§ 4. *On the Union of Original Powers and Stimulants*.

If you hold something before a young child, it turns its eyes to look at the object, perhaps seizes at it with its little hands in order to touch it, and possibly brings it into contact with its mouth in order that it may perceive (apprehend) it the better (on more sides than one).

We look at a distant object, but are unable to make it out distinctly. In that case our faculty of sight strains eagerly after the few stimulants of light in order to suck in (as it were) at least all that there are.

We hear a noise: it is not perfectly perceptible: we, as it were, set our auditory powers* on the watch for the least stimulant of sound, in order to make quite sure of that much.

---

* Every sense possesses not one power, but several, which from the first exist *separately*. The proof that this is so will be given below. But without proof we may here assert that it is not one and the same power of feeling which I affect when, for example, I stick a needle first in the right, then in the left foot; then in the right, and afterwards in the left arm; next in the neck, &c.: and, in like manner, it is not one and the same power of taste that is affected when I take different grains of pepper, salt, &c., on to the tongue, just as it would be impossible for me to hear per-

Briefly: *our original powers do not receive the impressions (stimulants) of the external world passively, without exertion, but they strive and strain after them.* (Cf. § 23.)

I shew somebody a plant. Immediately his powers of sight strain after the stimulants of light which proceed from it: stimulant and primitive power unite, and he says, I *see* the plant.

A bird is singing his joyous song on a tree. My faculties of hearing are directed to it; and when the sound-stimulants proceeding from the bird are united with them, I say I *hear* the bird.

Which of these two sorts of paper is the smoother? You run the tips of your fingers over both until the soft stimulants proceeding from both are sufficiently united to your sense of touch, and then you say, I find *by touch* that this kind is the smoother.

Here you have a bit of sugar. Directly you put it on your tongue and break it up by chewing it, the stimulants unite with your powers of taste, and you say, I *taste* the sugar.

I hold a violet before somebody's nose. He will keep his head down over it until the fragrance (stimulants) exhaled from it has united with his powers of smelling. When that is done, he says, I *smell* the violet.

Take a nettle in your hand. The very moment your powers of feeling unite with the stimulants proceeding from it, you say, I *feel* a nettle.

For *seeing*, *hearing*, *touching*, *tasting*, *smelling*, and *feeling*, we also use the general expressions *feeling* or *perceiving*[d], and because this is effected through *the senses* (original powers) we

---

fectly distinct tones at the same time if I only had one power of hearing. What is implied if three distinct colours are seen at the same moment? If the power of feeling, for example, were one and one only, must it not feel every impression at once *everywhere*, and therefore all over the *whole* body over which it is extended? Here, too, it would be more correct to say that each sense *consists of* several powers.

[d] The difference between sensation and perception is explained in § 50. In the present place we cannot enter into further details.

call this feeling or perception *sensation*, or sensuous *perception:* or, in one general term, *sensuous apprehension*.

Accordingly, a sensuous feeling or perception is produced when the original powers of the soul unite with the stimulants of the external world, and hence we may say, *Sensuous feelings or perceptions are formed by the human soul in consequence of impressions or stimulants which reach it from without.* Law of the Appropriation of Stimulants.

§ 5. *On the Sensibility of the Original Powers to Impressions.*

There are people who perceive the smallest objects by sight, while others pass them by as if blind to their existence, and this too when they are not otherwise engaged.

In like manner we find persons who catch up and distinguish in a moment the faintest sound that falls upon their ear, while others close by do not hear it at all. Savages and uncultivated people in particular are remarkable for this acuteness of sight and hearing.

Many can find out by the sense of touch the smallest unevenness in a smooth object; others are incapable of doing so.

Some notice the smallest addition of seasoning in their victuals; with others a considerable quantity is necessary in order to strike their notice.

Many are rendered faint by a disagreeable smell; others are not in the least affected by it.

A good many are extremely sensitive to warmth and cold, to stuffy air, &c.; others feel the same impressions without inconvenience.

Amongst brutes also we find proofs that the receptive power of the senses is in the highest degree different. Everybody, for instance, knows what a keen sense of smell is possessed by a fox or a dog; what sharp eyes a hen or an eagle has, &c.; how acute is the ear of a cat, how dull the touch of so many of the larger brutes, &c.

Doubtless the construction and perfection of the bodily organs have a great influence here: the chief ground of those differences, so far as they are constant, depends however (both in man and brutes) on the different constitution of their original psychical powers. The bodily organs are formed with more or less perfection according to the peculiarities of these powers.

From all this we draw the following conclusion. The original powers are not all constructed alike. Thus in one man the powers of sight are fitter for, or more sensitive to, stimulants, in consequence of which they seize on very slight ones and unite them with themselves, whilst in others *stronger* stimulants are necessary to excite their psychical powers. And yet the *auditory powers* of the first may be duller, while he may perhaps have a more delicate *sense of touch* than one who hears acutely; and so on through all the senses. In proportion then as the original powers of this or that man, whether it be in one sense or another, are more apt or ready to receive these external impressions, in that same proportion do we ascribe to them a greater or less *sensibility to stimulants*. This is not anything *apart from* the original powers, it is *only a property of them*. The *special* original powers of *one and the same* sense do not differ in such a manner that, e.g. in me one power of hearing has a greater, another, a less capacity for receiving impressions of sound: these distinctions are only found generally in kinds of senses (in classes). The subject is pursued in further detail in § 80.

Each sense is a totality or class (system) of powers *each exactly like the other*; and this is what we mean when we speak of *systems of powers, systems of senses*. These systems, however, differ from each other in the peculiarity above described, as well as in some other respects.

The word 'sensuous' has two meanings: (a) *material*, as sensuous objects = material objects—sensuous impressions = material (external) impressions (stimulants); (b) *capable of receiving external impressions*. In the second signification only are the original psychical powers called sensuous, or powers of sense. Yet they are, and continue, *pure spiritual* powers; and hence a more accurate designation for them is *spiritual-sensuous* powers. They do not require the co-operation of the organs of sense when (as will be shewn below) they perform *purely internal* acts: they require these organs only for the purpose of receiving what comes from without. For details see § 75 at the end, and in particular § 81.

§ 6. *Trace.*

Somebody shows me a flower which I have never seen before to-day. As always is the case when I see anything, so now my original powers unite with the light-stimulants proceeding from it. What will be the consequence of this? If I am questioned about the plant to-morrow, I shall be able to recollect it with perfect distinctness, while another who has not seen it at all will know nothing whatever about it. The same result would follow if somebody sang me a song, or let me smell and taste some aromatic substance, or indeed with respect to any object which I apprehend by the senses of touch or feeling.

How does this happen? It is certain that the stimulants which proceed from all these objects and were united with my original powers must remain in them, i.e. in the soul. By this we are not to understand that particles of light, air, or odour, continue to exist in the soul *independently* or *in themselves* as they existed before that in the external world, but that they have become *incorporated with* or *subjected to* the original powers by which they were appropriated, and by that have become constituent parts of the soul, i.e. have become *psychical* elements. That this may be done without the introduction of 'matter' into the spiritual soul, as well as the mode in which it is done, is explained in §§ 81 and 82. By this appropriation of stimulants our original powers attain that definite development which corresponds to the objects affecting them: that object is represented, as it were, mirrored forth in them; and I am able to represent it to myself internally (to recollect it) although no stimulants may be now passing from it to my soul, when e.g. I am not seeing, hearing, &c.; and such an act is impossible to one whose original powers have not appropriated any stimulants from the object.

If these powers were lost when I no longer thought about the objects, or if the stimulants united with them were all to disappear, this internal repetition or recollection would be impossible. Only a small portion of the stimulant however disappears, and the *powers* can in no case be torn from the soul—

indeed they *are* the soul. Although therefore the product of an act of sense becomes lost to consciousness, yet the original powers and the stimulants united with them continue in their mutual connexion, and with powers so developed I can set the object before me internally almost as clearly as if I were actually perceiving it. All that happens in such a case is that the powers which had sunk out of consciousness are again brought into consciousness. This continuance requires no explanation, for it is tolerably self-evident that what has once been firmly connected must continue to exist in that connexion, unless the two elements are disconnected again (resolved into their elements); and as the separation of a closely connected whole hardly ever occurs, it follows that the (developed) powers with their contents cannot be lost, although they seem to disappear (cf. § 17), when we become unconscious of them. The only question is: What *deprives* them of consciousness and how do they recover it? For the answer see §§ 12 and 13.

Therefore, the *formed* primitive powers still continue to exist after they have sunk into the unconscious, i. e. have become unconscious; and in becoming so they do not lose the formation or development which they received. They have only lost (as will be shewn) their activity; and hence their consciousness, *which can only assert itself under excitement*, is for a season quenched (as it were arrested) until it is revivified, and returns on a fresh excitement of the power. This may be expressed as follows:—

Whenever external stimulants act on the original powers, **provided they do so with anything like completeness, a Trace** *of that stimulation remains in the human soul.*

Consequently, every such Trace consists of two elements: the stimulant itself is never a trace, but the original power considered as connected with the stimulant received and retained is called a trace.

Traces therefore are the formed original powers in their **unconscious** *mode of existence.*

It may be further observed, that not merely the original powers developed by external stimulants continue as Traces. The same thing occurs with every product formed in the human soul with any degree of perfectness, and consequently we shall in what follows meet with Traces, which owe their existence to other acts besides those of the bodily senses.

Again: in common language 'Trace' generally means only a small portion of what has taken place—a mark of it from which we may infer what has occurred, but which does not enable us to reconstruct, to reproduce it. Thus cinders are a trace, a mark of a fire: from them however you cannot renew the fire. In psychology on the other hand the word 'Trace' has a more extended meaning; here it indicates a product in which the occurrence itself continues in an arrested (latent,=concealed) manner, because its factors are to a greater or less extent preserved; and in proportion as they are so preserved the act may be internally repeated. The Trace therefore turns to an act, as the act turns to a Trace.

How *long* do such Traces continue in the soul? To this no definite answer can be given. This however seems clear, that if no special cause intervenes to destroy or change them, they must last as long as the soul itself: of this there are many striking examples. Cf. *Beneke's* 'Die neue Psychologie,' p. 126 sq.[a]

---

[a] The passage is this: "*Reil,* in his Theory of Fevers, reports the case of a peasant who during the paroxysm of fever declaimed Greek verses fluently: after his recovery he recollected that when a boy he had been instructed in that language along with the son of his clergyman, but in his healthy condition he knew nothing of Greek either before or after his illness.

"*Abercrombie* mentions a man born in France who, from living in England (which he had done from his earliest childhood), had entirely forgotten his native language: in consequence of an injury to the head followed by a violent fever he recovered his knowledge of it. In consequence of a similar accident a patient in St. Thomas's Hospital began to talk Welsh, which in his sound condition he had quite forgotten from not having spoken it for thirty years.

"A Roman Catholic peasant-girl (aged 25) during the paroxysm of a fever, began to declaim passages from Syriac, Chaldee and Hebrew works. She had been left an orphan as a child, and been taken into the house of a Protestant minister who was in the habit at set hours in the day of walking up and down a long passage and reading in a loud voice and with much emphasis out of his pet authors in those languages. The kitchen where the young girl was generally sitting unoccupied opened into this passage, and thus her whole attention had been directed to these strange and imposing sounds, and in consequence they had become deeply impressed upon her."

§ 7. *On the Tenacity of the Original Powers. Memory.*

Still there is a great difference between these Traces. Twenty persons see the same plant to-day. The same stimulants, therefore, affect the visual powers of all; and yet how different is the Trace left on the souls of each of them! The morning after, some will be able to give an exact description of the plant; others know nothing or little about it, and easily confound it with a different one. What is the reason of this? They say the latter did not notice it carefully. Very good: but what is the reason of *that?* Were they unwilling to do so? No. The reason is a very different one. A Trace is, as we have seen, nothing else than a power in which a stimulant has been received and *retained*, although the power, along with its stimulant, may have become passive and unconscious. The more closely it adheres to that power, or the more perfectly it is *held fast* by it, in exactly the same proportion is the Trace more perfect, and in the same proportion we are able afterwards to represent the object internally with more vivacity and clearness. *It is obvious*, by the way, *that larger objects consisting of divers parts, e.g. a tree, give rise not to one, but to as many Traces as there are distinct stimulants from it affecting the original powers.*

Hence, when experience proves that many men are unable to represent to themselves with such clearness as others objects which have equally affected both, we may infer that they do not retain such a firm hold over the stimulants as the others do, and the reason of this is not to be sought for in any difference in the stimulants themselves.

Hence, whether a man retains a clearer and more permanent hold over objects which have affected his senses than others do, or not, depends on the peculiar qualities of his *original powers*, and we hence attribute to the original powers *a greater or less degree of* tenacity *or* strength *according to the different degrees in which they* retain *the stimulants which they have received*[f].

---

[f] In the examples mentioned above, sensibility is a matter of considerable importance (§ 5); e.g. suppose the child had caught up only a very

What in common life we call a good or bad, a long or short, *memory* depends on this property of the original powers.

A memory is *good* or *long* when the stimulants appropriated by the original powers *remain* firmly fixed in them, so that afterwards we are able to represent *internally* to ourselves an object with all the clearness with which it appeared outwardly to the senses. A memory is *short* or *bad* when the external stimulants appropriated are *not held at all, or not held with sufficient firmness*, so that the original powers lose more or less the peculiar development wrought in them by the external stimulants. In that case the object cannot be represented internally with clearness without the help of fresh stimulants.

Consequently, memory is not a particular power *beside* and *distinct from* the original powers, it depends simply and solely on a *property* possessed by them in consequence of *which they* hold fast *to a greater or less degree the stimulants which they have received.* Briefly, it consists in the special amount of their *tenacity*[s].

§ 8. *Gradations of the Original Powers in Respect of their Tenacity.*

Somebody shews us a beetle, which we have never seen before. Directly after he mentions a peculiar name, sounding like nothing we have heard before.

---

few stimulants emanating from the plant, he would not be able to describe it *accurately* even if those few were retained in extremely firm connexion with his original powers. But supposing him to possess the necessary amount of language, he must be able to describe that little correctly. If we suppose him incapable of doing so, we are justified in inferring that the stimulants were not retained with sufficient firmness by the child's original powers because the latter were too weak to do so. In many cases firm connexion is wanting because the act of apprehension was defective, i.e. too faint and too fleeting. See the preceding section.

[s] For details see § 75, where we shall have to speak of the case where we retain with firmness that which has not been produced by the reception of external stimulants, and also shew how this derivative memory is to be accounted for.

Next day we are asked about the object, and its name. Which of the two shall we remember with most ease?

Unquestionably the beetle, which we *saw*: the word which we *heard*, as a rule, we should not remember.

Having experienced this frequently, we generally write down names, by which means they are more exactly imprinted on our minds the more deliberately we do it, and thus we retain them so firmly that we no longer need to look at the word we have written. How is this to be accounted for? Why does everybody in general retain a clearer remembrance of what he has seen than of what he has heard? Does not the proverb say 'One eye is better than two ears?' From what has been already said we know this much about it:—

We know that when an external stimulant is actually united to an original power a *Trace* is retained in the soul. (§ 6.) This trace is *more perfect* in proportion as a greater amount of the stimulant is *retained*—in short, in proportion as the original power is more *retentive*. (§ 7.)

If then, as appeared above, a *visible object* is *more firmly* fixed in the soul than an *audible one*, it follows that the power of sight must be *more retentive* than that of *hearing*; and that is the reason why we take better note of a word which we have *seen* written than of one which we have only *heard*.

'No!' it may be objected, 'that is not the reason: but what we gain through two senses we hold as it were *twice over*, and therefore with greater firmness. What right have you to infer that sight must be more retentive than hearing? All that follows is that the visible and the audible in some way or other mutually support each other.'

But certain as it is that such a mutual support is real, still that does not explain why everybody would sooner *see* an object than *hear* it described, or why the most uneducated man is convinced that he shall retain a *simple* visible impression with more certainty than one simply audible—and in consequence of which he always prefers seeing to hearing. The fact is comprehensible when we reflect that while sight gives us *things*, hearing only gives us *signs* of things, and that signs without a knowledge of the thing signified are valueless. Besides, the sign requires to be supported by the thing if it is to be *permanently* retained; and as we are able to form a more perfect image by sight, as it gives us in general a higher enjoyment of life than is the case with hearing, every one would sooner part with the sense of hearing than with that of sight, if a cruel fate required him to give up one of them.

This superiority of sight explains several phenomena, e.g. a child when it hears the clock strike turns its head to *see* it as well: when we are at church we want to *see* the preacher as well as hear him. The visual powers not only form *more perfect* Traces than those of hearing, but such Traces of objects have in themselves more value as representations than those derived from mere signs of things. Signs which we can *see* acquire by that something of the essence of the thing, and when apprehended they become rooted in powers of more decided retentiveness.

Blind persons find their way about by *touch*. Their tactual perceptions are so clear that they are able accurately to distinguish coins, faces, and other tangible objects. And this is possible only because this sense forms Traces with some important completeness, and it must therefore possess a retentiveness sufficient to enable it to do so.

When a blind man recovers his sight he gradually gives up touching objects: he is satisfied with *visual perceptions* of them, just as all who enjoy that sense from their birth neglect the sense of touch because they find that the perceptions of sight are *clearer* and *more definite*.

Hence it follows that the powers of *sight* have a stronger retentiveness than those of *touch*.

What I have once *seen*, *heard*, or *handled*, I can afterwards see, hear, and touch (feel) internally almost as perfectly as if the former stimulants of light, hearing, and touch were operating on my senses. Take your absent *relations* for instance. You can see and hear them internally almost as clearly as if they were actually standing before you and talking to you.

Now think of the taste of *sugar*. It tastes sweet, you say.

Very good! but represent to yourself the taste of it as though you had at this moment a bit of it on your tongue. You will succeed but very imperfectly in doing so.

What is *the smell of coffee?* For this odour we have not so much as a special name. *To smell of, to have an odour, to stink*—these are almost all the words not figurative that we possess to indicate odours.

And what do we chiefly think about when sugar, coffee, &c. are mentioned? About their colour, shape, &c.—therefore about that which we have perceived by our more *powerful* and *retentive* senses. Our sensations of the taste and smell of such objects are associated with our other sensations of them: and without the help of these more retentive senses we should have but very obscure representations of things which we can merely taste and smell.

Lastly, why is nobody able to recall the *heat* or *cold*, or the *toothache*, which he experienced, with the same vividness as if they were actually now present? Why has everybody at the best a faint and imperfect feeling of them?

The reason is the same as that mentioned above. *The powers of taste, smell, and feeling, are too* weak, *too much wanting in retentiveness;—they do not retain their stimulants with sufficient* firmness *to enable those traces to be left behind which are necessary for reproducing the object internally as if it were now present to our senses.*

Since the powers of sight, hearing, and touch possess a greater retentiveness than those of taste, smell, *or* feeling, *the former are called* higher, *the latter* lower *senses. Touch can only be reckoned among the* lower *senses in the case of those who can see, and who therefore cultivate the sense of touch slightly, if at all.*

In all mentally healthy men the retentiveness of the original powers exists in the above order: in all, sight is the strongest, feeling the weakest. (Compare § 1.) As to the immediate impressions of things, it seems indeed that one sense is just as strong and retentive as another; but this is accounted for by the sensitiveness which in all the senses allows weak as well as strong impressions to be made. The degree of their retentiveness, however, can only be measured by the permanence of the impressions so made.

No brute comes into the world with the same original powers (*senses*) as men possess, *and consequently even at birth the souls of men and brutes are totally different.* Though many brutes surpass men in the sensitiveness and vivacity of their sensitive powers, still the noblest brutes, like the elephant, horse, dog, &c., do not possess that *retentiveness* in any of their senses which man does in those of sight and hearing. They retain what they have seen or heard with about the same perfectness that men retain what they have tasted or smelt. Hence it is that the cultivation of brute souls ceases after they have by the guidance of man reached with pain and difficulty a few of the lower degrees of improvement. Left to themselves they never advance. Compare § 80 at the end.

§ 9. *The Similar and Allied unites with the Similar and Allied.*

We have all seen a good many kinds of birds. When I mention *dove*, why does no one think of *sparrow?* I say *bench*, and nobody recalls *table;* I shew a *knife*, and no one says, That is a *fork*. Touch this stone; will you say it is *soft?*

Suppose I tried to convince a child that sugar tastes bitter and salt sweet; that a rose has a choking and hemlock a refreshing smell; that the warmth of spring is painful and a prick with a needle pleasant. He laughs and thinks to himself, 'I know better. I might be persuaded that it is so had I never *tasted* sugar or salt, never *smelt* a rose or hemlock, or never *felt* spring warmth or the prick of a needle.' But all this he *has done*, and traces of all that he has *seen*, *heard*, *touched*, remain behind in his soul. (§ 6.) If he *sees*, *hears*, &c., the same objects again, he gains a new apprehension which leaves a fresh trace, in case, that is, an original power was not excited too faintly and momentarily; for all seeing, hearing, touching, &c. is (be it well noted) never directly rendered possible by the traces left, but solely *because an empty* (unemployed) *sense-power* (original power) *receives the stimulant*, with which, if sufficiently stimulating, it unites, so that it becomes a similar trace if the object producing the *impression* is like. Now what will happen? Will the fresh trace remain solitary and alone in the soul, or will it connect itself with the traces already there resembling it, or with those which do not resemble it? It unites only with those like itself. This is clear from the fact that on any impression being made we always think of the like which we have already within: the present perception comes to us therefore as one already known; it only appears to us new when there are no traces like it already existent there with which it can associate itself. I pronounce the word *hare* to somebody who only knows English, and instantaneously the stimulating sounds of the word unite with the traces which he has retained from former hearings of the word. Had I uttered the word *lepus* he would have regarded me with astonishment, for those sounds could be connected with nothing resembling them in his soul; and the same would be the case with *alauda:* whereas say *lark*, and the traces immediately operate, he recognises something before known, the fresh sound-stimulants and the old ones resembling them coalesce [h].

In the notions which we owe to the senses of sight, touch, and taste we meet with this same union of the like. Look at this *plate*. Do you think of a window? Touch this rough *stone:* what kind of traces are excited in you by it? Certainly not those of *soft* or *smooth*, but those of *hard* and *rough*, although you possess the former as well as the latter within. Taste this *cherry*, smell this *pink*, hold your hand to this *warm stove*, and you certainly will not think of *bitter*, *mouldy*, or *cold*. Things however which we see for the first time, words heard for the first time, fruits tasted for the first time &c. we call *strange;* we do not *recognize* them, because the new perception finds no answering traces within us.

---

[h] Do not confound notions of words with notions of things for which they are the names. The former reside exclusively in the sense of hearing, the latter in other senses as well (in fact, things produce very different effects on the soul), and whilst the former consist of our powers of hearing and sound-stimulants, the latter are composed of stimulants and totally different powers from the others. That they arouse each other is not therefore to be explained from the nature of their constituent parts; it is caused by particular associations whereby *dissimilar* forms are connected together. On this see § 38.

Accordingly, we may and must say that—

In the human soul everything that completely resembles another ites with it, fuses into one whole (form)[1].

Moreover:

I was at the annual fair. A person whom I did not know ne up to me, held out his hand, and said in a hearty tone: ow glad I am to see you again!' I looked at him full of asishment, and enquired to whom I had the honour of speak-;? He then saw that he had made a mistake. 'I beg your rdon,' said he, 'I thought you were an old friend of mine: you extremely *like* him.' The same thing has no doubt happened most people.

Little children who have not yet experienced the like of what now presented to them use the analogous in its place: hence y call shillings, sovereigns, sixpences, flat buttons, '*pennies;*' rything hairy and soft is a '*pussy cat;*' clarionettes, hautys, flutes, are '*whistles;*' all men whom they do not know are *apa,*' women '*mama,*' &c. Even grown-up people talk about *doctor,*' which includes very different persons—surgeons, veinary doctors, &c.

Such expressions also as 'this feels, tastes, smells, *like* this or it,' prove *that in the human soul* analogous *stimulants* (*imssions*) *unite with* analogous *traces already formed.*

Hence:

What arises in the human soul by sensuous apprehension unites a whole, *in* one *form, provided the several elements are* e *or* analogous. Speaking figuratively therefore, we say ey coalesce,' 'fuse with each other;' and the reason is, *they ract each other. Law of the Mutual Attraction of Similars.*

Hence is explained how and why the primitive sensations of the child st gradually harden into *perceptions,* or into what in the following agraph are called *notions.*

---

[1] Every *individual* trace is of course a something formed (after birth), l therefore a psychical form: by a Form however we generally undernd a something composed of *several* traces, and in that sense we shall erally use the word.

§ 10. *Rise of Consciousness; Notions.*

The whole activity of the newborn soul is confined to this: it forms sensations or apprehensions by uniting external stimulants with its original powers; in short, *it apprehends sensuously* (i.e. through the senses). (§ 4[k].)

No one is able to remember the first apprehensions of sense formed in his soul. No one's consciousness reaches so far back as that. The newly-born child sees, hears, &c., it is true, as the grown man does, i.e. external stimulants are united with its original powers, as they are with those of the adult; but the child *knows* nothing of that: its sensations or apprehensions are all of them as yet *unconscious.*

How do they become *conscious?*

How this is managed we have experienced more than once. When we first went to school, the teacher showed us, let us say, the letter B. We apprehended it (§ 4), and *a trace* of it was left (§ 6). But were we at once clearly conscious of the letter? Unfortunately we were not, as was proved when we were asked about it the next day. What did the teacher do? He made us look at it repeatedly and carefully, and pronounce its name after him; we gained new apprehensions of it, and they all united themselves with the first trace which was left by it (§ 9). At length we became clearly conscious of it: though in other children whose original powers were not so strong as ours (§ 7) it did not yet become perfectly clear. The teacher, therefore, shewed them it again and again, until all had gained a clear consciousness of it. He treated the other letters in the same way; and the result is that we are so fully *conscious* of all the letters of the alphabet, that our notions of them will certainly never be obscured as long as we live.

---

[k] 'To apprehend'=to seize upon, take up; 'comprehend'=understand. It is only in the developed soul that apprehension can be an intelligent, a clearly conscious act; not that it is always so even there; why? the reason will appear with greater clearness in what follows. [A note of more consequence to the German than to the English reader, since it turns upon the difference between *auffassen* and *fassen.*]

Some children have to learn a tune, and have already learnt many. How do they set to work? The teacher begins by singing to them a few notes slowly and clearly, and the pupils sing them after him. The process is repeated again and again. Then a whole series of notes are similarly repeated, until the whole tune is learned. Scholars soon notice that a tune of which they at first knew nothing becomes, by repetition, more and more conscious; and at last they can sing it from beginning to end without the aid of the teacher.

Now how did the consciousness of all the letters and of tunes arise in the souls of the scholars?

Simply by this: they formed numerous apprehensions of them and consequently many traces.

The same has been found to be the case with grown-up persons who were born blind, and who have recovered their sight by a successful operation. At first they did not in the least know what they saw. All was obscure and irrecognizable; nothing offered itself to their eyes as determinate and distinguishable; although they had a clear consciousness of what they *heard* or *touched*. In proportion, however, as they accumulated more traces of the same objects by repeated impressions of light, in the same proportion did they learn to see the clearer, and at last they beheld them with full and distinct consciousness.

But since original powers are one and all at first unconscious, how does each *single* original power which is necessary for every single apprehension gain its consciousness?

Answer: *These unconscious powers possess from the very first an inherent capacity of becoming conscious, which capacity becomes actual, as soon as they are excited by stimulants, and the two are united:* this is the sole condition of consciousness.

Therefore *original powers and stimulants, both of which are in themselves unconscious, yield consciousness by their union:* such is the psychical law here predominant. *Consciousness, however, depends more on the powers than on the stimulants.*

How was it that consciousness became stronger and stronger in the examples given above?

Because each of these apprehensions was retained in the soul, and in consequence of their likeness they coalesced into **one whole.** For each particular apprehension has its own consciousness, only it is very faint; and though extinguished for the moment it is not really lost when the act of apprehension is converted into a trace (§ 6). *The greater the number of such similar traces that come together, the stronger must be the consciousness of the whole* (form) *so formed, when it is afterwards excited in all its parts.* Further details in §§ 12 and 71.

He who has seen an animal *ten* times obtains a clearer consciousness of it than one who has only seen it *once*, *twice*, or *thrice*; supposing, that is, that the original powers of both are equally strong, &c.

He who has heard a tune *ten* times will be more clearly conscious of it than one who has only heard it *once* or *twice*; provided the original powers of both are equally strong, &c.

The original powers which exist side by side with the traces naturally remain completely unconscious until they are developed by the appropriation of stimulants, and thenceforward continue to exist as traces.

Why then is repetition so useful? Why must a pianoforte or violin player repeat the movements of his hands and fingers many hundred, indeed many thousand times, in the same way before the needful dexterity is acquired? Because here, too, all improvement depends on the formation of traces.

When so many like traces have been united into **one** *form that we become clearly conscious of the object from which the stimulants proceeded, we say that we have got a* **notion** (*representation*) *of the object, or that we can* **form a notion of it**[1].

---

[1] This notion is called a *perception* or *intuition* when it owes its present consciousness to the presence of an object now acting; it is called, on the other hand, an *imaginary notion* [Einbildungsvorstellung] (=a reproduced notion) when it is called up into consciousness not by the object itself, but by something else. (Details in § 75.) Moreover the term notion [Vorstellung] is applied not merely to the forms of the kind described produced by external objects, but also to the concepts and perceptions of our own self-consciousness. See § 15 and §§ 77—79.

The more receptive of *finer* stimulants our original powers are, and the greater the firmness with which they appropriate and retain them, the more *exact* must be the notions which we gain of the object (§§ 5 and 7).

With the rise and strengthening of consciousness there arises what is called *mind*, using that term in a vague and general sense. 'The mind awakens' only means that *consciousness arises*; for where no clear consciousness is produced, e.g. in the souls of brutes and idiots, no one talks of 'mind.' The healthy human soul is spiritual-mental, i.e. one capable of *clearer, more definite, more comprehensive* consciousness than the powers of brutes are susceptible of; and this consciousness from the first, and up to a certain period, is necessarily developed with greater or less perfection. By education, instruction, and careful self-culture this development may be infinitely continued, since the formation of new powers never ceases. The *more tenacious* these powers are (§ 7), the stronger and clearer is the consciousness formed in them, and hence may be explained the fact, that with man the mental and spiritual is produced mainly out of what he gains through the eye and ear: this strength and retentiveness proves to be the main source of his *higher* consciousness, of his spirituality or mind. The souls of brutes are not spiritual and mental because their powers are so much less retentive than those of man. For a somewhat narrow meaning of the words mind and spirit, see below, in the note to § 69. Compare especially the end of § 79.

Has the human soul a consciousness independent of these forms,—has it therefore a *general* consciousness? See below, § 71.

§ 11. *Relation of Stimulants to the Original Powers.*

Whether a notion arises in the soul with *clearness* or the reverse depends also upon something else as well.

I arrived in the evening twilight in a strange neighbourhood. Somebody afterwards asked me to describe it accurately: I was obliged to say that I was unable to do so, for when I got there it was too dark to see it. I had, it is true, united (light) stimulants with my original powers, only they were too *faint*. Suppose I were to be often in the same place, but always *when it was twilight*, what would be the invariable result?

We hear a word quite unknown to us pronounced at a tolerable distance, so that it falls very faintly on the ear. We are asked, What was that word? 'We don't know.' It sounded like this. The sound (stimulant of hearing) was too weak. And if we were to hear that word a hundred times, but always as faintly, we should never get a clear notion of it.

Now suppose we visit a place *in broad daylight*, or hear a strange word *distinctly pronounced*, and we shall have a *clear* notion of both. The reason of this difference is obvious. In the former case the stimulant was too *little*; it did not sufficiently, so to say, *fill* the original powers: in the present case there is as much stimulant as they *require* for their modification: they appropriate it and retain it; and as the magnet is strengthened when you give it as much to carry as is suitable for it, so the original powers are perfected and strengthened by a full degree of stimulant. In such a case a perfect trace remains; and the more there are of such *perfectly formed* similar traces that unite in one whole because single original powers are excited fully and perfectly by the same object, in that same degree does the notion of the object perceived become *clearer* [m].

Hence we learn that:

If a clear notion is to arise in our soul, there must be sufficient stimulant *from without, i.e. there must be as much stimulant as the original powers require for their formation, or, so to say, for their satisfaction:* too little *stimulants yield* no *notion, or at best only* an obscure one.

If we gather together all that is required to produce a clear notion, we arrive at the following result:

1. *The original powers must naturally possess sufficient* power *to retain the stimulants received* (§ 7).

2. *Like apprehensions must* unite *along with traces of the same kind* into one whole; and

3. *The external* stimulant *must be* sufficient, *i.e. such as the original powers require for their perfect* formation, *or as it were to fill them* [n].

---

[m] The remaining modes in which stimulation may be effected may be more suitably discussed in § 24.

[n] The latter expression is purely *figurative*, for our psychical powers are not hollow: still it is a fact that they take up a greater or less *quantum* of stimulants, and assimilate them, and that they are never satisfied and perfected by too small a *quantum of them*. Compare § 24. Such figures of

It is self-evident that no sharp limit could be laid down where we could say that this amount of external stimulant is, and that is not, sufficient. This obviously depends on the different degrees of sensibility possessed by the original powers (§ 5) in this or that man. In every instance, however, the law holds, that an exactly suitable amount of stimulant strengthens our powers, whilst too little makes them listless, too much over-excites and weakens them.

§ 12. *Perpetual Alternation of Consciousness and Unconsciousness.*

Suppose a child has reached the age of ten, it has already obtained, in the way described, more notions than it could possibly count. No one knows the number of his own notions; and, fortunately for us, they are never all present to consciousness at the same moment. For what confusion must arise if only twenty different notions were to start into consciousness at once! When reading a book we have only those notions present which are necessary in order to understand it. All others are unconscious. When a man takes up a sum to do, he ceases to think of what he was just reading; he only thinks of the *numbers* which he wants at the moment: and so on in all other cases.

We are never conscious of more notions[a] *than we require*[b] *at the moment: of all the rest we are unconscious*, i.e. they are not conscious.

What was consciously present to us at one moment we very likely cease to think about the next; and during sleep, when not dreaming, all our notions are in an unconscious state, i.e. they are all unconscious.

Accordingly there is a perpetual coming and going amongst our notions. Those that were conscious become unconscious,

---

speech are, moreover, used in everyday life when we say: his heart is 'filled' with sorrowful care, with fear, &c.; his understanding is 'full' of errors.

[a] We cannot here speak of our feelings and acts of will where consciousness alternates in exactly the same manner; they will be considered afterwards.

[b] The fact that, as well as the reason why, all the notions which we require are not always consciously present, cannot be discussed till a later paragraph. Compare §§ 31 and 76.

those that were unconscious again become conscious. How does this happen?

In § 10 we explained how consciousness *arises* out of the original unconscious state of the powers; out of something therefore which had up till then not been conscious. Consciousness thus arising is therefore the opposite of the *not yet conscious.* Traces, on the other hand, are, as such, unconscious and latent also; yet a developed consciousness is implied in that kind of unconsciousness, and it is not actual only because an exciting cause is absent (§ 6). Hence when they again rise into consciousness, we have a form of consciousness with a completely different opposite, viz. mere quietude from, or absence of, excitement. The renewed consciousness of these traces is accordingly no new product; it is only a repeated (reproduced) consciousness, the renovation of former consciousness. The condition of this renewal is excitement, which implies the presence of exciting elements. Hence

If we are to become conscious of anything afresh *the Traces already formed must be excited by becoming united to external stimulants.*

Accordingly, the moment we hear the bird's song, the notion 'bird' starts into consciousness. I should never at the moment I write have thought of a carpenter, if there had not been one thumping and hammering outside. (Cf. § 9.)

The bird and the carpenter I have already *seen*, and consequently my notions of both have been produced by *stimulants of light* affecting my *powers of sight* and afterwards continuing in those powers in the shape of Traces. At the moment, they are excited by stimulants of *sound*, that is, by *dissimilar* stimulants; whereas in other cases they are excited by *similar* stimulants. I only require to see the bird and the carpenter, and I should immediately become conscious of them both afresh, but then by stimulants of light. When I read a book the stimulants of light proceeding from the letters affect my soul, and by that means objects that I have seen, or heard, or tasted, or touched, &c., are excited into consciousness; yet the present stimulants (the letters) are at any rate different from the earlier ones through which I originally gained those notions (the notions of the letters themselves excepted). Hence it follows that the external stimulants by which Traces already formed are again brought into consciousness may be either *similar* or *dissimilar*.

But how do *conscious* notions become *unconscious?*

This must be produced by a similar but opposite process.

If notions are brought into consciousness = excited by being united to fresh stimulants, we must conclude that when they become unconscious the reverse must take place; i.e. a part of the fresh stimulant must be *separated from* these notions, *must disappear* from them. In that case the notion ceasing *to be excited* becomes *unconscious.* A similar effect is produced by unemployed void original powers. (See the following section.)

We have seen what is the reason of the disappearance of stimulants in §§ 7 and 8. We there discovered that

The original powers, owing to their different degrees of tenacity, *retained the stimulants received by them, some in a greater, some in a less degree;* to which we must now add that even under the most favourable circumstances some stimulants are inevitably lost. *The Law of the Disappearance of Stimulants.*

Whether these vanished stimulants completely disappear *from* the soul or not will be examined by-and-by.

§ 13. *Second Manner in which the Unconscious in the Soul acquires Consciousness and again loses it.*

I am sitting alone in my room. It is dark and perfectly still = no stimulants from without are acting on me. Is it impossible for me *to be conscious* of any notions?

Certainly not. I may be conscious of many. Very often in such solitude notions come tearing in one after the other.

(*a*) *Without my willing it,* I fall to thinking of my past life, of the places I have seen, the men with whom I have associated, of ways and means to plans the execution of which will require me now to save up against the future, &c.

(*b*) Besides this, however, notions come to me which *I will* to recall. For instance, *I will* to bring before my mind's eye the lovely groups of rocks in the Saxon Switzerland, and they rise up before me, although no external stimulant from them was acting upon my soul. You, dear reader, have the same power. Choose some object to think about which is not present to you, and from which, therefore, no stimulant can act on you. (The house of your friend, villages, cities, plants that you have seen.)

Therefore notions existing unconsciously in the soul must be capable of being excited into consciousness by something else besides external stimulants.

What is that something?

If it does not come from without, it must be in the soul. As yet, however, we have discovered nothing in the soul except original powers *modified* by the stimulants which they have received (Traces), and *empty, unmodified* original powers. Cf. §§ 3 and 4. Is there anything else in the soul?

We shall shew in §§ 30 and 31 that, besides the stimulants which continue to exist in the *Traces*, there are also stimulants contained in the *unmodified* original powers, which we may call *free* or unappropriated stimulants, and that the *involuntary* excitement of notions may be produced by them (therefore by *internal* stimulants) just as well as by *external* ones. The example mentioned under (*a*) may be explained on this principle: for the present, however, we shall not discuss them further. What is to be said of *voluntary* excitement, which, everybody knows, can only proceed *from within?*

I reflect in the evening (because *I will* to do so) for a long time in complete solitude on a certain object, = a mass of notions which were unconscious are for a long time *excited* (into consciousness), and that too *without the help of external stimulants.* After a time I find it impossible to continue my reflections. I observe that what excited these notions in me must have *diminished.* So I go to bed and fall asleep. In the morning I attack the same object in the same solitude (it is winter time and not yet light) again, and I find that the notions in answer to my will recur to consciousness with double vivacity and freshness.

This leads me to observe that what excited them into consciousness must have been *repaired* during sleep. During that time no *external stimulants* entered my soul; therefore *original powers* must have been formed in the soul during sleep (see § 82), which now *excite* these latent notions *into consciousness*. I infer this from the fact that the excitement is not *involuntary*, but *voluntary*, obtained by effort; the night before it was impossible to effect anything when the void and unemployed original powers (these also are *active*, see § 4,) had decreased.

In accordance with the results hitherto arrived at there are therefore two ways in which *unconscious* notions may be brought into *consciousness* from within, and therefore be *excited*:

1°. *internal stimulants* resident in the *unmodified* original powers meet with these notions (find them out) and unite with them, and

2°. *original powers as yet unstimulated*, formed by the soul mainly during sleep, which also attach themselves to the stimulated original powers (notions). *These, like the internal stimulants, may again break loose from such notions, in which case these notions become latent.* But in all this nothing actually leaves the soul. See § 31.

These two kinds of internal exciting elements are also called elements of consciousness [Bewusstseinselemente] or movable elements.

As already observed, the former kind of excitement is *involuntary*, the latter *voluntary*. The result of both is more or less *uncertain*; whilst *involuntary* excitement produced by external stimulants is always quite *certain* in its operation. For details on this see § 72.

When psychical forms are excited into consciousness out of their unconscious condition we say 'they are reproduced,' or that they are 'reproductions.' It appears from what has been said above that such expressions ought not to be understood as asserting that these psychical forms *arise* afresh: are we to suppose that the consciousness of them does so? No! rather that consciousness is restored to freedom—it becomes again active, for if once obtained it is never lost again. See §§ 6, 10, 12, and below § 71.

§ 14. *Vivacity of the Original Powers and its influence in rendering Notions conscious.*

Somebody brings a sheet of pictures on which a number of familiar every-day objects are depicted, and there are twelve of us who want to look at it. He unrolls it, we all fix our attention on it, and directly he whisks it away from before our eyes.

He now asks, 'What were the things represented on it?' Some are able to describe several; others confess that they have no distinct knowledge of any of them. What is the cause of this? *Some must certainly have been able to see* **quicker** *than the rest.*

We notice the same thing with people reading. Some require time to look over a whole line, others catch it up in a moment.

We catch stimulants quickest through hearing. Let any one think how rapidly the several sounds, syllables, and words succeed each other in talking, and yet we do not miss one of them.

With what rapidity do the notes in a piece of quick music follow each other, and yet we detect them all.

No doubt there are differences in this respect between different men, some hear quicker than others; yet on the whole the sense of hearing is in all men the quickest. As to the degree in which this may possibly depend on the bodily organs, see the middle of § 5.

To the qualities therefore hitherto attributed to the original powers, viz. *sensitiveness* (§ 5), and *retentiveness* (§ 7), we must add **Vivacity (Quickness)**, i.e. their *efforts* follow with greater or less rapidity, as we have already seen was the case with them in seizing stimulants[a].

---

[a] The soul at the very moment of birth, before it has received any external impressions, when therefore it is *objectively* void [has acquired nothing from the outer world], still possesses a very important content in these three qualities of its original powers, to which must be added its innate laws of development, laws which we shall gradually become completely acquainted with in the course of this work. Two souls acted on by the same objects must be very differently developed, if the *sensibility*,

This vivacity exists in a lower degree in the original powers of the other senses. Touch and the muscular sense (on the latter see the end of the present section) appear to possess it in the highest degree; and it is notably manifested in the muscles of the fingers of practised pianoforte or violin players, in rapid writers, pillow-lace makers, &c., in a degree which almost equals the quickness of hearing. Stimulants of taste, smell, or feeling, if of different kinds and succeeding each other rapidly, no one can seize and distinguish with accuracy. This class of original powers is naturally far slower and sluggish in operation.

We must go a step further; for the *vivacity* of the original powers is reflected *internally*.

We find men who are all life. They not only seize with extraordinary quickness all that meets their eyes and ears, but their internal changes also are very rapid, which would be im-

---

tenacity, and *vivacity* of their respective original powers are different. If sensibility is low, little will be taken up; if not tenacious, what has been apprehended is lost again; if slow and sluggish, the elaboration and assimilation of what has been preserved must be a very slow business. Therefore external agencies affecting the original powers can exist in them and be there elaborated, only so far as the nature of those powers allows; the qualities in question, and especially *tenacity* and *vivacity*, are impressed on all that the soul receives, and give it a permanent subjective character, which, however insignificant it may appear at first, must increase as the process of development goes on; for as traces are multiplied this subjective impress is multiplied to infinity. Is it true, then, that the soul is (as has been asserted) at birth '*an unwritten tablet*' (*tabula rasa*)? Certainly not: it can only be called so as respects the *objective*, not as regards the *subjective*. Objects inscribe themselves upon it not as on a dead passive wall; for the soul is not a dead thing passively receiving impressions from without: it is something instinct with life, which necessarily imparts its own character to the impressions which it receives. Compare §§ 4, 23, and following, especially § 80. The reason why brutes never attain to human development is that their original powers have not the *tenacity* which is possessed by those of man.

When, therefore, in the course of this book we talk of 'void' unemployed original powers, we mean by the expression those which have not yet taken up anything *objective*—anything from without, or which have done so and afterwards lost it.

possible if their original powers were not extremely lively. The notions which they have already *gained* are perpetually rising into and passing out of consciousness, as though one were chasing the other. This characteristic is apparent in their talk and in all that they do. We can see it in their very eyes. No other property belonging to our powers speaks so clearly as this does.

Others, on the contrary, are in all their acts far more deliberate and quieter; whilst some are so very deficient in this vivacity that they dawdle over what ought to be done quickly, and only think, when it is too late, of what they ought to have said, or might and should have done.

This greater vivacity therefore in the original powers not only produces a quicker appropriation of external stimulants, but also causes unconscious notions to start into consciousness with greater rapidity (§ 13). As has already been observed, it is the inherent effort and tension of the powers which exhibits itself as this special kind of vivacity.

When a man is extremely deficient in this quickness, we call him '*stupid*,' just because he requires too much time to 'recollect himself,' i.e., to arouse those notions which may be needful in this or that case. He may possess them, but before his sluggish original powers have excited them all into distinct consciousness, it is too late. We must not therefore confound a stupid man with an ignorant one; though dulness and ignorance often go together.

The following may be observed as regards the muscular sense above mentioned:—

In so far as there are muscles in our body which we use for the purpose of performing external acts, in so far we have a muscular sense. It is divisible into several distinct systems; the muscles of the finger, hand, arm, legs, eyes, vocal organs, &c.; and we may with equal propriety talk of several muscular senses as of one. For each system has its special degree of quickness; the muscles of the finger being the swiftest of all. Since the fingers include the sense of touch, it may be asked whether both are equally quick? It can hardly be said that they are; since even blind people (see § 8) cannot perceive a number of *different* tactual sensations in succession so fast as they can move their fingers. Still more sluggish is the vital sense[1] (see the remark in § 46), where, as often happens, it is used as a sense of touch. That these muscular systems together constitute a

[1] ['Gemeinsinn,' here used as equivalent to the sensus vagus, vital sense.]

completely special sense is shewn (*a*) by the peculiar sensations which arise from long-continued movements of the muscles, as well as from long disuse of them, and is still more clearly proved (*b*) by the important circumstance that the normal excitement of the muscles is always produced *from within* (*by the soul*), whereas their excitement from without is abnormal, and gives rise to the phenomenon known as *cramp*. Cramp is rarely produced from within, e.g. in many persons at the sight of a spider, &c.; in which cases it arises from a too great mass of transferred movable elements. (See § 30.)

In many brutes muscular movements take place with greater rapidity than they do in man, whence it might be inferred that they must do more than man does in the particular dexterities to which they have been trained. But man alone possesses in his muscular powers the requisite strength for retaining his past movements (as Traces), so as to raise his acquired dexterities to a high degree of perfection.

§ 15. *Origin of Concepts.*

Everything which we apprehend through our senses, with anything like perfection, leaves a trace behind it in the soul (§ 6): and similar traces unite into one whole. It is thus that notions (intuitions), whether clear or not, of external things are produced; and of these we possess not a few. (§§ 9 and 10.)

Now it will often happen that we become conscious of several different notions *at the same time*, or at least in *immediate succession*. For instance, we go out and see willows, limes, birches, alders, beeches, poplars, firs. What occurs? We represent these things to ourselves in a mass. And what then? What always takes place in the soul when things of the same kind come together, i.e. when we become conscious of them together: *what is common to all these notions is strengthened and more closely connected together*, because they are mutually attractive. In the case before us these are the constituent parts common to all trees: *roots, a trunk, branches, twigs.*

Another thing also takes place.

As we already know, *exciting elements* (movable elements) are the condition on which our psychical forms acquire consciousness, which increases or diminishes according as they flow to or away from these forms. (§ 13.)

Now these movable elements of consciousness, by a constant law, always flow in the *largest quantity* to those forms which are most intimately connected with each other, or united. (See below, § 73.) Consequently these *similar* constituent parts in such intuitions, must, since they are most intimately connected, receive the largest share of those movable elements, whilst the dissimilar (diversities of colour, of leaves, height and thickness of stem, &c.) are more or less deprived of them. But this is not all. The prevailing consciousness of what is similar according to § 10 becomes at the same time *stronger* and *clearer the greater the number* of the similar parts which are excited together. In seven trees, however, which we see and figure at the same time we have the *similar* repeated seven times, while that which is peculiar to each, and therefore the dissimilar, occurs only *once*. Consequently we shall represent that which is common to every tree *seven times more clearly and strongly* than what is peculiar to each; and as the movable elements are withdrawn from the dissimilar, it is natural that it should become, if not wholly, yet almost wholly, unconscious *.

Thus the *concept* Tree arises, i.e. a form in which what is common to the trees *seen* is as it were *connected together* for our consciousness, whilst their dissimilarities are (so far as consciousness is concerned) obliterated; and this is the way in which all Concepts are formed. Every concept is a *general* or *aggregate* notion; for it is always applicable to the whole class of things (intuitions) from which it was formed; whereas an Intuition is only a *singular* notion—the notion of one thing which is exactly applicable only to the *single* object which produced it.

Is the Concept dissolved again into its parts when consciousness leaves it? No! it only becomes unconscious, or a Trace; for what is contained in it has been specially and strongly connected—how? On this see the middle of § 38. We are not to suppose that the Concept tears itself loose from the special intuitions to which it owes its existence: it is really the more

---

* For the reason why the concentration of consciousness on particular points in the soul necessarily implies its withdrawal from others, see below, § 73.

intimate connection of their similar constituent parts. Unless the intuitions which contain the similarities are simultaneously excited, no concept arises; whereas it always does start up when they are sufficiently excited in this manner[1].

When, therefore, there are no intuitions there can be no concepts answering to them. Hence a man born blind has no concept of 'Colour,' although he knows the name, the man born deaf has no concept of 'Sound,' nor can such persons ever obtain these concepts. Similarly those who live in equatorial regions are destitute of the concept 'Ice,' nor had Luther any concepts of coffee, tobacco, steam-engines, &c., &c.

§ 16. *Gradation of Concepts.*

In the last paragraph we have seen how concepts arise: *that is to say, they arise of themselves, when the similarities contained in certain intuitions are thought of together, whether they are excited simultaneously, or one after the other in immediate succession.* Concepts are readily interchanged with intuitions because we have no special words for the latter: for as language has only names for concepts, we are obliged to call the intuitions *by the same name* as that which is applied to *concepts*. The only exception to this is in the case of words for *unique* objects, like Elbe, Danube, Blocksberg, Dresden, &c., &c., i.e. *Proper names.* All other words except these are class-names; and hence the

---

[1] Concepts, therefore, are not produced, as is usually asserted, by 'abstraction' (by the withdrawal of consciousness), but by the *combination in consciousness* of those parts in our intuitions which resemble each other. No doubt consciousness is withdrawn, turned away, but only from that out of which the concept neither is nor can be formed. Abstraction, therefore, is a process which goes on coincidently with the formation of concepts; but the important thing is the combination of elements (and the act by which the several points in common become conscious together). In calling concepts *abstract* (abstracted) notions we must be cautious not to let that expression lead us into error, not to misunderstand its purport.

When we let anything fall out of our thoughts, or, in common parlance, when we forget it, consciousness is withdrawn from similarities and dissimilarities alike. But who ever gained concepts by forgetting something?

word *house*, for instance, is not the name for some one definite house, but for the whole class; and if we mean some particular house, we must say, *this* house, *that* house, *Henry's* house, &c., &c. A general name requires such limiting terms in order that it may denote an individual.

In order to shew how the formation of concepts proceeds from the more special to the more general we will first form a few concepts out of intuitions. Represent the following things to yourself:—

Coat, waistcoat, jacket, trousers, boot, stocking, shoe, glove, cap.

Every one has noticed these articles to be coverings for certain parts of the human body. The moment, then, he grasps all these one with another in consciousness, this common point forces itself upon him, and so there arises the concept, 'Article of Clothing.' These objects have many other marks besides this, as, made of cloth, or leather, green, variegated, black, large, small, &c., but, very naturally, no one's consciousness is turned so strongly upon them as upon the mark of 'clothing.' For the latter occurs here nine times over, whereas the other marks are all different from one another, and consequently only occur once. Is it possible, then, for the mutual attraction of similars to produce in this case any other concept than that of '*article of clothing?*'

Exactly the same thing happens when we represent in immediate succession (as intuitions), knife, fork, spoon, plate, dish, table-cloth, napkin. These objects also are very different from each other: yet, as we are accustomed to see them used at meal-times, that mark forces itself into more distinct consciousness the further one proceeds with the representation of such things. Naturally! for the same thing *seven times* repeated must yield a stronger consciousness than that which only occurs once, and thus we gain the concept, '*table furniture*.'

Again, Dwelling-house, Barn, Stable, Shed, Brewery, &c. No one ever saw them grow out of the ground as trees do; everybody when he thinks of their origin finds that they have been produced ('built') by the hand of man; and if this mark strikes us in the first, it will certainly not fail to strike us in the rest: it is, in fact, common to them all, and so they lead us to form the concept *Building*.

Now think of these three *concepts*, Article of Clothing, Table-furniture, Building, together. They will yield the *higher* concept, *Product of Art*, as soon as consciousness is directed to the fact that articles of clothing, &c. cannot exist where there are no men to make and produce; while, on the other hand, the concept, '*Product of Nature*,' must arise when one is conscious of the already acquired *concepts*, Tree, Bush, Fish, Mountain, Stone, Cloud, Star, &c., simultaneously: for in this case every one allows that such things are not produced by man.

Moreover, the concepts, Product of Nature, Product of Art, have this common mark, that all such objects are 'extended in space and perceptible to the senses,' and if consciousness is turned away (a more difficult matter no doubt) from all their other marks and fixed on these two only, we gain the *still higher* concept *Body*[a].

Accordingly we find that,

Concepts *arise in the human soul because the similarities in different notions of individual objects (intuitions) mutually attract each other and fuse together into one whole; and as concepts so formed have also points in common, they in their turn coalesce, and hence arise* **new** *and continually* **higher concepts.** The condition on which this depends is, that the several fundamental notions (the intuitions and the lower concepts) should be excited together, should be roused into consciousness simultaneously. Compare §§ 15 and 38.

On more attentively considering the *gradations* of these concepts, it is apparent that the higher the concept is, the more does it embrace—the larger the number of objects to which it can be applied. The lowest embrace merely the intuitions which are the *only* forms contained under them; the higher embrace the

---

[a] Of course concepts are not formed so rapidly as is represented in these examples: all that we wish to point out here is *the manner* in which, and the *materials out of which*, they are made.

lower concepts as well as their intuitions; for they are formed out of these fundamental forms, and cannot be formed out of anything else. The common points in these fundamental forms constitute the *content* of the concept, and what it embraces are the fundamental forms in general abstracting from their common constituents[a]. Accordingly the higher concept has a greater, a *wider compass* in proportion as it includes *under it* a larger number of lower concepts and intuitions, and so it is briefly called a *wider* concept.

Do 'concept' and 'the content of a concept' differ as, say, a bottle differs from the contents of the bottle? Never: the content of the concept is the concept itself. 'Concept,' however, and 'compass or sphere of a concept,' are always two distinct things. Thus Fir, Birch, Pine, Ash, Larch, Lime, &c., are the *compass* or sphere of the concept 'Tree:' its marks, on the contrary, Roots, a Trunk, Branches, Twigs, are the concept itself or its content. The *whole* compass of a concept is indicated by the word *all* (or *every*), a *part of it* by the expression *some*, &c.; as in the judgments, *All* trees are vegetable products; *some* trees are Scotch firs.

The greater *the content* of a concept the lower that concept is (the nearer it is to the intuitions), and conversely; and the smaller its content the more objects does it embrace, the greater is its *extension* and the reverse.

Is it possible for the higher concepts to be formed before the lower ones? In the natural order of development it is not. Yet a child's attention is generally directed by its teachers to the *universal* before the particular; e.g. it hears the word 'bird' before 'lark,' 'tree' before 'lime,' &c.; and thus it is not directed to the *special* marks of these objects: this being

---

[a] ["Das Gemeinsame der Grundgebilde macht den *Inhalt* des Begriffs aus, und was er umfängt, sind die Grundgebilde überhaupt, abgesehen von ihren gemeinsamen Bestandtheilen." Unless I am mistaken this sentence is somewhat carelessly expressed. 'Rational mortal animal' (or any other definition that we choose to adopt) is the content of the concept 'Man;' but the latter is applied, says our author, to each and every man, 'abstracting from their common constituents;' whereas his meaning, I imagine, would be more clearly expressed had he said, 'abstracting from their special and peculiar constituents;' i.e., the concept man is affirmed of a Negro, or an Esquimaux simply when considered as 'rational mortal animals,' and therefore when not regarded as being (what they are in fact) black, olive-coloured, of a certain height, age, &c.]

so, no wonder the more general is formed in its mind before the particular. Such concepts are as a rule imperfect, and consequently of very little benefit to the child, whilst they easily impede the formation of the more exact and lower concepts.

Concepts are more *perfect* in proportion as the original powers are stronger and more sensitive, and as the intuitions are more *definite* and *richer*.

Why is it that those brutes which are most sensitive are never able to form concepts properly so called?

§ 17. *Understanding.*

The concepts hitherto considered always arise ultimately from different *perceptions* (intuitions), and therefore from the primitive union of external stimulants with the corresponding original powers. Hence, as they consist of the same elements (excluding dissimilarities) as the perceptions, and are produced by a more intimate fusion between the similarities of the latter, and at the same time by a peculiar and permanent connexion being established between them (see § 38), it follows that these concepts must remain in the soul unchanged until some special cause operates to destroy that fusion or to dissipate the perceptions themselves.

We may convince ourselves of the truth of this by facts at any moment. If concepts once formed continue to exist, then those which were formed in us years ago must also continue to exist in us.

Such are, e.g. the concepts long, short, light, heavy, white, green, mountain, house, man, brute, horse, dog, fish, &c. Do they still exist in us? Every one will find that he has them. To concepts, then, may be applied the general principle: *When once anything (a form) arises in the soul with any degree of perfection, it continues to exist there until some special cause destroys or dissolves it.*

In this respect it is with the soul exactly as it is with the external world. There all that has come into existence lasts until some special cause destroys it. Take, for instance, stones, mountains, trees, houses, furniture, &c. Hence the permanence of any product in the soul is not a law peculiar to the soul, it is a *general law of nature.* We saw in § 6 that whatever has been produced in the soul with *sufficient perfection* is hardly wholly destructible: though it seemed to disappear, still it was only *unconscious* for a long period.

Now according to §§ 15 and 16 new concepts not only are produced from fresh perceptions which we gain, but these concepts themselves give rise to *higher* concepts. Such is the case in every man of sound mind. Their number increases the more perceptions we gain, the longer we live, especially if we are assiduous in seeking out the similarities of things.

What is the advantage of gaining concepts?

The similarities of *many* notions constituting the stock of a concept are united and concentrated in it; hence concepts must be psychical forms accompanied by *great clearness of consciousness*, for that clearness increases in proportion as more similarities are accumulated. (Compare §§ 10 and 15.)

Consequently concepts bring *light* into the soul and impart their brightness to that with which they are brought into relation (= that with which one brings them into simultaneous consciousness). Thus we arrive at an *understanding* of the object represented; and this is the reason why we say of a man who does not understand a thing, that he has no conception (concept) of it. Farther on we shall meet with more exact details concerning the enlightening nature of concepts [7].

On this account we call the sum total of concepts formed in the soul a man's **understanding.**

Hence it follows that:

Concepts are not the products of understanding, but that the understanding is produced by concepts.

Before the formation of any concepts whatever, there is no

---

[7] 'I understand that,' 'I see or I comprehend that,' is tantamount to saying 'it is clear or obvious to me.' It is to be noted that the word 'concept' (Begriff) is frequently interchanged with 'intuition' (Anschauung): in everyday language the terms are used very inexactly. [A note rather for the German than English reader, 'concept' being with us a technical term never used in common life.]

such thing as understanding in the soul—there is only a *disposition* for it partly innate, partly acquired: viz. the law of attraction, and the sum of intuitions from which concepts are and must be formed. But if there is a total want of all intuitions that law cannot operate.

Why do we say, and say with truth, of a child a year old, that it has as yet little or no understanding? When can the child be first said to have it, and how far does it then extend?

Why has the shoemaker no understanding in painting? Why does the painter not understand how to make boots and shoes? How comes it that the carpenter has no understanding in the building of ships, though he knows well enough how to build houses?

When we meet with men who understand, if not all, yet a great many things, what must previously have happened to them all without any exception?

The nature of Understanding will be found thoroughly investigated in Diesterweg's '*Pädagogisches Jahrbuch auf* 1858,' in an essay by Dressler, '*Ueber das Abstracte.*'

§ 18. *Propositions. Power of Judging.*

I shew the following objects to a number of people—coal, soot, pitch, ink, a raven, mourning clothes. What will every one think when he sees them? 'These things are *black.*' This proves that the concept 'black' exists in the persons present, and that it has been added by them to these intuitions.

I exhibit an emerald, and they say, 'the emerald is *green.*' Here, beside the perception of the emerald, the concept 'green,' a completely different one, starts into consciousness.

I shew a bell, strike on it, and people say 'the bell *rings.*'

Thus it may be proved in a thousand instances that, *when we perceive anything, as a rule a* concept *rises into consciousness in addition to that* perception.

But why do not people say, pitch is *red*, the emerald is *blue*, the bell *runs?*

The reason has already been given in § 9. The similar only can unite in the soul by mutual attraction. The concepts 'red,' 'blue,' and 'run' have, however, nothing in common with the intuitions in question, and there being no similarity between the several forms, these unsuitable concepts are not excited.

Hence, when we perceive anything, *such* concepts only start into consciousness as have been produced by the coalescence of the *similar points* in numerous perceptions of that kind.

Moreover, if the similarities in the concepts black, red, green, blue, grey, violet, &c., coalesce, the higher concept, 'colour,' results.

Suppose now I mention red or black, what will a man say? 'Red (black, &c.) is a colour.'

Consequently, a *higher* concept of like kind is often summoned into consciousness along with another.

When that takes place—when, that is, (a) *either a like* concept *is called into consciousness along with a (simple) perception, or* (b) *a* higher *concept of like kind along with another concept —the soul is said to* judge.

Now what happens when anybody judges that the sphere is *round?* that roundness is a *shape* or form?

It follows from what has been said that in the judgment we have the same Traces which occurred at first as intuitions (perceptions), and were then formed into concepts because the similarities contained in them coalesced with increasing force. A definite bond holds the constituent parts of the judgment (subject and predicate) together (see § 38), supposing them to have been excited together with sufficient strength; and so long as this connexion holds, every judgment must continue *to last* in the soul (§ 17); it cannot vanish, it can only become unconscious.

Thus we gradually accumulate a large number of judgments, which lie ready for use in the soul as we may require them.

The totality of all the judgments that have been formed and that are permanent in the soul we call its judgment *or judging power.*

Is there any ground for the common assumption that judgment is an innate *special* faculty?

At what period may we say that the soul possesses the power of judging.

and by what means is it rendered greater and richer? Where is it, where must it be totally wanting?

What is the meaning of the proverb, 'He judges as a blind man does of colours?'

§ 19. *Reciprocal influence of Concepts and Perceptions when simultaneously present in a Judgment.*

It may be asked what advantage is conferred by judging on the two forms concerned in it?

As regards the subject, we already know that it is *brightened* and *rendered clearer* by the predicate (by the concept), since the concept is always more *vividly present to consciousness* and *clearer* than is the intuition or *lower* concept, one of which constitutes the subject in the proposition. (See § 17.)

But what does the predicate gain?

Suppose that the intuition *oak* as a subject is attached in consciousness to the concept *tree* (for a predicate). Intuitions are always younger than concepts, and therefore they consist of more lively or, as one might say, of more vivacious elements—for the stimulants are the freshest thing in the soul.

Now when such fresh and lively elements are added to a concept, the latter is rendered more vivacious; its depressed condition, so to speak, arising from the monotonous elements of which it consists, is rendered as it were more sonorous, or more full of colour; and by that it is made more impetuous, it is in a sense made young again.

In brief: *the concept renders the perception* more clear *to consciousness, while the concept is rendered* more fresh *to consciousness by the perception.* In this consists the beneficial influence exerted by perception and concept on each other, when they are called up into consciousness together in the act of judging.

§ 20. *Inferences. Inferential Powers.*

In the human soul there are very often *several judgments* conscious at the same time. Take the judgments.

All men are mortal.
A Moor is a man.

Here we have three concepts side by side, *man*, *mortal*, *Moor*. While the first judgment affirms 'mortality' of *all* men, i.e. of the whole compass of that concept, the second declares that the Moor is included in that compass.

What takes place? 'Man' and 'Moor' are similar concepts, for Moor is but another name for man—it only signifies a particular kind of human being. Hence these two concepts will coalesce, but in such a way that Moor will remain present to consciousness. In fact, this concept is *forced* with special strength upon the consciousness, the consequence of which is that not it, but 'all men' is obscured, and almost vanishes from consciousness. The movable elements which kept it consciously present are withdrawn from the latter, and are attracted to the more strongly emphasized term 'Moor.' Hence the only thing the dissimilar concept 'being mortal' can do, is to attach itself to the term Moor, now *vividly* conscious: and so the inference (the inferring judgment) is drawn—(Therefore) *the Moor is mortal* also.

If in two judgments there is a total want of similar concepts, though they may co-exist in consciousness, yet they can give rise to no new judgment, no conclusion, no inference. Suppose, for instance,

The bird flies.
The fish is aquatic.

Here each is *outside* the other, and no inference is possible in such cases. As the concepts in the judgments, Iron is hard, and Honey is sweet, can never coalesce, so neither can the former.

When therefore two judgments are rendered simultaneously *conscious, and in them are contained similar concepts together with one* dissimilar *one, the similar concepts fuse together and a new judgment is produced; because the* dissimilar *concept must attach itself to that one of the similar concepts which in one of the judgments has been brought definitely and prominently into consciousness.*

This process is called 'drawing a conclusion[1],' and the assemblage of three such judgments is termed an *inference*. The first judgment is called the *major proposition*, the second the *minor*, both together the *premisses*, the third the *conclusion*. It is the function of one of these judgments to put prominently forward in its subject or predicate that concept on which stress is to be laid in the new connexion, or new judgment. As a rule the *minor premiss* does this, but the *major* may do it as well, because the syllogism is not affected by the external arrangement of the judgments composing it. Consider the following examples:

All ignorant persons ought to learn.
Little children are ignorant.
Therefore, little children ought to be good and learn.

Some animals are birds.
All birds lay eggs.
Therefore, some animals lay eggs.

The emphasizing judgment is placed first in the second example (instead of All birds lay eggs, Some animals are birds), yet the conclusion is drawn in spite of it, because the attraction of similars is not affected by the position of the fundamental judgments.

Accordingly an inference, as the preceding clearly shews, is nothing more than a complex judgment, which leads, without any act of ours, from the mere constitution of the concepts composing it, to a new judgment, to a judgment which is produced solely by the mutual attraction of similars[2].

---

[1] 'Schliessen' [to conclude, draw a conclusion] is derived, not from 'zuschliessen' [to lock up, close, conclude], but from 'anschliessen,' to attract, to follow, be added. [A note for the German reader merely.]

[2] It is impossible in this place to give a more minute account of the nature of inferences and of the judgments on which they are based. For complete information concerning all these logical phenomena, see Dressler's '*Praktische Denklehre, nach* Beneke's *Vorgange auf die Thatsachen der innern Erfahrung gebaut.*' Bautzen; published by A. Weller, 1852. Price 27 Ngr.

A *conclusion* once drawn continues to exist in the soul, partly because it arises from Traces which are already permanent, partly because the concepts composing the several judgments have been definitely and permanently connected. (See § 38.) Hence the soul perpetually becomes richer and richer in *ready-prepared* inferences. But as a rule we do not express them at full length, we abbreviate them: the first example may be thus shortened: being a man the Moor is also mortal.

Here belong, if any one likes, *negative* judgments[b], e.g. *This* flower is not an auricula. The major premiss would run thus, The auricula has one pistil, five stamens, &c.: the minor, This flower has two pistils, &c.: the conclusion, Therefore, this flower is *not* an auricula.

As a rule, however, it is unnecessary to go through this lengthy process in order to draw a negative judgment: it may arise from the fact that we find something *affirmed* (by others, or by ourselves in consequence of an error), the contrary of which we now know, or afterwards discover to be true. Suppose, for example, somebody has declared, This book is a bad one; we should correct the mistake, and say, This book is *not* a bad one, as soon as we discovered the error. It is just the same with our own mistakes: we shall and must sweep them away by negative judgments, the moment we are better informed.

What we have hitherto said yields this result:

The sum total of all the conclusions formed in the soul and permanently existing there constitute man's **Inferential Powers.**

When then may we say that Inferential Powers exist in the soul? By what means are they rendered greater and fuller?

Since the souls of brutes, owing to the weakness of their original powers, are incapable even of forming concepts properly so called (at the best they only approximate to them), it is natural that they should be still less able to form *Judgments* and *Inferences*.

---

[b] Judgments with a merely grammatical negative do not belong here: they are only verbal turns equivalent to logically affirmative propositions, e.g. that does not cost much = it costs little; he is not industrious = he is lazy, &c.

The mutual attraction of similar elements—a law which governs the souls of brutes as well as our own—conducts them however to combinations which may resemble judgments and inferences. The *nobler* brutes not unfrequently exhibit such; though no brute attains to the *clearness* which is conspicuous in man under like circumstances.

§ 21. *Additional Remarks on the Power of Judging and on the Inferential Faculties.*

In the majority of cases when we judge or infer, judgments and conclusions *already formed* are roused into consciousness; *for that which already exists in the soul does not need to be formed afresh.*

All that is required, then, are fresh exciting elements which cannot be wanting, and we have already learnt what they are in §§ 12 and 13. Whether they proceed *from within* or *from without*, they unite with one of the forms of which the judgments or inferences consist, and in consequence of this, the other forms connected with them are excited, and the whole complex act returns again into consciousness. Compare § 38.

But new judgments and inferences arise with the greatest facility, when concepts (whether already worked up into judgments and conclusions or not) are brought into connexion with new perceptions (notions): e.g. suppose I have the concept 'Reptile,' I am able to judge, the first time that I set eyes on a lizard, 'The lizard is a reptile;' though without this concept I could not do so.

At the same time it would be impossible for me to form this judgment, even if I possessed the concept 'Reptile,' unless it were excited into consciousness simultaneously with the intuition of the lizard. Hence as regards *the power of judging* and *the inferential powers* the following important principle holds:

The power of judging, and that of drawing conclusions, only acts on condition that the constituent parts of the judgments or conclusions presently to be formed **are brought into consciousness together**: *consequently there must be no want of those elements which are necessary to* **excite** *unconscious forms.*

A man may possess the concept 'metal,' and yet when he sees

platina it is possible he may not judge 'platina' to be a metal, either because the concept 'metal' may accidentally remain unconscious, or because he thinks that platina is something else. But if *I say* to him, Platina is a metal, the sound of the word 'metal' will infallibly excite that concept into consciousness (why?), and then he judges that platina is a metal. In this manner such judgments must arise in every one who has already obtained both the name and the concept answering to it.

Accordingly we find that 1°. external stimulants *cause judgments and conclusions to arise in the soul or merely to return to it, and that too* involuntarily, unwilled, *because such stimulants light unerringly on those concepts and judgments with which they were already at an earlier period connected.*

I suddenly think, 'People coin ducats out of gold.' This is a judgment which has not been suggested from without by any one's having at this moment mentioned either 'gold' or 'ducats,' nor is it one that I *willed* to make. It occurred quite involuntarily, and the question is, what led me to think of it; that it is not now formed for the first time is clear. From what has already been said we know what the answer is, for there are also

2°. internal stimulants *which attach themselves to unconscious mental forms, and thus rouse them into consciousness; and this form of excitement often occurs so much* against *our will, that it disturbs, checks, and confuses the desired course of our thoughts.*

But these are not the only ways in which unconscious forms attain to consciousness, and we should often be obliged to wait a considerable time and in vain, if we waited for such *external* and *internal stimulants* to arouse our judgments. For while they not unfrequently awaken more unconscious notions than we wish for or require, so they at other times leave us completely in the lurch. In that case there is yet a third means of excitement in our power.

A man has to prepare an essay on a difficult subject. For this he requires concepts, judgments, and conclusions, all of which must already be slumbering unconsciously in his soul: for if he did not possess them he could never succeed in writing his theme: at present he will not have the opportunity of producing much that is positively new; he is mainly concerned with fresh combinations of what is already familiar to him. So he sits down pen in hand. A number of sentences occur to him spontaneously and unsummoned which he writes down, but really good propositions to the point are yet wanting. Indeed, on carefully reading over what he has put down, he notices that he cannot make any use of many of these suggestions, because they do not set his task in a right, possibly they set it in a wholly false, light. He now *tries*, strives to hit on something better, and lo! the effort assists him. In spite of much unsteadiness in his quest after suitable judgments and conclusions, what he wants gradually makes its appearance, and what does not occur to him to-day, because his powers are weary, is suggested next morning with greater facility, the better he may have rested during the night: the freshly accumulated original powers give him new vigour, and his task is happily accomplished. Therefore the power of judging and the inferential faculties are

3°. *more vigorous, the more* **free unsatisfied original powers** *there are in the soul which* **voluntarily** *excite the unconscious forms.*

But there is yet a fourth thing of supreme importance here.

We meet with men who are certainly not deficient in concepts, the main constituents of judgments, nor in the void unemployed original powers necessary to raise the unconscious into consciousness,—for these are formed in them as they are in all other men,—and yet in all their judgments and conclusions (whether spontaneous or voluntary) they are so helpless that they, often to their own detriment, only awake to what is required when it is too late.

Their original powers are deficient in the needful vivacity or quickness, as we have already seen, § 14.

For the more lively the original powers are, the quicker do the internal stimulants act, the more quickly does the unconscious rise into consciousness, and the more quickly therefore do judgments and conclusions make their appearance.

Therefore it is proved, 4°. *that the* vivacity *or quickness of the original* powers is the main thing required for the activity of the judging and inferential faculties.

Finally, if we consider the relation in which the power of judging and of drawing conclusions stands to *Understanding,* it is clear from the preceding observations that

1°. both are identical with *Understanding, i.e. with the sum total of all the concepts already formed and existent in the soul, in so far that no judgment or conclusion can be formed* without *concepts; seeing that the latter are in fact the essential parts both of judgments and inferences;*

2°. but *that both are* different *from the understanding in so far as that, in judging, definite notions are required to serve as subjects in addition to the concepts forming the predicates; and in drawing conclusions besides the* inferred *judgment (conclusion), definite singular* fundamental *judgments (premisses) are necessary.* Add to this,

3°. *that in order successfully to handle judgments and conclusions, there must be no lack of internal and external stimulants, nor, in particular, must there be any deficiency in unmodified free original powers. And lastly,* that

4°. *in addition to all this, a higher degree of vivacity or quickness on the part of the original powers is requisite, since neither understanding, power of judging, nor the inferential faculties can operate, if the forms of which they consist remain unexcited, or are only excited too slowly.*

Besides this the following is clear. Since by all these forms [conception, judgment, and inference] we do more than *understand,* we may with perfect right distinguish between understanding in *a narrow,* and understanding in *a wide,* sense of the term. To the former belong concepts only, to the latter judgments and conclusions as well; and consequently, in calling all these phenomena '*intellectual developments or evolutions,*' we employ a title long since in familiar use, and one eminently suitable to express their nature. Man has no innate faculty for this kind of understanding (understanding in the widest sense) given to him, except the greater strength and retentiveness of his original powers, especially those of sight and hearing; and hence you may, if you choose, call this strength and tenacity man's *innate power* of understanding (= capacity of acquiring understanding).

It is evident then that we must distinguish carefully between the *formed*, and the as yet *unformed* understanding. Of the latter there are several degrees; for it consists at first in the mere *strength* or tenacity of the original powers, at a later period in the possession of *acquired products* necessary to the formation of concepts, judgments and conclusions;—therefore, as regards concepts, in intuitions; as regards judgments, in concepts; and as regards conclusions, in judgments.

§ 22. *Recapitulation.*

What have we learnt hitherto?

I. The original powers of the human soul.

What do we mean by these? (§ 3.) Three different properties attach to them in different degrees:

1°. *Susceptibility to stimulants* or *sensitiveness*, by which they seize on stronger, or it may be, weaker stimulants, and by so doing attain to a development corresponding to those stimulants. (§ 5.)

2°. *Tenacity* or *retentive power*, by which they retain in a higher or lower degree stimulants once received (§ 7); and,

3°. *Vivacity* or *quickness* in their action, by which they apprehend, with greater or less rapidity, passing stimulants, and awaken consciousness in the soul with more or less quickness. (§§ 14 and 21.)

Consequently the original powers of the soul are not something merely *passive* or quite *dead*, they are on the contrary in a high degree *living* and *active*, they catch up and assimilate external stimulants. The properties inherent in them and the laws of their development constitute a very important content for them, even while yet unexcited by external stimulants, without which they could never be developed into anything truly and characteristically human (§ 14, note). What especially causes them to be manifested as *mental* and spiritual *powers*? (§ 10.)

The original powers which have been *used up*, i.e. formed

into Traces, are *replaced* by fresh ones which are engendered for the most part during sleep. (§ 13.)

II. The stimulants of the external world.

They are divided into those which are appropriated by the powers of Sight, Hearing, Touch, Taste, Smell, or Feeling. As far as we have at present gone it has been found that their mass or quantity relatively to the original powers is *of two kinds*.

For either these stimulants affect the original powers in a *sufficient* degree (and this produces *clear* notions), or they are *too small* and little for them; (in which case *no* notions result, or at best only *obscure* ones. § 11.)

The psychical powers, at first unconscious, develope their *capacity* for consciousness into *actual* consciousness by uniting with the stimulants which excite them, and consciousness so produced continues to be connected (though arrested) with the act, after it has ceased to be excited: (it continues connected in the 'Trace'). (§§ 6 and 10.)

III. The fundamental laws operative in the soul*.

1°. *Sensuous* (what is the meaning of this?) *impressions*[d] *and perceptions are formed by the human soul in consequence of*

---

* By the expression *Law of Nature* is meant all those exertions of force (processes) which take place in a uniform and harmonious sequence; and the superior leading laws are also called fundamental laws, or processes. It is only the latter kind that are here intended; derivative or subsidiary laws are deducible from them at once, for they are only particular modes in which the more general laws work together. Since the soul is of a spiritual nature there are such things as *spiritual* laws of nature.

Let not Force and Law be confused together. Along with forces are always included the laws of their activity (action), for the term 'law' means nothing more than *regularity*, uniformity of action. Similar (regular) action, however, is something totally different from similar force. Thus men, trees, and grasses always grow upwards, i.e. they act similarly, or obey, as the expression goes, one and the same law. But does that imply that they are themselves (= the forces of which they consist) similar?

[d] ['Sensuous sensations' is somewhat nonsensical English for *sinnliche Empfindungen*; I have therefore been driven to depart from the equivalent for the latter word elsewhere constantly employed.]

impressions or stimulants which affect it from without. (§ 4.) Law of the Appropriation of Stimulants.

This follows from the fact that the original powers strive after, tend towards, satisfaction by means of stimulants (§ 4), and that they are at the same time *retentive* (strong, tenacious); in consequence of which impressions once made on them must be *permanent.* What is a *Trace?* (§ 6.) What is *Memory?* (§ 7.) The permanence of these Traces is no special law of the *soul*, but a universal law of *nature* (§ 17.)

2°. *Everything which is of the same kind unites, fuses in the soul into one whole*, for similars are mutually attractive. (§ 9.) Law of the Mutual Attraction of Similars.

The new stimulant coalesces with the Trace allied to it; and thus all Traces of a similar kind are more intimately united when they are excited simultaneously or in immediate succession. *Consciousness* becomes *clearer, the larger the number* of similar Traces united in one whole*. (§ 10.) In like manner the similarities of many different notions or perceptions blend together, and hence arises a *concept.* (§ 15.) Again, when the similarities of several distinct concepts coalesce, the result is a *higher* concept. (§ 16.)

What is the *Understanding?*

When, along with a perception, a similar *concept*, or along with a concept a similar but higher concept, rises into consciousness, a *judgment* is produced. What is the *Power of judging?* (§ 18.)

What are the mutual influences exerted in a judgment by Concept and Perception? (§ 19.)

---

* The original powers, as well as the newly-formed ones afterwards added to them (which must also be termed original powers, seeing that their performances and functions are identical with the former), are, notwithstanding their individual character, indissolubly connected together, and constitute one completely *unextended* (unspatial) whole, namely, the soul. These, therefore, are connected together from the first. The mutual attraction of similars, however, leads to still more intimate union between them: they fuse together, and by thus doing, they, without giving up their original connexion, constitute smaller wholes, which are still more strongly and intensely united. Cf. p. 5, note.

When the similar concepts in two judgments coalesce in consciousness we have an *inference.* (§ 20.) What are the *inferential faculties?* (§ 20.) What is particularly *advantageous* for the exercise of the power of judging and inferring? In what does the deficiency of stupid people consist? (§§ 21 and 14.) On the relation of the judging and inferential powers to understanding. In what sense may it be said that there is an understanding in a higher and a lower sense of the term? What is the difference between *formed* and *unformed* understanding? (§ 21.)

3°. *The* full *stimulant is not permanently retained by the original powers: on the contrary, a portion of it is always released by them (though it does not therefore disappear from the soul); and more of it disappears in proportion as the original powers are less* tenacious (§§ 5, 7, 8, 12.) Law of the Disappearance of Stimulants.

In consequence of this, the *excitement* necessary to bring psychical forms into consciousness is withdrawn, which effect, however, is also produced by the transference of original powers: in this case these forms become *unconscious*, and they only return to consciousness when that loss has been supplied by fresh internal or external stimulants, or by void unemployed original powers. Hence we gain a simple explanation of the perpetual *alternation* between *consciousness* and *unconsciousness*, whether it be spontaneous or voluntary. (§§ 12 and 13.) Amidst this incessant change, consciousness is, so to say, alternately fettered and then again set free (by the recurrence of excitement). In other words, the act becomes a Trace, and the Trace in its turn an act.

The powers involved in concepts, judgments, and inferences, or of which they consist, are the same which, as original powers, are developed into sensations and perceptions. They only coalesce in a peculiar manner because they are evolved in a similar manner; and that they, amidst this fusion, preserve their special forms as other traces do, is owing to a special connexion established between them, and caused by special elements, concerning which we shall meet with further details hereafter. (§§ 15—21.)

PART II.

CONATIVE POWERS [STREBUNGEN].

§ 23. *The Original Powers are by nature Active.*

WE have already seen in §§ 4 and 14, that the original powers of the human soul do not *passively* receive the stimulants of the external world—in the way in which a tablet with nothing upon it quietly lets me paint or engrave on it whatever figures I choose—on the contrary, they *strive after* stimulants with more or less quickness; they are essentially *active*, *impulsive*, or *impulses*, because they are *living* powers. Compare the note on p. 30.

Examples of all kinds prove this, not to repeat those mentioned in §§ 4 and 14.

Rich Englishmen, unable any longer to endure the torment of ennui, i.e. ignorant how to pacify their original powers, which desire to be satisfied and made use of, have before now committed suicide.

I have seen children who, from superabundance of spirits, did not know what to do with themselves, and so amused themselves with the silliest pranks, merely because their instructors did not give them some suitable occupation.

In the prisons of New York, if criminals will not obey the rules of the place, they shut them up for a few days, without work of any kind, in solitary confinement. After a short time, they earnestly beg for something to do. They are unable to resist the striving of their original powers after stimulants.

We see from this that,

The original powers of the human soul are *naturally active;* for, before they begin to be developed, they are endowed with a definite *impulse* after the satisfaction derivable from stimulants. Therefore the *activity* (striving) of the human soul is contained *originally in its primitive powers.*

Moreover we find that in a young child its active visual powers have absolutely no preference for one kind of light-stimulant over another: they join as readily with the blue stimulant as they do with red, yellow, &c.; they seize on what is angular as easily as upon what is round, long, &c.

The same thing is true of the powers belonging to all the other systems. The auditory powers *strive* generally after stimulants of *sound*, the tactual powers *generally* after those of *touch*, the powers of smell *generally* after those of *smell* (*odours*), and so on.

The inference is that,

The original powers tend naturally and at first, not after this or that individual definite *stimulant; but rather their activity is directed, in* a completely general *manner, to satisfaction by means of their corresponding stimulant.*

An innate *determinate* effort or desire exists in them only in so far as the powers of *sight* strive after stimulants of *light*, those of *hearing* after *sounds*, &c.; or as, generally, each system of powers strives after those stimulants which *correspond* to its peculiar constitution.

No soul brings into the world with it any *articulate* desire or striving, i.e. a desire for any *definite, individual* object.

How, then, do these *definite* desires for *special* objects come to exist in the human soul? In other words, how does it attain to impulses of a *definite* kind? We shall endeavour to obtain a clear answer to this question in the following paragraphs.

§ 24. *Relations between Stimulants and Original Powers. Different degrees in which Stimulants are retained by them.*

We have already been introduced to two of these relationships between stimulants and powers in § 11, where we learnt that,

1°. *The external stimulant is often so weak, that the corresponding original power is not completely filled by it, and is consequently not satisfied and perfected:* e.g. when we look at an object in the twilight, or from too great a distance; or when a sound is too faint for us to hear it clearly, &c.

This is what is called *half-stimulation*. In this case stimulant and power are only very loosely connected, and if repeatedly excited in this manner, the power soon loses its activity. The feeling immediately produced in the power by this treatment is called *dissatisfaction* or *dislike*.

2°. *The stimulant is exactly commensurate with the power that receives it*: in such a case it is firmly appropriated: e.g. when we look at an object in a clear light, or hear a sound at a convenient distance.

This is called *full stimulation*. When fully excited, the power is better able to appropriate and retain the stimulant, and our immediate feeling in such a case is that of *satisfaction*.

But it is, 3°. somewhat different when *a number* of lights are burning in a room, as all children know in the case of a Christmas-tree. The mere recollection of it brings a smile into their faces. It is true that they would have been pleased enough with their Christmas-boxes, if they had received them by the light of only one candle, or by daylight: but to get them when ten, twenty, or more little candles are sparkling on the tree is certainly an additional pleasure. What is the reason of this?

Somebody repeats to us Uhland's charming poem,—

> "Bei einem Wirthe wundermild,
> Da war ich jüngst zu Gaste,
> Ein goldner Apfel war sein Schild,
> An einem langen Aste." &c.

This pleases us. Then he sings it, and that causes us still more pleasure. Next, he accompanies his song on the piano, and that quite enchants us.

How is this to be explained?

The more light the more stimulant: again, the greater the volume of sound, the more stimulant.

But the light of a single candle suffices to enable us to see an object clearly; i.e. our visual powers are sufficiently filled by it. (§ 11.) Moreover, in order to make that poem perceptible to the ear, there is no need that it should be *sung*; for our auditory powers are sufficiently filled when it is distinctly recited.

Consequently when ten or twenty lights are burning, or when that poem is sung, and the piano accompanies it, more *stimulants affect the original powers than they* require *for their satisfaction.*

*They are thus thrown into a state of still greater excitement; they are, as it were, set swinging**, *and the immediate feeling attendant upon this is* Pleasure.

Hence we call it *pleasurable excitement.* The power in this case loses in ability to retain the stimulant, but gains in activity and tension. Compare § 32.

But 4°. this not unfrequently leads to a different result.

In my neighbourhood somebody kept a trained starling which whistled the old Dessau March in a very comical manner. It was indefatigable, repeating it certainly ten times in an hour. At first I was much amused, it no doubt produced in me a pleasurable excitement; but in a few days I became so heartily sick of its whistling, that I wished the industrious musician further.

I suppose that you have some favourite dish. Just eat it every day, and you will soon become disgusted with it.

Brandy drinkers have been cured by soaking everything they eat in their darling brandy. At first they like it, but that does not last long; they acquire such a loathing for it, that they can scarcely endure its smell.

In all these cases *more* stimulant acts on the original powers than they really *need* for the purposes of satisfaction. They are thus set, as it were, on the swing, which at first causes a feeling of *pleasure.* But if this great abundance of stimulant affects our original powers *constantly* and repeatedly, they must naturally be *over-stimulated, fatigued, deadened;* and we immediately perceive that by a feeling which gradually arises, and which we call *satiety, disgust.* Even full stimulation, if long continued, leads not unfrequently to the same result.

Hence we call all these *gradual* over-stimulations of the original powers, *excessive stimulation,* (stimulation to satiety). In this case a large number of stimulants are collected together,

* ['*gleichsam in Schwung*'— made to oscillate, quiver with excitement.]

but naturally they are only loosely connected with their corresponding powers.

Lastly, 5°. it occasionally happens that a stimulant much too strong affects our original powers *suddenly;* e.g. when we suddenly come out of darkness into a bright light. This causes us considerable *pain*, and we are unable to endure the sudden glare.

Or a gun is suddenly let off near us, or we take a large dose of some pungent essence into the mouth, or we smell at a phial full of some strong smelling liquid, or unawares put our hand into the fire, or receive a violent blow on some part of the body.

In all such cases *over strong stimulants* are at work which the original powers cannot assimilate, and they act *suddenly*. These powers must be at once *overcome*, *over-stimulated*, and *weakened*, and all this we perceive directly with a sudden feeling of *Pain*. Hence, all such sudden over-excitation of the original powers we call *painful stimulation*. In such cases the appropriation of the stimulants is at its minimum; indeed, a considerable portion of them are not appropriated at all, and only a few of them are retained by the power.

This excess of stimulation may, as experience shews, be so violent, that the original powers once weakened in this manner may never recover their strength again, in which case the freshly formed ones prove equally weak; and hence impaired vision, and even blindness, difficulty of hearing, and perhaps deafness, &c., may follow from it.

It is hardly necessary to mention that these five different relationships between stimulants and powers do not actually occur in the sharp and definite forms in which we have described them; half-stimulation sometimes approaches to full stimulation, and this to pleasurable stimulation, &c.

It is equally clear that any power receives a different inclination or tone, and retains it in the shape of a trace, according as it is developed under the one form of stimulation or the other. Under what relations do pleasurable dispositions arise? or the three different feelings of dislike? The *internal disposition* of the soul, so far as it is permanent, depends, in the main, on both these leading kinds; and hence we may call these acts, when continuing as Traces, *forms of disposition* (*affective* or emotional forms). May we include among them *notions* which are neutral between pleasure and dislike? Unquestionably: they dispose the soul to moderation, to peaceable behaviour.

What common language designates as '*Temper*' [Gemüth] is only the sum of those dispositions which are caused by *joy* and *sorrow*; and a joyous and cheerful temper, as well as one melancholy and depressed, &c., is no innate force or power of the soul, but only an assemblage of individual, single *forms* of disposition [Stimmungsgebilde]. For further details on 'Temper' see below, § 69 at the end.

§ 25. *Desires are developed out of Forms produced by Pleasurable Stimulation.*

Let us first recapitulate what we have just stated.

It often happens that a more powerful *stimulant acts on the original powers than they* need *for their satisfaction;* and yet without its being, properly speaking, immoderate. This sets them directly, so to say, on the swing, i.e. it *more thoroughly* excites them, (§ 24). Pleasurable stimulation.

When the stimulant is exactly *suitable* to the original powers, they take firm hold of it: it is thus that clear and distinct notions arise (§ 11). Full stimulation.

Now the question arises, what is the *further effect* of a pleasurable stimulation; that is, of the *preponderance* of stimulant over the original powers?

In such a case we generally express ourselves as follows: 'we were dazzled by the presence of so much beauty and splendour,' or 'the magic of those sweet sounds enchanted us;' 'we know very well that what we saw or heard, &c., was uncommonly lovely, beautiful, glorious; but we are unable to describe it exactly.'

Therefore when the stimulant preponderates over the power, we do not gain such clear and distinct notions as we do when we observe an object which only produces an effect exactly *suitable* to such a power. Powers greatly excited, set *as it were* on the swing, are not so ready to appropriate stimulants which pour in upon them with such extraordinary force, they can therefore only appropriate them *loosely* and *imperfectly*. But that yields no clear and distinct notions.

Therefore *when more stimulants affect the original powers than they are able to assimilate* (which is the case in pleasurable stimulation), *it follows that the stimulants can only be* retained *in a diminished degree.*

From this it follows further that,

If it be true, as it is, that even when a stimulant is *firmly* appropriated, a portion of it is always detached from the power (in consequence of which conscious notions again become unconscious § 12); *then when a stimulant is only retained in the* loose, imperfect *manner above described, a still* larger *portion of it must vanish from the power that appropriates it.*

What will the effect of this be?

I have eaten an apple: its taste was delicious; how I wish that I had another like it!

Somebody sang a lovely song: I shouted *encore!* until he sang it again.

There was a splendid picture hanging there: I felt impelled to come back to it again and again to gaze at it, and could hardly satiate my eyes with the sight of it.

Somebody had a snuff-box. He kept on constantly opening it and taking a pinch. How is all this to be explained?

We already know that,

The original powers are *from the moment of birth, active,* and they continue to be so until they are satisfied by stimulants (§§ 23 and 11).

Therefore in so far as a power that has been satisfied with stimulants afterwards loses any of them, so far does it again become active and desiderative.

When I ate the apple I experienced *a pleasurable stimulation;* accordingly that stimulant was only *loosely* appropriated, and on that very account a portion of it vanished from the power. What was the consequence? The original powers thus rendered *poorer* in stimulants began to strive and desiderate afresh, and what is more, they strove after that stimulant by which they had just been filled: what I desired was another apple *like* that which I had eaten.

Thus, also, in the above instances, our auditory powers desiderated *the same* melody, the visual powers *the same* picture, the powers of smelling wanted to be satisfied again with the stimulant of *snuff*, because they had all of them lost a portion of the stimulants which they received We find then that,

When the original powers* have lost a portion of the stimulant which they have received, *they immediately recover their original activity and desiderative power; only with this difference, that they no longer desiderate satisfaction by stimulants* generally and vaguely, *but they strive after* that exact *stimulant by which they have been already modified. That is to say, they never lose the whole of the stimulant; and the portion of it that is retained, determines what direction the renewed longing is to take, that is, towards a like stimulant. This brings about *definite* impulses.

***Therefore in the void unmodified original powers there exists only a* general *striving after stimulants; whereas after they have been stimulated, and have lost a portion of the stimulant, this impulse is directed to a* Definite object, *and is called* Desire.**

How, then, do *special, definite* [illegible] arise in the human soul?

Never when stimulation is full and perfect. It must be *pleasurable stimulation* which leads to the formation of *most* of our desires; for our whole nature is so constructed that what does us good cannot be otherwise than welcome.

§ 26. *How far Desires are engendered as a Consequence of the other Modes of Stimulation.*

If you shew a child half of any object it will want to see the whole of it. We take pains to make out that which we only hear indistinctly. The same is the case with insufficient stimulation in all the other senses.

Since the original powers are not completely filled by such half-stimulation, the part in them which is left unfilled directly seeks to be satisfied, and hence, under such circumstances, we always find a desire generated for the object which causes this unsatisfying stimulation. Now if you continue to stimulate a child's powers in this unsatisfying manner, and never give it full, complete stimulation, it will be found that its efforts after satisfaction will cease. Its powers are *relaxed*, *lowered in tone*, *weakened* by the recurrence of unsatisfying stimulation, and therefore at last they cease to act at all[b].

If it were possible to bring any one up *exclusively*, or *for the most part*, under the influence of such half-stimulation, he must become short-witted, however promising his disposition might be. Experience has proved this in the case of those unhappy persons who have been immured for a considerable time in damp, dark, gloomy dungeons.

When an exactly suitable amount of stimulant acts on the original powers, it is firmly appropriated, and they are perfected into clear and distinct notions. Notwithstanding, however, a portion of the stimulant always vanishes from the power afterwards, as we saw in § 12; the consequence of which is that what was excited *ceases to be so*, and thus becomes *unconscious*.

The loss of the stimulant always causes a renewed appetition for one like it on the part of the deprived power. Hence, full stimulation must also produce *desires*, though in a lower degree; because, owing to the firmness with which the stimulants are appropriated, only a small portion of the power is deprived of them, becomes void of stimulant, and therefore active or appetent. Thus, it often happens that we wish to see again a work which we have contemplated when the stimulants operated fully upon us; we desire to hear sounds *again* which have caused us pleasure, &c. In most cases, however, full stimulation so entirely satisfies our powers that their activity and appetency is completely pacified, and they only retain a disposition to renew the past *in consciousness*.

In the case of *over-stimulation* (stimulation to satiety) it is impossible to deny that the powers may be moved to desire satisfaction again by the same stimulants. We see this in

---

[b] *Repugnancies*, however, are hence generated; see below, § 33.

drunkards, gluttons, debauchees, who often desire fresh gratification at the very time when they feel disgust at their past excesses. But there can be no more than a *dull* appetition in each particular power, because it has been over-excited and *weakened* by long-continued stimulation, which naturally requires some time to disappear. That the drunkard, &c., however, feels a strong impulse towards fresh enjoyment, is explained from the great *number* of traces which have been for so long kept alive within him.

If we turn to *painful stimulation* we shall find that it yields no results as far as the question before us is concerned. I have never yet met with anybody who, after being deafened by some sudden and violent report, *desired* to hear such an one again. The same is the case with blinding by a dazzling light, sudden and pungent impressions on taste or smell, burning, hard blows, &c.

And it is very natural that a desire for a second effect of the kind should *not* be formed. For the powers are so weakened by such sudden impressions, that they must lose their original elasticity.

From all this we see that no kind of stimulation is so suitable for the formation of Desires as the *pleasurable*.

In such a case the power not only remains at nearly its original force, but it also acquires, through the fulness of the stimulant, a peculiar modification which consists in this, that its original appetency or activity is intensified. In it also, owing to the *loose* unstable connexion between stimulant and power, a very considerable portion (but never the whole) of the former vanishes directly, and thus we have a case where both conditions are fulfilled under which in particular a *definite* appetency, i.e. a *Desire* is possible. Compare § 32.

§ 27. *Desires are at the same time Notions. Two different shapes in which Pleasurable Forms* [Lustgebilde] *may be re-excited.*

Before, therefore, a desire can arise in the soul, an object must have acted on our powers, and the most favourable mannin which it can do so is, as we saw in the preceding §, *pleasurable stimulation.*

Now we already know from § 4, that when external stimulants unite with our original powers, *sensations* are produced, and by constant repetition (§ 10) *perceptions* or *notions*[c].

If, therefore, a flower has often excited pleasure in my sense of sight, there will have been formed in the same powers not merely *a desire* for it, but also at the same time *a notion* of it: *for a union between stimulants and original powers took place*, and *all the stimulants* have not vanished. Only *a portion* of them disappear, and it is only to that extent that our powers become again appetent—only to that extent has *a desire* been engendered.

Hence *we form a notion* of all things that *we desire* simultaneously in *the same* act, or, what amounts to the same thing, in *the same psychical form.* As is clear from all that we have hitherto said, all the forms of our soul spring from *acts:* they are, whether they be simple or complex forms (see the note on p. 19), nothing but acts *in repose*, or traces; and when they are aroused from that repose they recur as *acts.*

Consequently one and the same form of the human soul may be of a twofold nature; partly *a desire*, partly *a notion.* It is *a notion*[d] in so far as the stimulants are *permanently retained;* *a desire* in so far as they have *vanished* from the powers, and are now again sought after afresh in *definite* stimulants (§ 25).

Notion and desire accordingly are in such cases only two different *shapes* (modes of development) of one and the same form (act); they are positively not two different forms. When any such form (engendered by pleasurable stimulation) is again excited, one or other of these shapes or aspects may be brought into special prominence; it may be reproduced sometimes in the one shape, sometimes in the other. If the pleasurable stimulant has been firmly retained, or if what it has lost has been

---

[c] On sensations and perceptions, see § 50.

[d] This notion must always be one of *pleasure*, because it was formed under *pleasurable* stimulation.

replaced perfectly by other like stimulants (see § 13 and in particular § 31), the form excited takes the shape of a *pleasurable notion* [Lustvorstellung] (recollection of pleasure); if, on the contrary, it has not been retained, nor had its place supplied, it returns as *a desire* for pleasure *.

Hence we arrive at this very important principle, *that pleasurable forms are capable of a twofold re-excitation* (reproduction): partly as a recollection of pleasure, partly as a desire for pleasure; or *they are manifested in two modes of reproduction.*

Is it possible that in many forms one of these shapes may become *permanent?* Certainly it is. There are men who must always desire again what they often desired at an earlier period (see the following §); because the powers in the Form in question have become incapable of permanently appropriating the stimulant which they receive, and which forthwith vanishes from them. The powers of the lower senses are naturally less capable than others of firmly retaining their stimulants, and hence they reproduce their pleasurable forms almost exclusively

---

* We shall see below in § 49, how far a third form, that of *Feeling*, may belong to it.

Moreover, no psychical form, not even one of dislike, is totally divested of all traces of a notion: we always form to ourselves notions of what causes us unpleasing emotions, and in fact, in the very *same* act; for a portion of the stimulant proceeding from the object abides in the power receiving it, and, at the moment it produces its effect, the stimulant cannot have yet disappeared entirely. Notional forms are more prominently conspicuous in the class of desires, [i.e. whenever we feel desire of any kind we have a more distinct notion of the object required, as well as of our subjective state, than is the case with the other psychical forms just alluded to,] because in them stimulants are more numerous and more intimately incorporated with our powers, than in forms of displeasure or dislike when the notion is always obscure. Under all circumstances the clearest notions arise in the second mode of stimulation (i.e. full stimulation), and they are then neutral between pleasure and displeasure: it is exactly for this reason that they cannot be the source of our actions; they mainly furnish us with the knowledge (theory) of objects: they constitute us *theoretical*, speculative, and not practical beings.

in the shape of desires (§ 29). In the higher senses, on the other hand, cases often occur where a former pleasurable impression always recurs as a recollection of pleasure, simply because these powers are vigorous enough permanently to retain their stimulants.

Other pleasurable forms are susceptible of both modes of reproduction, either always, or at least at first, and until one or other of them has become definitely fixed to the exclusion of the other.

§ 28. *Like Desires coalesce. Inclination, Propension, Passion.*

We have already seen, in §§ 9, 16, 18 and 20, that in perceptions, concepts, judgments and inferences, the law holds *that similars in the soul always coalesce with similars.* Are we to regard the desires as forming an exception to the rule?

Whenever I eat new potatoes, I ought, as I am told, always to drink a small glass of kümmel [carraway-brandy], for health's sake. I am not fond of brandy; however, I asked for some. I relished the first glass because the kümmel was capital, excellent—I was pleasurably stimulated—and it did me a world of good. The second time I liked it far better than the first, and so matters went on till I had finished the bottle. I ate potatoes again, and in a moment I felt as if I must again take a drop. I was on the very point of getting the bottle refilled when I became aware how strong my desire had become, and, as I believe, not a moment too soon. I got the better of myself, and thought of that woman who *was obliged*, as she used to say, to get up in the night and have a talk with her bottle. She, too, began by taking a small glass of liqueur after dinner to promote digestion. And does not every drunkard do the same?

That man, then, who is perpetually opening his box to take a pinch, at first very seldom took snuff, only perhaps when some one offered him his box. But presently so strong a desire was formed in his powers of smell that he could no longer wait until somebody offered him a pinch; he bought himself a snuff-box.

A rich Englishman was very fond of beautiful flowers, of which he possessed a large number of kinds. One day somebody offered him some handsome and rare birds; he bought them; by-and-by he added to his stores a collection of minerals, which cost him a good deal of money. The more people praised his 'taste for natural history,' the more did he *increase* the objects of which he was so fond, nor was he able to resist this inclination until he found himself beginning to run in debt.

These examples suffice to prove *that similar desires coalesce in one whole or form, though the objects which engender them may be very different.*

Thus arises what in common life we call *inclination, propensity, passion,* according as the number of desires which unite into a whole is *small, great,* or *very large.*

In common usage, however, propensity and passion are often both called 'inclinations,' so that this expression is sometimes taken in a narrow, sometimes in a wide, sometimes in the most extensive sense[f].

---

[f] "These three species of strongly associated traces may be distinguished from one another in the most precise manner by considering *the modes in which they can be awakened into consciousness.* '*Inclination*' [Neigung], in the narrow sense of that term, is excited into consciousness when the diffused elements (see §§ 30, 31,) are *directly* transferred to it; '*Propension*' [Hang] is aroused even when an opportunity for its display is *indirectly* and *distantly* suggested: whilst '*Passion*' [Leidenschaft], owing to the *extraordinary multiplicity* of the traces united in it, lies so near to consciousness, that it may be said to always exist in a state of semi-consciousness; it is always, so to say, on the very point of attaining to full and perfect excitation the moment the soul is left free from other activities and modes of development.

"The highest degree in which this multiform association of such traces or forces can exist, and the products thence determined, is, in common life, called by the name of *Vice* ['*Laster*' = vice, crime, what weighs down or oppresses]. The inclination weighs down the soul to such a degree that it is totally unable to free itself from the burden."—(*Beneke's* "Lehrbuch der Psychologie," Ed. III., p. 126 sqq.) [A note of more consequence to the German than to the English reader.]

Can we be astonished then at the extraordinary *strength* and *power* which the inclinations manifest in so many men? As the trunk of an oak consists of thousands and thousands of fibres, so are these the aggregate of thousands upon thousands of desires. Every desire was at first simple. But as fresh ones were perpetually being formed, each fresh impression of pleasure exciting and modifying some fresh and single original power, we must suppose the law of the Mutual Attraction of Similars to have become inoperative, if similar and allied desires did not coalesce and mutually strengthen each other.

The only question that can now be raised is how *the real*, the objective element in desires, can allow them to flow together, since undoubtedly that element is not unfrequently very heterogeneous, as the above example of the Englishman shews. The following § will afford a partial answer to this question; but the important point in such a case is the well-known law of experience, that a variety of *different* objects mutually obscure each other in consciousness; and the more so in proportion as a larger number of them are excited together. Bring only ten different notions into consciousness at the same moment, and not one of them will be clear, however clear they may be when presented singly. But this *obscuration* does not *diminish* the appetency of the powers of desire. Compare § 73 at the end.

The sum total of all the desires that are engendered and permanent in the soul (whether simple or complex) is called *man's* **desiderative power**, *or his desires.*

With what does it begin?

§ 29. *Influence exerted on the Formation of Desires by the* **qualities** *of the Original Powers.*

1°. *Tenacity.*

If a desire is to be engendered in the human soul we have already seen in § 25 that a portion of the pleasurable stimulant must *vanish* from the power, and *a desire is produced only in so far as this occurs* (§ 27). Now, since, when the tenacity of the original powers is very great, the disappearance of the stimulant is proportionately less, it is clear *that a very high degree of strength and tenacity is not requisite in order that desires may be formed.*

Hence it is that we find most of our desires and passions engendered in the *lower senses:* examples are furnished by gluttons, drunkards, snuff-takers, tobacco-smokers, &c.

And yet, on the other side, the formation of strong desires[*] and passions *necessitates* a certain degree of tenacity on the part of the original powers.

For such are produced solely in consequence of the fact mentioned in the preceding §, viz. that *all similar desires coalesce into one Form, which implies that the individual desires are* permanent *in the shape of traces* (§§ 6 and 17.)

If, then, the original powers were so weak that *no Traces*, or only *insufficient traces*, were left by each fresh desire as it arose, what we call inclination, propensity, passion, could never be produced to all eternity.

Hence may be explained why idiots and brutes never develope passions, though they do inclinations. *Congenital* idiocy consists essentially in an abnormal weakness of the original powers, a weakness which is always to be found in brutes, but is, in their case, normal. Such powers let the greater portion of the pleasurable stimulant which they have received loose again, they do not retain that *high tension* which is produced in strong powers by pleasure, and consequently nothing but faint, weak Traces, are left behind. In consequence of this,

---

[*] Between *Begierden* [strong desires] and Begehrungen [desires strong or weak] there is, properly speaking, no difference. Still, as commonly used, Begierden indicate over-strong desires [zu starke Begehrungen] and, therefore, inclinations manifested with some notable vehemence. To talk of inclinations *and* strong desires [von Neigungen *und* Begierden] as though these words indicated two different kinds of things, is an error; just as there are no "Impulses" [Triebe] *beside* and apart from inclinations and strong desires, for the desires in all their shapes are impulsive, or impulses. [Again a note of less interest to the Englishman than to the German.]

therefore, they no more exhibit *passions* than they do clear notions and concepts; but it must be admitted that both idiots and brutes have inclinations. Are not our domestic animals inclined to do repeatedly what they have been taught and trained to perform? Do they not acquire likings for particular persons, places, enjoyments, &c.?

A very high degree of tenacity, therefore, is not required to form inclinations, but a certain degree of it is indispensable in order to form **strong desires** *and* **passions.**

All desires, even those of the *lower* senses, grow, in healthy men, into passions, if pleasurable stimulation is perpetually repeated, and they thus acquire a strength and fixity which is often quite invincible. Take such instances as love of drink, of gaming, of ruling, of money, of finding fault, &c.

The inclinations of the *higher* senses, though they are strengthened by the coalescence of desires, never, *of themselves*, attain to that *clearness of consciousness* which is acquired by notions which grow as Traces are accumulated; the reason is, that in the desires the stimulants are no match for the powers. Clear consciousness only arises where stimulant and power are in equilibrium. Compare §§ 11, 24, and 32. Hence may be explained why most men know so little about their own inclinations, although the obscuration mentioned in p. 69 contributes largely to that result.

2°. *Sensibility.*

If a desire is to be generated in the human soul, the powers of the latter must be *pleasurably stimulated* (§§ 25, 26). Now, when the original powers are such that they can seize on *weaker* stimulants and unite with them; in short, when they possess greater *sensibility* (§ 5), it follows that *pleasurable stimulation* will the sooner be produced in them.

A small quantity of seasoning in his food produces pleasure at once in one who has naturally a delicate and impressible sense of taste: one less sensitive requires, perhaps, the addition of pepper or salt.

A man with a delicate ear for music feels, at once, great pleasure when he hears a soft low melody: one with less susceptibility requires the rattle of kettledrums and the blaring of trumpets to cause him any delight, &c.

In a word, *the greater the sensibility the quicker and more frequently is pleasurable excitement produced.*

Now if these pleasurable modes of excitation are the peculiar centre where desires are fashioned (§ 26), it follows *that sensibility is of great importance in their production.*

3°. *Vivacity.*

The more lively the original powers are, the quicker do they appropriate stimulants; but in the same degree the sooner do the latter *disappear* (§ 14).

Since we can only desire what we have not got, and powers when satisfied want nothing, it follows that no desire makes its appearance in them so long as no stimulant has escaped from their grasp. The sooner that takes place the sooner must desire arise; *consequently the vivacity of the original powers also exercises an important influence on the generation of desires.*

The phlegmatic man, whose original powers are defective in sensibility and vivacity, is, for this reason, never betrayed into passion. Even his desires are very weak, and it is rarely that anything is permitted to ruffle his darling repose.

§ 30. *Original Powers and Stimulants as Movable Elements.*

A. All the psychical forms hitherto considered (Perception, Concept, Judgment, Inference, Desire, Inclination, Propension, Passion,) are products of original powers and stimulants.

Original Powers, therefore, *and Stimulants*, are the *constituents* or **Elements** of those forms.

In forms produced by *full stimulation* both elements are *firmly* connected; they are less firmly connected in those arising from *pleasurable stimulation.* This stability is still less in the case of *half-stimulation, over stimulation* (to satiety), or *painful stimulation* (§ 24).

There are, therefore, in our souls, forms the elements of which may be separated again more or less completely, and if separation takes place they lose the peculiar stamp which they fornerly received, and turn into *general*, *free* elements, which may be employed in other ways. We shall call both these kinds of elements *movable*.

This is the *first kind* of movable elements.

B. Every evening sleep comes on, and announces its approach by an increasing disability on my part to see and hear, so that it appears almost as if I had lost the power to do either: the other senses also, shortly before falling asleep, become more and more incapable of seizing on their appropriate stimulants. At last, even my clearest notions sink into unconsciousness; but whether I will or not, they start up next morning into consciousness, fresh and lively. It again becomes perfectly easy for my senses to seize on their stimulants. No wonder! for during sleep *fresh original powers* have been formed (§ 13), they cause this renewed activity of my senses, and thus excite consciousness afresh. For details see § 82.

Now we are justified in calling these newly-formed original powers *movable* elements also. True, they attach themselves to psychical forms already existing, for they cannot dwell apart, as it were, in some corner of the soul; but for all that they are not firmly attached to them, for fixity can only pertain to the developed, to what is definitely modified. As yet, however, they have received no stimulants, they are as yet unable to coalesce with them, and have not yet been definitely applied to any purpose. This they will be during the day. For the present they are *un*modified, *un*formed, objectively *void*, *unemployed*, *free* powers, which may be employed in one way or the other, simply because they have not yet been actually used, actually *appropriated* in any. Their relation, therefore, to the *modified and formed* powers is that of general elements.

This is the *second kind* of movable elements.

C. Were it possible for the powers *already developed*, i.e. the *Traces* (Forms), immediately *to seize upon stimulants* (to see, hear, smell, &c.); if, moreover, *consciousness* could be kept going or awake merely by the *Traces* in which it, as a fact, resides; then any acquisition of fresh original powers, and sleep as well, would be completely unnecessary. But it is a law, that every stimu-

lant coming from without must be first taken up by s
unemployed power, before it can take its place amo
already developed and formed; on which account seei
ing, &c., cease directly these free powers have been
during the day, i.e. have been converted into traces,
rendered unfit for the immediate apprehension of st
It is, moreover, a law, that the Traces can maintain t
sciousness only so long as they are excited by elemen
solely on condition that they themselves are excited,
not yet *constituent parts* of the traces. They are, it
taken up by the traces, but are not, therefore, *app*
by them.

Now, invariable experience shews that as long as I a
and have my eyes open, light-stimulants are constantly s
into my visual powers, and yet they do not all of them
perception in me. I only have an intuition when I l
attention, with a certain effort, and not in the superficia
in which I frequently do (see § 71). If I am to kn
I am looking at, those Traces within me which suit t
now affecting me must be aroused for the purpose, th
the only way in which I apprehend impressions, and so
perceive objects. Now, very often no perception ta
notwithstanding that my eyes are open, whence it foll
the light-stimulants operating in such cases are discha
the *void*, *unemployed* powers of sight (original powers)
becoming firmly attached to them. Were they so u
them they would become to a certain extent consci
§§ 6 and 71) without the assistance of the Traces, whi
ever, is not the case. They are, therefore, for the
unappropriated.

The case is similar with hearing. I frequently rec
my auditory powers stimulants without gaining by t
clear perceptions of sound, for I am not always listeni
attention. The products previously formed in the soul
suitable for perception often do not flow towards the im
of sound at all, or, at least, only in such insignificant
that at best I only half hear, sometimes less than h

and in many cases fail to do so at all. The sounds produced by men and brutes, strains of music, the ringing of bells, the noise of hammering, &c., are often producing some effect upon me, and I am almost always surrounded by a busy hum of all sorts. These stimulants of sound therefore can, in those cases where I remain half or entirely deaf to them, only attach themselves to the *void*, *unemployed* auditory powers (original powers) in the shape of *unappropriated* elements. It often occurs to me afterwards that I had some sort of faint inkling of these stimulants of light and sound: what does that prove?

With the other senses the case is similar to a greater or less extent. That of touch is frequently affected by objects which we take up and hold, and yet no perceptions of touch, properly so called, are produced, and the sense of feeling (vital sense) is perpetually influenced by air, warmth, &c. Yet I have no clear sensation of them; in both cases for exactly the same reason. In like manner the sense of taste is being perpetually excited by impressions produced by the saliva; that of smell by odours and exhalations of all kinds: but who clearly perceives all these at all times? I do not notice that the vital powers in the lungs are perpetually taking up out of the air minute portions of oxygen, which form (in a waking condition) one of the supports of consciousness; and yet when I breathe stifling air, or am prevented from breathing at all, consciousness is certainly extinguished, if not life itself.

Briefly: external stimulants of all kinds are perpetually pouring in through all the six doors of our soul, and they are from the first properly denominated *general* stimulants. They are taken up, for the most part, without our noticing them, for they are received merely into the void, unemployed, unconscious original powers, and, as a rule, we become aware of their existence only when they wholly cease to act, e.g. when sudden darkness comes on, or when the clock or anything else that produces a familiar and monotonous noise suddenly ceases, when the warm room in which we are begins to be cold, that is, becomes rapidly cold, &c. That, however, such stimulants are introduced into the original powers, that those powers need them, and are perpetually on the look out for them, is clear from this; that you have only to cover anybody's eyes and ears, and he will soon push your hands away, for the original powers are bent on being constantly occupied by stimulants, on being, as it were, fed superficially by them. Powers, on the contrary, which have been *developed* and thus *satisfied* very often do not require fresh external stimulants for weeks, nay, for months and years together.

These *stimulants* thus *received within*, which are only *loosely* attached to the *original powers*, are also to be called *movable* elements.

This is the *third* kind of movable elements.

If we sum up what has been said it appears that we have learnt this much:

One portion of the movable elements is produced thus: *powers and stimulants already* united *may partially be* separated again from each other, *and thus lose the special impress which they had received*, and this in proportion to the *want of firmness* with which the stimulants have been appropriated.

A second portion arises from *the daily* formation of fresh *original powers in the soul, which there await some definite employment.*

The third and last portion are thus produced: *stimulants of many sorts are perpetually, and without our being aware of it, attracted to the soul during our waking hours, and therefore attach themselves to the* original powers, *but are* not firmly and definitely appropriated by them.

All movable elements are as such unconscious, and as they on this account are transferred or transplanted to forms of all kinds in a greater or less degree, they are obviously one and all *general* elements.

If we compare these movable elements with the fixed which are permanently connected in the Traces, it is easy to see that they can never be so numerous as those of the latter kind are. For, granting that the powers and stimulants in the traces may afterwards separate, still experience shows that comparatively few Traces are in this way resolved absolutely into their elements, and that to this process we owe but a small portion of the movable. The only Traces which can be thus resolved and lost, are those produced by a stimulation which was too dull, too fleeting, or too defective. Just so stimulants which continue for a time to be movable can only enter the soul, if void unemployed original powers are at hand to which they may attach themselves; for they cannot, as it were, float about in the air—they are not self-supporting. But the number of such original powers can never be so great as that of those which are already elaborated into Traces, for that which is produced during six or eight hours sleep can never be so abundant as that which has been engendered and rendered permanent during a longer period of life, therefore in the course of many years: consequently, the *general* stimulants cannot be so numerous as the fixed. All this necessarily follows from three facts. If these free powers were more numerous, or even as numerous as formed powers, the soul must develope, i.e. add to its traces, with enormous rapidity: but it only does so *very gradually*. Secondly, only a small number of Traces are ever present to consciousness at the same time, which could not be if the exciting movable elements were equally numerous with the Traces. The strongest proof, however, is—that, in the third place, the new powers acquired during the night, however they may be applied, are only sufficient for one, or at most for a *few*, days, which certainly could not be the case if they at all approached the developed powers in number. Hence a young child, after it has busied itself with looking, hearing, &c., for some time, must go to sleep, in order to obtain fresh powers to receive fresh impressions (stimulants), and even an adult, after looking and hearing for a long time, must, at least, rest, if he does not sleep, in order to let those powers which were only slightly modified and affected again divest themselves of their stimulants, so that they may be applied elsewhere, i.e. to apprehend other objects or be otherwise employed. All further psychical growth must be arrested, unless the traces already acquired are supplemented by fresh original powers: the former alone would never suffice for the purpose[h]. Compare § 82.

§ 31. *Transference of the Movable Elements.*

Now what is done by these *movable elements* in the soul?

We know something about this already. Fresh original powers are destined directly to produce new traces by uniting *firmly* with the stimulants of the external world. When these *external stimulants* flow towards Traces already formed, they excite them into consciousness (§ 12).

---

[h] [This is not a close rendering of the original, which runs thus: Eine zu grösserem Umfange und Reichthum fortschreitende Entwickelung ist durch die schon erworbenen Spuren allein niemals möglich. A literal translation would probably be unintelligible to most readers].

But *internal stimulants*, also, and void (as yet unformed) *original powers* do the same, by attaching themselves more definitely to the Traces. (§ 13.)[1]

It is easy to add to the examples which we have already given in § 13.

[1]*a*. What joy does the first fine spring day cause the traveller; it sheds pleasure and delight over his whole soul.

b. A man hears of an unexpected legacy. You should see how *he was excited*, i.e. how countless forms, hitherto unconscious, passed through his soul—became conscious in rapid succession.

c. I was sitting peaceably at my work, and my thoughts were pursuing their usual course, when I received a long-wished-for letter from my friend. My calmness vanished; thousands upon thousands of notions, judgments, desires, &c., were awakened, and caused me delight.

How is all this to be explained? Only by stimulants which are partly projected into the soul from without, partly which, being already existent within, are passed on from one psychical form to another.

In case *a*, the extraordinary abundance of stimulants which thronged into the soul of the traveller at the glorious sight of nature were not held fast each by its correspondent power (§ 30),

---

[1] Carefully note that the term '*movable elements*' is applied only to the two latter species. So long as stimulants exist externally they are, it is true, also movable, and they do, as a fact, move into the soul and affect it, but as external elements they are not as yet psychical elements, and only elements of the soul are intended when we contrast the unfixed or movable with the fixed. How hard it often is, moreover, to firmly attach stimulants to their powers, no one knows better than the teacher: it is the business of his life to contend with the want of fixedness prevalent in the psychical elements of children. What to-day seemed to be firmly appropriated is, in the morning, loose and imperfectly retained; indeed, it has often vanished altogether from the powers which had taken it up.

In the external world, as well as in the internal, the opposition between fixed and unfixed elements (constituent parts) prevails, and here, as in the soul, the fixed and consolidated is formed, not unfrequently with great slowness, out of the unfixed or movable.

the larger portion remained *movable*, and flowed over other psychical forms which were at the moment in repose, *excited* them, and thus made them *conscious*. As the feeling of spring is a pleasurable stimulant, it cannot produce dislike in what it excites, and as, at the same time, according to the law of the Mutual Attraction of Similars, other pleasurable stimulants *already possessed* must be excited as well, we may explain the joy which manifested itself in the traveller's mind.

In case *b*, the news of the inheritance was conveyed by stimulants as indifferent (in audible words) as the impressions derived from the characters of the letter in case *c*. Neither is any pleasure contained in them; and yet they both excited much pleasure. Why so? The movable portion of the abundant stimulants already *inherent in* the notions of 'inheritance' and 'friend' passed to other psychical forms which were not at the moment conscious, caused them to be vividly excited, and thus to become conscious. Indeed, the notions of 'inheritance' and 'friend' are pleasurable notions, hence full of stimulants, and by them only homogeneous; i.e. pleasurable notions can be excited, while, to some extent, ordinary notions by this kind of excitement receive the stamp of pleasure, and the more so since *general* stimulants also (which are only absent when we are exhausted) are carried along by this violent excitement, and transferred with special fulness to ordinary notions.

Had the contents of the letter excited unpleasant emotions they would have occasioned an equally strong but opposite effect, which would have been propagated to the rest of our psychical forms, and thus, not unfrequently, a veritable storm is excited within. (See §§ 33 and 34.)

Furthermore. Somebody pronounces before me the word 'pinnacle,' excites the corresponding *notion*, and he requires me to think of that and of nothing else. I am quite unable to do this. Against my will the whole spire comes into consciousness, indeed, it carries me still further, and I think of the church belonging to the spire—its exterior, interior, &c. 'Think of the road that leads to Dresden and of nothing else.' But in attempting to do so I think of the adjoining fields, localities, &c., and do what I can I am unable to banish from the notion 'road' the stimulants of sound which proceed from it: they spread irresistably towards other notions. Again: six and three are ——? four times five is ——? London is situated on the ——? in the beginning God created ——; and so on. The omitted portions of these imperfect sentences start up into consciousness in a moment, provided they already exist within, but, of course, not otherwise. Who ever experienced the reverse of all this? Or will any one venture to say that the notions themselves spread one into another? What would become of them if they fastened one on the other, and so got mixed together?

These examples will render clear what is meant by '*the Disappearance of Stimulants*,' an expression which we have often used. It is not that they disappear out of the soul, but that stimulants actually taken up, yet not firmly appropriated, are transplanted from form to form, are transferred from one to the other, in the same way as external stimulants are communicated to them [h].

The same thing happens with freshly produced void, original powers; since they are naturally *active*, they generally attach themselves directly to those forms which are homogeneous with them, and therefore to the *Desires, states of will, inclinations, disinclinations, &c.* In such forms the powers are predominant, the stimulant retires more into the background, and thus free original powers lean on them, so to speak, and become mainly serviceable to them by transferring themselves from them to that which has to be excited by them. To their action we owe volitional, *arbitrary* excitement. The following example will illustrate this:—

I have forgotten the name of a hero in a play, and want to

---

[h] We may, therefore, banish the process of the Disappearance of Stimulants from consideration, seeing that it is contained and implied in that of the diffusion or transference of movable elements. See below, the note in § 43.

In order to explain those internal excitations it was formerly usual to assume the existence of *an innate power of recollection*. But that hypothesis is totally incompetent to account for those violent perturbations of soul which so frequently occur under circumstances of joy, ecstacy, &c.; and on the other side, in a remarkable manner, in terror, fear, despair, &c. In such cases there must be a good many exciting causes at work, not one merely. Moreover, a definite and independent power of recollection could not leave us in the lurch so often as we actually are left: it must, if it existed at all, act uniformly.

recollect it: what is the man's name? Albion? Ilion? I think the letter A formed part of it. That big bandit, as Zschocke represents him, the man with the frightful nose and satanic laugh—what *is* his name? I plague myself ever so long without success. If I could see his name on paper—if *external* stimulants were to affect me—I should know it directly. But *these* are absent. There are *internal* stimulants enough present, but I must wait a long time if I wait till they chance to excite it into consciousness. I want, if possible, to recover the name at once, and all I have for the purpose are merely free original powers which, by the act of desiring, I have already sent on the search through my soul. I have already excited the forms Ilion, Albion, but that is not the name. Albion, Ilion: no! not that, but something like it. Stop! now I know it: *Abällino* was what the fellow was called.

Who has not often experienced the like?

Now we learn from this, *that it is not* **movable stimulants** *alone that pass in the soul from form to form and excite the unconscious into (involuntary) consciousness:* **movable, loose original powers** *as well transfer themselves to unconscious forms, and so* **excite** *them (voluntarily) and render them* **conscious.** *Forms thus rendered conscious immediately cease to be so when the exciting elements are withdrawn from them.*

Thus these *loose* or *movable elements* are what first bring *life* into the soul, if the expression be allowable: and we can now perfectly understand the following proposition:—

Original Powers and internal stimulants, in so far as they exist as movable elements, are perpetually flowing during our waking state from one form to another, and thus cause that alternation of consciousness which exists at every moment in the human soul.

The law thus enunciated we call the law of *the Diffusion of Movable Elements.*

Should any one object that 'this explanation is false, for *we are totally unaware of any such transference,*' he may be reminded that the objection proves too much, and consequently that it proves nothing. We do not in the least notice the transference of *external* stimulants to the soul which, nevertheless, takes place at every moment in seeing, hearing, &c.; we are naturally inclined to suppose that seeing, hearing, &c., are acts which are and remain quite external, and yet, after seeing, hearing, &c., those stimulants exist *within* us, for we can recall into consciousness the effects which they produced, and that, too, without fresh external excitation. In like manner, we do not in the least notice the circulation of the fluids and of the blood in our bodies, nor the motion of the earth, nor the movement of light reflected from a mirror to our eyes, &c., and yet do not all these things take place? Nor need we be in the least anxious about the question how such individual, singular elements can generate an intelligible order and law in the process of becoming conscious. See § 38 and §§ 73. 74.

§ 32. *Strong and Weak Psychical Forms.*

We shall frequently have occasion to refer to the movable elements and their constant transition from one psychical form to another, for the purpose of explaining facts in the human soul. At present, however, we wish to interpose some remarks which are easily deducible from what we have already said, and which will serve to throw light on what is to come.

When an *insufficient stimulant* acts on an original power and is by it appropriated, the latter is, of course, *modified* or *formed* by the stimulant, only it is so in a *weak*, *insufficient* manner: at best only an *obscure* sensation is produced, and a faint effort on the part of the imperfectly satisfied power after full satisfaction (§ 26).

Now suppose a man were mainly brought up only under such half-stimulation, would he ever attain a strong psychical development? Never. And though the Traces of thousands of similar imperfect stimulations were united in one whole, still they would never yield a *strong* and *clear* form (§ 11[1]).

---

[1] "The fresh weakness increases the former weakness, and as a thousand poor people do not make one rich one, so a thousand weak traces do not make one strong one." (*Dressler's* Beiträge zu einer bessern Gestaltung der Psychologie und Pädagogik. I. Theil, p. 119.) It is here exactly as it is, for instance, with water; a single drop of water is not a fixed, stable thing, nor will it become so even if you add to it a thousand other drops. The kind of evolution then referred to is, properly speaking, degeneration—the reverse of development.

We learn from this, that *half-stimulation never produces* **strength,** *never a* **strong psychical form** : *on the contrary, when subjected to such influences, the soul must eternally remain* **weak** *and* **imperfect** : *and although it constantly enlarges, still it only increases the number of imperfectly-formed original powers, i.e. of* **weak psychical forms.**

When thus half stimulated we have no feeling of perfection or satisfaction—we rather feel a sense of *dislike*, of *dissatisfaction.* Hence we may call those weak forms, *Forms of Dislike* [Unlustgebilde]. —Moreover,

If too *full* a stimulant acts *constantly* on an original power the latter becomes *wearied, stupified, over-stimulated:* we perceive this by the gradual rise of an adverse feeling, which we call *Satiety, Disgust.*

But if an *immoderate* stimulant acts *suddenly* on the original power, then follows a *sudden depression* of it, *over-stimulation, weakening*, and the feeling attendant on it is one of *Pain* (§ 24).

Therefore, in both cases, we find the opposite of what occurs when the soul is developed perfectly and strongly (we have a kind of degeneration—reverse development).

The character of our original powers is decidedly *changed* by both these modes of stimulation. Not merely is their original strength diminished in different ways, *the stimulants are also retained by them in different degrees*, which explains why these kinds of Traces produce such different effects afterwards. In the case of *stimulation to satiety, a tolerably large amount of stimulant must remain* in the weakened power; for satiety and disgust previously felt, only require to be internally excited, when a stimulation is manifested almost as strong as if an immediate and direct impression were being made, and this may, in some cases, even produce vomiting. The stimulant would accordingly seem to have gained a sort of independent existence, and yet the weakened power must, after all, be that in which it is deposited, so that we may regard these Traces as being, to some extent, *subsequent formations* produced in consequence of the weakened power not having sufficiently retained its stimulants. Hence, loss of stimulant occurs principally in the case of *painful stimulation*, on which account, when the traces are again excited from within, we find no such effect produced by stimulants as in the former case, although a minimum of the stimulant is retained even by the most debilitated power. In the case of *half-stimulation* less of the stimulant must be retained firmly because less was taken up.

Therefore the original powers are very decidedly *developed* (*modified*) when stimulated to pain or disgust, only they are not thereby *perfected* but *weakened*. Hence, the more the soul is stimulated in these two ways, the more *weak forms* must it gain instead of *strong* ones. Or are we inclined to call sated, timid, anxious, depressed, mournful, despairing, souls, *strong* souls? These weak forms may be termed 'Forms of Dislike' in a wider sense.

Hence it follows that *the soul is not* **strengthened** *by half-stimulation, by painful stimulation, or by stimulation to satiety, but* **weakened**: *not* **strong** *but* **weak forms** *are* **engendered** *by them, and such forms are just as capable of permanently existing* (*in an unexcited condition*) *as the strong are.*

Now consider *full stimulation.*

The mere feeling that immediately accompanies it (we find ourselves pacified, improved, perfected, in short, *elevated*), shews that the soul has gained in strength, and the more the original powers are satisfied by stimulants in this manner the more strong forms does the soul gain. Compare §§ 11 and 24.

How does the case stand with *pleasurable stimulation?*

Here the stimulant *preponderates* it is true over the power, yet it does not *subdue* or *weaken* it. On the contrary, the power gains a *more intense appetency for the stimulant*, a kind of *abandonment to it*, which is manifested in the augmented strength with which it seeks the stimulant which it has lost. Very naturally! for the stimulant *nearly* overcame the power.

From this it is clear that pleasurable stimulation must produce *strong psychical forms*. But since the stimulant is not in this case so firmly appropriated (especially when the tenacity of the powers is small) as in full stimulation, the result is, that, on the other hand, pleasurable stimulation does not *strengthen* the soul in the same degree as full stimulation does.

Accordingly, pleasure produces, it is true, *Desires*, but they are not *strong psychical forms simply*, or *as such*, even when they have been so accumulated as to produce passion; they are, in fact, *defective* in that very thing which assures a power of perfect development, namely, perfect *stimulation*, for, in their case, a portion of it has vanished: hence they strive after *fresh*, repeated satisfaction from the same stimulant.

Consequently, *pleasurable stimulation* produces in a power an intermediate condition, half *strength*, half *weakness*: *strength*, in so far as the stimulant received is permanently retained in the power, or in so far as the pleasurable effect produces a notion of pleasure (which becomes clearer in proportion as more Traces are accumulated): *weakness*, in so far as the stimulant again disappears from the power, or the pleasurable effect engenders a desire. (Compare § 27.)

The result of our enquiry is this:

The human soul acquires strength or weakness according as its original powers are modified and developed by different modes of stimulation. These powers are strengthened *only in so far as external stimulants are intimately united with them: they remain* weak, *or are* weakened, *if that intimate union is hindered in any way by unfavourable modes of stimulation, and thus either* a defect of stimulant *is created in the power, or such a* fullness *of it, as* lames *and cramps its original force* (as in stimulation to satiety).

It has already been observed at the end of § 24, that powers developed under these circumstances acquire a permanent tone and character of their own, and therefore become Forms of Disposition and Temper.

We may call the original powers original forces, provided that we do not forget that in no case can they be so strong as developed powers are. They are forces in a lower state of existence, and hence the child, when compared with the developed man, is not only weak in body, but in mind as well. Still forces they must be, they must have some strength, for otherwise they could not form the ground and *condition* for those higher forces which are developed from them by training in the right direction; nor, on the other hand, can they lose in energy by an opposite mode of treatment. Are the *fresh* original powers subsequently formed stronger than those which first existed? Certainly not. For, if that were the case, the original powers in their earliest stage of existence would be weaker in a baby, and that would cause it to be perpetually over-excited, for the external world acts as strongly on the child as on the man. The man (or even a biggish boy) can bear more, simply because he possesses, in addition to his original powers, a *large number* of developed powers on which the surplus of stimulants may be diffused and expended, and thus rendered harmless.

§ 33. *On Repugnancies.*

I went out to take a walk. A wasp flew at me and threatened to sting me. I involuntarily lifted my umbrella and struck it to the ground.

A child has to take some bitter physic: the moment it hears of it it opposes itself to the operation.

A certain man considers himself a capital singer: somebody says to him, 'You sing abominably,' which so offends him, that he almost strikes his critic, &c., &c.

How is all this to be explained?

During our waking hours the movable elements are never still, but are constantly flowing from one psychical form to another (§ 31). As they (according to § 15, p. 33) are transferred to what is most intimately connected, movable *stimulants* in particular flow by preference where there is a defect of stimulation; *for in the soul, as in the external world, the fluid and fluent always tends to spread in all directions, and immediately in a direction where some void has to be filled up.*

When I went out for a walk I was clearly conscious of the bodily comfort and security which I was enjoying. This was a very complex and *strong psychical form*. Directly the wasp threatened to sting me another form was instantly aroused, that of pain left by other wasps' stings (or something of that kind). This was a *weak psychical form*. Now, seeing that the former was *rich in stimulants*, and the latter *poor* in them, what must happen? (§ 32). The movable elements belonging to the first passed in a moment over to the other, so that the powers of the first were deprived or *emptied* of a portion of their stimulants. By this they recovered their original tension or appetency, which was necessarily directed to similar stimulants, and therefore to those which it had lost, and thus was produced an effort *counter to* or *against* that weak form which was answerable for having deprived the strong one of its stimulant. In order to put a stop to this loss of stimulant, my hand was raised and struck the wasp to the ground. But how is this explicable? A *mean series* (see § 40) already existent within me was simultaneously excited by the movable elements (these are in fact always ready to spread *in all directions*, see § 73), and since by this the end (i.e. to preserve to 'my corporeal comfort' its fulness of stimulation unimpaired) was attained, the repugnance immediately ceased. But it continued to exist in the shape of a Trace.

Why did the child resist taking nasty physic? Two forms were conscious in his soul at once; in his gustatory system a complex *strong form* of pleasure previously experienced, and a *weak one* (arising from some previous over-stimulation by nasty physic or the like): the movable stimulants of the former poured over into the latter as being poor and feeble in excitants: this converted the powers of the former into *efforts*, and to *efforts* directed *against* the weak form which was the cause of its losing its stimulants. Hence the child resisted the taking of physic—a *repugnance* was generated in him.

The like is the case in the third instance. The strong form, abundant in stimulants, 'I am an excellent singer,' was faced by the weak one, poor in stimulants, 'you are a wretched singer.' (Compare on this § 54.) The first immediately began to lose its stimulants, and simultaneously it took the shape of effort to check that loss, which effort did not remain permanently directed to the weak form, owing to the tendency stimulants have to spread in all directions. The muscular powers, in which the insulted person possessed the means of permanently removing the blame, were affected by the excitation, and hence, as people say, his fingers itched to close his critic's mouth by a blow. Suppose he mastered that disposition, it would have been a proof that nobler and very powerful forms were also excited, which rendered violence impossible, by taking such decided possession of the movable elements exciting them, that for the moment they were unable to produce an effect in any other direction.

How then do *Repugnancies* arise?

In all cases two kinds of things must be conscious, a strong form *beside a* weak *one. This causes the movable elements to flow from the former to the latter, and thus quickly converts the strong form into* a form of effort *which defends itself against that loss of stimulant, and thus a counter effort,* a Repugnance *is engendered.*

In what respects, then, do Repugnancies differ from Desires or resemble them? (compare § 25). Why is it that in repugnancy the *stimulant* only and not the powers is equalized? Because the sensations of pleasure or dislike depend sole'y on stimulants.

The explanation above given makes three points clear.

1°. Strength and weakness must lie in a like direction, i.e. they must relate to a similar or at least analogous object. The strong forms which, as a musician, I owe to corresponding impressions made by musical tones will not enable me to feel any repugnance to grammatical mistakes, nor does the knowledge of what is grammatically correct create in any one a repugnance to false or blurred musical sounds—that implies a knowledge of correct musical sounds [m]. In like manner the repugnance disappears, unless the false and the correct are simultaneously and consciously opposed in the soul. How many are there, who, when correcting an exercise, let errors pass merely because the correct expression did not happen to occur to them simultaneously with the incorrect phrase which they have just read. But the repugnance to the mistake is felt the moment the correct expression rises into consciousness.

2°. Repugnance is only another kind of effort (desire) generated when the usual striving of the powers after stimulants has vanished. No force in the world can produce opposite effects: the eye can only see the external, not the internal; fire can heat, but it cannot chill; a stone can fall, but cannot of itself rise, &c., and thus also the (*unawakened*) powers of the soul can no doubt strive after stimulants, but they cannot immediately strive in an opposite direction, cannot reject them (or have a repugnance for them). They are invariably directed to *receiving* stimulants and appropriating them so far as possible, never to rejecting or keeping them at a distance. Now since in repugnancy stimulants actually are rejected and resisted, the only explanation possible, is, that the *diffusion* of stimulant is interrupted in the following manner: the powers of the strong form strive after the stimulants of which they have been deprived—endeavour to recover them, and in

[m] The correct, or what is accounted correct, is always felt as strength, the false always as weakness; why? See below, § 54, at the end.

thus acting, the powers of the weak form which received them are relieved from an unwelcome burden[a]. In cases of anxiety, alarm, terror, &c., a number of weak forms are simultaneously excited, so that an extraordinary amount of stimulant is withdrawn from the strong ones. Now if among the latter there are none powerful enough to check this diffusion by recovering some of those stimulants, no repugnancy is produced; the stimulants spread further and further in the soul, indeed even to the body, and occasion exclamations of woe, crying, trembling, convulsions, &c., and they not unfrequently lead to a total deterioration of our psychical forms, so that mental disease may be the result. Naturally, Traces are left in this case as in others, but they are not Traces of repugnancies.

3°. When the diffusion of stimulants and the condition of repugnancy has ceased, we find that the psychical forms are preserved in their original shape, however violent the diffusion and repugnance may have been. Hence, it is impossible that the *powers* lying at the bottom of the psychical forms can have been equalized along with them, for in that case the latter must have been dissolved, and for the same reason only the *unfixed, movable* stimulants can have been transferred. *Free, void*, unemployed powers, in consequence of the mutual attraction of similars, are diffused solely over the fixed *strong* forms: for the weakened powers in the forms of dislike are unable to attract them, and the more such free powers there are, and the more they attach themselves to strong forms, the more powerful is the repugnance and the consequent check on the diffusion of stimulants. Weakening diseases only damage the free powers: but the more this happens, the less energetic are the repugnancies which the debilitated patient still possibly manifests.

§ 34. *Repugnancies are frequently connected with a Sensation of Pain, and are then more violent than they otherwise would be. States of Dislike* [Unlustaffecte].

A vain girl who thinks a great deal of her beauty, partly because she has often admired it in herself, partly because foolish parents or other silly people have often given her to understand that she is handsome (compare the second note in § 54), is a person whom we must treat with particular caution. Only shew the least disregard for her good looks, and of a certainty she will

---

[a] It has already been shewn, in § 26, that *weakened* powers do not care for stimulants, and why they do not: not only their retentive power, but their active (striving) power as well is impaired. To desire disagreeable impressions is unnatural in a healthy soul.

not easily forget or forgive it, so grievously insulted does she feel. Or take the case of a child who is particularly pleased with some toy or other. Try and take it away from him, and he will resist tooth and nail, cry and howl as if the greatest misfortune were befalling him. Or suppose somebody takes great pride in the neatness and cleanness with which he keeps his book; if any one were to soil it, would he not feel very much pained?

This is obvious: *if repugnancies are formed, they are frequently connected with a feeling of* pain.

Why so?

If we consider the vain and pretty girl, it is clear that the psychical form, 'I am beautiful,' engendered by much gazing in the glass, and by constant laudations, cannot continue to exist in her without a *full stimulation*. It is in fact a *pleasurable notion*, and therefore *a strong form, very full of stimulant*. To this now is added the *disagreeable* form, 'want of beauty.' This has been engendered in the girl's soul from her having, as we all do, often received impressions from the shapes of ugly people. Such impressions do not elevate, they depress and *weaken* our powers. Now if this form is reproduced with its weakened powers, powers therefore *deficient in stimulants* (§ 32) when want of beauty is thrown in any way directly or indirectly in the girl's teeth, then in a moment (see § 33) the numerous movable stimulants belonging to the strong psychical form pour over into the weak one and act on it as an *over-stimulation*, and hence not merely a repugnance, but *a feeling of pain* must be engendered as well*.

It is equally easy to account for the greater *vehemence* of such repugnancies.

---

* Why is no repugnance excited when one is reminded of some disagreeable thing *overcome* and therefore past? Because there is no reason to guard oneself against it. Repugnance can only arise if fresh injuries (troubles) are actually present or threaten to annoy us. Nevertheless, even in the former case, a faint tendency to repugnance is scarcely ever wanting. But who could, for instance, feel the same repugnance to hunger *past* and *gone* as he would if it were now present?

The child screams, cries, and fights tooth and nail, when his beloved toy is suddenly snatched away from him. Why?

When many powers lose their stimulants many are converted into efforts: if that loss is *rapid*, so is the effort. Now as both are present in the pleasurable form 'possession of a toy,' it follows that the effort directed against the loss of stimulation must be *more vehement* in proportion as the pleasurable form consists of more Traces, and hence it is natural that the child in the supposed case shews no listless and unenergetic repugnance.

It is clear, then, that *the more abundant in stimulants the strong psychical form is, and the less rich in stimulants, and weaker the weak form is, the more vehement is the repugnance which is engendered, and the more acute is the feeling of pain with which it is connected.* Such processes are called **States of Dislike** [Unlustaffecte].

Most repugnancies, however, occur without any feeling of dislike. We quietly push aside what stands in our way, we calmly remove from a place which we do not like, or correct the faults of speaking or writing made by our pupils: we seek for what we have lost patiently and composedly, &c.

§ 35. Repugnancies *of a like Kind Coalesce. Aversion. Detestation.*

The Similar and Allied unites with what is Similar and Allied (§ 9). We have already had occasion to prove this psychical law several times. In the *case before us* also its operation cannot be denied.

A child is frequently ill-treated by its nurse. This does not last long before it shews unwillingness to go to her. When it is handed to her it always begins to cry, and scream, and fight. At last the parents are compelled to send her about her business.

The first time it was ill-used a form of dislike was formed in the child's soul in regard to the nurse, and—since this must be simultaneously conscious along with the pleasurable form of kind treatment on the part of its mother—the first *repugnance* is engendered. On the second occasion, the same thing was repeated: but both repugnancies *united* because they were homogeneous. On the third occasion, a third repugnance was attracted to the two others, a fourth on the next occasion, and so on. At the same time, a determinate connexion was formed between the strong and the weak forms, for a portion of the exciting elements always remained behind attached to them, and then produced a joint effect.

And thus it happened that this *decided* aversion to its nurse was gradually formed in the child.

Or, suppose that the howling of a dog has stimulated us unpleasantly, and that hence a *repugnance* has been developed: the same effect has been also produced by the cry of the pewit, the owl, the mewing of cats, &c.: all these *homogeneous* repugnancies will coalesce in one psychical form. We shall acquire a *decided aversion* to all such sounds.

We should as a matter of fact meet with few men who, instead of *repugnancies to such sounds based on many traces* (*aversion*) feel a *desire* to hear them. We should find many who neither *desire* nor *feel any detestation* for them. With whom will this be the case? With those who from not having experienced them at all, have neither been stimulated by them agreeably or disagreeably.

Hence we learn *that homogeneous repugnancies also coalesce in one form, and thus increase in strength.* Such accumulated repugnancies produced by many traces we call *Aversion*, a higher degree of it we name Detestation.

In this case, as in the rest, what we said in p. 69, as to the obscuration produced by the existence of opposite and contrasted forms, holds good.

§ 36. *The Influence exercised on the Formation of Repugnancies by the Qualities of the Original Powers.*

We shall arrive here at the same result as that to which we came in § 29.

Since *repugnancies* can only be engendered in so far as *strong* and *weak psychical forms* are present in the soul, it follows that they are promoted in general by all that favours the formation of such *strong* and *weak forms.*

The *sensibility* of the original powers (their susceptibility to stimulants) is here of supreme importance.

Where it exists, a tolerably small stimulant may produce *full stimulation*, a little stronger one, *pleasurable stimulation*, and then *satiety* is soon caused; and who is ignorant that delicate ears, &c., may be *painfully* affected just when others less sensitive begin to feel pleasure? Therefore, far more *forms of pleasure* and *dislike* are produced in *more sensitive* powers than in those endowed with *less sensibility;* consequently the *former* must lead to a far greater number of *repugnancies.*

But if repugnancies are to be engendered, *the movable stimulants belonging to the strong psychical form must* flow from it to *the weak one.*

The more speedily this takes place (and living powers impress their own lively character on their stimulants), the *more speedily* does a repugnance arise: accordingly *vivacity* promotes the formation of repugnancies.

The phlegmatic man is, in his *repugnancies*, as in his *desires*, dull and sluggish, whereas in very lively people we observe a veritable effervescence, as it were, both in their desires and in their repugnancies.

Moreover the movable elements are more abundant where impressions are *less powerfully* appropriated by the powers, and less so where the reverse is the case. Hence it follows that power and *tenacity* are *prejudicial to* the formation of repugnancies.

But since repugnancies of a like kind *coalesce* they will do so more completely in proportion as their several Traces have been so formed as to be *more permanent*, consequently in proportion as the original powers are more tenacious, and thus it is obvious that a certain degree of strength and *tenacity* is indispensably *necessary* for the generation of *aversions* and *detestation.*

As idiots and brutes, owing to the defective tenacity of their original powers, are unable to attain to *concepts, &c.*, and *pas-*

sions, they are equally incapable (and indeed for the same reason) of arriving at *detestation*. They do of course feel *repugnancies* and even *disinclinations*, often of a vehement description (§ 34), but they are wanting in that something which in healthy men holds all repugnancies together, unites them into a whole, and thus multiplies their strength in proportion as their numbers increase; viz. strength or *tenacity*, and consequently they are wanting in the product which depends on that quality, viz. such an *accumulation* as amounts to *detestation*. (Compare § 29.) Instinctive *detestation* in brutes is of course something completely different.

§ 37. *Goods and Evils.*

Directly any object affects us *pleasurably*, *a desire* for it is engendered, as we learnt in § 25, and such an object we call —*a Good*. Before coffee was known in Germany, i.e. before it produced a pleasurable effect on our faculties of taste and smell, none of us reckoned it a good, none desired it, nor is it now-a-days desired, or accounted a good by those who have not experienced the pleasure which it causes. But where it has done so, we find it pursued everywhere as a good, by many so intensely that they could hardly live without it. So in all cases and with all objects (persons and things).

Whatever has affected us pleasurably becomes a Good to us, and we desire it so long as we do not possess it.

So long as we do not possess it: of course! For directly we do possess it, it affects our powers pleasurably, and although individual stimulants from it may vanish from those powers, still they are constantly replaced by fresh ones (in part from within —§ 31), so that they never become *void of stimulant*, or take the shape of *effort*, and consequently can never be formed into a *desire*. The psychical form, therefore, remains in such a case *a pleasurable notion*, and when this is recalled to consciousness it is called *a pleasurable recollection* (§ 27).

Hence our desire, our want ceases when we get what we desire

(the *Good*), *and continues in abeyance so long as we possess it.* Examples :—

Some time ago I had never seen or tasted pineapple, and had, therefore, never been pleasurably stimulated by it. And yet, will it be believed? *I desired* such fruit.

Soume (the poet) had never in his life seen Italy, and yet there arose in his soul so strong a desire to visit that country, that he suddenly started off and traversed it all on foot.

I have never heard Weber's glorious music to "Oberon," but I assure you that I would gladly give a good bit of money if I could manage to hear it.

How is this? How can we regard as goods and desire things which have never affected us pleasurably?

The case will be found to be pretty much the same as those mentioned above.

True, I had never tasted pineapple, but I had tasted *other* fruits, which at least resemble it in this respect, that they produce a very pleasant effect on our gustatory powers. Now, I was told that pineapple tasted as agreeably as those did, and therefore I represented it to myself as pleasant to the taste (I obtained the corresponding *Imaginary Notion* of it). What happened? The manifold desires after pleasantly tasting fruits already existent in the soul attached themselves, owing to their similarity, to my notion of 'Pineapple,' and thus arose a *desire* for it in the soul.

Seume would not have developed so strong a desire to go to Italy, if he had not already possessed in his soul manifold traces of pleasure derived from *other* beautiful localities. These insinuated themselves into his Imaginary Notion (imagination) of Italy, connected themselves with it, and the desire to see *Italy* was generated.

And I desire to hear Weber's "Oberon" because other pieces of music by him and other composers have affected me pleasurably. Thus music in general has become a good for me. Now, these similar musical desires formed elsewhere have merely to be connected with the imaginary notion of Weber's "Oberon" to generate a desire to hear that opera. Hence one who has developed no desires for good music at all will never desire to hear *this*.

Therefore things whose effects we have never experienced may become Goods for us, And they become so from the fact, that forms of pleasure resembling *them already acquired, and the desires thence arising, attach themselves to the Imaginary Notions* (*imaginations*) *which we have formed of these objects, and impart to them* (lend them) *their tension and activity.*

On the mode in which Imaginary Notions are produced, see below, § 75.

Directly any object affects our original powers *disagreeably* or *painfully*, effects which may be produced indifferently by half stimulation, painful excitation, or stimulation to satiety, there arises in our soul *a weak form* (§ 32), and in consequence of that, if the necessary conditions are complied with (§ 33), a *repugnance*.

Whatever affects us painfully, whatever *weakens* our psychical nature, that we do not desire; we avoid it, *detest* it, *resist* it, and all such objects as cause these repugnancies in us we call *Evils*.

Illness is an evil. Why? How far do we regard fire and water as good, how far as evil? Why are industry and order great goods to many people, and why do some avoid them as onerous evils?

Lastly, what is produced by *full stimulation?—Perceptions, Notions*. But as these imply a firm union between original powers and stimulants, and, therefore, do not directly produce either desires or repugnancies, it follows that we neither *desire* nor *detest* objects which *fully stimulate* us, we regard them neither as *goods* nor *evils*. Yet they would much sooner become *goods* than *evils* to us: for full stimulation promotes and perfects the original powers, and since even when firmly appropriated a portion of the stimulant vanishes, it follows that even in this case *desires* may be generated, though of lower intensity

(Compare § 26). It must, too, be borne in mind, that in reality there is no such hard-and-fast line of demarcation between full and pleasurable stimulation, &c.; on the contrary, they resemble the winds, which do not always blow exactly due east, west, north, or south.

§ 38. *Unlike Forms also Unite with each other. Groups and Series.*

The proof of this is soon given. I name the word 'tree' and wager that every one of my readers will immediately think of several totally distinct things at the same time. Did not the notions, roots, stem, branches, twigs, leaves, tree-top, become conscious together in every soul that represented a tree to itself? The reason why I suppose so is, that these different things are united together in my soul.

I say 'house,' and again entirely distinct notions become conscious, as 'walls, windows, doors, roof, chimney, rooms, bed-chambers,' &c. Just so if I say, *your* father, *your* brother, *your* sister, &c.

Hence we learn that dissimilar[p] *psychical forms may also unite together with some degree of closeness.*

But how and why? That is another question. We will attempt to answer it.

The first time we saw a tree, what did we apprehend?

Answer: why those different things just mentioned: roots, stem, branches, &c. They were therefore all *formed* in the soul *at the same time*[q], for we gained the corresponding intuitions from them. As often as we have since looked at the same or a similar tree, these objects were again *simultaneously* conscious,

---

[p] The union between *like* and like has been treated of in §§ 9, 10, 15—20.

[q] At least they were formed directly after one another, and were then simultaneously present to consciousness: for the larger a tree, house, &c., is, the greater the necessity that their parts be apprehended singly—be singly formed or copied in the soul, and it is only subsequently that they can be all united in one act of consciousness. Compare § 7.

and were *strengthened* by the addition of one Trace, provided that fresh examination and apprehension was only strong enough. Now we already know, from what has been said, that not *all* the stimulants and original powers applied for the purpose of generating and elaborating a notion are definitely united, but that a certain portion of them remain *movable.* We know, further, that *similar* stimulants exist in those original powers which have been *otherwise* excited, that they rest in them in the shape of *general* elements, and that they are also *movable, transferable.* These movable elements, to which also the free original powers themselves belong, flow during our waking hours from one psychical form to another, and so produce the constant alternation of consciousness and unconsciousness in the soul (§§ 30, 31). What must be the further consequence of this, when different notions are thus made conscious at the *same time?*

Two cases are conceivable. Either the movable elements are entirely withdrawn from the notions (psychical forms) excited by them, or else a portion of those elements remain attached to the notions, are appropriated by them, this portion forming a kind of *tie* or *cement* around them, which fastens one firmly to the other. Experience proves that the former is the case when the excitation is of too faint and transient a kind, but that the latter takes place when the forms are excited with sufficient force. Under such circumstances the movable elements are retained by them as a connecting *Trace*, and this trace must be *augmented* by another produced by the fresh diffusion of the movable elements, when these different notions again become simultaneously conscious, provided the excitation is sufficiently strong, so that at last they arrive at such fixedness and strength, *that the different heterogeneous notions held together by them always preserve that union or connexion, and consequently always become conscious together.*

We call this trace *which holds such notions together* a *connecting Trace*, and also *a condition of awakening to consciousness* [Weckungsangelegtheit], because it predisposes, prepares the way for, the future restoration to consciousness of notions so connected.

Such associations of *heterogeneous* psychical forms arising in the manner described—we shall call them Groups; why?—are uncommonly numerous in every human soul, for everything in any way perceptible by us is always complex; even such a thing as gold, a chemically simple body, is so: we apprehend it as something yellow, hard, heavy, &c. But as often as we notice it as being a something so complex, so often must that complex whole be *simultaneously* overflowed by movable elements, and as a portion of them are permanently retained by it, the several parts constituting that whole must at last become connected in *a group*.

Since these movable elements are able to excite *things the most different* together, need we be astonished that the oddest and most arbitrary groups of notions are formed in the soul? A superstitious person, for example, when he hears the word 'devil,' always thinks of a being in human shape with horns, hoofs, and a tail: and every one when reminded of Frederick the Great thinks of his stick and pigtail. How is this to be explained?

Again, though we always find that word and thing, or generally sign and thing signified are connected by us, still very few, I fancy, notice that they are groups of notions, and that their component parts belong as a rule to entirely different senses, and have consequently grown out of totally dissimilar elements. The *notion* Swallow, for example, can exist nowhere but in the sense of sight, for it is produced from the union between stimulants of light and our visual powers: the (audible) *word* swallow, on the other hand, was generated by stimulants of sound affecting our ears, and therefore can only exist in our auditory powers. The same is true of the *twittering* of a swallow, which proves that it consists of stimulants of sound and powers totally different from those which constitute the word swallow. Consider, moreover, the sounds of music and the notes representing them, (here the thing lives in the sense of hearing, the sign [the note] in that of sight), the odour and form of a rose, the taste, the form and colour of an apple, the coldness and smoothness of ice, &c.,—all mere groups of notions which arise in different senses and dwell there, the several members of which only awaken each other, because by the help of movable elements which become attached to them, they gained that definite connexion which they now exhibit. As these elements are of a completely *general* character, they are adapted to join together notions the most opposite.

More than that!

Every proposition, every line in a song, every narrative, is a *series* of different notions, not *a group*. He who recalls them often into consciousness in the same order, e.g. by external stimulants, by reading or hearing them, will soon know the proposition or verse by heart, i.e. he will fix in *his own* soul the series of notions in the order in which they exist in the proposition, verse, &c. How?

After what has been already said, it is not difficult to answer this question. How else should the several notions be linked together, if not by movable elements which have been appropriated and *rendered fixed?* In this case, therefore, they pass from one notion to another, only not over all *alike*, they rather flow from the end of the first to the beginning of the second, from the end of that to the beginning of the third, and so on, and therefore *one after the other;* and the more frequently this is repeated, (the more we con over the proposition, &c.,) the firmer does the connexion become, because a connecting trace is left behind after every effective repetition.

And here it must not be forgotten, that as our notions of their corresponding *objects* grow together, so also our notions of signs —visible word and audible word—come into play. Our notions of words are, in fact, linked to those of things, and form groups with them, since we learnt the names at the same time that we got the notion of the things, or soon afterwards. At first we connected with the notion of the thing, the *audible* name which people pronounced for our information; at a later period when we learnt to read, the *visible* name or word became connected as well—but it was immediately associated with the audible name, (in the case of deaf mutes alone thing and *visible* sign coalesce immediately); and now when we read, the *visible form* of the word preserved in its Traces is awakened by the letters, the *visible* arouses the *audible* word, and that excites the notion of the thing[r].

[r] In one who understands and reads Latin the process of reproduction is often a more complex affair: first, there is the *visible* form of the Latin word formerly seen and preserved; this leads to the *audible* Latin word, that to the German equivalent given in the Latin-and-German Dictionary,

How would it be possible for any one to recall to consciousness such series of totally diverse psychical forms in the same order in which they previously occurred, unless they were bound together by something or other in that exact order? Naturally the stock of movable elements by the partial fixture of which this is effected must gradually become exhausted if they were not constantly replaced by fresh ones, a process however which takes place daily. See § 30, and below § 76. Observe how tired one becomes in learning anything by heart; this fatigue is caused solely by the decrease of the movable elements.

From this we learn that,

Whole series of psychical forms of the most diverse kinds, (notions, desires, feelings,) are united into a common whole which we call **groups**, *by the diffusion of movable elements over them: and this connexion is firmer, more intimate, the more frequently such diverse forms have been effectually brought into consciousness in the given order, and effectually permeated by those movable elements. The connecting trace thus produced grows therefore in this case as it does in that of group-forms.*

That such *series* must frequently arise in the soul is almost self-evident, for consciousness is changing every moment, and therefore the several psychical forms which rise into consciousness must become connected in continued series[a] by the continual diffusion of the movable elements.

A very frequently *repeated* diffusion of the movable elements is doubtless necessary in order to so *completely unite* notions that they may continue to exist in the soul for years afterwards in their original connexion. But if we reflect how often some things throng upon us from our very

---

and as the *thing* depends on this last word, the exciting cause traverses a group consisting of many members, a group, however, which may be considered as a series, because its parts are aroused successively. It is only after long practice that we learn to connect the object directly with the *audible* Latin word. It needs hardly be remarked that the process of excitation takes place with more than lightning speed.

[a] *All* our notions *of the external world* are notably groups and series of notions. Where whole masses of objects succeed each other, we have groups and series together, as, for instance, in a chorale, where melody and harmony proceed simultaneously; the same is the case in the recollections of a journey, the incidents of our life, historical events, &c.

birth, either at the same time or in succession, and how much there is that we bring into this double connexion within us by assiduous exercise, we shall not be astonished at the remarkable stability of so many groups and series of psychical forms.

Moreover, since that which has once been sufficiently established does not need to be made a second time, we may hence explain how it is that many persons apparently gain at one stroke what others can only obtain gradually and laboriously. The former have merely to rouse into consciousness what already exists there bearing on the matter before them, and so are able to apply all their free powers to the insignificant portion of it which is new to them: how then could they avoid being quick and handy about it? In like manner we can understand from this, that on the occasion of fresh perceptions, we can form a perfect picture of the object before we have apprehended the one now before us on all its sides. When we see a fresh stem of a tree never viewed before, we believe that the portion concealed from us is round as well as the front of it, which is all we see at the moment, and we hold the back of a new house to be flat, and not running into a point, for instance, even while we are only examining the front of it, &c.

Law: *every psychical form already obtained is ready to form a part of any fresh product with which it suits, exactly in the same way as, for instance, the note A on a piano is ready to form part of the scale not merely of A major, but also that of F major, D major, F sharp minor, &c., and thus renders the creation of a fresh note A unnecessary.*

Concepts are in a special manner adapted to thus form part of groups and series, because the most characteristic points in the intuitions are absent from them, and therefore, owing to their general nature, they may be fitly applied to a large number of objects. But intuitions as well, which are properly only applicable to one definite object, must resemble each other in many points, seeing that their objects have so much in common. Consider a number of different men, different trees, different houses, different localities, &c., and see how many similarities there are between them. See below, § 75, what is said about *imaginary notions.*

What then is the origin of the associations of which we spoke when treating of *concepts*, *judgments*, and *inferences?* The homogeneous not only coalesces, but it also underlies the association effected by the help of movable elements. For why should the like elements in concepts, judgments, &c., which are after all excited into consciousness by the movable elements, not themselves experience the binding powers exerted by the latter? They must experience it, and all the more, because similarities even of themselves, from their mutual attraction tend powerfully to unite, and the movable elements penetrate into them and increase, the more intimate their conjunction is. Without the assistance of movable elements the similar would merely meet together, but would not permanently hold together; it is those elements which give similarities their abiding conjunction, which in this case must naturally be of a twofold kind, because they are assisted by that attractive force which fuses those elements together. Hence, no forms are so indestructible as concepts and what springs from them, provided always that they were perfectly formed to start with.

§ 39. *Some Important* Series of Psychical Forms: *Cause and Effect; End and Means.*

When I light a fire in the stove, it becomes warm. When it rains, the ground becomes wet.

When I perceive an object many times, my notion of it becomes clearer.

When beside a pleasurable form in my soul an unpleasant one arises, and the movable stimulants flow from the former to the latter, a repugnance is produced.

I have never yet experienced the opposite of any of these things. Whenever I have lighted a fire in my stove it has always become warm. Whenever I have seen it rain, wet has invariably been the consequence, &c. Now these, it is clear, are (twin) series in which different forms (rain—becoming wet; frequent perception—clear notion; pleasure and dislike coexistent—repugnance, &c.) are presented, which, by being frequently repeated, become so closely connected that when only one member of the series, e.g. 'lighting a fire,' becomes conscious, it immediately imparts full consciousness to the other member 'becoming warm.'

Now series which are engendered by *such constant* and *invariable* succession in the different processes in the soul or in *the external world* ought certainly to be distinguished from other series. For in this case we regard every single member as *necessarily belonging to this series of events*, or we attribute to them *a causal connexion*, and we call the antecedent member '*Cause*,' and the consequent '*Effect*.'

Psychical Forms which stand in the relation of "cause and effect" are therefore series which have been formed by constant *and* invariable *sequences in different processes (as well in the soul as also in the external world*[1]). We call them, for brevity's sake, *Causal Series*.

We will now reverse the above series, and put the effect first, the cause last. Therefore, he who wishes to produce a *repugnance* in his soul must bring simultaneously into consciousness a *pleasurable* and a *painful psychical form*: he who desires to obtain clear *notions* must *perceive* the same object many times:

---

[1] It does not follow that *all* sequences in the *external world* are *causally* connected because we see them succeed one another in an *uniform and absolutely invariable manner*. If a given star invariably rises after another, are we to suppose that the first causes the second to rise? Is night the effect of day, summer of spring, winter of autumn, &c., &c.? Are not such sequences rather *mere connections in space and time*, differing decidedly from the *causal* sequence? When merely connected in space and time, objects exercise no mutual influence on each other, whilst when causally connected they always do so: in the latter case, one acquires its existence or qualities *through and by* the other, whereas in the former each is or takes place merely *beside* or *after* the other. Hence, we call the causal connexion an *internal*, the other an *external* (contingent) connexion of objects and events. As respects the external world, it is often a difficult and uncertain matter to distinguish one of these kinds of connexion from the other, for in its case we only perceive *external phenomena*, which may, but also may not, be internally connected. As regards the processes of our own souls we stand in a better position. Here every change produced *by* and *out of* another is directly manifested as being so produced: it is not concealed, as it is in the external world, under cover of a mere antecedence and consequence in time, which is all that our senses can perceive externally: they can never penetrate into the inner being, the inner processes of external objects: but in all changes taking place in our souls, effect and cause are exposed to clear immediate observation, and hence we apprehend them not merely as they seem to be, but as they really are, and can estimate them accordingly. Compare *Beneke's* "Psychol. Skizzen," Theil. II. p. 264, sqq.

he who wishes to get a *warm stove* must light a fire in it: if the ground is to be *wet* it must *rain*.

Such reversals of the series of 'cause and effect' occur in the soul very frequently, and we are indebted for their existence merely to excitations and connexions *of a contrary kind* to the causal, for the forms connected are in both cases the same.

I desire the effect, warm stove; instantly there starts into consciousness, fire makes it warm! I should like to obtain a clearer knowledge of an object, directly there rises into consciousness, observe it afresh with care, &c.

In this way the effect becomes an *end* and the cause a *mean*.

Therefore those psychical forms, the members of which stand in the relation of "end and means," are series, and, what is more, they are the same as cause and effect, only taken in a reverse order[a].

We shall, for shortness, call them *mean-series* (final series). They are, therefore, causal series reversed.

Those mean-series in which muscular powers are concerned, i.e. powers by which we produce movements in the external world (§ 14, at the end), deserve particular attention.

If a young child has once used the movement of its arm as a mean, say, to convey the fruit that it sees to its mouth, that movement remains in the shape of a Trace (in the muscular powers), and it becomes associated with the notion of fruit. Now directly that fruit, or any like it, again falls under the child's eyes, the muscular act connected with it will be again excited, and thus the child will reach after the fruit again, and obtain another Trace of the movement by which it does so. In this manner not merely the most diverse muscular acts are formed gradually, and in part laboriously (take as instances the first very uncertain movements of children, of beginners on the violin or piano, &c.), by the coalescence of similar Traces of move-

---

[a] It would take too long to explain in this place *how* this reversal is managed in the soul. Those who desire further information on the point may refer to *Beneke's* "Neue Psychologie," p. 221, sqq., and *Dressler's* "Beiträge," &c., Theil. II. p. 289, sqq.

ments, so that they grow at last into the most marvellous "*dexterities*," but the different modes of movement enter into permanent connexions with notions, desires, repugnancies, &c., which they serve to execute, because they are capable of being excited on both sides one after the other. The corporeal and the psychical consist, it is true, of very distinct powers: but the law of association operates between both of them as effectually as it does between two purely psychical forms.

It was therefore very natural that the 'wretched singer,' spoken of in § 33, should feel his fingers itch (= that muscular acts should be excited in him): it was natural that I, without thinking about the matter, should move my arm and strike to the earth the wasp that threatened me: it is not astonishing that an expert pianist strikes every key with certainty without looking at them, or taking any trouble about it, &c.

§ 40. *Willing: Wishing.*

I want to warm my room, for I find it chilly. My powers of feeling (vital powers) desire a higher degree of warmth in order to be stimulated sufficiently or pleasurably. There is, therefore, existent in my soul a *desire* for warmth; warmth consequently becomes an *end* to me.

What happens? The void movable original powers, according to what we saw in § 31, attach themselves to these desires, and thus not merely give them greater vigour, but thereby also excite other psychical forms, and especially those which at some earlier period were permanently united to them. Consequently, I think (and the case will be the same with others) of the stove, the wood, matches, muscular movements, which are available for lighting a fire: these are the *means* for bringing about my end. Hence, my desire for warmth excites into consciousness a whole series of notions: warmth, stove, fire, &c. (a mean-series), or, briefly, *the corresponding mean-series attaches itself to my desire for warmth*. Is that enough for willing? It is not. A poor man might have the same desire for a warm room, and most of the members of the mean-series might attach themselves to it, but he does not think of *willing*, for he has had no wood for a long time, and even if he had any now, he is so ill on his hard straw pallet that he is unable to rise and perform the necessary muscular movements.

I am more fortunate in this respect. The wood lies under the stove, the matches are on the table, and I am perfectly capable of performing the needful muscular movements, and, what is more, they have acquired such *dexterity* in doing it that I shall certainly not go blunderingly to work, and so defeat my own end. I am able, therefore, to *perfectly employ* the means which lead to my end of 'warming the room,' *and thus can actually attain what I desire.* And although *I have* not yet so employed them in the present instance, *yet I am able* to figure to myself with full confidence beforehand *that this will take place, and thus that what I desire* may be actualized *by me.*

I do so accordingly: hence I say briefly, I *will* to make my room warm.

The poor man, however, could *not* represent that desire beforehand as feasible, at least not with *conviction* as feasible to him, because, for one thing, he had no wood, and in the next he was prostrated with sickness: hence he might *wish* for a warm room, but could not *will* to have one.

We have, accordingly, convinced ourselves that *willing* is a very complex affair.

Willing implies—

1°. *that a desire is consciously present in the human soul, and that it is connected with movable original powers;*

2°. *that the corresponding mean-series attaches itself to this desire*, and that we

3°. *are able to represent confidently and beforehand the object desired as feasible to us, by knowing that we not only completely possess the requisite means, but that we are able to apply them.*

When the third condition is not fulfilled we may *wish* for a thing, but cannot *will* it. What is the distinction between *willing* and *wishing?* In what does it consist?

Why was it impossible some time ago for a man to *will* to go from Dresden to Leipzic in three hours? Why can he now will it?

Frederick can *will* to raise this stone, Charles cannot. Why can he not?

Writing requires a certain dexterity of finger, singing a certain dexterity of the vocal organs. Suppose these means present, can a man with them *dance, play the piano, or violin, reflect, &c.?*

Therefore, every different kind of willing requires a special series of means.

§ 41. *All Similar Acts of Will coalesce. Formed Will.*

This is, I suppose, self-evident from what has already been said. *For from everything that takes place in the soul with any approach to perfection a Trace is left*, and consequently from the first act of will that arises, however faintly, in a child's soul. Directly another act similar, or at least analogous to the first arises, it coalesces with it in proportion as it resembles it, and increases it by a fresh Trace, and so on.

We have discovered that every act of will implies *two* parts: a desire, and a mean-series which attaches itself to that desire, (§ 40). Both were originated separately from one another, or *independently*, and hence a man may be able to figure to himself all the means subservient to the satisfaction of a desire without generating an act of will. These two constituent parts must be *connected* before such an act is possible. Hence, the Trace which was left by the second and similar act of will, and which went to strengthen the first, is *primarily* only a *connecting-Trace* (see § 38), as indeed the first was. Still, since desire grows stronger the oftener it is repeated (§ 28), and as the notions referring to the means are rendered more perfect the more frequently their traces are increased by their objects (the means), it follows that the second, third, &c., acts of will may produce a second, third, &c., Trace even in relation to both its constituent parts, in case the desire and the mean-series are repeated in such a manner that the relative objects themselves act on the soul. In children this is almost always the case so long as their willing is in process of formation; the adult, however, requires no such practice, when he determines to will afresh: supposing him to possess the constituent parts needful for the purpose ready formed within, all he has to do is to connect them. But even in his case, as with young and old alike, they grow stronger at least in their '*accressive space*' (see § 54, note, and § 75) the oftener they are excited within.

If, therefore, the act of willing at its first rise is uncertain and weak, yet the more often it is repeated the more definite and stronger does it become, and then by way of distinguishing it from its initial condition, we may call it a *ready* or formed will *which has been engendered by constant repetition and by the accumulation of Traces*: consequently, when it retires into unconsciousness it does not vanish into nothing, it is now always ready for renewed action, and merely requires to be excited afresh in order to exert its powers.

§ 42. *On the Will of Man.*

The human will must be a strange thing, for to-day it wills *one thing* (in the same individual) and to-morrow *another*, indeed in very fickle people it may will ten different ways in an hour, and what is more, some of its acts may be in flat contradiction to others.

Who will solve this riddle for me?

After what we have already learnt it really involves no difficulty whatever.

Directly the corresponding mean-series becomes attached to a desire, and we are able in consequence to confidently represent to ourselves beforehand the object desired as feasible to us —when, consequently, we confidently *expect* its realization, then we *will* something. If this process is repeated several times in the soul, it becomes a psychical form supported by many Traces, and thus a definite *ready willing* arises. Let any one ask himself how many such formed acts have been already engendered within him. It would be an endless task to enumerate them all. The same is the case in every man: for under certain conditions *every* single desire may be converted into an act of *willing*. (What are these conditions? [§ 40]).

In every human soul there are a countless number of formed acts of the Will.

When David had charmed King Saul by his harp-playing, and gratified him by overcoming Goliath, Saul was resolved to have David continually about him. When, however, in consequence of many circumstances, a profound melancholy had seized on the king, and he—after the thoughtless praises of David by the rejoicing women—saw in him an enemy, the scene suddenly changed, and Saul resolved to kill him.

When afterwards, while sleeping in the cave, he had experienced David's great magnanimity, his feelings again changed, and he resolved to do David no more harm. But when fresh mistrust re-possessed his soul, he again resolved to lay hands on him, &c.

Acts of will the most contradictory had been developed in Saul's soul.

We find the same thing in others, to a greater or less degree. But one is very often puzzled by it, and unable to comprehend why many men, otherwise of a really benevolent nature, exhibit to-day such animosity against this or that person; or how a child, generally so obedient, happens at the moment to be so obstinate. How are these phenomena to be explained? After all, the matter is very simple.

Since acts of willing are formed out of desires (§ 40), *and since the latter are produced in every conceivable variety according as this thing or that causes us a pleasurable impression* (§ 25), *it follows that the multitude of acts of willing must be just as manifold as they are, and therefore we have no reason to be astonished at finding contradictory acts of willing engendered in one and the same human being.*

All these various, often contradictory acts, taken together, constitute a man's *Will.*

The Will, therefore, is not something simple; on the contrary, it is something in the highest degree complex (consisting of thousands and thousands of individual formed acts of willing). As Understanding is the totality of all concepts that have been formed in the soul (§ 17), Judgment the totality of all judgments (§ 18), the Inferential power the totality of all the conclusions that have been drawn (§ 20), *so also man's* Will *is nothing but the totality of all the particular acts of willing which have been formed and are permanently retained in his soul.*

Willing becomes more powerful in proportion as the one constituent in it, viz. desire, strengthens into inclination, propension, or indeed, into passion; and hence inclinations, &c., belong to the will as soon as they become permanently connected with a mean-series.

With what, then, does the will of man begin, and how far does it extend? What does it require in order to increase its sphere? The correct answer to these questions is easy; if, in accordance with the present and two preceding §§, we distinguish between the *developed* and the *undeveloped* will. The latter consists simply in the *states or forms antecedent to* (or the factors of) acts of willing: the former is ready for immediate use, and only requires to be reproduced. But an *absolutely finished* will exists in no man: whatever its condition may be, it always admits of further growth by other and fresh combinations of the forms or states antecedent to it.

According to the invariable usage of language, the will is properly only *positive* (it desires), not *negative* (it does not reject or feel repugnance), and, in fact, it is not easy to unite willing and repugnancy under any common term except that of effort [Streben]. Nevertheless, the not willing what before one willed, and, in particular, *capricious* and *defiant* acts of willing, depend for the most part on repugnancies, and common language talks of a 'stubborn' will in all those cases where rooted repugnance (aversion) is apparent. Add to this, that to carry out repugnance into act, mean-series are requisite, and they are not unfrequently permanently connected with them, and thus a large proportion of the repugnancies become part of the "will," if that term be taken in a somewhat wide sense. When Saul 'resolved' to kill David, he could have been actuated only by a dislike, a repugnance to him; and whoever 'resolves' to do any harm to another is at bottom moved to do so by a *negative* estimate (see § 56), which leads to a repugnance (§ 33), however keenly he may at the same time *feel* a pleasure in the misfortunes of others, or in revenge. Even when parents punish their children from a feeling of duty, their will to do so is as much, nay, even more determined by a repugnance than by a desire of right. In especial, the '*corrupted will*' is characterized as well by over-strong desires as by repugnancies which have acquired exaggerated strength. Compare § 61.

The nature of the Will is thoroughly explained in Diesterweg's "Pädagogisches Jahrbuch auf 1861," where an essay by Dressler "über das Wesen und die Bildung des menschlichen Willens," enters into every particular about it.

§ 43. *Recapitulation.*

I. The Original Powers of the Human Soul.

They are essentially *active* because *living:* but their impulses are quite general and directed merely to satisfaction derived from corresponding stimulants, and at first there is no striving after definite stimulants (§ 23).

It is not until they have been pleasurably affected, and have lost a portion of the imperfectly appropriated stimulant, that they tend towards the exact stimulant which they have lost. It is thus that a *Desire*, i.e. a tendency towards particular definite stimulants, arises out of the primitive activity of the original powers (§ 25). How far is this effect modified and conditioned by the other modes of stimulation? (§ 26.)

For the formation of such desires the *sensitiveness* and *vivacity* of the original powers are of great importance. Why? Their *tenacity* is rather an impediment to their formation: yet a certain amount of this quality is indispensably necessary for the formation of inclinations and passions. Why? (§ 29.)

These qualities of the original powers exercise a similar influence on the formation of *Repugnancies* (§ 36).

So long as the original powers have not been affected by stimulants, we may call them *movable* elements, which during our waking condition flow, or are transferred from one psychical form to another, and thus cause the perpetual alternation of consciousness in the soul, even the *voluntary* change of it (§§ 30, 31).

II. The Stimulants of the External World.

We have learnt that their *mass* or relation to the original powers is *fivefold:* viz. *half, full, pleasurable, over,* or *painful stimulation.* The traces left by these form the foundation of our *emotions—affections*, which determine the kind of '*temper*' we have (§ 24). Stimulants are retained by the original powers with varying degrees of tenacity; they are most perfectly retained when the stimulation is full, least so when it is painful (§ 24).

The powers are strengthened, perfected only by *full* or pleasurable stimulation: by the other modes of excitation they are weakened. Thus *strong* and *weak psychical* forms arise in the human soul (§ 32) by which things become *goods* or *evils* in our eyes (§ 37).

Those stimulants which, owing to their imperfect, loose appropriation by the original powers, are again separated from them, or which never from the first were firmly appropriated at all, we may also call *movable* elements, because they, like the former kind, flow, or are transferred during our waking hours from one psychical form to another, and they contribute their share to the constant alternation of consciousness in the soul, but in their case it is an *involuntary* alternation (§§ 30, 31).

III. The Fundamental Laws which prevail in the Soul.

The *first*, according to which *external impressions are taken up by the original powers and become permanent in them*, we have seen operating in divers ways in this section, as in the preceding. In general, everything which occurs in the soul with anything like perfection leaves a trace behind it. Compare § 22, iii. 1.

The *second*, according to which *everything similar fuses into a whole in consequence of mutual attraction*, is operative in strengthening single desires into *inclinations* and *passions* (§ 28), it unites single repugnancies into *disinclinations*, *detestation* (§ 35), and converts simple willing into definite *formed* willing (§ 41). What is the Will of man, and how wide is its range? (§ 42.)

The *third*, according to which *the* whole, complete *stimulant does not remain permanently in the original powers, but a portion of it invariably* vanishes *from those powers*, converts pleasurably excited powers into *desires*. (§ 25.) How far can desires also arise out of the other modes of stimulation? (§ 26.) What are a man's *desiderative* or *orectic* powers? (§ 28.)

Lastly, the *fourth*, according to which *the movable elements in our waking condition flow or are transferred perpetually from one psychical form to another* (§ 31), was one which we had not met with before[1]. It is called the Law of the Diffusion of the Movable Elements.

It leads to the formation of repugnancies. How are they different from the desires? (§ 33.) When are they connected with a feeling of pain, and consequently more vehement than usual? (§ 34.)

Again, it causes *dissimilar* psychical forms to unite in a whole. Groups and series are the consequence (§ 38). What are *connecting Traces or conditions on which awakening to consciousness depends?*

Two very important formations are the series in which the several members are connected as *cause* and *effect*, as *end* and *means*. What is a causal series? What is a mean or final series? (§ 39.)

When a mean-series is rendered conscious by the transference of the movable elements to a desire, and we are able to figure to ourselves confidently and beforehand the object desired as feasible to us, an act of *willing* is produced.

How does this differ from *wishing?* (§ 40.)

In this part, as in the last, we have seen all derivative psychical forms arise out of the same powers, which, as original powers, are developed at first into certain elementary forms. All effort, desire, repugnance, willing, wishing, so far as we were able to follow them here, arose out of a mere elaboration of these powers: all groups and series of forms, however complex they might be, all pleasure and pain, &c., presupposed these powers and no others. Will the same be found to be the case in the following part? Compare § *22* at the end, and § 69 in the middle.

---

[1] So far as the movable elements are *stimulants*, this fourth law is a continuation of the third, for stimulants once actually taken up no more vanish from the soul than the powers do, they are only diffused or transferred to other psychical forms. Or, to express the same truth better: the disappearance of stimulants is really no *special* fundamental law (or process), it is only one side or aspect of the *fourth* law, since all that is unfixed, unstable, (whether powers or stimulants,) is transferred to, or diffused over, what is fixed (the Traces). Compare, moreover, below, § 84, iii. 3.

PART III.

FEELINGS.

§ 44. *During our Waking Condition there are always two or more Psychical Forms present to Consciousness simultaneously, or in immediate succession.*

PROOF of this is furnished at every moment in our psychical life.

Let any one read or hear the proposition: the tree bears fruit, and three notions become conscious in his soul: the tree—bears—fruit.

In company, if we wish to understand the conversation, all the notions, &c., which answer to the words employed must become conscious one after the other.

Even when we are alone, too, and no external stimulants affect us, as during the darkness and stillness of night, one psychical form rises after another, and indeed at such a time we often notice that our thoughts are varied and complicated in an astonishing manner; take the case of a timid man for example.

It would be difficult to determine exactly in any case how many psychical forms are conscious at the same time; nor have we any definite measure of the velocity with which they succeed one another: for though we are accustomed to compare our quickest thoughts to lightning, or even to attribute to them a still greater degree of rapidity, still this is no more than a rough approximation.

Notwithstanding this, there are hours, and they make up the largest part of human life, when this hurry and bustle does not exist, but rather a calm and equable flow of thought and feeling, e.g. when we sit down to dinner in a good temper. Of course we see the table, the table-cloth, plate, knife, fork, &c., as well as the viands which we are enjoying; we converse quietly with our neighbour on one subject or another, or we think of the work which we are going to do when the meal is over. So also while we are quietly dressing, we figure to ourselves not only the articles of clothing, but the engagements of the day, the persons we shall have to see, and so on. In short, if we only attend to what passes within us, we find that during our waking condition the soul is *invariably* conscious not of *one* but of *several* psychical forms. Even a lazy Turk who lolls on his divan, and with listless gaze smokes his pipe, forms no exception to this rule. What are the forms of which we can assert with great positiveness that they are consciously present? A man even when dreaming proves that,

Consciousness in our soul is never confined to one psychical form alone, but is invariably extended to several, *which are either co-existent, or occur in immediate succession.*

§ 45. *All Psychical Forms differ more or less from each other.*

"When so many like traces have been united into one form that we become clearly conscious of the object from which the stimulants proceeded, we say that we have got a notion of the object." (§ 10.) This union of similar traces into one form is *common to all notions.*

But the notion of the colour *red*, for example, was produced by different stimulants from those which engendered that of *green*, the notion of the *word* 'green' arose not merely from other (sound) stimulants, but also from other (auditory) powers, the notion 'hard' from tactual stimulants and powers, &c.; therefore to this extent all our notions are more or less *different* from each other.

Moreover one form may consist of more, another of less, Traces, and therefore the powers of the one will be formed and modified by a greater, those of another by a less fulness of stimulation, and this produces a different *tone* or disposition in them.

Concepts, *Judgments*, and *Inferences*, originate from single notions (perceptions). Now, as it is impossible to deny that manifold differences exist in the latter, it follows that the more complex forms educed from them must not merely be as different as the former, but considerably more so.

Concepts *resemble* each other only in this, that they are all produced by the coalescence into one form of what is common to, or similar in, a number of distinct things (perceptions): they *differ* in that one arises out of these similar parts, another out of those; one out of many, another out of few; one out of great fulness of stimulation, another out of a lesser amount of it—for in fact the perceptions which lie at the bottom of all differ from each other in all these respects.

The same is the case with judgments and inferences.

If we compare *desires* together, we find that they *agree* in the fact that they all arise from the disappearance of a stimulant which has been but imperfectly appropriated by an original power. (§ 25.) But the most hasty glance at the mode of their formation must prove that the original powers sometimes lose more, and sometimes less stimulant, that this may occur with greater or less quickness, and that these circumstances in themselves occasion particular desires to assume the most varied forms.

Add to this that two desires must always differ as respects the stimulant (object) which they strive after: one desire tends towards *one stimulant*, another towards *another*, and again each may imply a different *tone* or disposition *in the powers* in which it is produced (§ 24).

In *repugnancies* the same relations occur (§§ 33, 34), and the tone of the powers is notably, in this case, as varied as it is possible for it to be.

Special *inclinations* and *disinclinations*, *passions* and acts of *detestation*, must differ still more widely from each other, since they are forms of still greater complexity, in consequence of which both the quantity and quality of their traces must vary in the highest degree.

An *act of willing* always presupposes a desire (§ 40). If, then, we are compelled to assert that all special desires are more or less different from each other, the same must naturally be true of willing also; and the more so, inasmuch as every particular act of will requires a different series of means, &c., (§ 40).

We have then said enough to convince ourselves *that all psychical forms differ to a greater or less extent, and that there are no two which are in all respects exactly similar*[*]. *Not merely are the stimulants* (the objective element) *different in each case, but the modification and tone of the powers* (the subjective element) *dependent on the degree of stimulation varies endlessly: and then, again, the number of these powers in every psychical form, on which depends the strength, clearness, &c., of the latter, is always different in each case.*

Accordingly, amongst the billions of objects in the external world, we never find two which are *exactly alike.*

§ 46. *When Two or more Psychical Forms are present together in Consciousness, we are immediately and simultaneously made aware of their Difference (the interval between them): Feelings.*

a. When we go out of a stuffy room into the open air we feel refreshed.

b. When, on the other hand, we merely pass from one stuffy room to another equally so, or from fresh air in one place to fresh air in another, no such feeling is observed.

How is this to be explained?

If we analyse the two cases, we find,

1°. That in both two psychical forms are *simultaneously* conscious, viz. in *a*, the perceptions 'close air' and 'fresh air;' in *b*, the perceptions 'close air' and 'close air,' 'fresh air,' and 'fresh air.'

2°. That in *a* there was a considerable *difference* (*interval*) between the forms (perceptions) simultaneously present to consciousness, whereas in *b* both were *similar*, or quite alike. In the former case, the stimulants being different, gave a different

---

[*] If this were the case, there would be no longer *two* psychical forms, but *one*, for all that is homogeneous in the soul fuses into one form or whole (§ 9).

disposition or tone to the powers apprehending them; in the latter, both stimulant and disposition are alike.

What happened in the first case?

We immediately felt refreshed. How was that caused?

Without any other circumstance coming into play, there rose up beside the perception 'close air' the very different perception 'fresh air.' The difference between the two was simultaneously forced on our consciousness; in other words, there directly rose up beside the two simultaneously conscious perceptions a third something: *the Feeling*, i.e. the consciousness *of their difference or interval*, which was necessarily a feeling of *refreshment*, because the newly-introduced perception, 'fresh air,' possesses that very quality in relation to 'close air,' but *only in relation to it*. For in *b* there were also two psychical forms (perceptions) simultaneously conscious, and yet no noticeable feeling was produced. The reason is obvious. *There is, in fact, no difference or interval between the two;* and if so, how could we be conscious of any? Being *similar forms*, they must rather coalesce in accordance with the law of the Mutual Attraction of Similars (§ 9) into one *single* whole, and therefore no noticeable *feeling* can arise in such a case.

What do we learn from all this?

If a *Feeling* is to arise in our soul

1°. *Several psychical forms (at the least two) must be conscious together, whether simultaneously or in immediate succession.*

2°. *These forms must be different from one another, or there must be a difference or interval between them.*

This difference or interval is immediately and of itself presented to our consciousness, and it is just this immediate and concomitant consciousness *of the difference or interval between our several psychical forms that we call* Feeling[b].

---

[b] The word *Feeling*, therefore, bears a different sense here, from what it did when we were speaking of powers of feeling, meaning thereby the sixth class of sense powers (original powers). It would therefore be, perhaps, a good thing not to call the latter powers of feeling at all, but to coin some other name for them. The expression, 'Sensitive Powers' [Empfindungsvermögen, powers of feeling], which might be proposed, would certainly

Similar forms yield no feelings; nor do a succession of similar sensations—they remain mere sensations.

In order to render this matter still clearer, I cannot refrain from adding a remarkably lucid passage out of *Dressler's* "Beiträge," &c., Part I. p. 152, sqq. He there says:

"We two are standing together, when, unexpectedly, a sound strikes upon our ears. You observe, 'that was a very deep note.' 'Deep!' I reply, 'how can you know that, seeing you are no musician?' 'O!' the answer is, 'this is not the first time that I have heard a sound, and I am therefore perfectly able to say what note is high and what low.' You compare, then, as I see, the tone which you have just heard with others which you have formerly heard, and which you now reproduce within: you compare them both internally as respects their interval, their difference from each other, and so you are, of course, able to say, 'my ear tells me, by an immediate feeling, that it is not a higher but a lower note.'

"Had it really been the first that you ever heard, it would have been impossible for you to say that it was a lower note, just as the man born deaf can make no assertion as respects notes and sounds, although, according to the view hitherto maintained, he has as much power of feeling as another; for it is only a damaged organ that interferes with his sense of hearing. Again: 'The colours in this picture are very glaring.' I wager that if

---

not be suitable, for all original powers are such. Besides which, not one, but several classes of original powers are indicated by the word, 'powers of feeling;' that is to say, all those which are diffused over the whole of the interior and exterior of the body without being bound, as the organic senses are, to *particular* corporeal organs. To them belong, *a.* the powers which digest and assimilate food derived from without (they approach the powers of taste most nearly, so far as their sensations are concerned); *b.* powers subservient to respiration (which have most affinity with the powers of smell as regards their sensations); *c.* the powers of the so-called common feeling [Gemeingefühl]—for warmth, cold, sultriness of the air, tickling, pressure, &c. (closely allied to our powers of touch, and frequently used as such); and *d.* the muscular powers (see p. 32). They are all inferior to the organic senses in point of tenacity. As the body of the new-born child is first manifested by these powers, and as they are in the adult the fundamental conditions for the *preservation* of life, Beneke calls them *vital powers* (= powers of life). If we conceive of them all as one, we ascribe to man one vital sense; but if we consider them as falling into certain classes or systems of powers differing from each other, we then talk of vital senses. Common language sums them all up together in the expression, *Body*. Compare § 50, and particularly § 81.

these colours had been the first you ever saw, you would not have pronounced them either glaring or tame, nor, indeed, have attributed any qualities at all to them: comparison with other colours reproduced internally, enables you to form such a judgment, which expresses the immediate consciousness, i.e. the feeling of glaringness; and this explanation is correct, however sceptical you may feel respecting it, on the score of its being new and unfamiliar to you.".

§ 47. *Further Details on the Subject. Factors of Feelings.*

In order that a feeling may exist, it is necessary that *several* (at least *two*) psychical forms should be conscious together, and both must be *different* (§ 46).

Suppose, for instance, that some one is conscious of the notions concerning his means of subsistence. Let him be poorly off in this respect: he earns just enough barely to get on, yet he does manage to get along.

If these psychical forms are the only ones that attain to consciousness in his soul, he will experience no special feeling at them; we see, in fact, thousands in such narrow circumstances, *contented*. The usual remark is, 'they do not know any better,' and, in reality, there is a good deal of truth in the saying. For suppose we assume that our poor man has *known* better days, in that case the notions of his earlier and *better* condition will be associated with those of his present poorer and worse condition*, and then farewell to contentment: he cannot escape *a feeling of pain*. And this is produced simply because, to use figurative language, the forms of his present poor condition *measure* themselves by those of his earlier and *better* state: or he becomes conscious of the difference between the two conditions because they become conscious *together*.

For the sake of greater clearness we might call *the forms* by which *the others are, so to say, measured*, the **foundation of feeling** [Gefühlgrundlage] or the **measure of it**; for by **reference** to it the present condition is felt. In the example just made use of, the notions of the man's former and more pros-

* It need hardly be observed, that the latter imply painful, the former pleasurable, moods or feelings.

perous condition are the *measure*, those of his present poverty-stricken life *what is measured by it*, or *felt*. Both these—measure and what is measured—are called the *factors* or *constituent* parts of feelings. They need not, therefore, as in the former instance of close or fresh air, be strictly simple; they produce the same kind of effect whether they are complex or simple, provided that in the former aspect they, when united, produce that tone or emotion which belongs to them in the latter aspect as well.

Now let us suppose the same man again to become prosperous, what effect will that produce? Three cases may be supposed: either

1°. His *earlier* and better condition remains the standard by which he measures his present improved circumstances: and as there is no serious difference between the two, they will restore to him a feeling of contentment and peace; or

2°. His *poorer* condition is made the rule by which he measures his present *happy* lot: this will cause him a feeling of *joy*, because the present is advantageously contrasted with the past; or, lastly,

3°. His present state is left totally out of sight, so that his *first* and better condition remains the standard by which the notions of the *hard* fate which succeeded it are measured: in that case he cannot avoid his former *feeling of pain*.

This last will happen often enough at the beginning of his new happiness. For, as when he was poor both states (his earlier happiness and his subsequent misery) were often thought of together, it follows that, as the movable elements are perpetually permeating our conscious psychical forms, *both must become connected into one group or series*. (See § 38.) But as long as *the same* pair of factors are conscious at the same time in the soul, *so long, of course, must one and the same feeling be produced*.

Now we not unfrequently meet with men, upstarts as they are called, who seem so rapidly and so completely to forget their previous unhappiness, that they are no longer able to figure to themselves what they formerly experienced, nor, indeed, what a poor man's feelings are at all. How are we to explain this?

In the following way. Their present good fortune takes such

entire possession of their soul, that all their thoughts are concentrated on their good fortune. This causes a gradual dissolution of the groups formed in the earlier condition of poverty and subsequent prosperity,—the several members of these enter into other combinations, and therefore the first *feeling* must cease, simply because it was merely the consciousness of the differences between the several members in these groups.

Consequently *a feeling lasts only so long as both its fr . (by the simultaneous consciousness of which it arose) remai he same connexion; if that conjunct consciousness is imped* any thing, or if the connexion is *totally dissolved*, the re ng *feeling* must also vanish.

This is the difference between the *Feelings*, and *notions*, and *efforts*. *The two latter continue to exist in independent Traces: the former*, on the other hand, only so far as the *factors of the feeling are formed into permanent groups or series by the appropriation of movable elements:* for the feelings are nothing more than *the consciousness of different psychical forms present to consciousness together;* they are not, like notions and efforts, something *based on independent Traces.*

The result is this: in the feelings we have not a new and peculiar kind of *psychical forms*, but only a new and particular kind of *consciousness* of such forms [d], which consciousness implies that forms already conscious in themselves exist side by side, and that then one of them enhances the other. As a white object appears still whiter when contrasted with one less white, a red one still redder when contrasted with one less red, so also conscious psychical forms raise and elevate each other by their being present to consciousness together.

And note that *the elevating form* (= the standard) *is, as a rule, that which is* less constantly *conscious, what sinks back into unconsciousness with greater rapidity:* the feeling (what is felt) is not *this*, but that which

[d] Hence, we neither feel the pleasure nor pain which we might so long as we do not think of their causes and occasions (= do not render them conscious): consequently all feelings are drowned in the total unconsciousness of sleep: hence the expressions, 'I feel joy, trouble,' 'the feeling of joy or trouble is vividly before me,' &c., are identical in meaning with, 'I am *conscious* of joy or trouble,' &c.

remains longer in consciousness: where, however, both are equally strong in consciousness, there they are *both feelings*, and both are *foundations* or conditions for feeling as respects each other.

§ 48. *Extent of the Feelings: Freshness of Feeling.*

During our waking condition there are always *several* psychical forms, conscious either at the same time, or in immediate succession (§ 44), and all such forms are to a greater or less extent *different* (§ 45).

Now if, as we have proved in the preceding §§, forms cannot be simultaneously conscious without the difference or interval between them being immediately manifested, it follows that we cannot be without feeling *at any moment of our waking life*. Is this justified by experience?

Apparently not. For what sort of a feeling has a reader had of the numerous forms which were just now present to, and have now vanished from, consciousness? On a superficial examination he would reply, that he had not experienced any particular feeling. And that answer is true, if, as is the case in the usual current of our life, only ordinary notions rise into consciousness together, notions in which our powers are rather affected joyfully or painfully. All this is quite in order, for where there is no great difference between one state and another, then there can be no feeling at all, or none which is specially *remarkable*.

Yet, at such times, feeling is not totally absent. It is at once natural and necessary that feeling there should be. Where any distinction (interval) exists, be it ever so small, it must manifest itself in feeling; and this fact deserves a more careful observation. For instance, I certainly feel a greater degree of *clearness*, when the *concept* belonging to any *perception* becomes conscious along with it: for the concept is distinguished from the individual perception by its greater clearness (§ 15). Hence the expression, 'at length a light dawns upon me.' In like manner, no one would be tempted to take a conscious *notion* for a *desire*, or a *longing* for a *repugnance*, a *recollection* for a *percep-*

tion, a *resolve* for mere *indifference*, inspiriting *courage* for *fear*, *&c.*, *&c.* The difference between all these forms is too great for us to confound one with another.

But no doubt in common life the term feeling *is confined exclusively to the recognition of* noticeable *and* remarkable *differences.*

Hence, there is a considerable difference between feelings. Some are *stronger*, others *weaker*, often so weak that, unless examined with great attention, they might pass for non-existent. The one important point here to be insisted on is, the *greater* or *less* difference between the psychical forms conscious together.

A man constantly in good health derives scarcely any feeling of pleasure from his health: at the best, he merely feels comfortable. But let him fall ill, and get well again: what joy will health then cause him.

Do you imagine that a wealthy man feels himself particularly happy on account of his riches? It would be a mistake to think so. Suppose he gains a hundred dollars in addition, he would scarcely notice the fact: but a poor man would jump for joy at getting such a sum. The result is this: *the greater the interval between the psychical forms simultaneously conscious, the stronger or* fresher *is the feeling; the less that interval, the weaker or* duller (*more languid*) *it is.*

We may express the fact in the following way: *the greater the difference between psychical forms simultaneously conscious, the greater is the* freshness of the feeling *by which that difference is manifested to our consciousness.*

Who, then, would have a *fresher*, keener feeling of joy at a beautiful landscape; the man who dwells in the midst of it, or a stranger who lives in a dull locality?

Who must feel a *fresher* and keener sense of the uneasiness (pain) of sickness; one who is constantly ill, or one who was but a short time before in good health?

When should we feel a very *keen* pleasure in a hearty meal of dry bread?

When does dry bread cease to give us any more pleasure?

§ 49. *One and the Same Psychical Process may be at once a Notion, a Desire, and a Feeling.*

A father comes amongst his children, and says, 'Look at this picture that I have brought you! Have you looked at it enough? Then I will put it away. Now, Henry, describe to me what you have seen.

'I observe from your description that you have obtained a *notion* (a copy in your soul) of the picture. Have matters stopped there?

'Your joyful looks tell me that you were pleased with it. The perception of the picture was added to the forms which were already conscious in your soul when I came in. These forms were purely indifferent notions, e.g. of tables, chairs, of the walls, &c., of this room, and they were obscurely present to your consciousness, when you were looking at the picture. But that differed in a very marked manner from them. This difference, which arose from an act of involuntary *comparison* in your soul, immediately became conscious; your consciousness turned by preference to the more vivid and stimulating effect produced by the picture, and so there arose that *special* consciousness which we call *feeling*. It was naturally a feeling of *pleasure*.

'Why do you keep standing with such a wistful look at the place where the picture is kept? I observe that you would be glad to look at it again. Apparently your visual powers have already lost some of the stimulants which they received from it. Hence, they have become to some extent *void of stimulants*, and as such they are striving after fresh satisfaction to be given by the same stimulants. You *desire* to see the picture again.'

Who could fail to recognise in this instance the multifarious effects which are produced by the painting? They are the following:—

1°. *So far as its stimulants were firmly united to the powers* *of sight, there arose in the soul of the spectator a* Notion *of the picture* *.

2°. *So far as this perception was different from other forms conscious along with it a* Feeling *of that difference was manifested.*

3°. *So far as particular stimulants disappeared from the powers of sight (and the Traces excited in them), there arose a longing, a* Desire *for fresh satisfaction by the same stimulants.*

Therefore, one and the same psychical process was at once a Notion, a Desire, and a Feeling.

This is very frequently the case.

We have already seen in § 27 that *desires* are also at the same time *notions.* In order that they should be feelings as well, nothing more is required than that they should be conscious along with other psychical forms tolerably different from them. When, then, this difference is immediately manifested, then the desire at once becomes a *feeling.* For when *I desire* an apple, I figure it to myself—*form a notion of it in that same act of desire;* and in so far as the apple when compared with other edible objects *more fully* stimulates my gustatory powers, that difference *is manifested as a feeling of pleasure; hence one and the same psychical process may be at once a notion, a desire, and a feeling.* Usually one of these forms preponderates more or less over the others.

Notion, desire, and feeling, therefore, are only three different *forms of development,* they do not in the least imply distinct powers; indeed, not even distinct acts (processes), except so far as the form 'feeling' requires that the fundamental form with which the others are compared and measured should exist in consciousness beside, and along with them (§ 47). Compare § 27.

* It need hardly be mentioned that in this instance many Traces suitable for the present perception are excited, and that the stimulants spread over them as well as over the others. For the (void) visual powers as now affected merely, would of themselves produce a sensation, but no notion properly so called. See the following §.

§ 50. *Feelings of Pleasure and Dislike. Difference between Sensation, Feeling, and Perception.*

From § 24 we know that *pleasurable* forms are engendered within us by thoroughly *full* stimulation, which, as it were, sets us on the swing, e.g. if we perceive vivid colours, powerful full tones, &c. If, at the same moment, other psychical forms less full of stimulants are presented to consciousness, it follows, from the preceding §§, that these different forms are compared or measured together, and so the *perception* of pleasure is converted into a *feeling* of pleasure.

Now, as there are also *sensations* of pleasure, it may be asked, how they differ from other species of pleasure? As respects this we offer the following observations.

In the new psychology, the term sensation *in general* is applied to every *simple* act of sense, when a single original power so connects with itself a correspondent stimulant, that nothing already formed and elaborated within is concerned or employed in the act, [i.e. it is the bare union of a stimulant and an original power, abstracting from every other change or process with which it may as a fact be connected]. Such an act is attended by an extremely faint consciousness, so faint, indeed, as to be almost = 0, as we find to be the case with a new-born child when its soul is receiving its first impressions. Each of these sensations are retained in the soul in the shape of a *Trace*, and all these Traces, so far as they are *of like kind*, fuse into *one* whole; and it is in consequence of this that the psychical forms thence resulting arrive at *full* consciousness (§§ 9, 10). After the soul has in this manner attained a certain degree of development, stimulants still continue to unite, as they did before, with the isolated original powers, i.e. *sensations* are still constantly engendered: but since they, as a rule, instantaneously attach themselves to Traces homogeneous with them, and excite them into consciousness (§ 12), the simple act of sense gains strength from within in proportion as the homogeneous Traces there found are numerous; *sensation*, which was in itself and alone almost destitute of consciousness, is thus converted into *percep-*

tion. We may, therefore, say that *Perceptions* are *sensations* which have been *strengthened* (multiplied) by elements derived from within.

The case is exactly similar as respects sensations of *pleasure*. They differ from those which imply no pleasure merely because they are the results of *fuller* stimulation than the others, as we have already proved in § 24. Now, if the homogeneous Traces of pleasure are attracted to a pleasurable sensation, the latter participates in the accumulated consciousness contained in them, and so there arises a *perception* of pleasure. It usually happens that other psychical forms less full of stimulants become or are already conscious along with the perception of pleasure, which measures its greater fulness of stimulation or its pleasure by them as by a standard. This yields that difference which is manifested as a *feeling* of pleasure.

The difference, then, between the sensation and the perception of pleasure is precisely that which exists between sensation and perception in general. The former is nothing but a *simple* act of sense, which may, it is true, be accounted a feeling, but only so far as stimulant and original powers may, in its case, be compared together, which can, at best, be but very obscurely felt: the latter, on the contrary, is a *fully conscious* pleasurable form, which cannot exist at all at the earliest period of psychical development. The further, however, that development is carried the more numerous do such pleasurable forms become, and, on being compared with others, in the manner described, they lead at last to *feelings* of pleasure properly so called. An adult finds it more difficult to form purely simple *sensations*, but yet he does form them, for the assemblage of like Traces already existent within is not always aroused by every sensation, as is noticeably the case in transient impressions; and many sensations of both the former and latter kind remain, as we shall see in § 69, in their original and elementary condition.

The careless language of everyday life frequently confounds the *sensation* of pleasure with the *perception* and *feeling* of it: it applies the term sensation to every act of consciousness, whether it be attended with pleasure or the reverse; whereas the word can only be properly used of the *lower* senses; for in them no form attains to that *clearness* of consciousness which is requisite for perception, properly so called. At least everything which is *reproduced* in the lower senses remains so obscure that it cannot properly be called more than sensation.

We have already observed in § 37 and elsewhere, that, in point of fact, it is impossible to affirm generally what will be the exact effect produced on the original powers by a given amount of stimulant: it cannot be said that so much stimulant produces full stimulation, and so much pleasurable stimulation. Hence it is self-evident that a greater or less difference must prevail amongst our *feelings of pleasure.* Such terms as delight, joy, bliss, transport, ecstasy prove this, for they are intended to indicate different degrees in which pleasure is felt.

All other sensations that arise in the soul are converted into feelings in precisely the same manner as that already described.

If the stimulant is too *small* for the original power, two things are rendered prominent; that part of the original power which was filled, and that which was not, are manifested side by side, and therefore we have, to some extent, a feeling, though a very obscure one, of *dissatisfaction*, of *displeasure.* As a rule, the Traces of former and similar cases of half-stimulation are excited by the present sensation, and coalesce with it. If, as often occurs, a psychical form produced by full stimulation is aroused into weak semi-consciousness at the same time, the consciousness of the first will be heightened, and we have a *stronger* feeling of dissatisfaction (of *dislike*).

If the stimulant *gradually* becomes *too strong* for the original power we become aware of a gradual *over* stimulation, i.e. the feeling of *satiety* or *disgust* arises. As long as it remains in this simple shape the feeling is naturally very obscure. As a rule, however, homogeneous traces are excited along with the simple act: moreover, this complex form is compared with more perfect ones, which then rise more weakly into consciousness, and thus the feeling of satiety gains in strength.

Finally, if the stimulant affects the original power *suddenly* and with *too great strength*, so that the latter is *overborne* by it, we shall experience *a feeling of pain*, stronger in proportion as the number of similar traces which co-operate is greater, and in proportion as they attain to clearer consciousness, by measuring themselves by more perfect psychical forms. So long as stimulant and original power are *alone* concerned in the act, the pain is only felt obscurely.

The feelings of dissatisfaction, of satiety, and of pain, being all the opposite of pleasure, might be embraced under the common term 'Feelings of Dislike' [Unlustgefühle]—a term usually employed only in a wide signification. All these feelings, whether of pleasure or the reverse, may be greatly intermixed—they run into one another; indeed, a weaker feeling of pain may even appear pleasant when contrasted with the recollection of a more violent one.

It must be carefully noticed, that most pleasures and pains (as, indeed, to a great extent, their different forms) are caused by the *degrees and modes in which our powers are stimulated*, from the perfection or weakness which the original powers are then subject to: their perfection (elevation) is immediately pleasant, their weakening (depression) immediately painful[f]. This pleasure and dislike in immediate *sensation* is suspended, but only suspended, when the (so excited) act changes into (an unexcited act or) trace; and it, therefore, returns in the shape of *formed* pleasure or pain when the act is re-excited. Compare § 24, at the end. In *feeling* (= when different acts are mutually compared), this pleasure and pain is only modified; it is partly, as it were, thrown into the shade, partly set in a brighter light. Feeling, therefore, would be totally impossible, unless several conditions were fulfilled: the fundamental differences between the various psychical forms must first have been caused by the different ways in which they were stimulated. Again, the several powers must, from the first, have constituted distinct systems; they must have received a real *objective* and differing development by being affected by different objects; and, lastly, all these differences must have been manifested to consciousness.

---

[f] Hence the expressions *elevation* and *depression* always denote two kinds of things as contained in one and the same act: in the former, pleasure and perfection; in the latter, pain and weakness (damage). That something real (objective) is also necessarily implied—the powers are the subjective, what is *attuned* to pleasure, dislike, &c.—is self-evident. See the note on p. 66.

§ 51. *Similar Stimulation does not always call forth the same Feeling.*

Invalids are often unable to endure ordinary daylight, and start with pain if people talk within their hearing in their ordinary tone. How is this to be explained?

The *stimulants* cannot be to blame in the matter, because, then, healthy people ought to be pained in like manner; therefore the cause must be sought for solely in the peculiar *quality of the sick man's original powers*[8]. They are, doubtless, so weakened by sickness, that an ordinary stimulant (one not in itself too strong) over-excites them, and so produces a feeling of pain. It is as clear as daylight that this explanation is correct; for when the invalid gets well again, i.e. when his original powers have recovered their original strength, ordinary stimulants instantaneously cease to produce over-excitement.

Therefore the kind of feeling produced by like stimulation depends (1°.) *on the quality and condition of the original powers.*

Again, a poor and hungry man will experience great pleasure if he can obtain a good hearty meal of merely humble fare, and yet a rich man, whose palate is daily tickled by delicacies, would make but a wry face at it.

The native of a large city passes by with indifference all the gay and sometimes prettily ornamented shop-bills, the grand display in the windows, the monuments, and so forth; whereas a countryman, who looks on such objects for the first time in his life, stares with open eyes and mouth, to the great amusement of the bystanders, in order to draw in the unaccustomed glory at all inlets; and if we ask him how he likes it, we shall find him untiring in his praise, &c. Here, also, the same stimulant produces totally different feelings. The *stimulant* cannot be the cause of the difference, for it is *identical* in both cases. The *original powers* are not responsible for it; for we presuppose

[8] Therefore not in that *of the traces*; they retain their full vigour, and are not weakened. Generally speaking, in such cases, the bodily organs alone are affected, and the pain arises chiefly *in them* (consequently in the vital powers).

them to be *sound* and healthy in all alike. Therefore, there must be some third thing.

When the poor man satisfies his hunger by simple food, that satisfaction is compared and measured with the depression which was existing just before, and which had been produced by want of nutriment. Compared with this defective state, satisfaction must manifest itself in immediate feeling as *a more perfect* condition, or as *a feeling of comfort*.

In the case of the rich man driven to eat common food, the latter is contrasted in consciousness with the recollection of the dainties which he usually enjoys: these are made the standard, and therefore the effects now produced on his organs of taste must needs appear something *imperfect*, when compared with his ordinary feelings, or as something *displeasing*.

If the countryman felt great pleasure at the grandeur of the town, and the townsman none, it is obvious that the former compared the brilliant impressions which he received with those common things with which he is acquainted, and that naturally yields a great difference: the townsman, however, takes the splendour to which he is accustomed as a standard, and as he has nothing to compare with it, it produces in him no feeling either of pleasure or the reverse.

The same is the case in all the other instances. The question always is this: *with what kind of forms* is the present one simultaneously conscious, or *what is the standard* (or *foundation of comparison*) *by which an act is measured*. Hence it is not merely 1°. the quality of the original powers, but 2°. *also the psychical forms which are then and there conscious, that cause similar excitation not to produce always the same feeling*. *Different standards give different estimations, i.e. different feelings.* But let it be constantly remembered that the standard is, as a rule, that psychical form which is maintained less steadily and clearly in consciousness. (§ 47.)

Hence, it is explicable why often the same object may at certain times call up a feeling of pleasure, at another of pain. For example, dip your hand into decidedly cold water, and then into warm, and you will feel much more warmth than there really is. Conversely, the warm water would have felt cold, if you had previously dipped your hand into hotter water.

§ 52. *Feelings of the Agreeable, Sublime, and Beautiful. Immediate Factors of these Feelings.*

These feelings are naturally only produced by the *third* mode of stimulation. They depend not merely on the special qualities of the stimulants causing them, but also, and mainly, on those of the original powers; and besides that, in the case of the Beautiful and Sublime, an interpretation must be put upon the phenomena drawn from the *more deep lying* yet still acquired possessions of the soul. This will become clear in the following § [h].

When a lively and simple dance is played, or if bright colours are contrasted in a small picture, when a sweet fragrance in spring breathes through the air, when we once and away enjoy highly-seasoned and tasty viands instead of our usual dry and insipid food,—all this causes us a *sense of pleasure* (a feeling of pleasure).

When, during the stillness of evening, the pure full tones of a chorale echo down from a tower, when the departing sun streaks the sky with purple, when before us far away in the distance mountain and plain succeeds mountain and plain, when on a clear night we gaze into the infinite depths, where suns revolve round suns, and worlds round worlds: then also a *sense of pleasure* (a feeling of pleasure) seizes on our soul.

But there is a great difference between the two, as is clear from the feelings immediately attendant on them: our language calls the one *pleasant, agreeable*, the latter *sublime*.

In what do they both essentially consist?

Now, if for the moment we disregard all that which in the case of the sublime must be sought for in the *depths* of our own soul, it is evident that in the examples of the first kind of plea-

---

[h] [This is not very clear, but it is difficult to express the original, which runs thus: *wozu beim Schönen und Erhabenen noch eine Unterlegung aus dem tiefern, sonst schon erworbenen Inhalt der Seele kommen muss.* He means that whenever we view an object as Beautiful or Sublime, we attribute to it human qualities, we give it a meaning by analogies derived from ourselves.]

sure, the stimulant is of a tolerably simple kind: hence it acts as an *easy* and *lively excitant* on our original powers, and presupposes on their part nothing but sufficient *sensibility* and *vivacity* to enable them to appropriate these rapid stimulants. At the same time, however, unless the impression made is to remain a mere *obscure*, scarcely conscious *sensation*, it is clear that all that we have hitherto experienced of a like kind, and now retain in the shape of traces, must be excited along with it, and so convert this mere apprehension into a conscious *perception* of pleasure (see § 50).

In the instances of the second kind, the impressions (stimulants) are more complex, more massive: hence they make a heavier impression on the original powers, the strain they produce is steadier and *longer*, and therefore these powers must be endowed with more than ordinary *strength and tenacity*, in order to withstand such treatment. In this case also, unless the result is to remain a mere obscure sensation, the homogeneous traces formerly acquired must be added to the present impression, they alone being capable of strengthening a mere *sensation* of pleasure into a *perception* of it (§ 50.)

Again: when a fresh green clothes fields and hedges, when good sterling and yet not elaborate music excites our ear, when an agreeable neighbourhood opens to our view, and is not too extensive, but diversified by houses, thickets, commons, lakes, &c., all this also produces in us a sense *of pleasure* (feelings of pleasure), but these we call neither agreeable nor sublime, but *beautiful.*

When this arises, the already existing and homogeneous traces must, as in the former cases, co-operate: but here, on the other hand, the stimulants have a certain *intermediate mass or weight;* their effect, therefore, though vigorous and lively, still takes place with *tolerable* sedateness, which naturally requires original powers possessing the requisite *vivacity, strength, and tenacity.*

From what has been said, two things may be explained: 1°. the fact that, as well as the reason why, brutes though capable of feeling the *agreeable* are never capable of feeling the *Beau-*

tiful and *Sublime*, notwithstanding that the same stimulants act on them that act on us. They do not possess the requisite tenacity and strength in their original powers, and consequently they cannot accumulate that number of homogeneous Traces, which in men raises their bare apprehensions of objects to the strength of clear consciousness. On the other hand, the brute often possesses powers of great vivacity and sensibility, and is therefore perfectly able to form agreeable feelings, or (to speak more correctly), sensations. In men's lower systems of powers, impressions are, owing to want of strength and tenacity, only so transiently appropriated, that most of them are lost again, and this explains, 2°. why we are unable in like manner to form the feelings of *beauty* or *sublimity* in our senses of taste or smell, or in our vital or muscular powers. No one, therefore, when he speaks correctly, talks about beautiful or sublime tastes, smells, vital or muscular acts; they are *agreeable*, and that is all.

Now as the feelings of the Beautiful and Sublime are called '*æsthetic* feelings,' it is obvious that man alone, and he only as regards his higher powers, is capable of æsthetic developments.

We know, from § 49, that one and the same psychical process may be at once a notion, a desire, and a feeling, but that usually one of these aspects preponderates over the rest. What we have said in the present § about the Sublime and Beautiful shews clearly that both incline towards the notional side, that therefore they consist of pleasurable notions (see § 27), and belong to the class of *emotional* psychical forms, (modes of feeling). (See § 24 and 50 at the end.) Hence, it is correct to say that the æsthetic region is that of *affective, emotional notions*: it would, if it could, assume the form of feeling properly so called, (see the following §), and yet remains essentially distinct from it. The æsthetic, therefore, can only be called a feeling, if that word be used in its most extensive sense to denote every kind of disposition and sensation.

§ 53. *The more Remote Factors of the Æsthetic Feelings.*

The origin of the æsthetic feelings (of the Beautiful and Sublime) has up to this point not been perfectly explained. We have still to answer the questions—in what does their essential nature consist? how comes it that many men remain completely cold and unmoved by beautiful or sublime phenomena?—why is it that similar æsthetic feelings are produced by objects so different? and, lastly, what is the reason that many men find it more difficult to feel the agreeable than the sublime? The following remarks may serve to resolve these queries in their order.

Suppose a violet affects me (my visual powers), and because it flowers so quietly and secretly, I attribute to it the quality of modesty. I have added to it, in thought, something which really comes from within myself. Whether a violet really is modest, I do not know, but I am sure that I could not think of the nettle as modest, but rather as malicious, because, when touched, it makes a destructive impression on my vital powers. Is the rose animated by love, the lily by innocence, the tulip by pride? I do not know; but the impression which these flowers make on me is such as to excite involuntarily the notion and sensation (the tone and temper) of these qualities. These qualities I ascribe to them: I have *given* them an internal something derived *from my own mind*, which corresponds to their external appearance: I *deepen* my apprehension of such objects (take a deeper view of them), by attributing to them my own dispositions, according to the impressions which they make on me. I do the same when I regard the oak as a symbol of strength, or a rock surrounded by the roaring sea as an emblem of stedfastness, the rapid stream as representing the fleeting nature of human life, a ruin as the sign of the transitoriness of all earthly things, &c. So long as such objects merely impress their outward forms on me, they simply produce on me a *sensuous* impression; they cause an *æsthetic* impression only when I render my apprehension of them deeper in the way described. I thus penetrate through their outward form into their *inner being*, seize them as they (from an emotional aspect) might be *in themselves*.

That which by this union between the external and internal produces in us a gentler form of pleasure, as the rose, the lily, enamelled meadows, &c., we call *Beautiful:* that which causes a stronger and more intense pleasure, as the oak, a rock, the starry heavens, is called *Sublime.* Our psychical powers are manifested in the latter case as raised (enhanced) to *a higher and more vigorous condition.* This is the special characteristic of the æsthetic feelings.

Who are the persons, then, who remain quite cold in the presence of beautiful or sublime objects? Those who are incapable of giving to external things the kind of interpretation described; as, uncultivated people and young children, neither of whom have any consciousness of modesty, stedfastness, &c.; and again, adults, who, though they are conscious of such qualities, have never been assiduously excited to underlay what they see with such notions, or who, at least, have not yet been educated sufficiently to perceive certain kinds of beauty and sublimity. Without special training at the hands of those whose *æsthetic* feelings have been already developed, the Beautiful and the Sublime remain to many persons an unknown world.

According to § 48, feeling always implies a something by which we can measure it, *a standard of comparison:* if that changes, the feeling changes also (§ 51). Now, as the development of man is progressive, it is impossible that his earlier standards should not change: the paintings, poems, pieces of music, which as children we admired, no longer come up to the more perfect patterns which we now are acquainted with as adults, and these patterns consequently prevent us now from viewing objects as we did, i.e. our changed feelings prevent us from doing so. While the little girl fancies that her doll smiles responsive to her, because she ascribes to it her own joys (joyous tone); the higher standard which a maiden of twenty has gained by her knowledge of men and things no longer allows her to fancy anything of the sort; and, however pleasing a doll may still be to her, she would feel ashamed to attribute to it life and laughter as she once did. It is thus that we may explain the fact that the feelings of Beauty and Sublimity are excited by very *different objects,* not merely in different men, but even in the same man, at different ages and in different tempers; and, on the other hand, it is clear why objects which remain *unchanged* no longer continue beautiful or sublime as they once were. He who is satisfied by artistic products of little value, or who is insensible to the real beauty of objects of higher value, proves that his mental education is still seriously imperfect.

Lastly, the fact that many men find it difficult to attain to feelings of the agreeable, and easy to acquire those of the sublime, is intelligible enough. Sublime feelings will never be found in those whose powers are weak and dull, but solely in those whose faculties are conspicuous for a high degree of force, *tenacity* and *sensibility*. To the rich, strong, and deep development produced by such qualities, that which merely tickles the senses agreeably must appear insipid and commonplace, must therefore be felt only as dislike; and it is impossible to interpret objects pleasurably in such a case, because such an interpretation could only consist in something low, which souls strongly developed in the direction of what is noble do not care about. When, on the other hand, such tempers are affected by objects which harmonize with their high and lofty development, either in the kind or fulness of their stimulants, there some striking interpretation will not be wanting, and feelings of sublimity will easily and quickly start into existence. Consequently feelings of the agreeable are found more commonly in children and weak adults, since their powers possess greater vivacity and sensibility. By corresponding comparisons and interpretations, they are able of course to convert their feelings with ease into what they personally regard as beautiful and sublime: but such Beauty and Sublimity must always be very flat and unsatisfactory to minds better endowed; and as this cannot be otherwise, it simply proves the truth of the adage, *de gustibus non est disputandum* (we have no business to quarrel over matters of taste).

When the impression made is too violent and perturbing, as a thunderstorm is to many men, the æsthetic mode of viewing the object is checked. All objects which by their strength are adapted to produce the sublime feelings of majesty and might, presuppose a strong soul; in feeble minds they cause the painful *emotions* of fear and terror, because they too vividly excite the consciousness of their weakness.

If we gather up all that has been said, we arrive at the following results:—

a. *The æsthetic feelings are a union between external impressions and emotions already existent within us. They are produced by our not stopping at the sensible impressions made by things, but pushing on to their internal being and life, by our thinking* their *internal nature as analogous to* our own, *and thus spiritualizing the object of sense.*

b. *In order correctly to lend external things our internal emotions, we must interpret them in such a way as is actually suitable to the impressions which they make on us, which mirror forth to us their internal condition.*

c. *Since, however, we do not know the internal essence of external objects as we do that of our own internal states, our interpretations are very liable to be erroneous, and the more so because every one in apprehending anything æsthetically is necessarily restricted to his own (often very defective) stage of cultivation. And as the latter is dependent to some extent on the constitution of his original powers, it follows that a man's degree of æsthetic cultivation depends very largely on the amount of strength, tenacity, and sensibility possessed by them, but also very largely on exercise.*

d. *Merely agreeable feelings may be produced by suitable stimulation of the senses; as they require nothing more than this, they cannot be accounted æsthetic feelings.*

The language of everyday life pronounces much to be beautiful which ought to be merely called agreeable, because it not unfrequently regards sensations as feelings.

Lower stages of the Beautiful are, the pretty, neat, charming, graceful, naive, &c. The noble, estimable, splendid, glorious, &c., are more allied to the Sublime.

Why does the æsthetic please us without any 'selfish interest?' Because it carries its own satisfaction with it: the main thing in it is not the feeling *proper* (which may easily grow into a selfish desire), but the notion of pleasure which it implies.

Painful sensations may also be trained æsthetically; how? This is a question into which we cannot here enter, any more than we can into the still more profound fact, that æsthetic emotions may be engendered when no external objects are at the moment presented to us. See *Beneke's* "Pragmatische Psychologie," vol. ii. p. 222 sqq.

A remarkably good account of æsthetics will be found in the treatise: "Das Aesthetische nach seinem eigenthümlichen Grundwesen und seiner pädagogischen Bedeutung dargestellt. Eine gekrönte Preisschrift von *Friedrich Dittes.*" Leipsic, published by Julius Klinkhardt, 1854, price 15 ngr.

§ 54. *Feelings of the Strength of particular Psychical Forms.*

In consequence of the Mutual Attraction of Similars, every psychical form has a new trace added to it, directly the act with which it commenced is repeated with sufficient perfection, and at the same moment a void unemployed original power becomes modified and formed (§§ 6, 9, 10).

Hence my notion, for instance, of the dome of the Frauenkirche at Dresden, which I have seen perhaps twenty times, consists of that number of traces: the notion of my room, on the contrary, consists of many hundreds of them (§ 9).[1]

If I have desired an object once, my desire consists of a *single* trace; if a thousand times, then of a *thousand* traces (see § 28).

If a pleasurable activity has existed once in my soul, I retain only one trace of it; if ten thousand times, a psychical form consisting of ten thousand traces has arisen, (always supposing, of course, that actual traces have been left behind, and, therefore, that the processes in question were not too imperfect).

Who has ever calculated the number of traces out of which his psychical forms have grown? No one: and yet our consciousness, if it does not furnish us with their numbers, will give us very exact details as to the strength of these forms. How?

---

[1] It often happens that we see, hear, touch, &c., so momentarily and inexactly that these acts are not performed with *any* degree of perfection; the condition under which alone traces can be produced is not then fulfilled. When I merely casually cast a look round my room, &c., this would generally be the case, and thus we may explain why such notions do not increase in strength. For the same reason also, no one will learn anything who does not exert himself to do so. Moreover the remark in the note to § 49 holds good of the example of the dome of the Frauenkirche at Dresden, and in similar cases.

Let any one ask himself: Which do I know better, my dwelling-house or the church? The former would certainly appear a more strongly conscious form than the latter, and from this it follows that it is *richer in traces.*

In the drunkard, which desire is stronger, more abundant in traces, that for brandy, or that for the comfort of his family? Suppose he squanders his last farthing in drink, what would be our judgment then?

Which gives us more delight, to do a sum in arithmetic or to compose a letter? If the former, I infer that the pleasurable form which has arisen from correct solutions of sums is stronger and richer in traces than that which has been produced by writing letters; and conversely.

In a word: *the psychical form which consists of a larger number of traces, always manifests itself with a feeling of greater* strength *than another which consists of a lesser number, directly both are conscious together* [h].

Apart, however, from the number of traces, the feeling of strength depends largely on the kind of thing taken as a standard of comparison, and its peculiar constitution. This is especially the case in everything which

---

[h] The number of traces of which a psychical form consists may be *figuratively* called its space. Hence, we may say that this form occupies a greater, that a less, space in the soul. Even in common life we use this metaphor, e.g. 'this anxiety occupies a large space in my soul,' i.e. it is very strong = consists of numerous traces. But the strength (or space) of a form may also increase without an augmentation of its traces: this is the case if the form is reproduced merely internally, when a portion of the movable elements which cause its reproduction become permanently attached to it, and thus strengthen its traces without adding to their number. There are, therefore, two ways in which the space (strength) may be increased, and *Beneke* calls the first 'strengthening in *increscive*,' the latter 'strengthening in *accrescive*, space.' We cannot enter into further details on the matter in this place. For additional information, see *Dressler's* "Beiträge," &c., vol. ii. chap. 12 and 13, and *Beneke's* "Psychol. Skizzen," vol. ii. p. 417 sqq. Compare also § 75, below. [A more clumsy metaphor it would be hard to imagine: the absurd technical terms, *eingewachsener* Raum, and *angewachsener* Raum, I have rendered by the best barbarisms that occurred to me.]

we call 'correct.' A psychical form is consciously pronounced 'correct' only when it is compared with a normal standard with which it should and does agree. The united notions which constitute this normal standard, are associated with the form compared with it, and this produces a group of notions which must assert itself with considerable strength; while the (incorrect) form which stands isolated beside that normal, and deviates from it, must be felt as weak. If the standard itself is false, the agreement of a form with it will lead no doubt to error; an error, however, which cannot be discovered so long as that particular standard is adhered to: in such a case, the false passes for the correct. Hence the principle: the correct, or what is held to be so, will always be felt as *strength*; the incorrect, or what is considered so, always as *weakness*. See above, p. 87, and compare §§ 57 and 58. It is self-evident that *in such cases* the strength will be manifested as pleasure or satisfaction, weakness as pain or dissatisfaction.

§ 55. *Feelings of the Clearness, Obscurity, and Indistinctness of Notions.*

Whoever has learnt anything, knows that he did not get it into his head at one stroke. Let us take the simple letter A for an example. The child first hears some one say, look! that is A! And again, A! and so on for many times running. After the first three, five, ten traces, A is still a dark affair in a child's soul. But the more similar traces increase, the *clearer* does it become in consciousness: and I should like to see the conjurer who could persuade a boy of twelve years old that he does not know A yet, although he has looked at it some hundred thousand times during six years of school. The multitude of similar traces renders the letter so *clear* to him, that he would very sceptically laugh in the fellow's face.

He might succeed better with a child of six just beginning his alphabet, the first time he walks out of school with book and slate, to whom the teacher has just thrown out the letter A as a kind of bait. Being as yet deficient in traces, it cannot naturally present itself with the feeling of clearness. As compared with the notion of his hobby-horse, he would figure it to himself as *obscure*, or with the feeling of *obscurity*.

Hence, for the first few weeks, children often confound the letters together. They do this most frequently when they have been taught too fast. Tiresome as this interchange of letters is to the teacher, it is easily accounted for. The letters resemble one another. But like fuses with like—hence the traces left by A may coalesce in the child's soul with those left by O, or the reverse, and therefore with *analogous*, though, at the same time, *different*, traces. Grown-up people very often fall into the same error. How many mistake lead for tin, wheat for rye, quinces for apples, hemlock for parsley, &c.; indeed, many take bats for birds, blindworms for serpents, and so on. In all such cases, *similar* parts of notions are intermingled with *heterogeneous* ones, because we do not examine objects resembling each other on all sides with sufficient care, but only apprehend them in the rough. But let a man only have cause to be puzzled about such notions, and let him compare them with those which are decidedly clear, and then, in spite of all their strength, he will feel that they are *not clear* (confused).

Hence, the feeling of strength in our notions is distinguishable into three kinds: the feeling of *clearness*, of *obscurity*, of *non-clearness* (confusion), according as a form was produced from *many* similar, *few* similar, or of similar and dissimilar traces.

What psychical forms must manifest themselves in the soul with the *freshest* (§ 47) feelings of clearness? and why? (Compare §§ 15 and 16.)

The remarks made in this § are applicable in particular to *pleasurable notions*. Compare §§ 24, 27, and 50.

§ 56. *Estimation of Worth.*

In § 37 we have already seen what it is that mainly renders objects (persons and things) *Goods* or *Evils* to us. But as we could say nothing about Feelings then, though they are always concerned in the matter, we must now descend into particulars.

Suppose that a bird so affects me by its form and colour, or even by its song, as to stimulate me pleasurably. By this means it produces in me a psychical form which, as being fuller of stimulants, deviates noticeably from those forms which have been engendered simply by sufficient stimulation. The pleasing form is compared with these latter as soon as they are excited into consciousness along with it, as they usually are: in this manner it becomes a form *felt* or *Feeling*, and at once the bird becomes a *good* to me, not merely in the way of immediate *sensation*, but also, at the same time, in the way of *feeling*. I should estimate it otherwise, if other forms were conscious along with it (§ 51). Hence it is inferred, that *we estimate the* worth *of an object by the degree of* pleasurable feeling *which it produces in us by its special mode of operation, and the object is then called a* (greater or lesser) good.

Just think of fire. It may be so beneficent as to be a great good to us, but when it over-stimulates our vital powers, depresses or damages them, the result must be a distorted form, which, when contrasted with more perfect forms, is felt as serious *pain;* while that is less the case when that misformation is measured by other depressed sensations. And thus fire becomes to us a greater or less *evil*.

Or take hunger, which causes us more or less pain. That pain is caused by the fact that the digestive forces are *weakened* (not by over-stimulation, as by fire, but) by defective stimulation—by want of food to stimulate—their violent striving after satisfaction by means of stimulants remains unsatisfied, unappeased. This yields a psychical form poor in stimulants, which, when contrasted with the numerous forms full of stimulants existent in men, is manifested now as a weaker, again as a stronger *feeling of dislike*, in a higher degree as a feeling of *pain;* and hence everybody justly calls hunger an *evil*, especially when it is very violent and cannot be appeased. With thirst it is the same.

Now, are these *determinations of worth?* No doubt they are, but they are diametrically opposed to those we first mentioned. Hence, we infer that,

We estimate the value *of things also by the amount of dislike, satiety, and pain which we feel them to cause us: hence, their value becomes a* negative *worth, commonly called* worthlessness *and* damage, *and the relative object is then called* a (greater or less) evil.

Now, as all things (compare § 37, at the end,) may, in this

manner, acquire a value in our eyes, which is essentially distinct from the mere notion of them, it may be asked, what is the general estimate of value that actually exists in a man?

It is the sum total of all pleasurable and painful forms which are produced in him as (very complex) **sensations** *by the different stimulants of things, and then subsequently, by comparison, converted into* **feelings.**

Therefore, what we call goods and evils are *feelings of value* relative to things; they are either *positive* (pleasurable feelings), or *negative* (unpleasant feelings). They are revealed to consciousness in *three* different manners: 1°. when they are *being formed*, as *nascent;* 2°. on their reproduction, as pleasurable or unpleasurable *recollections;* 3°. as *desires* and *repugnancies* into which they have been internally developed. In the second case, these feelings of value exercise, as yet, no influence on our acts, they are regarded internally as something acquired, and give us what is called *practical wisdom, prudence* (in contradistinction to theoretical knowledge). In the third case, on the contrary, they form the foundation of our *actions:* they act here as *efficients* (motives) for what we do or refuse to do, and are what, in common language, are called good or bad *sentiments* and *principles.* In all these *three* shapes the values of objects are, for the most part, determined *immediately*, the concepts into which those objects may have been developed are not necessarily reproduced: the mere elevations and depressions directly caused by objects may, by their *mere juxtaposition in consciousness*, suffice to determine their value.

Before we discuss the further effects of this, we beg to call the reader's attention to the following remarks.

§ 57. *Gradation of Goods and Evils.*

So long as they are conscious together, the factors of every feeling are permeated by the movable elements, a portion of which remains and connects them into a stable group, so that when one member of it is excited the remainder are reproduced in consciousness (§§ 38 and 47). This furnishes *ready formed feelings*, which merely require to be reproduced. Now, as *void* unemployed original powers are transformed and used only when affected with sufficient strength by fresh stimulants (§§ 9 and 30), and since when so transformed into new traces, they coalesce with those traces *like* them which already exist and strengthen them, it follows that the divergence between the several factors of feeling must also change. The factor that is strengthened must assert itself with *redoubled consciousness*, as contrasted and compared with that other which is connected with it, and thus the feeling itself increases in strength. This is true both of unpleasing and of pleasing feelings.

Suppose I meet a man totally unknown to me—how shall I value him? Exactly as I value all persons unknown to me, i.e. I measure his worth by that *general* standard which I have formed for men in general, a standard generated by the impressions which they made upon me, excluding such cases as those where men had something particularly remarkable about them. The impression hitherto made by this person upon me exactly agrees with that standard. Let us suppose, on the contrary, that this unknown person lives with me a long time, and that by causing me pleasure a thousand times he produces a pleasurable psychical form, consisting of a thousand traces; then the strength of that form would raise him far above other men in my estimation; I should value him more than I do them; indeed, he would become more decidedly a higher good for me than one who had caused me pleasure a hundred, or even five hundred times.

If he had depressed me, produced feelings of dislike in me, I should value him *negatively*, I could not consider him as other than an evil to me. Still this need not lead me formally to hate him, supposing me, by good training, to have acquired such strong psychical forms as would enable me to despise his perversity: I should then, at the most, only feel disposed to pity him.

The following example may illustrate the gradation of negative estimates:

I have been often obliged to go about in rainy weather, when the roads were bad. From this an unpleasurable form, caused by 1000 traces (I choose purely arbitrary numbers), has been produced as respects the roads; by bad roads, caused by snow, I have a form, consisting only of one hundred traces. I should, therefore, not account such roads good. The standard which I employ for comparison is the notion and value of *dry roads.* Now it is only natural that I should feel the first disagreeable form more strongly, for its traces are more numerous. Hence, by mere pure internal consciousness, I accurately distinguish the values of the two states of road respectively.

And so it is with all objects (persons and things). Whether we estimate an object as a greater or less good or evil depends primarily on the strength of (the number of traces in) the pleasurable or non-pleasurable form which it produces in us, and also on the comparison implied in it. Such a form is always judged by reference to a standard allied to it, which has been produced by similar objects, but which is now not so strongly present to consciousness.

Thus all goods and evils assume in all souls a definite gradation. Whether this arrangement is that which is implied by genuine morality is another question, which we shall endeavour to answer afterwards.

Is there, then, anything astonishing in the fact, that there are people who assign a great positive or negative value to things which are to others quite indifferent?

A little girl cries her eyes red, if her doll, with, very often, only half a face, is in question; and many a lady feels herself unhappy if she cannot follow the last fashion, though it may even deform her. There we see a man rummaging every dunghill, and his countenance is lighted up with joy if he manages to meet with some dirty beetle. Here another marches on undismayed for hours together in sweltering heat to see, for the first time, some petty flower, or to look at it again. Many an one sits all night long in a smoky room at the card-table, as if fascinated, and is more delighted even at losing than others are with glory and honour.

A good many people say, we cannot comprehend how men

can take pleasure in such things. Of course they do not, and cannot comprehend it, for it is impossible for them to *feel anything as others do.* Such objects have either never affected them at all, or only very slightly. But if they had been so affected, if they had gained many a pleasant impression from them, they would be perfectly able to comprehend it; and conversely, if they had experienced the sense of displeasure in their own persons, which have produced in others an apparently incomprehensible repugnance to certain things, they would find that repugnance no longer incomprehensible.

Thus we perpetually come back to the statement, that *a thing becomes a good or an evil for us only in proportion as it produces in us a stronger or weaker* pleasurable *or* unpleasurable psychical form, *which is in part enhanced, or otherwise modified by the* feelings *excited along with it.*

§ 58. *The original Constitution of all Men determines for them all a* like *Gradation of Goods and Evils.* True *Estimate of Value.*

The preceding §§ have shown how objects become goods or evils to us. Now we already know from § 7, that every trace is more perfectly formed, and is more permanent in proportion as the original power, which is transformed into a trace, is more tenacious and strong[1]. Therefore these traces must be formed most perfectly in the *higher* senses (in those of sight and hearing, and especially in those of touch, compare § 8), whether those powers are developed into estimations of value, or into mere notions.

---

[1] We beg to remind the reader, that traces are nothing but the powers themselves developed and modified by stimulants, and to caution him against falling into the mistake of supposing that the stimulant taken up constitutes the trace. Compare § 6. In the *more highly developed soul* there are, indeed, traces which have been, to some extent, divested of their stimulant, because they have been left by processes in which psychical forms have been excited only on their subjective or *power* side. For further details see § 77.

Similar traces connected in larger numbers yield *strong* psychical forms. Now let us suppose that, in a man *fully developed*, every psychical form, in all his six senses, consists of an equal *number of traces;* then it will necessarily follow, that those of the *higher* senses must possess a *higher* degree of strength than those of the lower. For, owing to their want of tenacity, the impression made on any of the lower senses is far too faint to permit a form produced by a hundred traces to have that degree of strength which must be possessed by one engendered by an equal number of traces in any of the higher senses. In the former case, the powers are much less perfectly developed by the stimulants than they are in the latter, and, consequently, those traces can never be so perfectly reproduced in the one case as they can in the other.

As the higher senses are capable of a greater elevation, so their depression (*weakening*) must be greater than is the case with the lower senses, so that their forms admit of a greater degree of misformation, are exposed to greater perversion, than the others. Take, as a special example, those who have been rendered idiotic by over-stimulation.

It follows, then, that the feelings of pleasure and dislike must be manifested in the higher senses with greater *strength than can be the case in the lower*, supposing, that is, that the accumulation of traces is equal in both cases.

The tenacity, therefore, of the original powers is graduated, but the difference between them in this respect does not resemble that of their vivacity and sensibility; for those qualities vary largely in different men, and the mode in which they vary is not subject to any precise and constant law (Compare §§ 5 and 14). But, with regard to their tenacity, the case is different. Among men mentally sound it is impossible, as we have already seen in § 8, to find one whose lower senses possess that tenacity which the higher senses have in other persons, and conversely. The tenacity of the powers is always alike, in that their order and *gradation is the same:* the higher senses are *in all men higher*, merely because they are more tenacious and stronger. In like manner stimulants are essentially the same for all men; so that, for instance, the same stimulants of light or sound elevate or depress the powers of all alike, so long as they are not actually diseased. Lastly, in all men the law prevails, that all traces left by such acts coalesce in proportion to their similarities. Consequently, the factors which *produce* our psychical forms are for all men the same. *Like factors, however, produce like results.* Hence, all *feelings* must, in point of strength, be graduated in all men in the same manner, so that every one *feels* the *pleasures* or pains of the higher senses to be *stronger* than those of the lower, always supposing that each form in each sense consists of the same number of traces, and that, on becoming conscious, it is compared with the same standard, as is actually the case with feelings *already formed.*

Now, if the *value* which we attribute to an object depends on this strength of pleasurable or painful feeling (§§ 55 and 56), it follows finally,

That (on the supposition before mentioned) *there must be for all men* a like *gradation of goods and evils*, in accordance with which all must necessarily value those objects which produce pleasure or pain in the higher senses as *greater* goods or evils; and those objects, on the other hand, as *inferior* goods or evils, which only cause pleasure or pain in the lower senses.

If we reflect that every object that affects us leaves only one trace behind it, it will be quite obvious that this gradation must be identical for all men.

The acquisitions of the senses, especially those of the higher senses, are further developed into concepts, judgments, conclusions, ideas, principles, &c., and thus forms are engendered which transcend all that has been obtained from without, and they constitute the non-sensuous, the purely mental and spiritual in man. The original powers *are, in fact, spiritual and mental*, and they are only *called* sensuous for the reason mentioned in p. 8. Compare the preceding note and § 77. During this progressive development the greater tenacity of the higher powers cannot be lost, it must rather be increased, since, as we have seen, a greater amount of similar [impressions] are accumulated; and when once these forms are presented to consciousness side by side, and have thus been formed into feelings, no one is able to feel what is then manifested in them as a lower kind of thing. Again, since these forms constitute a graduated series, the same number of traces must yield one and the same gradation among them for all men.

Hence, this *similar* gradation of goods and evils is shewn to be *necessarily* valid for all mankind, because it is based, in all cases, on the same factors: *on the various grades of tenacity possessed by the senses in all men, on the identical nature of the stimulants affecting them, and on the law of the coalescence of like traces which prevails in every soul.* Accordingly, all men must *value* things, and *act with regard to them* in a *similar manner*, because their desires, repugnancies, and acts of will, &c., &c., cannot differ, if they spring from estimates formed *in a similar manner*, and they spring only and solely from such estimates. Hence, what incites to action must be everywhere developed with greater or with less intensity and force, according as higher or lower estimates prevail. We call this gradation the true *estimate, the* true *standard of practice.* It is the rule by and with which all that men value or do has to be measured and judged; and hence it forms what is called *the supreme Moral Law* (the fundamental principle of morals). Accordingly, the *highest* moral rule and standard *is that gradation of goods and evils, or of the value of objects, which is valid for all mankind equally* [m].

---

[m] Every one knows that it is only the like that is commensurable, i.e. only like can measure like, can determine its worth and validity; it is only by the like that it is possible to judge whether anything is true and correct, or false and wrong. Length can only be measured by length (perches, ells, feet, inches, &c.); duration of time only by periods of time (days, hours, &c.); weight by weights (hundredweights, pounds, ounces, &c.); forms and colours in a picture by other forms and colours; sounds in music only by other tones; numbers only by numbers; and generally notions only by notions. The reason why it appears as if our estimates of things were measurable by notions is that from them, as from all other practical forms, concepts are produced in the process of abstraction: but the *concept*, desire, for instance, is something totally different from a *concrete* actual desire; and similarly the *concept*, estimation or valuation, is very different from a *concrete* estimate. The latter forms are capable of moving us to act, the former are not. Consequently, estimates can only be measured by estimates. In all cases, the correct standard grows out of that which is to be

That this rule is not a *theoretical* one, not a rule for the mere formation of notions, is self-evident. We may express it in an imperative shape, and say: *So estimate things as goods or evils, and so act, that your deeds may accord with that gradation in the values of things which is identical for all mankind.*

If expressed so as to be applicable to special cases, it would run thus: "*In every particular case, do that which the true estimate of things shews to be the highest good.*" Therefore, prefer the enjoyment of a higher sense to that of a lower one, a mental perfection to a fleeting pleasure, the weal of a larger community to your own limited happiness; for that which gives happiness to thousands is a thousand times more valuable than that which merely gives happiness to an individual. If you act thus, you prefer the higher to the lower, the noble to the ignoble, the permanent to the transient, and no system of morals, however it may be expressed, essentially requires anything but this. See § 67 at the end.

On this and the following paragraphs compare an excellent treatise by *Friedrich Dittes* called "*Naturlehre des Moralischen und Kunstlehre der moralischen Erziehung.*" Leipsic, published by Gustav Mayer, 1856.

---

measured by it: it is (excluding the cases of favourite measures of length, time, and weight) that which is for all mankind universally similar [*das Allgemein-menschlich-Gleiche*] as conditioned and determined by the similarity of the factors of which it consists. Take, for instance, the supreme law in music. It is involved in the scale C, D, E, F, G, A, B, C. That alone is musically correct which accords with this scale of notes, or others like it. It is not *innate* in any man, it does not actually exist in him ready-made at his birth, but arises in all men in and along with the notes of which they gain a knowledge, and never before that; but when they are once known it arises necessarily, for the powers of hearing and the stimulants of sound, the two conditions on which such a law or scale depends, are the same in all men mentally healthy, in all men possessing the sense of hearing in a healthy condition. It is, therefore, a natural *rule*, or standard (it grows up naturally), in exactly the same way as the moral rule is so. It is called a *musical* standard, or rule, only because sounds which accord with it yield music; and, in like manner, the natural standard of our estimates of objects is a *moral* one only because estimates formed in accordance with it have morality (virtue) for their result. It is obvious that every standard must become perverted and erroneous, if the development by which it is engendered, and therefore by which it becomes a rule capable of immediate application, is in any way upset or hindered.

§ 59. *Solution of Apparent Contradictions;* false *Estimates.*

Our experience both of ourselves and others frequently appears to be in flat contradiction to what has been said above.

How many men are there who set a so-called *sensuous* enjoyment, i.e. one which excites the *lower* senses and the forms connected with them, far above a *mental* pleasure, i.e. one which arouses the *higher* senses and their belongings? How many selfishly desire that which they ought to exert themselves to acquire and expend for the common good. Where is there any appearance of a necessity that *all* men should esteem the higher as of *greater*, the lower as of *less* value, or that they must exhibit such an estimate of things in all their actions?

This question has been to some extent already answered in the preceding §§. The moral rule *arises* out of those germs which at a human being's entrance into the world form his entire stock of means for estimating objects: it does not therefore exist at birth *ready-made*, it is a something *dependent* on our natural dispositions (a something presupposed and implied by them), and, therefore, it is liable to numerous checks and disasters in the course of its development. It stands on the same footing as the rules and standards of thought and speech; these, like it, are universally *valid*, and yet their *validity* is not universally acknowledged, because they are not in all cases perfectly evolved. It is not, therefore, difficult to solve the contradictions mentioned above. Let the following remarks be considered.

If a feeling of pleasure or of dislike is to grow to *permanently greater strength*, one of their factors, the pleasurable or unpleasurable *form*, must arise in one of the *higher senses*, and must be compounded of *numerous* traces (§ 57).

Now there are parents, for instance, who, from foolish love for their children, indulge them in all kinds of dainties; and who, therefore, *excite frequently and pleasurably* the low-lying gustatory powers; while they take too little pains to educate the higher senses. What will this lead to? Although the higher senses form and preserve far more perfect traces, yet they will very soon be surpassed, as far as the strength of pleasure is concerned, by those traces which are so constantly being produced in the lower senses. The little that does or can arise in the higher senses, under such circumstances, remains *poor* in traces, whereas what is developed in the lower ones becomes abundant and *rich* in them. No wonder, then, that such children, when they grow up, value a good table more than a good book, for instance, or any other mental enjoyment. In like manner, thousands of children acquire a large number of pleasurable traces in their muscular powers, by being allowed to run about idly, to make a noise, and play the fool, &c., by all of which their powers are, of course, not disagreeably excited. Meanwhile their powers of sight and hearing are not properly educated by appropriate impressions, and therefore remain proportionably destitute of true genuine development (in fact, a host of useful intuitions are completely lost by them); these lower estimates are constantly adding to the number of their traces, and thus there is nothing to be astonished at, if such children find no pleasure in the learning and observation to which school compels them, or that a wild and dissolute life possesses far more attractiveness to them. The attempt to restrain low propensities in such souls, by higher considerations afterwards pressed upon them, and to diminish their tendency to become conscious, is rarely successful; such persons belong all their life long to those who have no taste for refined and elevated pleasures.

If, in the cases mentioned, the neglect of the higher powers might very well have been avoided, yet there are other circumstances in which the training received by children must almost inevitably be detrimental to their faculties. Consider, for instance, races that live in inhospitable regions, who are scarcely able to protect themselves against hunger and cold; and on the other side, the higher powers cannot thrive where nature is so prodigal that she holds captive, so to say, the lower senses by continual enjoyments.

Hence, if a large number of traces are accumulated, forms in the lower senses may attain to far greater strength than those of the higher, although the former senses are naturally less tenacious than the latter.

No doubt this is a perversion, wherever it occurs; still it does occur, and thus originates a *perverted* order in the gradation of goods and evils. Then that alone is valued which flatters the lower senses: what elevates the nobler senses passes for worthless. Hence, we may comprehend how the *true* valuation (the *correct* practical standard) remains undeveloped, and how that which we call a *false* estimate or a *perverted practical prudence* (folly) is produced. Life furnishes abundant examples of this.

It hardly needs be observed that false estimates of things are formed as slowly and as gradually as true ones. A *sudden* deterioration is as impossible as a sudden improvement, (as suddenly becoming noble, and good, or virtuous). At any rate, no one passes from ignorance to knowledge suddenly—no one suddenly becomes a savant[a]. That the moral rule may be *partially* right, and in other respects false, and therefore partially incorrect, is obvious, and is amply confirmed by experience.

§ 60. *Feeling of Strength in Desires and Repugnancies.*

Every one gains a more or less comprehensive *view* of the world: it is *theoretical*, in so far as it produces in him notions: it is *practical*, in so far as it causes him pleasurable or unplea-

---

[a] Are there, then, no such things as sudden "conversions?" Has not many a criminal been rendered quite another man in a short time by spiritual advice given in a prison? He has not been rendered *quite another* man, it only appears as if he had: when the minister has wrought such a seeming miracle, goodness must have been long existent in the criminal: it was concealed as it were and smothered by the false, and has now at length been raised strongly into consciousness. Thus it again became active, whilst his bad qualities are driven back into unconsciousness, and so rendered impotent. Where goodness is totally wanting, the most eloquent clergyman can do nothing, as is proved by the case of *hardened* criminals confirmed in wickedness. A Saul can only become a Paul if the latter, in all essentials, lies already dormant in the former.

surable forms. The former do not impel us to act, they are a mere dead inactive picture of the world; the latter move us to act or forbear action; for pleasure or pain produce desires and repugnancies, and hence this is *ipso facto* a *practical* view of the world. There is, therefore, a great difference between a theoretical and a practical view of the world. He alone is properly a wise man whose *practical* view of it is *correct*, and he alone is properly a fool whose *practical* view is perverted, consists in *false estimates*.

In the preceding § we merely shewed that a *false* estimate of things is often developed in the place of a true one, and why it is so; but we said nothing as to the way in which the former is manifested in *action*. So long as the false estimate remains a mere estimate, it is simply manifested *internally* as a feeling, and even when it is expressed in words and propositions, nothing more is revealed than what in common parlance is called *Folly*, i e. a perverted *practical view of the world*.

But such estimates are also reproduced in the shape of *desires* and *repugnancies*, seeing that they are internally converted into them (see § 56 and compare §§ 27, 33, and 34); and they thus lead to *action* in a totally different manner; for when they take these shapes they may increase to any amount of strength. They stand in the same position as the original pleasurable and unpleasurable forms (felt *notions* of pleasure and displeasure, § 27). The more complex their formation, i.e. in proportion as they grow into forms consisting of *more numerous* traces, the greater must be the strength with which they manifest themselves.

All the psychical forms which we denote by the names '*inclination, disinclination, detestation, propension, desire, want, passion, vice*,' furnish examples of this. We frequently find persons in whom they have been developed with such immoderate strength and might that they extinguish all opposite notions, impulses*, and feelings, and thus hurry away a man to do evil, often against his better judgment.

---

* That is to say (opposed) desires and repugnancies. Man has no innate impulses and desires, nothing existing *apart* from and *beside* his active

§ 61. *Immorality* [Unsittlichkeit]: *Corrupt Will.*

The preceding § may and will throw light on the following phenomena.

Here is a man who really believes health to be a greater good than a low and transient enjoyment; for his own experience has often proved to him that health is a more lasting blessing than a fleeting pleasure which shatters it. But when the opportunity for a fresh gratification presents itself, his violent desires are too strong for him to resist.

There is another, who depicts to himself with honest conviction the blessedness of benevolence, for he experienced it in his own person when, in earlier days, he felt inclined to succour the unfortunate. But now he is in a state of lazy self-indulgence, to which he has become accustomed; is he to sacrifice it in order to assist the miserable? It is too hard for him; he cannot do it.

Another acknowledges to the full the utility of good schools, for he owes his best knowledge to one of them. A new one is to be established: ask him to contribute to it, and he will warmly recommend it; but do not expect that he will subscribe money, though he is well to do.

Here, lastly, is a fourth, who so shuns the inconveniences of bad weather that he will not venture out of his room, and would rather imperil his health than risk a walk, while another pays attention to it in spite of wind and rain.

In all these cases, each man estimates objects correctly enough, and yet is not sufficiently influenced by his belief. How is that to be accounted for?

Psychical forms of *too great strength*, and *opposed* to what they believe to be advantageous, had been produced in them, and what is more, they have been produced in the shape of *desires* and *repugnancies*. In the first instance, such a form was the desire for low sensual indulgences; in the second, the love of ease and

---

original powers and developed forms (whether corporeal or mental). Compare the note on p. 70.

laziness; in the third, love of money; in the fourth, dislike to inclement weather. Therefore, in all of them a false and exaggerated *impulse* tyrannized over their correct estimate of things.

This kind of perverted growth, which frequently mars a man's better self, is called in common life by the name of *immorality* [Unsittlichkeit] or *corrupt will*.

Immorality in a narrower and stricter sense[p], therefore, is *the immoderate strength of the* desires *and* repugnancies *overriding the true value of objects.*

If we sum up what has been said in this and the preceding §, we arrive at the following results:

Deviations from the *true* estimate of things, as described in § 58, may be engendered in two ways:

1°. Particular *feelings of pleasure* or *dislike* may gain exaggerated strength by a too abundant accumulation of traces: this we call a *false estimate of value, Folly*, or *a perverted practical view of the world.*

2°. Particular *desires* and *repugnancies* may acquire immoderate strength when and because the pleasurable or unpleasurable forms are too frequently reproduced in these shapes: this produces 'immorality,' properly so called, or '*the corrupt will*[q].'

A third deviation *essentially distinct* from the other two is produced, in many men, by the fact that their practical education has not been carried far enough to enable them to form any estimate of what is really of *higher* value. As is well known, a good many value the merely speculative, e.g. history, mathematics, astronomy, &c., simply because their training was stopped before it ought to have been, generally through no fault of theirs; and in like manner, patriotism, the public good, national education, general enlightenment, &c., are accounted to be no goods by some, merely because they have never had an oppor-

---

[p] Taken in a wider sense, immorality includes not only false estimates, but also false impulses and efforts.

[q] On "*Maliciousness*" [Bösheit], which forms a distinct kind of corrupt will, see *Beneke's* "Lehrbuch der Psychologie," § 274, sqq.

tunity of becoming practically acquainted with them. This we call *defective moral development*, or *moral crudity*. In order to remove it, nothing more is required than increased education; whereas, totally different means are necessary in order to correct false estimates of things and a corrupt will; for these false growths have first to be removed before anything better can take their place and assert itself. See the end of the following §.

§ 62. *Feeling of Duty: Conscience.*

This *shalt* thou do, that thou *shalt* not do! so speaks a voice which I in common with other men often hear within. Thou hast done *rightly*, thou hast done *wrongly!* This also I hear not less frequently in my soul.—What is this voice, and how is it produced? Is it something accidental and capricious, or is it necessary, inevitable, constant?

When the man mentioned in the first example of the preceding § felt that health was something of more value than a fleeting enjoyment prejudicial to it, there were *two* psychical forms present to his consciousness: one was an *estimate* coinciding with the moral rule, and the other a *desire* at variance with it. The first form sprang from the very depths of human nature, from something towards which that nature inevitably strives and tends, because it is naturally disposed to uninterrupted and harmonious development: the second form did not correspond to that disposition, it was something alien to it, a mere contingent addition to that correct and normal development, for *it need not and ought not to have been there*. Can we wonder, then, that the former proclaimed itself as an *ought*, (as something which *ought* to be,) when contrasted with the preternatural desire? Thus, then, arose that feeling which we call *a feeling of Duty*.

Now, let us suppose that the *desire* conquered because it was stronger than the correct estimate; it would then be impossible for the man not to be conscious that he had acted perversely. For as soon as the tumult of enjoyment was over, the natural and normal estimate of the value of health returned into consciousness and measured itself with (compared itself with) the detrimental pleasure which he had indulged in. He felt the undutifulness of his conduct; and that feeling we call *conscience*, which must in this case be a *remorseful* ("*evil*") conscience, because it disapproved of the deed committed.

Now let us suppose, on the contrary, that the *correct estimate* won the day, because it was at the moment stronger (as, at first, it always is,) than the desire rendered violent by constant repetition; this must engender a cheerful and approving feeling. He was conscious of the conformity of his act with the moral rule (the subjugation of the desires), and thus he had a *peaceable*, *good* conscience.

Hence it is clear that *Duty and Conscience are at bottom the same*. Both of them are *a feeling*, a comparison drawn between our *estimates and impulses*, which partly accompanies, partly precedes, and partly follows our actions. As a feeling preceding, it either *encourages* or *warns*, according as we feel an impulse to be conformable to, or discordant with the moral rule. It is then called especially *a feeling of duty*. As subsequent, it either *disapproves* or *approves* of an act performed, according as it contradicted or harmonized with the rule. It is then especially called *Conscience*; in the former case a bad, avenging, gnawing, &c., (in particular called *Remorse*); in the latter a good, peaceable, joyful, &c., conscience.

As regards the *names* given to this feeling, it is further to be noticed, that it is, in particular, called "conscience" when it vindicates the moral rule as against *our own* actions; whereas it is usually spoken of as 'a feeling of duty' (the voice of duty) where the moral rule proclaims what all ought to do under like circumstances, so that it points out what duty is *in general* under certain combinations of circumstances. But as most men act under circumstances and in relations different from my own, or those of any other individual, it is clear that the 'ought' which we call duty, has a far wider range than the 'ought' which reveals itself as conscience [r].

[r] Be it remarked that while it is easy in theory, it is yet often difficult in practice, to decide whether a psychical form deviating from the true

Now it may be asked, to what extent does conscience (the feeling of duty) prevail among men?

We see savages slaughter their enemies, and tear them to pieces, and sleep as peacefully as Christians who have returned good for evil.—In the middle ages torture and horrible mutilations, &c., &c., were employed as means of getting at the truth, and for punishment, and conscience raised no objection to it. Rude uncultivated men ill-treat brutes, cheat or slander their neighbour, &c., &c., without any twinges of conscience. Represent to them the injustice of their conduct, they will only wonder that you should be moved by such 'trifles.' "Where's the harm of it?"

How are such facts to be accounted for? Is conscience *sleeping* here? No! *In such cases it is not present at all, it has not yet been engendered.*

Where conscience is to reveal itself, there, as was previously shewn, the *true* estimate of things must come into consciousness along with the false estimate or the exaggerated impulse. Now savages have no such estimate of *men*, who, though enemies, still remain men, hence it does not restrain them from barbarity: the

---

estimate of things in an over-strong *feeling* of pleasure or dislike, or an over-strong *desire* or *repugnance*; for, as has been shewn several times, both are in general mixed up together, since every desire is in fact a *pleasurable* notion which has lost some of its stimulants, and in which stimulant and power mutually measure each other, not to mention that the whole notion will also measure itself by other co-existent forms. In the case of repugnancies, the opposing form is likewise one highly excited, and possessing a pleasurable tone or tension brought into contrast with one of an *opposite* kind; and as a pleasurable notion can hardly equal the original *sensation* of pleasure, because by the process of diffusion some of its stimulant is lost (yet see § 27 at the end), it follows that a weak kind of *effort* will almost always be implied in it. The distinction between the two is this: an over-strong *feeling of pleasure* will be marked by a simple internal *liking* for the enjoyment, an over-strong *desire* by a weakish, self-forgetting, *abandonment* to it: and this with regard to both where the enjoyment consists at the moment in nothing more than the *internal reproduction* of a pleasure previously enjoyed. Compare *Beneke's* "Psychol. Skizzen," Part I., p. 116 sqq., and p. 121.

uncultivated man has none of *brutes*, of the *property* of others, &c., &c., hence it does not prevent him from acting cruelly and deceitfully, &c., &c.

Thus, then, it is clear that conscience in men extends only so far as *the true estimate of things has arisen or been engendered in them.* If that estimate is wanting, conscience cannot shew itself as advising, disapproving, in short, as judging right or wrong, and to that extent men are wanting in the feeling of duty, in *conscience.* Consequently it is an error to talk of an *innate* conscience, if by that is meant a ready-formed one, as it is equally erroneous to ascribe to a developed man only *one* conscience. On the contrary, they are as numerous as are his particular feelings of the agreement or disagreement of his several estimates and acts with the true moral rule. Duty and Conscience are in fact essentially one, and our feeling of duty in individual cases is itself always individual. The moral rule consists of purely individual forms, *each of which is itself a rule:* it is only when considered *abstractedly* that the moral rule can be denominated one.

The '*erring*' conscience may be explained from the fact that in many cases *false* rules and standards take the place of true ones, and the so-called "*unconscientiousness,*" consequently, when fairly viewed, is, for the most part, not an absence or utter want of conscience, but only a perversion of it, and in such cases, if conscience is, as people say, to be awakened, i.e. if *the true conscience is to be engendered,* the first thing to be done is to set up the *correct* rule or law. This is a difficult task, because the false rule already in existence is not unfrequently so strong, that it is impossible quite to annihilate it;—under the most favourable circumstances the best that can be hoped for is to permanently banish it from consciousness. A '*sleeping*' conscience, properly so called, is only to be found in cases of great absence and confusion of mind, when, though it exists, it is not able to act.

§ 63. *Moral Freedom, or Morally Free Will.*

Judas Iscariot had certainly a feeling for the goodness of his Lord, who had shewed him nothing but kindness, and yet

Judas betrayed Him for thirty pieces of silver. Catherine dei Medici well knew what general love of one's neighbour meant, and yet she could not repress her hatred of Protestants. She contrived the massacre of St. Bartholomew.

Which was more strongly developed in Judas, love of money or love for his Master? Which was more powerful in that queen, hatred of the Protestants or love of her neighbour?

Experience has answered these questions for us. Both were under the yoke of sin, i.e. in both of them the *false* estimate and impulse prevailed over the *true* rule, *false* pleasure over *true* pleasure [*].

Now let us think of examples of an opposite kind: of Joseph in Egypt, when he rejected the temptress; of David in the cave, when he spared his enemy Saul; of Luther at Worms, when he declared before king and emperor, "I neither can nor will retract."

In these latter cases, the *true* estimate declared itself with *greater* force than the estimates and desires *opposed to it; the moral outweighed the immoral;* in fact, the latter was wholly absent. But this preponderance was produced, in the one case as in the other, only gradually, for an external object can only leave *one* trace behind it at a time, and consequently it exercises no sudden converting compulsion upon us. When it seems to do so, the simple external impression merely *helps to reproduce* that which has been already gradually formed within us, and which corresponds with that impression. Consequently, all the power which impels to, or restrains from action, lies, at the moment of acting, simply and solely in *the interior of a man;* in the sum of his psychical forms, which are either conformable to, or discrepant with, duty. Now as these, if we pay no attention to the influences of external things on us, are consoli-

---

[*] It is well known that the term 'pleasure' is not used always to denote the lower and reprehensible pleasure, but rather for our higher and nobler emotions [Steigerungen]. Thus, the Bible says, "The works of the Lord are great, sought out of them that have pleasure therein." [Ps. cxi. 2. Substituted for the original German, "habe deine Lust am Herrn," "habe Lust am Worte Gottes."]

dated quite quietly, badness may have taken root before we have noticed it, and in this manner most people are deceived who fall into moral corruption. They, in such cases, are inwardly disposed to yield to the impressions which they receive, they reproduce them frequently, and so strengthen them in the *accrescive* space which they occupy. (See the note on p. 142). Therefore be watchful as to the external influences under which you live. This is a holy precept; and the educator's first duty runs thus: Be watchful over the circumstances which surround your pupil, and the more so the younger the child is.

We are, therefore, absolutely free from any *compulsion* exercised by the external world over us. At the moment of action we are determined simply and solely by our *internal* constitution; the external world merely excites it, and, at most, strengthens it by one trace. In this consists the *practical Freedom*, the *practical Free Will* of man. The wicked man possesses it just as well as the good. Both are able to bid defiance to the outer world so completely, that present death itself does not deter them from executing their will: they would sooner die than yield; and hence thousands have, are now, confirmed the old truth, that "*he who can die cannot be compelled.*" "No one is obliged to be obliged[1]," as Lessing says in his *Nathan*. Now, may we call this practical freedom "*moral* freedom?" Unquestionably we may, if we understand the word "moral" in a *wide* sense, but not otherwise[2]. For only the good man possesses *true* or *genuine* freedom: in his soul alone a true estimate of things (at least) reigns, if it does not always govern; it is stronger than other estimates and impulses diverging from the true view which may co-exist with it, and thus it prevents them from prevailing. But the internal struggle which often

---

[1] [Niemand muss müssen.]

[2] In the wide sense of the term, everything that a man does externally or internally, be it good or bad, is called moral [sittlich]. Consider such phrases as—his moral condition is equivocal, is not to be applauded; Ferdinand is not worth much, from a moral point of view. The context immediately determines whether it is used in the wider or narrower signification: 'Moral freedom' is generally understood in the *wide* sense.

takes place proves that the freedom has not as yet become a perfectly moral freedom. This can only exist when all such contests are over, because right has at length annihilated all opposing wrong, and this *perfect, all-sided* moral freedom we find in no one except in our master *Christ*. He was free, not merely from all compulsion of the external world, but also from the influence of anything immoral within.

Man can *choose* between evil and good, and he will always be choosing between them, so long as he bears both about within him. This constitutes his arbitrariness, i.e. his choosing will. Yet it is not the weakest, but the strongest thing within him that will turn the scale. If his *false* estimates and impulses are the strongest, he will act *immorally;* if, however, the universally valid, the *true* estimate of value, has the upper hand within, then he will act *morally*, i.e. in a morally *good* manner. The weaker forms will determine his action only when the stronger are partially or totally precluded from acting by the *immoderate excitation* of the weaker; a thing which occurs exceptionally in conditions of bewildering anguish, violent anger, &c., &c., especially in the imperfectly educated. In all other cases the stronger forms prevail over the rest.

Does a man, then, choose *freely?* Yes; that is to say, when he chooses he is free from external compulsion, but he is not free from, or independent of, his internal development. To this he remains bound, *because he never can escape from himself*, and hence he possesses no *absolute*, no *unconditional* freedom; i.e. he cannot resolve either for good or evil *without some* determining reasons, he cannot educe an act of will out of vacancy—out of nothing. The reason why this seems to be possible, in the case of many men, is, that their estimates and impulses, both for good and evil, are tolerably equal, or in equilibrium, so that sometimes the good, at others the bad, may be efficiently excited according to circumstances. Compare the preceding §, at the end.

Therefore, a man who is *really* morally free *cannot* do evil, just as, on the other hand, one in whom *false* estimates and impulses predominate, is ruled by them (see Matt. vii. 16—18); and hence the Scriptures declare him not to be free, and call him '*a servant of sin*,' notwithstanding his freedom from external compulsion. But they rightly call the truly free man '*a servant of righteousness*' (uprightness). See the noble passage in Rom. vi. 16—22.

All freedom, therefore, is, when fairly looked at, *the power of self-determination* [Selbstbestimmbarkeit]. Now, as man at first, and directly after birth, cannot determine himself, because that act presupposes psychical forms capable of becoming conscious, it follows that, at first, he is not free, and that the external world determines his acts absolutely. But he has an innate *capacity* of becoming self-conscious, and therefore of determining himself, i.e. of Freedom; and if his forces, one and all, were developed *naturally*, without let or hindrance, he would become free to do good, for originally no psychical power impels to evil, just as originally no corporeal power tends to disease. The correct expression for the condition which we call by the *negative*, and hence vague word, "Freedom" (= independency), is, therefore, *the power of self-determination*. It is, from first to last, a something which is always *growing*, always gradually *developing*.

Compare with this section two capital treatises: 1°. "*Ueber die sittliche Freiheit, mit besonderer Berücksichtigung der Systeme von Spinoza, Leibnitz und Kant. Gekrönte Preisschrift. Nebst einer Abhandlung über Eudämonismus*," by *Dr. Friedrich Ditter*, Leipsic, published by Klinkardt, 1860: 2°. "*Die Willensfreiheit, Zurechnung und Strafe in ihren Grundlehren*" (those of empirical psychology), by *Otto Börner*, advocate, Freiberg, published by Craz and Gerlach, 1857.

Besides this, further details on the subject, especially on the question of responsibility, will be found in the essay by Dressler, mentioned above, in p. 111.

What has been said in §§ 56—63, then, perfectly solves the apparent riddles and contradictions which occur in the region of human disposition and action: but we cannot conclude this § without adding a very important remark.

It is commonly thought that men's actions depend solely on notions; because the words, by which we encourage them to act, directly denote concepts, and our words are not unfrequently obeyed (though it must be admitted that very often they are not). Hence it is believed, that if we furnish any one with right notions we have given him sufficient motives for right action, and, accordingly, young people are abundantly thus provided, in particular by religious instruction.

But men's dispositions and acts spring from estimates of things, from *feelings of value*, and these can only be engendered by the objects themselves. Instruction may reproduce, and thus strengthen them; it may concentrate them, and bring them to a right focus; but it cannot directly furnish them. All that it can give are *notions* (in particular concepts), and *external aptitudes*; nor is it to be denied that concepts are very valuable, they are, indeed, indispensable for the light which they shed on the soul. Still thousands have this light, and yet how badly do they act! Hence *education* must step in here; it must take care that young people are placed in relations of life where they will set a proper *estimate* on such objects, and learn *to feel* their true value, which implies, that they are brought into contact with the things themselves; it implies *immediate experience*, and this can only be obtained when we are directly *occupied* with the objects (persons and things) themselves, and *act* in relation to them. In particular, the good example of others is of the gravest importance, because then the right course lies before our eyes, the proper estimation of things is *intuitively* exhibited to us. It is only in this manner that youth can be put into a position in which they can obtain correct notions and correct *impulses*; it is thus only that they can learn to be morally good. So far as a psychical form is a mere notion, effort is quenched in it, and how should any impulse spring from that?

No wonder then that thousands are good who have never had the advantages of education, as on the other hand thousands are bad in spite of the best instruction. Right estimates are the good ground in which alone the seeds of instruction take root and bring forth fruit a hundredfold. It was thus that even *Jesus* judged in the well-known and beautiful parable of four kinds of soil, which refers not to new-born children, but to adults to whom He applied it. Three parts of the seed, He complains, fall on thankless land (amidst 'the cares of this world and the deceitfulness of riches'), i.e. the instruction lights on false estimates of things, and hence it necessarily produces no moral improvement. Hence a Judas remained, in spite of the best instruction which he received immediately from Jesus Himself, loveless and a traitor: hence thousands heard the Master 'who preached with authority,' and their tempers were so little improved by it, that at last they cried out 'Crucify Him,' not to mention the malicious Scribes and Pharisees who might, one would have thought, have understood Him at first.

Moreover, let not instruction in *Morals* be confounded with instruction in *Religion*. Both are generally lumped together in the expression '*Religious Instruction*;' yet there is an important difference between them. The religious, properly so called, relates to objects which we do not *know*, but can only *believe* (embrace by faith), because they are not objects of experience, but lie beyond all that is earthly: it refers to God and the life of the soul after death: the moral, on the contrary, has to do originally with what is purely perceptible, it is confined to what falls within the circle of human experience: for every one experiences in life what is uprightness, modesty, falsehood, pride, moderation, debauchery, peaceableness, hatred, envy, &c.,—in general, what is right and wrong: he gains *a knowledge* of them. Now, as we are able still to love and reverence our relatives though dead, to listen to their behests, to be grateful to them: as such moral feelings and impulses may be transferred to those who lived long before our time (to the benefactors of mankind), so the same can and ought to be done in reference to God, and thus religious belief assumes a *moral* character, a character possessed in a marked degree by Christianity (the worship of the heathen gods was and is very often immoral). But, in spite of the close connection between religion and morals, the two remain totally distinct; and as there are men who possess much moral goodness and little religious belief, so there are others who join much religious belief to great immorality. So far as religion and morals consist of notions, and are therefore theoretical, they may be soon produced by instruction; but so far as they are rooted in feelings and impulses (and it is this practical side of them which constitutes their true essence), instruction can, for the most part, be merely of negative assistance, by pointing out and warning us against the errors and defects which may arise, by exciting the good opposed to them, and depriving the evil, so far as possible, of consciousness, and thus of effective existence.

That religion, when developed purely out of human nature without instruction from without, springs out of something totally different from morality, and what that source is, is explained *inter alia* in *Beneke's "Lehrbuch der Psychologie als Naturwissenschaft,"* 3rd edit., § 223, sqq.

The same subject is treated of in the following valuable treatise, "*Ueber Religion und religiöse Menschenbildung,*" by *Friedrich Dittes*. Plauen, 1855. It illustrates religion in all its aspects.

§ 64. *It frequently happens that several Feelings, some Harmonious, some Inconsistent with each other, are simultaneously Conscious within us.*

After spending a good many days in my room engaged in dull, uninteresting affairs, I go with some friends on a bright spring morning into the fresh and fragrant wood; larks are singing in the bright air, grasshoppers are chirupping in the dew-spangled grass, and we ourselves are singing and joking, &c. These are pleasurable impressions, which awaken in me large numbers of pleasurable traces. They are compared with my previous dry disposition of soul, and as they differ from them widely, they turn into feelings of greater freshness (§ 48). The total feeling which they produce in me is naturally one of great joyousness, for each single process is a pleasurable feeling, and all of them being of a like character, unite and form an aggregate disposition or emotion. How correct this explanation is, I know full well from having experienced it at other times, and every one may test it for himself. For when I visited the wood by myself, in unsettled weather, without merriment or song, it by no means produced in me the same pleasurable feelings: in fact, what I felt just now was so different from the joy of yesterday, that the latter seemed to me to be almost a dream.

'Why are you so sorrowful to-day?' 'I have got the headache.'—'You often have it, but I have never before seen you so downcast.'—'I was robbed last night.'—'I am very sorry to hear it.'—'And besides that, my neighbour wants me to repay him in a week the four hundred dollars which I owe him.' 'O! triple misfortune!'

We observe that *feelings that harmonize together, that are of the same kind*, **strengthen** *each other when they are conscious together*, for the homogeneous unites into one whole.

On another occasion, I was in a joyous company. All that heart could desire I found there: food and drink, wit and song. And yet I could not manage to be as cheerful as the rest, for I had the toothache, and beside that, I could not banish from my mind sundry vexations which I had just encountered. Thus there were certain painful feelings excited within, side by side with the pleasurable feelings aroused by the company.

Had I been free from toothache, &c., the agreeable society would doubtless have produced in me as great an emotion of pleasure (generally joyous tone) as it did in my companions: but if I had been left alone at home with my own thoughts and emotions, I should have felt the toothache and my vexations more keenly than I did. Hence it follows that,

Dissimilar, mutually opposed feelings, when simultaneously conscious in the soul, limit *or* diminish *each other's strength.*

In the following §§ we shall consider at greater length some feelings compounded in both these ways.

§ 65. *Feelings of Gratitude, of Favour conferred*[1], *and of Mortification.*

A poor man receives a present: it comes from his true benefactor, whom he has long known and valued as a worthy, intelligent, and universally respected man. His eye glistens: he would be ready to go through fire and water to serve the revered donor; in short, he is animated by the feeling of *Gratitude.*

Obviously, here there are several harmonious and homogeneous feelings conscious together. To the feeling of the benefit (the present) conferred are added the feelings already formed in the recipient's soul as to the worthiness, the intelligence, and the general reputation of his benefactor. This explains the *strength* of the aggregate emotion which now surges within, makes his eyes glisten, and disposes him to render any service in return.

Let us suppose, on the other hand, that somebody receives a benefit from a man whom he does not know, and whom he cannot suppose to bear him any particular good-will: let us suppose it a question of a few dollars which the unknown person lost in a bet, and which, because unclaimed by the winner, he resolves to give to the first deserving poor man that he meets. Here also the present would no doubt be attended by a pleasurable feeling, but it would be far from being so strong and high as in the preceding example: for it is a mere isolated emotion, and the homogeneous feelings present in the former case are wanting in this. Gratitude, therefore, in this case, remains a simple and hence weak psychical form.

This feeling may under certain circumstances lose so much of the pleasure attached to it, that the favour may scarcely be felt

---

[1] [*Gefühl der Gnade,* i.e. sense of having been graciously treated by a superior, for which, so far as I know, there is no English term.]

as a matter of congratulation. This would be the case, if opposite feelings were excited and brought into play.

Suppose, for example, somebody requires *speedy* assistance. Whoever serves him *at once* may be sure of his gratitude. But if the help only comes when by his own exertions he has pretty well extricated himself from his difficulties, this delay will chill his feelings as much as the gift warms them. If, in addition to this, he is driven to suppose that the gift was dictated by mere love of ostentation, the painful feeling thence produced will exercise such a restrictive influence on the pleasure caused by the gift, that it would be impossible to talk of an honest feeling of gratitude any longer. "He gives twice who gives quickly."

Hence, we may understand why benefits *openly* conferred always involve something humiliating to the receiver. They cause a feeling of depression, and that so outweighs the pleasure of the benefit as to rob it of all its delight. A sensitive man therefore declines such public gifts, unless extreme need forces him to accept them. He confers the greatest benefit who confers it with most delicacy.

The feeling of favours graciously conferred by a superior (and received) is allied to that of gratitude.

It is always a composite feeling. Let us suppose ourselves as contrasted with God: this feeling involves, on the one side, the consciousness of His sublimity (greatness) and goodness expressed in numerous benefits: on the other side, the consciousness of our pettiness and demerit. Now, if the greatness and goodness of God *predominates* in our thoughts, we shall feel ourselves powerfully raised: if, on the other hand, our own weakness is more emphatically presented, the vast distance between us and God, which then becomes clear to us, causes us to feel cast down and humiliated. Now, if we were dealing with men, we should find ourselves elevated, if the *beneficence* of the gracious donor were consciously and vividly contrasted with our humble position: but we should be annoyed if he treated us so as to remind us too forcibly of our inferiority, for we should then say (feel) that after all we are men as well as he, and not without value, and that no one has the right to place us lower than our own qualities put us[7]. Suffice it to say that, as in every feeling, so also in the complex feelings in question, the point prominent in consciousness is the *object felt*, the point thrown into the background is the *foundation* of the feeling, and thus at one time the pleasurable emotion of elevation, at another the painful one of depression, may predominate. Both emotions, however, must, if conscious together, restrict each other more or less.

The feeling of *Mortification* is generally a simple one, consisting, on the one hand, in the consciousness of blame incurred, of rebuff, &c.; and, on the other, in the consciousness of our innocence. In many cases, however, it is a complex feeling, implying, on the one hand, that we have been blamed and rebuked not altogether without deserving it; but, on the other, in the conviction that the *degree* and *manner* of the correction passed the proper bounds. Suppose, for instance, a man is not really a lazy fellow, but yet has not sent in his work when it was perfectly possible for him to have done so. He is then violently scolded in the presence of other people, and accused of being an idler. In this case, different unpleasurable feelings jar together (consciousness of exaggerated blame, the malicious joy of enemies now present, fear of the contempt of friends, &c.), and are compared with one's better feelings of oneself, feelings, however, not quite untroubled by a sense of half-guiltiness. The question is, to what consciousness turns with greatest strength, so that the consequence will be either a kind of anger with ourselves, or indignation will be excited, and both are often found together in the feeling of mortification.

66. *Feelings of Honour and Glory.*

A schoolboy has made arithmetic his favourite study, and has attained to great proficiency in it. The day of public examination arrives, and as usual he answers the questions proposed to

---

[7] How far this is modified when the person to whom the favour is shewn is a criminal, every one can easily determine for himself.

him with great facility. It was plain that such dexterity caused pleasure to the numerous audience, but the boy's arithmetical powers gave him then a feeling of pleasure stronger than he had ever before experienced.

Very naturally! For before that the pleasure of cyphering stood *quite alone* in his soul, he was at best merely conscious of the gratification felt and expressed by his teacher. To-day he sees this pleasure diffused over many persons, and in thinking of them he thinks of their pleasures as well, and consequently he gains more pleasure in proportion as the persons delighted by his calculating successes are more numerous. This gave him what we call the feeling of *Honour*.

The greater the number of men by whom we think and feel our good qualities to be recognised in this manner, the stronger must the aggregate emotion naturally be which grows up in us in consequence, and thus is produced that higher degree of honour which is called *Glory*. Glory is felt by the brave warrior whose exploits are in all mouths, the noble defender of the people whom a whole nation reverences, the great savant by whose genius and writings everybody is fascinated, &c.

The feelings of *Honour* and *Glory*, therefore, are those *aggregates of feeling in which we represent to ourselves our own perfections as simultaneously thought of, and felt by, a large number of other persons.*

If so, what must the feeling of *Shame* be?

§ 67. *Feelings of Liking and Dislike.*

We meet with men who agree with us in valuing the same objects as we do, so that they harmonize with us in their feelings, impulses, views, habitudes, &c.

Since like always attracts like, the views, feelings, impulses, &c., of others, which we have noticed in them and copied in ourselves, must strive to unite with ours, *they will be attracted to one another because they harmonize.* This is clearly manifested in the wish to be externally connected with such persons, to shake hands, embrace them, kiss them [1], &c.

Thus the feeling of *Affection* arises. It is rendered more vivid in consciousness, when side by side with it persons are thought of who are indifferent to us, or whom we positively dislike. As to its composition, it is an assemblage of individual pleasurable feelings which *attract each other*; it is a *harmony* of such feelings; for the notions which we have of ourselves and of others, and which are constantly combining in different groups, consisting as they do of parts so unlike, cannot, properly speaking, *fuse together*. The external impulse just noticed, is also connected with this feeling. It is, therefore, a very complex emotion, and is sometimes called *Friendship*, sometimes *Love* [2].

We find affection amongst the professors of a religion, the members of a state, the scholars of a school, inhabitants of a village, &c. How far does it extend, and why?

It is obvious from what we have said, when and why *dislike*, *hatred*, *enmity*, must be engendered instead of affection.

"Love God above all things, and thy neighbour as thyself," so runs the supreme law of Christian morals. It therefore establishes degrees of *Love*, just as the supreme law of psychological (natural) morals, stated at p. 152, established a (more minute) gradation in our *estimates* of objects. 'Loving' and 'valuing,' however, are expressions meaning precisely the same thing, and we love not persons only, but also things. "Love God above all things," when translated into the language of psychology, means, let Him be your highest good, the object most valued and esteemed: "love thy neighbour as thyself," means, let him be as valuable to you, as you are to yourself. Now, as it is impossible to love either God or man truly, if we do not truly value the *things* which refer to both, it is clear that, in this

[1] This external tendency towards union with another is but an expression of what passes in the soul. For (paradoxical as it may sound to a tyro in psychology) if we were able to see immediately in the souls of friends and lovers the aggregates on which their friendship and love depends, we should find that they, too, were equally *anxious to meet*, *equally appetent of each other*; only that all this implies no local movement, for in the soul there is no such thing as space. See *Beneke's* treatise "Die neue Psychologie," p. 161 sqq.

[2] On the difference between the two, see the masterly discussion in *Beneke's* work just quoted, p. 145 sqq.

Christian command, the correct estimation of things is tacitly required, and hence the farther conclusion, that the supreme law of morals dictated by psychology coincides exactly with that prescribed by Christianity.

§ 68. *Feelings of Hope and Fear.*

Winter was at hand. Potatoes had turned out bad: the harvest had been only middling: every week provisions were dearer: still, all were well at home, and there was yet a small nest-egg saved during the summer: besides, work was plentiful, wages good, and if the worst came to the worst, one of the cattle might without damage be sold for the household. Such were the feelings with which this family faced winter.

Matters were different in the neighbour's house. They had no savings, no beast to sell, and their labour was not so well remunerated. Fortunately all were as yet healthy, but health is a precarious blessing. How, with what feelings, did these people face winter?

This much is clear: *in the souls of both families pleasurable and painful emotions were intermixed.*

In the former case, they were able to say with tolerable certainty that they had the means of staving off the threatened want, and so their unpleasant feelings were, on the whole, overcome by agreeable ones. In the latter, on the other hand, painful feelings predominated, for their means were less, and want was far from being improbable. In the one case, then, there was considerable *security* against the future, in the other, great *uncertainty*. No wonder that their mixed emotions gave, in the former case, a feeling of *Hope;* in the latter, a feeling of *Fear*. These are the names given to the resulting feelings.

One can see that these feelings are conterminous, for they depend on a *plus* or *minus* of the same factors, and may, therefore, easily pass into one another. If, in hope, the means of warding off an evil grow less, it is transformed into fear; fear, however, changes into hope if the means of defence increase. Consequently these feelings are frequently interchanged.

If, on the contrary, in the first instance, the dearness of

provisions and the winter vanished, the remaining relations must produce an absolutely pure feeling of *Joy:* and if, in the second instance, sickness were added to the want which was already great enough, a feeling of total *Apathy*, or indeed of *Despair*, would be engendered. Accordingly, Hope ascends into Joy, and Fear descends to Apathy and Despair.

§ 69. *On the Faculty of Feeling*[b].

It may be enough to say that the same sort of explanation as that already given may be applied to all our other feelings. We now ask, *What is the Faculty of Feeling in the human soul?*

We gave the name of *Understanding* to the totality of concepts existent in the soul: *Judgment* to the totality of judgments: *Inferential Power* to the totality of conclusions: *Will* to the totality of all particular ready-formed acts of willing: consequently the Faculty of Feeling is nothing more than *the totality of all the feelings that arise in the soul, and are permanently existent in it, and ready to be exerted.*

Since, however, fresh feelings may arise beside those which have been already formed, seeing that whenever psychical forms are present together in consciousness, their difference or interval is also *present to consciousness along with them* (=*is felt*), two kinds of faculties of feeling must be distinguished, the *developed*, and the *undeveloped*. What is meant is this. Feelings already existent and produced by the past connexion of their factors (§§ 47 and 57),—are simply *reproduced;* having been once made they do not require to be made over again: on the other hand, new ones arise only because their factors are present, but have not yet been connected. In the former case, therefore, feeling rests on a firmer basis than it does in the latter. A similar distinction holds also in reference to Understanding, Judgment, Inference, and Will. (See §§ 21 and 42.)

---

[b] [*Gefühlsvermögen*].

The soul's power of feeling consequently extends, *generally*, as far as there is a possibility for different psychical forms to be present in consciousness together, whether those forms have been already fashioned into *ready-made* feelings, or whether they manifest themselves, *for the first time*, as contrasted with each other.

If, however, these factors are not yet existent, or if, though existent, they cannot be present to consciousness together, it follows, necessarily, that Feeling is, to that extent, an impossibility.

This is obtrusively manifest in the case of one who is, as it is said, destitute of feeling, *unfeeling*. But can there really be a man who has no feeling? It would bo a serious mistake to believe so; for very feeling people are unquestionably unfeeling in some relations. Take, for instance, a child who is delighted with the flowers scattered on its mother's coffin. Does that prove want of feeling? Obviously not; for whoever can experience joy cannot be totally devoid of feeling. Conjure into the child's soul the same estimate of the deceased that has been formed in the heart of the elder sister or the father, and you will find it bend over that coffin with grief as genuine as theirs. Consequently, an unfeeling man is merely one who has not a sufficient number of ready-formed feelings, or one destitute of those factors which are required to produce fresh ones. A good many persons, too, are accounted unfeeling, because they are not so demonstrative as others are. The female sex, so ready to weep and laugh, appears to be more feeling than the male; but, as a rule, their advantage over men is, that their psychical forms, possessing less firmness and strength, are more easily excited, whereas, in general, men's feelings are stronger and deeper, and, consequently, they are of a higher kind, than those of women *.

* In proportion as a man can, and actually does, realize to himself *another's* feelings and wants, we ascribe to him a *Heart*; and a good heart when these sympathetic feelings are connected with desires and acts tending to that other's benefit. The mode in which such feelings are realized is this: along with the notions which we have formed of other persons, we

Does, then, the soul possess any *special* and innate faculty of feeling *distinct* from the rest of its powers? Positively not. On the contrary, every developed power, as it is a power of forming notions and desires, so is it a power of feeling, and thus we find the question answered which was proposed at the end of § 43: feelings are produced by the same powers which, at first, appeared in the shape of *original powers*, whence follows the irrefragable and most important proposition, that *the* developed *human soul is a product of mere original powers, and of that which has affected them and been retained by them*—a proposition which, in the sequel, will be confirmed by additional facts.

The remark made in § 3 will now become intelligible: we there said that the child, apart from its original acts of sight, hearing, &c., would require for its subsequent activities "*special powers, which it would be obliged gradually to acquire.*" Have we not proved that every psychical form which remains permanent in the shape of a notion, &c., desire, repugnance, inclination, &c., is a *kind of faculty* [Vermögengebilde] (for the most part of a very complicated description)? and as all forms whatever are generated out of our original powers, is it possible that the relatively *small number* of those original powers existent at birth should suffice for these purposes? Whence, then, do we get the *fresh* original powers which must be in constant course of formation? The answer to this question will be found in §§ 82 and 83.

Only let it never be forgotten, that all our notions, desires, feelings, volitions, &c., are *forces*, and *individual* forces, however complex they may be.

Now, as all our original powers are what we, in common life, call *faculties of sense*, all the developments of the soul spring from our *senses*. But those powers are something totally different from our sense *organs*, which consist of *bodily* powers, and are therefore of a *material* nature (compare §§ 2, 5, 10, 81). The former are *purely spiritual* powers, in an elementary

---

reproduce our *own* feelings, and co-ordinate them with such notions. The meaning of the term *Temper* [Gemüth], which is often used as synonymous with *Heart* (often as identical with the soul in general), will be explained presently. Man, therefore, does not possess a "heart" as something mentally distinct, as a kind of special *innate* force in the soul; a good "heart" is the sum total of sympathizing feelings. It stands on the same footing as the expression "*mind*," which is used either as completely synonymous with "*soul*," or means the totality of intellectual forms, especially of the *productive* (compare § 10). On this latter point, see *Beneke's* "Lehrbuch der Psychologie," 3rd edit., § 160, and for the expression "*Heart*," § 292. On "*Character*," compare the same work, §§ 153, 192, 232, and others.

shape, and they cannot, therefore, in their development ever lead to *materialism*, but to a constantly higher *spiritualism*.

Now, as by "*Sensationalism*" (from the Latin word *sensus* = sense) is meant a psychological system, which, like that of *Beneke*, deduces and explains all psychical phenomena from the activities of the senses, people, from not distinguishing between bodily and spiritual powers of sense, have charged *Beneke's* theory with materialism; for sensationalism and materialism are commonly held to be identical. This is a vast mistake. On the question see *Dressler's* work, "*Ist Beneke Materialist? Ein Beitrag zur Orientirung über Beneke's System der Psychologie, mit Rücksicht auf verschiedene Einwürfe gegen dasselbe*," &c. Berlin, published by Mittler and Son, 1862. The charge of materialism brought against the new psychology is here refuted so triumphantly, that no one but a malicious slanderer would venture to repeat it.

We must now give an answer to the important question so much debated in the present day.

What is the "Temper" [Gemüth], *and how ought it to be formed?*

The temper is the *easy excitability* of internal emotions, not merely of a kindly, benevolent, but also of a melancholy, sullen, anxious nature, &c. It is not, therefore, a special innate power, but consists in single, and indeed simple attitudes of soul (affective or emotional psychical forms, see p. 59), which have been left behind as traces by previous sensations of pleasure, pain, satiety, dislike, and therefore of experiences by which such sensations are produced (see § 50, at the end). Now, as everything becomes, in the course of development, more and more rigid, it may be asked how the sensations, to which, collectively, we give the name of "*temper*," acquire their *easy excitability*? Simply from the fact that they have not become so rigid and fixed as *forms consisting of many traces* have; because *not all* sensations fuse together in proportion to their similarities. A portion of them remains *isolated*, and, in their *elementary* condition, they are not combined into pleasurable or painful *notions*, as we have already observed at p. 129; out of a hundred sensations, for instance, ten or more have not been fused with the rest. In point of fact, the new sensations produced day by day do not usually unite at once and firmly with their kindred forms already existent. It is, therefore, natural that the temper should have that shifting, fluent, indeterminate character that it has, because the elementary, whether produced by this or that mode of stimulation, requires only a small impulse in order to be instantly excited. It then bursts out into laughter or tears, as we find in light-hearted, sorrowful, anxious, &c., people. What temper is it we first clearly see in young children before their development has proceeded very far: they are one moment merry, and the next cross. As yet they possess but few fixed psychical forms (consisting of many traces), and hence, so long as the movable elements are busy in such unstable regions, the sudden change of emotions is quite what we should expect. We see it, secondly, especially in the case of fear, which may be found not merely in children, but also in many adults. A firmly developed man feels little fear: he who bears about with him many unpleasant traces in the form of *elementary* sensations is the one who feels most fear; and they, like all other sensations, may continually arise afresh, for every day furnishes us with impressions for new sensations. Women, in particular, abound in such elementary emotions, because in them the inferior tenacity of their original powers does not induce to the same extent the powerful attraction and fusion of what is homogeneous: and many women, therefore, remain all their life long mainly creatures of sentiment and temper, cheerful or timorous, often both at once. We see it, thirdly, in all those other cases where the clear understanding, the firm will, powerful feeling, are struck dumb by the violent excitation of our rudimentary powers, as we find, under circumstances of great, exuberant joy, or violent anger, sudden terror, profound grief, &c.

Between the fixed and the unfixed in the soul there is naturally no sharply-determined line of demarcation; but all that has been formed with some degree of strength, therefore all that does not remain in its original state of elementary fluidity, stands in man *above* the sphere of temper: and in particular, therefore, the pleasure or pain of a definitely developed desire or repugnancy, of feeling already formed, so likewise firm will, clear understanding, judgment, &c., &c. These latter forms cannot therefore be accounted to belong to the temper in the narrower and stricter sense of the word,—they belong to it only if it is understood in its wider or widest signification. Doubtless, pleasure and pain are manifested in them, and as the temper is characterized by '*moods*,' the inexact language of daily life considers both *desire* with its feeling of pleasure, and *repugnance* with that of pain, and in particular *feeling* properly so called, as belonging to temper, and therefore it considers the latter to be what impels us to action. But temper, in its narrow and strict sense, is not the true source of our actions, any more than it is the true source of our notions properly so called, although an *elementary* kind of notion is of course always involved in it: for in feeling we must always feel *something*: but for the formation of true notions or for action, temper, which is always condemned to remain in the *lowest* stage of psychical development, is something too immature, and hence the proposition holds good: *the temper is neither of a practical nor of a theoretical nature.* Of course, it always accompanies our acts and thoughts, and may exercise on them a favourable and also an unfavourable influence; it may strengthen our practical efforts, it may keep notions in consciousness, but at the same time it may confuse and darken both, according as it is excited with more or less violence, and is then allowed to influence them. It ought never to be forgotten that the temper may modify all that has been stamped into a permanent shape, and accordingly there may be a thought, a judgment, an estimation, an action, in which temper plays a considerable part. In particular, temper is quickly operative in cases of immediate intuition. It is well known that external impressions are not unfrequently viewed differently than they would be by *firmly-developed* psychical forms, if those impressions had not been directly encountered by particular emotions, by which they are instantly taken possession of, and invested with their own peculiar colours. When a man's temper chances to be a little ruffled, i.e. if elementary traces of displeasure (ill-temper) are excited in large numbers, he will receive a friend, or a request, quite differently from what he would if he had been excited by them directly in his *own proper character as a practical and rational agent.* Impressions then play on the elementary region of the soul as if on a musical instrument, but the tones produced depend on the qualities of the instrument (on its good or bad state of tune). From this one can see at once that there is an important difference between temper and sensation, although temper is produced by previous sensations, and that consequently it is more nearly allied to sensation than other psychical forms are, e.g. than understanding is. Temper is the state of our *internal disposition*, and therefore a condition already formed which merely requires to be *reproduced;* whereas thought and action cannot be effected by mere reproduction, but consist more or less *in new productions*, in *transformations* of what is reproduced.

One whose temper only is excited, yields himself almost *passively* to his emotions; at the highest he is pleased with 'good-natured chatter,' singing, jumping, laughing; or, on the other side, in complaints, sighs, tears, according as the elementary traces of pleasure or pain give him occasion: he neither reasons, nor wills, nor makes.

How temper is to be produced and trained is a matter which we cannot here discuss; fortunately there are works in which all this is clearly done. See in *Beneke's* "Archiv für die pragmatische Psychologie," vol. iii. p. 36, sqq., the essay entitled, "*Das menschliche Gemüth. Seine Bildungsform, Stellung, Umfang, Bedeutung; und in welchem Masse und in welcher Weise man dasselbe bilden soll.*" The same subject is treated of with greater detail, and in a more popular manner, in an essay by Dressler, "*über Gemüthsbildung,*" in *Diesterweg's* "Pädagogisches Jahrbuch auf 1857," p. 273 sqq. Trainers of temper, who in modern times have put forth so many perverted views on the subject, may here learn enough truth for their purpose, if they are only willing to open their eyes. Temper can neither be produced nor trained by instruction, which is, in fact, almost incapable of conveying external notions and external aptitudes; it can be obtained and trained only by experience of life, only by what causes *joy* and *sorrow*; and the true place, therefore, for its education is, not the school, but the *family* where joy and sorrow are to be felt, felt in common with others, and with sufficient frequency. True it is, that by clear notions the soul gains steadiness in its emotions, but such moods belong only very distantly to temper; and joy and sorrow are not so much at home in the school as they are in the family, and in public life. It is a particularly perverse view when the correct general and common culture of a human being is regarded as in the main the training of temper, and so is allowed to curtail the cultivation of the understanding. In order to have a proper sense of things, and to act rightly, man requires much more than mere temper, which, in its most perfect shape, always remains something blind, something *capricious and uncertain in its action*. See these hints carried out in detail in the two treatises above mentioned.

§ 70. *Recapitulation.*

I. The Original Powers of the Soul.

Fresh powers are being perpetually formed in the Soul. If they are decidedly *strong*, tenacious, and *sensitive*, the feelings of the Sublime are more easily produced; if, on the contrary, their *vivacity* predominates, the feelings of the *Agreeable* are sooner formed. A happy mixture of all three qualities is favourable to the feelings of the *Beautiful* (§ 52). The Beautiful and Sublime require, however, in addition, an *interpretation* derived from what the soul already possesses; this must answer to the relative impressions (§ 53), and in all three cases the proper degree of stimulation must not be wanting.

Again, the *stronger* and more tenacious the powers are, the sooner does there arise the feeling of the *strength* of particular psychical forms; in other words, the feeling *that they consist of many traces* (why? § 54). In proportion to this strength, all *notional* forms are attended by the feelings of *clearness* or *obscurity* (§ 55), and all forms of *pleasure* (or *dislike*) and *effort* likewise acquire their very peculiar character as feelings. We feel the stronger *pleasure* as of higher *value* (§ 56), and the stronger *desire* as a stronger *effort* (§ 60).

Now as the original powers, in point of *tenacity* and strength, are arranged in all men in a *similar* series, and the stimulants acting on them are always of *a like nature*, since moreover the law that *similar traces coalesce* is everywhere the same, it follows naturally that objects which stimulate the higher senses pleasurably, or the reverse, must be felt to be *higher* goods or evils than those objects which affect the lower senses; supposing always that, while the factors remain similar, there is a *like number of traces* accumulated *pari passu* in the products. In this fact is founded the *universally valid* (and therefore) *true* estimate of objects, the *moral rule* (§ 58), for like causes always produce like effects; and hence, in this case, produce a similar gradation of goods and evils, which can only be disturbed by *excess* or *defect* on the part of the impressions.

If the powers are not produced in their usual strength and tenacity, e.g. in sickness like stimulants do not produce the same feeling (§ 51).

II. The Stimulants of the External World.

According to their quantity or their relations to the original powers, they cause either a feeling of *dissatisfaction*, or of *pleasure*, or of *satiety*, or of *pain:* in brief feelings of pleasure or dislike (§ 50). What are *Sensations* (§ 50)?

In like manner, a peculiar relation of stimulant to the original powers causes the feelings of the *Agreeable*, *Sublime*, and *Beautiful* (§ 52), all of which arise from the third kind of relation between the two.

III. The Fundamental Laws prevalent in the Soul.

The *first*, according to which *external impressions are received by the original powers, and permanently exist in them*, is the origin of feelings in general; for since a feeling is only the consciousness of the difference or interval between two or more psychical forms (§§ 45, 46, 47), there could naturally be no consciousness of such difference, and therefore no *feeling*, if particular psychical forms, with the special emotions produced by them, had not previously arisen, and then been preserved as peculiar traces

(§ 50). But as everything which happens in the soul with any approach to perfection remains, with all its peculiarities, in the shape of a trace, it is easy to account for the *large extent*, as well as the *infinite complexity* and multiplicity, of the feelings; for one and the same psychical form may be manifested at one time as one feeling, at another as a different one, according as it co-exists in consciousness along with this or that psychical form (§§ 48 and 51).

What is freshness of feeling? (§ 48.)

The *second* fundamental law, according to which *all that is similar fuses into one whole, in consequence of mutual attraction*, continues the edifice commenced by the first.

It is thus that the feeling of the *strength* of particular psychical forms is produced which is manifested in *notions*, as *clearness*, *obscurity*, or *want of clearness;* according as many or few similarities meet together, or as like and unlike have been intermixed (§§ 54 and 55).

The greater the number of traces from which particular *forms* of pleasure or dislike have arisen in the soul, the greater is the *value* or *worthlessness* of the objects by which they were produced. In case the accumulation of traces has been *too great*, a deviation is easily caused from that (universally valid) order of goods and evils, which, from consisting of the same factors, is necessarily the same for all mankind. This is that *false estimate* of things which often prevails, in a special manner, among the forms of the lower senses (§ 59).

In like manner, this law leads to an increase in the strength of *desires* and *repugnancies* (§ 60). Where they are too strong in relation to the *true* estimate of objects, we call them *immorality*, or *corrupt will* (§ 61).

This *normal* or *immoderate* strength in our forms of pleasure, dislike, or effort, is always manifested by immediate feelings. The strength of an estimate commensurate to the moral rule is manifested as the feeling of *Duty*, which is called *Conscience* (§ 62), when we feel that duty in reference to our own actions. What is a *good*, what an *evil* conscience? (§ 62.)

When the moral (morally good) is stronger than anything

else in the soul it is called *Moral Freedom*, or *a morally free will;* and this freedom increases exactly as the morally good grows stronger (§ 63). Human action never springs out of mere notions, but exclusively from *estimates of value* (§ 63).

When several *similar* feelings are conscious together they *strengthen* each other according to their resemblance (§ 64). It is thus that the feelings of *Gratitude*, of *Favor conferred*, of *Mortification*, of *Honour*, of *Glory*, of *Affection* and *Dislike* are produced (§§ 65, 66, 67). *Dissimilar* feelings, on the contrary, when present together, impair or check each other's strength (§ 64), as is very clearly shewn in the case of the closely allied feelings of *Hope* and *Fear* (§ 68).

The *third* fundamental law, according to which *a portion of the stimulant always disappears from the developed original power* (not from the soul), is at once the foundation of *Immorality* and of *Moral Freedom*, because it is the cause of *Desires* (§ 25).

Lastly, the *fourth* fundamental law, according to which *the movable elements during our waking moments are perpetually flowing over, or are transferred from one ychical fo m to another*, causes the constant alternation of consciousness in the human soul, and is, in conjunction with the first law, the second originating cause of the Feelings in general; for the different psychical forms must be *conscious* either *together* or *in immediate succession*, before we can be aware of their *differences* or *intervals*. So far as this law shews itself active in the soul, so far do *Feelings* also arise; and, in so far as these movable elements are deposited on psychical forms, often excited together in such a manner that they are by them permanently *connected* (transformed into a group) to that extent, this law leads to the formation of *ready-made* feelings, which continue in the soul so long as their factors remain united (§§ 47 and 69).

What is *the Faculty of Feeling*, and how far does it extend? (§ 69.) The feelings, like all else that we have described, presuppose nothing but *original powers*, which are, therefore, powers of feeling, as well as of forming notions and desires (§ 69). Feeling is preceded by a certain tone and temper on the part of the original pow.s produced in and along with the impressions operating on them, so that in every sensation (emotion) so arising two kinds of effects are simultaneously produced: an impression or copy of the *objective* (of the object), and a sort of tone or emotion on the part of the *subjective* (of the power) (§§ 45 and 50).

What is understood by *Heart*, *Temper*, and *Mind?* (§ 69, in the note.) For further details on Temper see the conclusion of § 69.

PART IV.

SUPPLEMENTARY REMARKS AND FURTHER DETAILS.

§ 71. *Consciousness and Excitability.* (*What is Attention?*)

None of us know anything whatever about the first sensations which were produced in our souls; and every new-born child may serve to prove to us that it also is destitute of any consciousness either of itself or of its surroundings. *Consciousness, therefore, does not exist from the first in any soul; it must come into existence gradually.*

In what manner and by what means is it produced? By the union of external stimulants with our original powers, as we have aready seen in § 10. Beside that, we there learnt, that consciousness gradually attains to *clearness*, from the fact that every act of sensation leaves a trace behind it, and that similar traces coalesce into one whole. No mental form attains to *full clear* consciousness, unless similar traces are multiplied and accumulated.

Hence it follows, that in the very *first* sensation, i.e. satisfaction of an original power by a stimulant, there must be involved *the beginning* of the process by which that form afterwards attains to full consciousness, even though this consciousness exist in the very *simplest form and faintest* degree—so faint, that it appears to be almost non-existent. Unless a minimum of consciousness were implied in the first sensation, and unless it remained permanently attached to the trace left by it, where could the full consciousness implied in a form resulting from many traces come from? In the soul, as elsewhere, *ex nihilo nihil fit*, and the *second* sensation could involve no consciousness if it was impossible for the *first* to do so.

This fact may be illustrated by the following example, derived from the material world. A minute grain of sand laid upon the hand produces no appreciable sensation of weight, and therefore seems to be imponderable; a million of such grains produce a very decided pressure. How could this be possible unless every single grain possessed a minimum of weight? The whimpering of a new-born babe at any painful sensation shews that an obscure consciousness is already germinating in it.

Let us turn our attention for a moment to brutes. The *same* stimulants that affect men affect them, and yet they never attain in any of their psychical forms (the nobler brutes, especially those that have been trained, like dogs, horses, &c., are by no means deficient in them) to human clearness of consciousness. From this it unquestionably follows, that the origin of consciousness does not depend on any peculiarity in the *stimulants:* it must rather be sought for in some special quality of *the original powers* (elementary powers). This, as we have already seen in §§ 7 and 8, is the *higher strength and tenacity* of man's original powers, in consequence of which stimulants are more perfectly appropriated and *retained*, and this tenacity implies also the power of becoming conscious. As the steel involves the possibility of sparks, which, however, can only be actually elicited by contact with the flint, so also this potential consciousness is elevated to actual consciousness by and through stimulants.

This power of becoming conscious constitutes the peculiar difference between the brute and the human soul: both are *originally*, or at birth, distinct, not in *kind*, but only in *degree* (we are comparing here only the *nobler* brutes); but that difference of *degree* must very soon be transformed into a difference of *kind*, because the human soul necessarily advances, and is *able* to advance infinitely, whereas the brute soul is absolutely incapable of doing so. Observation of ourselves will tell us how much progress it is possible for the higher species of animals to make, and will enable us to form a *tolerably close* notion of their feelings; for our original powers are not all endowed with the same degree of tenacity, that property varying from that of sight, where it is strongest, down to the vital powers, where it is weakest (compare § 8), the consequence of which is, that even we never attain to *full clearness* of consciousness in the lower senses. It is probable that brutes, in their strongest powers, arrive at about the same degree of consciousness that we do in our lower senses*.

But even those forms which are richest in traces do not continue in permanent and unbroken consciousness: consciousness alternates with unconsciousness—at this moment they are conscious, then unconscious, and the next they become conscious afresh, and so on. In short: *in the developed soul there is a perpetual alternation of consciousness and unconsciousness.* Therefore, there is such a thing as a *recurring* consciousness, which must be *different in kind* from that which *comes into existence* at first, and with tedious slowness. What is the peculiar difference between them?

It is obvious, that the consciousness which first arises is the opposite of the *as yet unconscious*, while recurrent consciousness is merely opposed to the actually *unexcited*. If a form is to have that clearness, which we briefly call consciousness, it must be based on many traces. This kind of consciousness, however, vanishes the moment those traces pass from the excited to the unexcited and passive state, *it lasts only as long as their excitation continues.*

That other species, however, which springs out of the absolute negation of consciousness as yet [*aus dem Noch-gar-nicht-bewusst-gewesen-sein*] is a something which only gradually developes—it is not a something which has been merely arrested for want of excitation; and, consequently, we cannot affirm of it that it now manifests itself, and again ceases to do so. To be able to do that it must first exist, but the kind of consciousness now alluded to is a germinating consciousness, a consciousness in bud.

---

* That, however, the "*Spirituality*," the "*Spirit*," or *Mind* of man's soul, is nothing more than that higher strength and tenacity of his original powers (especially those of the nobler senses), which renders clear consciousness possible, is shewn above, § 10, and below, § 79. In the lower senses, there is often a stronger momentary consciousness than exists in the higher, but it cannot maintain itself, and therefore cannot be reproduced.

It is natural, then, that one who is unacquainted, for instance, with the letters of the Greek alphabet should be destitute of any consciousness of them. Had he learnt them, we might and must say that he had a consciousness of them, even when he is not thinking of them, for then they would be merely unexcited, or in a purely latent condition. In this way we all have a consciousness of our dwelling-place, of our name, of our furniture, &c., &c., even when they are absent from our thoughts; for the notions of them exist in our soul as the result or complexus of numerous traces. As the warmth of our body is by excitement (exercise) released from its bound or latent condition, not created by it (for it is already there, and only a corpse is deprived of it), so, also, the recurrent consciousness in our mental forms is not created by excitation, it is already existent in a bound condition, and it only requires excitement to make its actual appearance, and to be released from its fetters. Consequently, *psychical forms* are capable of becoming conscious in a totally different and far higher sense of the word than is applicable to the as yet *undeveloped original powers*: the former carry with them an already *formed* consciousness, the latter an *unformed*—a something which is a mere germ of consciousness one day to be actualized.

Excitation, consequently, is the indispensable condition, without fulfilling which, forms, however rich they may be in traces, must remain unconscious—so runs the psychical law here operative. When, therefore, only a portion of the traces constituting a form, and not the whole of them, are excited, *the intensity of the consciousness of that form is proportionate to the actual number of traces so excited*[b]. The as yet undeveloped elemen-

[b] This determines the degree of what is called *Attention*. We are more attentive when, along with a present impression, the traces previously acquired, and of like kind with it, are excited in larger numbers; we are less attentive when less of them are so aroused. To objects for which we do not possess any traces we can naturally shew no attention, e.g. for a language unknown to us: in such a case the impressions are apprehended by mere void original powers along with which, of course, similar sounds in our mother tongue may be excited, but they are incapable of giving us any

tary powers, on the other hand, cannot be so vividly excited: they never yield consciousness, as may be seen from the fact that none of us have any consciousness of those powers which we employ as movable elements: the new-born child proves this by the gradual evolution of his consciousness from its germinal condition.

We already know, from §§ 12 and 13, the cause of this constant alternation of consciousness and unconsciousness, in other words of *excitation*, and the reverse. We there found that if a *conscious* psychical form is to become unconscious, *it must either lose a portion of its stimulant, or of the void unemployed powers which attached themselves* (*flowed over*) *to it.* By this separation it ceases to be excited, and consequently loses its consciousness *. Hence, we necessarily infer that if it is again to attain to consciousness this loss must be somehow or other repaired.

That loss is made good either, 1°. by *external stimulants* (§ 12), or 2°. by *internal stimulants* (§ 13). or 3°. by *void unemployed original powers* (§ 13). When I unexpectedly hear

---

comprehension of the foreign language, because the sounds of the latter are not yet associated with the objects which they represent (compare pp. 99 and 100). In like manner, if we have sufficient traces within for comprehending any object, but they are not excited because too many other forms are aroused, so that the exciting elements do not reach them, we shall be completely unable to attend to it. Consequently, attention is only intense when the soul is free from excitation of a different kind, and when the traces on which attention depends do not take up the impressions in a mere passive way, but actively (in an already excited condition) meet them, and are, therefore, *on the look out* for them.

* The old psychology seems to have thought that the process of becoming conscious required an explanation, but not that of ceasing to be so: accordingly it assumes as the cause of the former a power of Recollection, but is completely silent as to the reason of the latter. And yet the question why what we were once conscious of should disappear, whether for a shorter or longer period, and how it comes about, is to the full as important as the question how the unconscious returns to consciousness. Moreover, Recollection is a different thing from becoming conscious. (See § 75.)

the name of an old acquaintance, the notion of him rises into consciousness, excited by *external* stimulants: when I think first thing in the morning, before external stimulants remind me of it, of that which occupied me yesterday, that excitation is produced by *internal* elements, and, therefore, partly by those mentioned under No. 2, partly by those under No. 3.

It has already been explained, in §§ 30 and 31, that the two latter classes are called *movable elements.* So long as the supply of them lasts they keep passing from form to form, and are as effective in producing that alternation of consciousness and unconsciousness, which continues every moment of our waking life as the external stimulants themselves. During profound sleep they are necessarily at rest, because, if not then entirely absent, yet they exist only in very small numbers, and because sleep deprives them of their peculiar vivacity; for their normal excitation implies waking, unlocked senses, which are, and must be affected before the soul can be definitely aroused to action. All this, however, requires further examination, for which see the following §. One remark, however, may be made before passing to it.

Where there are no forms excited, there there is no consciousness in our soul. On a superficial examination it may perhaps seem that consciousness is a *completely universal* condition of soul, i.e. a condition which belongs to the *developed* soul in *general*, and not one connected merely with the individual forms in it. Thus, for instance, a man who awakes in the morning from a deep sleep may suppose that at waking he has passed into a state exactly as general as the unconsciousness of sleep was a completely general condition. How is this illusion to be explained?

Simply from the fact that our psychical forms are excited one after the other without cessation, and without any gaps. Let there be only short pauses between them, and the appearance of universality on the part of consciousness vanishes. Reflect, too, that to the universality of the psychical condition which we usually call sleep, there is really no such wide step as there seems to be when it is viewed from our waking condition. In the waking state, it is only an extremely small portion of our soul that is alternately really awake, i.e. conscious; by far the larger part of it sleeps continuously, and for the production of *perfect* sleep all that is required is that the little which was awake should become unconscious. Hence, the great fulness of consciousness in which we find ourselves in the morning with our first waking notions, proves how uncommonly *abundant the traces* of our psychical forms must be. If you observe a child of two or three months old, you will perceive an important difference between its waking existence and that of an adult. Moreover, everybody who accurately observes himself, may occasionally be aware of actual stoppages in the current of consciousness, and in many conditions (e.g. after great exertion, in many maladies, in depressing emotions, &c.,) such cases are frequent.

§ 72. *Involuntary and Voluntary Rise of Consciousness. Certainty and Uncertainty therein.*

a. I take a walk, not for the purpose of meditation, but to refresh myself: yet involuntarily I think on one thing and another, and am incited to do so not by anything external, but purely from within. All of a sudden a hare crosses my path; can I avoid thinking of it? Without that external occasion, probably anything rather than the notion of a hare would have risen into consciousness.

b. I want to remember somebody's name, a song, an event, &c., and I succeed with greater or less celerity. (Compare p. 81.)

Everybody calls the two modes of becoming conscious, mentioned under *a.*, **involuntary**, because they follow purely without our will. It very often happens that we become conscious in this way directly *against* our will, as e.g. when we wish to think quietly over some subject, and a noise, music, or some internal uneasiness, &c., excites ideas which prevent us from doing so.

The second mode of becoming conscious (*b*), on the other hand, all call *voluntary* because it is caused by our will (§ 42). What is the difference between the two?

This we are already acquainted with from §§ 12, 13, and 21. Before I thought of the hare, *internal stimulants* were exciting my notions (thoughts), until the *external stimulant* of the hare affected me, and brought the notion of it into consciousness. In the second case, however, these external stimulants were the very thing absent, otherwise I should not have needed to *bethink* myself of the name (song, or event, &c.) If, then, what is willed or desired also becomes conscious, there must be *void original powers* to impart to it fresh excitement (compare the examples in §§ 21 and 31), and, as a matter of fact, these powers are the main constituents of every volitional act (compare §§ 25, 40, 41), i.e. of that from which it here follows that the name (song, or event) becomes conscious.

So, then, *involuntary* consciousness is produced when *external* or *internal stimulants* excite unconscious psychical forms into consciousness; *voluntary*, on the other hand, when *void original powers* do so.

The *ordinary intermediate* course of our thoughts, which is half voluntary, half involuntary, is caused by *a mixture of both kinds of elements.* For there is no exclusive opposition between the processes of becoming conscious voluntarily or involuntarily; every psychical form may become conscious, sometimes in the one way, sometimes in the other, and hence they may be excited in both ways at once. Very naturally! for as the movable elements, original powers as well as stimulants, may attach themselves indifferently to all forms, so they may be indifferently transplanted from any; as, on the other side, it is natural again that forms in which the developed *powers* predominate (*appetencies*) should transfer more original powers, and on the other hand that those in which appropriated stimulants predominate (*notions*, ideas,) should transmit a larger quantity of general stimulants, because the attraction of similars prevalent in every form has become connected with *such* movable elements as correspond to its more important constituents (compare § 31). Only let it not be forgotten that no transferred element requires any space to move in, because no local extension is required for any psychical processes—a main reason why, as people say, 'we are unaware' of this transference (see p. 81), i.e. we are unaware of any local process or change. Compare pp. 80 and 89.

But why is it that external stimulants are *certain*, internal stimulants and void original powers more or less *uncertain*, to awaken consciousness? This question, already touched on in § 13, may be easily answered thus:

Internal stimulants and void original powers suit, in the main, all traces, because they are universal, *general* elements, which have as yet received no special stamp (have not been definitely modified), or have lost it again when they released their hold over the traces and again became movable. The external stimulants, however, which e.g. are contained in the word *Hand*, will not fit on to the traces of the words, *Face*, *Arm*, *Eye*, *&c.*, the latter sound quite differently. Just so the light-stimulants of Red, Angular, &c., are completely different from the traces left in me by the light-stimulants of Green, Round, &c., and so on through the whole class of exterior stimulants. Among those there are but few that are quite universal and indeterminate, and hence it is natural that since the definitely similar attracts its like, the process of becoming conscious must in this case take place with more certainty; whilst the universal can only arouse this or that form precariously, because it is almost indifferent to any Traces, and is therefore not *exclusively* suitable to this or that particular one. When external stimulants are given in an indeterminate manner, e.g. in a sound, cry, &c., they only determine consciousness in an uncertain and indefinite manner. The moment a definite excitation is effected by some definite external stimulant, other forms are excited through the medium of the internal, movable elements, but this effect is more or less uncertain. The following §§, however, will serve to shew that notwithstanding this, these movable elements are subject to a stringent law, and that they do not arouse consciousness at haphazard, but that the constant change from consciousness to unconsciousness, and the reverse, is governed by this law.

§ 73. *Direction followed in the Process of becoming Conscious.*

I am convinced that when I excite the notion of 'Hunter' in any one's consciousness he will also think of 'Gun.' A wild

The movable elements are always transferred from any psychical form by preference to that which is most intimately connected with it, or is one with it.

Hence, in the native of Dresden the notion 'country' immediately suggests the environs of Dresden, and not those of the Breslau district: hence a soap-boiler, when he thinks of 'Soap,' is put in mind at once of tallow, ashes, boiler, &c., whereas a washerwoman thinks of dirty linen, and so on. Anyone may add examples for himself.

Those forms are most intimately connected (united) in our soul which have not merely frequently co-existed in consciousness (at an earlier period), but which, besides that, are constructed out of the same elements, e.g. the concepts, 'Tree,' 'House,' &c., consist of the same elements as the individual trees and houses that we have seen, to the exclusion merely of dissimilar elements of intuition: and the same holds of higher concepts in relation to lower ones (see §§ 15—17). Is it astonishing, then, that along with an intuition the homogeneous concept corresponding to it starts involuntarily into consciousness, and along with a lower concept the higher concept of like kind with it, and that in consequence we are, so to say, everlastingly forming judgments? (§ 18.) The number of judgments which we express in words is very small, yet the process of judging is constantly going on in the soul in proportion as similarities have been intimately connected together by the appropriation of movable elements, and are now usually excited together. Compare § 38.

One other remark may be added.

I said above, that in 1842, the notion of 'Hamburg,' though it suggested 'Fire,' was yet constantly associated with that of 'many ships,' but that the latter was at that time *less strongly* suggested, and in the merchant there can be no doubt that the notions of 'House of Business,' 'Loss,' &c., rose into consciousness in *different degrees* of force along with those of 'Conflagration,' 'Ships.'

If I remind any one acquainted with history of the Seven Years' War, the notion of '*Frederick II.*' will, to a certainty, be in a moment associated with a number of others, as *Ziethen*, *Keith*, the *Surprise at Hochkirch*, *Daun*, &c.; but it is also certain that all these notions are not *equally vivid*, some are more, some less fully present to consciousness, whilst others are barely excited at all, forming by their semi-obscurity the extreme horizon, as it were, the limit between consciousness and its total absence.

Hence, the movable elements, as it seems, are not transferred in *their whole fulness* to the individual psychical form which is most intimately connected with (or one with) that form from which the transference is made: no! *the movable elements rather flow towards all the psychical forms connected with it* (the waking notion), *but in a higher or lower degree proportionate to the closer or looser connection subsisting between them.* Compare § 33.

Thus may be explained the fact that some psychical forms excite a good many others into consciousness, whilst others only excite a few: it all depends on whether they were formerly connected with many or few other psychical forms: and hence it is comprehensible that the intensity of their consciousness is very diverse, varying according as the movable elements are transferred to them in a greater or less quantity, which transmission itself depends on the closer or looser connection existing between them, and thus a *larger or smaller number of traces* in the notions affected are excited. Compare p. 191.

When the movable elements are concentrated on a few forms, the latter are naturally excited and rendered conscious with extraordinary strength, whereas we find ourselves in a condition of *distraction* or *confusion* when those elements are diffused over too many psychical forms. As this renders *attention* to the objects surrounding and affecting us impossible, it follows that attention must be absent where the forms are either not excited at all, or too partially, so that the homogeneous impression which should be rendered conscious and received by them is only able to turn to a void original power, and must consequently remain an unconscious, or, at best, an obscure sensation. See the remark in p. 191.

If, then, these movable elements are, as it is abundantly clear they are, the exciting senses, why do they not excite all our psychical forms *at once*; why is it that they at the most only excite *a few* at the same time; why in the majority of cases do they only excite these forms in succession, so that the earlier members of the series must sink again into unconsciousness? Let any one try to repeat a poem, so as to be conscious of the first words and notions of it when he arrives at the last, and he will find that he is never able to do so. Why, then, do these exciting elements leave us in the lurch, and not enable us to retain continuously that which was first conscious?

Because (fortunately) there are only a moderate *quantum* of them, and there are, therefore, not enough of them to serve all the forms and their traces which we possess in such abundance (see p. 76). Accordingly, when they have done duty in one region of the soul they retire, and thus it is unavoidable that that which was this moment conscious should lose its excitability in favour of that which is afterwards to become so. And what an eloquent proof this is of the Creator's wisdom! If our internal possessions were so extensively excited, a confusion must ensue, which would render consciousness rather a curse than a blessing.

Besides this, there are three causes why the consciousness of these forms, *even in the presence of a sufficient number of exciting elements*, must occasionally remain more or less weak, so weak, that for a time it is hardly distinguishable from unconsciousness. In the first place, there is the *partial opposition* of forms, the effect of which is that they mutually obscure each other when simultaneously excited (see p. 69), because full clearness of consciousness pre-supposes similarity (similar elements or constituent parts), (see § 55). In the next place, a second cause is very often the *great number* of reproduced groups and series, in consequence of which the movable elements, as has already been observed, are *so diffused*, that none of them can attain to full consciousness; and, thirdly, the same effect may be produced by what frequently occurs, viz., the *quickness* with which the excitation takes place, which does not permit any sufficient connection to be formed between the movable element and the traces. These three causes serve to explain why it is that extensive excitement may occur in the soul, and yet that it may not manifest itself in consciousness, or that, at best, only the last member or step becomes conscious. Think of the dexterity of a pianoforte-player, of a rapid and practised writer, a well-trained reader, &c. If the reader were obliged to bring each letter and each sound into such full consciousness, as one who is learning his A B C is compelled to do, what wearisome tediousness would be the consequence!

Action in which the final step only is apparent to consciousness in the way described, we call 'Tact,' (practical tact, delicate critical tact, &c.)

§ 74. *The Explanation of these Phenomena according to the Old Psychology. Involuntary Suggestions.*

The old psychology enunciates different laws which regulate the constant alternation between consciousness and unconsciousness: and yet it falls into inconsistencies. Sometimes these phenomena are distributed under several laws, sometimes an attempt is made to explain them from as few as possible. I proceed to detail them.

The different psychical forms are said to be aroused

1°. According to the law of *Simultaneity:* for what we have seen, heard, &c., together, that we are again conscious of together. Quite right, but—*why?*

2°. According to the law of *Succession:* for what we have perceived as immediately consecutive, we reproduce in consciousness in a like order. True! but—*why?*

3°. According to the law of *Similarity:* for very often forms arouse others *resembling* them. True again! but—*why?*

4°. According to the law of *Contrast:* for black frequently suggests *white.* Right again! but—*why?*

5°. According to the law of *Locality:* for when we think of the church, we usually think of the churchyard also. Right! but—*why?*

6°. According to the law of the *Relation between Thing and Quality:* for when I think of a sphere, the concept 'round' is simultaneously suggested. Very true! but—*why?*

7°. According to the law of *Causal Connection:* for when I think of 'Fire,' I frequently become conscious of the notions of its effects, 'Light' and 'Warmth,' or conversely; but—*why?*

All these 'whys' to which we find no reply in the old theory, admit of a simple and easy answer, in accordance with the law of the new psychology explained in the preceding paragraph. We proceed to prove this.

1°. *Those things of which we are simultaneously conscious* are always permeated by movable elements; and since a portion of the latter remain attached to them, they are closely bound together (§ 38).

This connection is less perfect

2°. *in the case of Succession*, when, by the appropriation of movable elements, only *the end* of the first grows on to the *beginning* of the second, the end of that to the beginning of the third, psychical form, &c. Consequently, succession is only a *partial* co-existence in time, though, when often repeated, it leads to a close connection. Sign and thing signified, which belong here, are usually very closely associated. (See § 38.)

3°. *The Similar* is a mixture of like and unlike parts. So far, however, as psychical forms resemble one another, so far they always fuse into one whole (§ 9); consequently, owing to the similarity of their parts, like must in the soul be awakened by like. Naturally the dissimilar parts in such forms are also brought into consciousness, and, as a consequence, the otherwise similar forms are recognised as like. But while thus simultaneously co-existing, they are cemented to each other by the appropriation of movable elements, so that afterwards the Similar is able to attain to consciousness from this fact of connection as well. Hence, the excitation of the Similar rests on the law of Simultaneity in Time.

4°. Nor is the case different as regards *Contrast*. When am I able to say that two objects are contrasted? When I have thought of them both together, and have impressed on my consciousness their greater or less difference. Consequently, *the fact of their being simultaneously present to consciousness*, is the reason why psychical forms the most heterogeneous are interconnected by the retention of the movable elements; and then afterwards, if no other or stronger associations prevent it, they are restored to consciousness as united.

5°. *That which is connected in Space* is always perceived by us as something simultaneously or successively existing, and as such its parts must be cemented together with more or less firmness by the movable elements. Exactly the same holds of

6°. *The relation between a Thing and its Qualities*, as also of

7°. *The Causal Relation*, and depends *solely on a constant and unceasing succession* of different effects or processes in the soul, (and also for the most part in the external world, § 39).

Hence, all these so-called '*Laws of Association*' may be reduced to *a complete simultaneity in time, and a repeated sequence*, (= a partial simultaneity, or simultaneous consciousness); and they *must* be so reduced, because experience shews that what comes into consciousness at *separate* points of time is never associated together. That alone which is excited at the same time can appropriate to itself a portion of the movable elements, and thus grow into a whole.

Still this would not explain why, when a number of psychical forms once conscious together are reproduced, the current of consciousness should set from this particular form towards that, and not in some other direction, (compare the examples in the preceding §), if we did not know *that the movable elements are always immediately transferred from one psychical form to that other which is most intimately connected with it, or is one with it.*

The intensity of this connection depends, however, partly on the fact that psychical forms simultaneously in consciousness, are *repeatedly permeated* by the movable elements, and partly on *the greater or less fulness* with which those elements are, as it were, shed over the forms to be awakened. Experience, too, proves that the visible more easily excites the visible, the audible the audible, &c., than the visible does the audible, and conversely (all else being the same), which evidently depends on the *greater original similarity* and consequent *closer connection* subsisting between these powers.

Whether, then, in this or that case the law of *similarity*, or of *contrast*, or *any other* prevails, depends simply *on the intensity of the connection subsisting between the different psychical forms*, and if we were accurately acquainted with this in all cases, we should invariably be able to predict what psychical form would be aroused into consciousness by any other under any given combination of circumstances. In our own case, and in that of others with whom we are well acquainted, we do already, as a fact, know beforehand what the course of consciousness will be.

Involuntary suggestions (not to be confounded with *involuntary impressions*), which often arise suddenly in the soul, and are completely unconnected with the series of forms at present excited, admit of the following simple explanation. At every point of the human soul there are to be found, early in the morning, fresh or void original powers, with which general, vague stimulants enter into connection. Now, if they are both collected in any considerable quantity at any one point (as they possibly may be, in consequence of our other psychical acts), it is natural enough that they should arouse into consciousness that psychical form round which they cluster; for those powers are essentially living and active, and just as *external* stimulants press forwards to the soul (take sound and light for examples), so also it is impossible for *internal* stimulants to be passive and dead. Such *involuntary suggestions* are abundant in the morning at the moment of waking, but they also occur at any other time in the day; and then psychical forms become conscious, which certainly cannot have been excited by external stimulants, any more than they are awakened by forms *already conscious.* With these exceptions, however, it is an invariable law, that forms can only be excited *purely from within* by others already conscious and excited.

§ 75. *Memory, Recollection, and Imaginary Notions* [*Einbildungsvorstellungen*].

We have already spoken about memory in § 7, and discovered that it is not a special faculty beside and apart from the original powers of the soul, but that it consists simply and solely in the peculiarity which they possess of *retaining*, to a greater or less degree, the stimulants received by them. This memory is the foundation of all that which is further developed in us and retained (Concepts, Judgments, &c., Groups, Series, Feelings of Pleasure and Pain, Desires, Repugnancies, &c.), and in it the movable elements play a chief part as *connecting* elements. For most of the forms which continue to exist in our soul are groups and series, which have grown up out of connections established between the fundamental forms, i.e. from those which *first* came into existence; as, for instance, the notion, Tree, is a complexus of several different perceptions (roots, trunk, branches, &c.), which would not, it is true, vanish from the soul if that connection were broken, but which would cease to exist as this particular *notion*. The case is just the same with the notions, house, man, garden, apple, table, chair, stove, bench, &c. (see § 38). But of all fundamental, as well as of all derivative forms, the law holds that

What has been once produced in the soul with any degree of perfection *continues still to exist*, even when it has ceased to be excited, and has, consequently, lost consciousness. That which was conscious merely becomes unconscious, or lives in '*the internal substance of the soul*,' i.e. as a '*trace*' (see § 6, and especially the note on it). This unconscious *continuance of what has once existed in the soul is* Memory. It cannot, therefore, be limited to notions. Desires, states of will, feelings, &c., have their memory as well.

It is natural that every form should continue to exist *more perfectly*, in proportion to the *vigour* with which it was at first generated, and *the oftener* it has been *recalled into consciousness*, and thus strengthened. Hence the *perfection* of memory depends on two circumstances:

1°. *On the perfectness with which the psychical forms were originally produced.* The fundamental forms (sensations and perceptions) will be less liable to be lost *in proportion as the primitive powers are stronger and more retentive* (§ 7), *and in proportion as the stimulants act with greater strength and fulness* (§ 11), (but this fulness must not be inordinate, § 24): and the derivative forms will be more permanent *in proportion* as the elements combined are *similar* (§ 38, at the end), and the more intimate *the connection* between them is rendered by the movable elements (§ 38).

2°. On the *strength* infused by *repetition* into what already exists within: and here again two cases are to be distinguished. A form frequently repeated is either strengthened by fresh and homogeneous traces which are added to it (§ 9), or the number of traces is not increased, but, on being repeatedly excited, they attract movable elements, and so become more perfect, which is also true of *the general tendency to association* (see the remark in § 54 and § 38).

The latter mode in which forms are strengthened is particularly conspicuous in the process of learning anything by heart. Not only do the connecting traces increase, but the forms so repeated themselves appropriate a portion of the exciting elements, and, by so doing, grow, if the expression is allowable, in bulk. The same occurs when we are in a state of expectancy, or anxious, or in love, &c., when we are much teased by such matters, and, indeed, when any other state or act is reproduced, even when that is attended by disgust. Furthermore, what people call favourite inclinations, hobbies, whims, &c., are only forms of a similar kind which have been strengthened by movable elements. They are not merely very permanent in an unconscious shape (in memory), but they are ready to spring into consciousness at the least provocation. From continually appropriating exciting elements they have acquired an extraordinary facility of becoming conscious (a great "*nearness to consciousness*")."

Repetition, therefore, does two things, which ought not to be confounded together; increase in the number of traces strengthens the form and increases its *clearness*; the appropriation of mere movable elements strengthens and increases the fulness with which it becomes conscious[e]: in the former case, "*the incressive space*" of the form is increased; in the latter, the "*accrescive space*" (as it were heterogeneous and discontinuous) (see § 54, note). In both cases the old saying proves true, that Repetition is the Mother of Learning (Repetitio est mater studiorum[f]).

---

[e] An obscure notion, though repeated internally many hundred times, does not become any clearer, it only gains in strength of consciousness [is more ready to start into consciousness].

[f] New traces can never be acquired by merely reproducing internally (re-exciting) psychical forms which have been engendered by external objects: connecting traces alone can be increased in this way. But more than this; acts of reproduction, suggested by something external, yet not by the *object itself*, leave the traces exactly where they found them, unaugmented. You may, for instance, remind me by words ever so often of a melody, but I shall not know it any the better: I must hear the notes of it.

From this it follows, that memory is not a *special* and *innate* power of the soul, which is able to exhibit a *general* and higher activity when *generally* exercised: on the contrary, every single psychical form has its own memory; and in a more perfect degree the more perfectly it was originally formed, and the more it has been strengthened by repetition.

When, therefore, we ascribe to a man a greater or less perfection of memory, this must be understood as being true *on an average* of all his powers; for in every soul, however perfect it may be, there are always forms more or less imperfectly developed, and resulting from only a few traces, and these are, consequently, deficient in the property of a 'good and perfect memory.'

But is it not true, that a man who knows German and Latin can very easily learn English? If so, it would seem that increased tenacity of memory may be produced, say, by having learned a number of words. Let us look a little more closely into the case.

Consider the words, *der Vater*, *pater*, *the father*; *der Bruder*, *the brother*; *ich habe*, *habeo*, *I have*; *ein*, *unus*, *one*; *drei*, *tres*, *three*; *sechs*, *sex*, *six*; *zwölf*, *twelve*, *&c.* There is obviously a remarkable similarity between these words, and the resemblances are very extensive, because, as is well known, the English language is a product of German, Latin, and French. Now, if any one is

---

In like manner the number of traces in such a concept as 'bird of prey' can be increased only if I actually perceive more birds of prey, so that the combination of similar elements previously obtained is enriched by an actually new element: and so in all cases. Without *another similar or analogous* act there is no increase in the number of traces.

But there would be no harm in regarding this strengthening of a psychical form by means of the movable elements, as being, in a way, an increase in its *traces*, provided this *particular* species of traces was never confounded with those properly so called: on the contrary, since we do and must speak of connecting traces (see p. 98), there are many cases, especially in the act of learning by heart, &c., in which it would not be improper to call these secondary traces, *reproducing* or *reproductive* traces, and so mark them off from the *original* ones. These reproductive traces are obviously of great importance in strengthening our desires and repugnancies.

well acquainted with the *latter* languages, it must follow that, in learning English, the similar words already existent in his mind must be called up into consciousness along with the new English words (§ 74). It is thus that the new finds a firm foundation in the old: old acquaintances meet, so that the *vocabulary* of the English language has not to be learnt completely apart and from the beginning: the *pronunciation* and other *peculiarities* are the only points as to which a new and special consciousness has to be founded on an assemblage of fresh traces. Hence we may certainly affirm that: ***Memory may be so exercised and improved as to be able with greater ease to apprehend and retain new impressions***, that is, in so far *as that which is already rooted in the soul is able to coalesce with the new apprehensions as homogeneous with them, and is therefore capable of forming a constituent part of them.* But *only to that extent.* Hence, we may explain how it is possible for the botanist to apprehend and retain with such marvellous accuracy all that relates to his pet subject, and yet not to be anything like so successful in other matters. Or take the case of the so-called living chronicle—the village or town gossip, who carries about in his head and on the tip of his tongue every petty detail that he has ever heard relating to every house, every family. Another man, endowed with far more tenacious original powers, would possibly find it difficult to bear all these things in mind: the gossip finds no such difficulty, for the last piece of news meets with such a multitude of similar traces and forms, that it becomes fixed without more ado. Of course, the 'interest' which such people have in such matters plays a part; but that interest is, after all, nothing more than the larger number of traces which these kinds of mental forms have attained to in them: it is, therefore, a case identical with the others mentioned above.

But of what use are the strongest and clearest psychical forms if they do remain permanent within, and yet cannot be called into consciousness, or, as we are frequently accustomed to say, to *remembrance?* Since there is a difference between rising into consciousness and remembering, we must say a word or two on the latter.

"I was a boy of eight or nine years of age when Napoleon, in his wrath, led his soldiers to Russia. A division of his army passed through the little town of S. The Garde formed part of it. I can see the bearded, bold fellows now; how self-confident they seemed; in what upright, soldierly trim they marched along! They passed through in ranks of six men each: regiment succeeded regiment; the houses trembled, the earth groaned under the mighty throng. It was, indeed, an inspiriting sight, and I think I shall never forget it, nor will my sister either: she and I peeped out of a top window down into the street," &c., &c. Thus talks an eye-witness, and this much is clear from what he says: *Whilst telling his tale, a crowd of psychical forms become successively conscious in his soul, and they all belong to one another, because, at a former period, they were all excited at one and the same time;* or, more precisely, *to the leading notion, "Passage of the Guard," are attached those of the circumstances, the time, the place, &c., under which the main notion was formerly engendered.*

When repeating this narrative, not only the same series of forms become successively conscious which were excited when I heard the story, but I also think of the person who told me it, the time, the place, manner, when, where, and how he told me. When anything of this kind takes place in the soul, viz.:

When the process of becoming conscious starts from some main or leading notion, and proceeds so far that the notions of the circumstances, time, place, &c., also become conscious with it, under which we formed that notion, so that it is brought again into connexion with our former life, then we say *we have a* Recollection.

As recollection, then, is nothing but a *continued process of becoming conscious*, and as that alone can attain to consciousness which has been fixed in the soul with sufficient strength, and by a sufficient number of traces, it is clear that perfect recollection,

1°. *depends on the perfection of the memory* (see above).

It is useless having the strongest psychical forms, forms resting on many traces, unless *they are excited* into consciousness.

They are so excited by the movable elements, and the more completely in proportion as the latter are more numerous (§ 73): hence perfect recollection depends also

2°. *on the fulness of the movable elements.*

It often happens that movable elements are present in sufficient numbers, and also the psychical forms which might become conscious are in nowise deficient in the number of traces, and yet the restoration to consciousness which we desire does not succeed, or, at least, only with such slowness, that when it does occur it is too late (compare § 14). Perfect restoration to consciousness, and consequently perfect recollection, requires,

3°. *in particular, a high degree of vivacity on the part of the original powers.*

What, then, is *the Power* of Recollection? It is certainly not a *special innate* power: on the contrary, Recollection is *completely explained* by the fact that psychical forms are permanent, and that they are rendered conscious by the movable elements (§ 73) according to a definite law. Man consequently does not possess a single power of recollection, but as many as he has psychical forms capable of reproducing themselves as leading notions in company with those which are subsidiary to and allied with them.

All those notions which are excited (reproduced) purely *from within*, and not at the present moment from without, are called *Imaginary Notions*, using that term in its widest sense. As produced from within, they become *conscious* afresh in the manner described in § 73, (they are not actually produced or formed for the first time). The expression, Imagination [*Einbildung* — *Innenbildung*], dates from a time when Psychology was in a very backward state. The so-called *Power of Imagining* is therefore generally synonymous with *becoming conscious.*

Only in a very few cases do we know at what time and by what definite impressions these internally excited notions were *originally* formed or produced (as intuitions), and we are consequently unable to say which of the objects represented by them were *the first* to produce an impression upon us; when, for instance, we began to form the notions House, Tree, Bush, Water, Beer, Wine, Bread, Dove, Frog, Foliage, &c., (compare § 7, at the beginning). Innumerable objects of a like kind helped us to gain these intuitions: and the similarities in them soon coalesced into Concepts,—the consequence of which is that for the most part we reproduce those notions in the Concept-form, and especially so where the reproduction follows rapidly. It is at the same time true that all these notions of the Imagination, *supposing them not to have been elaborated into* Recollections, (see above,) bear, when they return unabbreviated and unchanged to consciousness, a stamp of generality, i.e. they are applicable to many objects indifferently, and hence are fitted to form constituent parts in distinct and new notions, which we are prompted to form by external or internal stimulants. The consequence of this is that the new product is, in the main, formed out of old materials (see p. 102). Hence the development of the soul depends in a special manner on the way in which these imaginary notions are applied.

When reproduced by the object which first caused them, or by one exactly like it, they give rise to *Intuitions:* when recalled to consciousness by something other than such an object,—by a mere word, (a word is of course never a thing—an object, except in the case of vocal intuitions),—or by movable elements, they remain mere notions of the Imagination: by merely connecting them with each other afresh, we obtain all those new notions (groups and series) which were produced in us when listening to a narrative, when reading a book, when being informed about some absent object, when reflecting on passed events, &c.[5] Compare § 38.

---

[5] Imaginary notions [*Einbildungsvorstellungen*] therefore are completely different from "Fancies" [*Einbildungen*], by which, in common parlance, are understood only such imaginary notions, feelings, judgments, &c., as are false, contrary to facts. That it should be extremely difficult for us to figure to ourselves with *perfect correctness* objects which we have never beheld, from a mere description of them, is natural, since nothing but actual perception can give the exact correlative and reality corresponding to a description. Hence every one, when he at length gains a sight of an object

Closer inspection, however, shews us that there is an important difference between these imaginary notions. Some return to consciousness in a *dull, dead* way, others *with freshness*, almost as freshly as if they were just this moment formed (as intuitions). *The latter class thus remarkable for their vivacity and freshness are called Imaginary Notions simply, or Imaginary Notions in the narrow sense of the term.* What is the cause of this freshness?

It depends simply on *the way in which they were originally formed:* for the more lively the stimulants were by which they were produced, the more lively will naturally be their return to consciousness, provided they retain the fulness of their stimulation. Now the appropriation of a higher degree of stimulation depends on the *higher sensibility of the original powers:* hence a more than ordinary sensibility on their part is the condition on which the formation of imaginary notions in the narrower sense of the word depends.

In cheerful company, when in the midst of fresh and charming scenery, in joy and anger, &c., we feel that imaginary notions, even those which at other times are dull and sluggish, briefly our ordinary ones, start forward with particular vivacity. Why? Because in such cases a considerable amount of movable elements, and also of movable *stimulants*, are transferred to them, which they receive from the lively and fresh intuitions then produced, or from violent emotions and inclinations (compare § 31). Accordingly, the formation of imaginary notions in the narrower sense depends also on *the greater abundance of movable stimulants* by which they are more completely perfected.

When such vivified notions of the Imagination, which are already to a greater or less degree connected with others, are led to enter into new groups and series, because the strongest and most lively of them attract what is similar to them, and bring them simultaneously into consciousness, the consequence

---

which he has frequently imagined to himself, says, "After all, I did not think it was exactly what I now behold." This is the reason why there neither are, nor can be, two men who represent God to themselves in exactly the same manner.

is, that the remainder lose their movable elements, and with that consciousness, and then arises what is called Fancy, or the *creative* (productive) *power of imagination.* Every poem proves this. Can it be said that a new poem represents new psychical forms? Not in the least! They are rather so inter-connected in subordination to one leading notion, the liveliest of them all, e.g. the notion of wine, love, harvest, &c., and in such a novel manner (form), that they assume a special relation to it, and so constitute a drinking-song, a love or harvest-song, &c. Such a poem we call 'original' and 'clever,' when the notions so connected represent a whole which has never existed in that precise shape, and which elevates and enlivens every reader capable of comprehending it: in the contrary case, we call it 'flat,' 'insipid,' 'common-place;' &c. The epithet 'creative' applies to Fancy not as regards the content (matter) which it represents, but only as respects the mode in which it combines notions, i.e. only as respects the form: and Fancy, again, is not a *special innate* power of the soul; it can have no existence at all until lively forms are obtained, and also is itself different according as those notions are different, and that is the reason why a Fancy capable of great things in poetry may be quite powerless in Music, in Form and Colour, in Architecture, &c. The exercise of Fancy is impossible, unless the special psychical forms which it postulates have been produced in us by their appropriate objects. Every species of Fancy extends as far as there are forms forthcoming to be combined in a novel manner, and it extends no further. The higher and more unusual activity of Fancy implies no other *innate* capacity on the part of the soul to which it belongs than *a more than ordinary degree of sensibility on the part of its original powers:* given that, all its manifestations may be perfectly explained by the law of the Attraction of Similars, and by the laws regulating the genesis of consciousness (§§ 73 and 74).

Now it may be asked whether all these internal activities occur in the case of one who has had the misfortune to lose both his eyes and his power of hearing as well. Does all that which we have previously seen and heard through the instrumentality of our sense organs disappear as soon as those organs themselves are destroyed? Certainly not: abundant experience shews that the power of remembering them, of judging, of imagining, &c., continues unimpaired,—a convincing proof that our sensitive powers do not reside exclusively in the organs of sense, but in the rest of the human being as well,—where they exist we know not, and hence we cannot assign any local habitation to the permanent traces. See § 2, at the end. It is only when their energies are directed to external objects that our sensitive powers require the co-operation of corporeal organs: for their internal activities those organs are not required at all, and there are cases on record where the brain itself was partially destroyed, and yet where the original powers and the traces were unaffected. Even in our muscular powers a trace once developed remains after the loss of the muscle, and we find instances where persons after losing an arm will to strike or perform other acts with the missing member, just as if they still possessed it. Nay, they even occasionally feel pain in the hand or foot that has been amputated. Will nerves or any other material elements serve to explain this?

On the other side, we are justified in saying that our sense organs are destined not merely to support (§ 2) the powers to be developed from without *positively*, but *negatively* as well. The minute corporeal eye and ear so restrict the great mass of luminous and audible stimulants which often pour in upon us, that they are thereby prevented from overwhelming our powers. What would become of us, if the whole body were an eye, or an ear, in the same way in which it is a vital sense?

§ 76. *Complete or Partial Quiescence in the Soul; Sleep, Dreams.*

Since every sensation or perception formed by the soul requires in order to appropriate its stimulant an original power which is thereby rendered incapable of forming a second sensation (§§ 9 and 30); since, moreover, in the constant alternation of consciousness the movable elements become more and more closely attached to forms, and so are rendered incapable of producing further excitement, it follows that every day a time must come when both these kinds of elements are reduced to an extremely small number, or are totally exhausted.

The body also is equally liable to a continual loss of its powers, partly by perspiration, partly by muscular movements[h], partly

[h] In such movement the free muscular powers are transferred to the objects set in motion. Perspiration is no doubt necessary for health, but what we lose by it is force, as is invariably shewn where this loss is excessive.

by contributions levied on it by our psychical activities (the soul is perpetually withdrawing something from the body in borrowing movable elements from it), and hence the body, no less than the soul, must experience a diminution of its powers. What happens then?

Forces which have suffered a loss immediately strive after compensation for it (see §§ 25 and 26), and this is equally true of the corporeal as of the psychical. This loss, and this tendency to reparation, is noticeable after a hard day's work. We feel tired: our acts and thoughts get slower and slower, first one psychical form then another sinks into unconsciousness, and at last we fall asleep. (Compare § 30.)

But increased activity then reigns in the body, in the powers of which the body consists externally and internally. They are material powers; on them mainly depends the preservation and continuance of life; and hence we call them *vital* powers = powers of life. (For further details, see § 81.) It is these corporeal powers which are exerted during sleep to supplement the losses of the day; their activity now becomes a vital activity, i.e. the act of *assimilation and appropriation;* and hence, in the morning, we find all our lost bodily forces more completely repaired in proportion as our sleep has been better and sounder. All our limbs are invigorated, *for the material prepared for their use by digestion is appropriated by them and converted into fresh bodily powers.*

Hence, *the peculiar characteristic, the essential nature* of sleep, does not consist in our being unconscious. Even in our waking moments we are always unconscious as respects the greater part of our psychical nature,—consciousness belongs only to a very small number of our psychical forms at the same moment, and must consequently be subtracted from one form when it passes to another. Can it be asserted that this unconsciousness strengthens those forms just as sleep strengthens the body? Certainly not: on the contrary, the longer they remain unconscious, the weaker they become; or if not, yet, at least, the more difficult it is to reproduce them. Morbid sleep also, as it is called, which is only a suspension of consciousness, never strengthens the body, whence it follows that healthy, refreshing sleep cannot consist in a mere inactive unconscious state.

In § 81 we shall see that Body and Soul are subject to similar laws, and this fact is apparent in the present case. *Psychical Forms are strengthened only when in an excited conscious condition, and corporeal powers only by their special activity in sleep.* This activity is scarcely perceptible from without, indeed it seems to be absolutely non-existent; for digestion, circulation, respiration, &c., proceed as a rule slower during sleep: but as an *assimilating* activity, that activity is quite distinct from these processes. Sleep, therefore, in a healthy condition, must perpetually and regularly recur the moment the body has lost its movable elements (forces), which are resident in its internal and external organs, themselves composed of definite and closely-connected elements or traces, and the greater the loss is, the quicker and more energetically do the forces of those organs strive after compensation or reparation. When we are awake, it is true that digestible matter is also in some degree assimilated and appropriated, especially on resting from fatiguing labour, but nevertheless what is effected under such circumstances is insignificant, and can never supply the place of sleep. The approach of sleep is favoured by everything which either depresses mental life (cuts off the supply of exciting elements, especially fatiguing mental toil, and also listless reverie, want of *external* excitement), or which gives increased impetus to the bodily act of *appropriation*, such as superabundance of food, hot drinks, great bodily exhaustion, &c., &c. That during sleep our *psychical forms* are unexcited, and consequently unconscious is natural, since the *psychical* elements, which as movable elements excite them, are very deficient. Nevertheless, that peculiar activity to which we are indebted for *new mental* original powers is not absent from the soul at such a time, such powers being obtained mainly during sleep: we shall have occasion to speak further of these presently in § 82. Suffice it to say that unconsciousness is merely a concomitant of sleep, the peculiar characteristic of which consists in the *corporeal act of appropriation*, by which new *bodily* powers are formed out of the nutritive elements taken in from without, and rendered fit for that process by digestion. In old age, in proportion as we lose this power of appropriating and assimilating material, so must sleep also diminish (see § 83), and a like phenomenon may be observed as temporally co-existent with many diseases.

During sleep, however, perfect quietude does not always prevail in the soul, as is proved by the phenomenon of dreaming. How is this to be explained?

As a rule, the movable psychical elements are not *one and all* used up when sleep overtakes us, as is clear from the fact that we remain awake for a longer period when any subject particularly interests us; while, on the other hand, we easily fall asleep (e.g. in reading) when these elements are but slightly excited by external objects, and especially when all around us is still. Now, amongst our notions there are some which were often present to consciousness, and for considerable periods during the day, because they related to objects important to us. Hence, when sleep overtakes us, they maintain a greater nearness to consciousness than others; they stand, so to say, on the threshold of consciousness, and only require a slight impulse to make them again start up so far as that is possible in sleep, whilst all the rest of our forms repose in complete oblivion. The movable elements, even in their diminished numbers, are sufficient to excite them, and thus we may explain why we so often continue in our dreams the occupations of the day. Most dreams remain completely obscure processes, because our notions, owing to the paucity of exciting elements, are only aroused in *some* of their traces. Naturally enough these elements, which during sleep have no definite direction, are able to light upon those forms also of which we have been long unconscious during our waking hours, and then we dream of things which were farthest from our waking thoughts.

There is nothing astonishing in the *chequered confusion* and *extravagance* which usually prevails in our dreams. Our notions are connected in groups and series so comprehensive and so extensive that even in a waking condition they cannot be perfectly reproduced in their entirety. What must be the effect then, when, as is the case in sleep, movable elements are only present in small numbers? A group will be only partially excited, a series will be broken off when only half excited—it will now be affected by movable elements at its beginning, presently it's the end: how is it possible that the orderliness of waking consciousness (only the clearly conscious can direct!) should be preserved? It is also possible that such fragments may arise now in that series or group and then in another, and then there is no limit to the extravagant confusion and combinations of dreams.

More order and more clearness is observable in dreams when sleep, towards morning, has already produced such an abundance of fresh original powers, that external stimulants again find an easy access; or when, shortly after falling asleep, there are still so many unemployed original powers at hand that the same effect may be produced without actually causing us to awake. At such a time it is possible to suggest dreams to a sleeper, he may hear the sounds of an Eolian harp placed near the window of his bedroom, and be excited by it to visions of wondrous beauty; and, as a fact, most of our pleasant dreams occur towards morning. Of course, that such an effect should be produced by an external cause on our auditory powers a peculiar *sensibility to stimulants* is necessarily implied.

The excitation produced by the higher senses falls to a minimum about the middle of the night: sleep then is really sleep, i.e. it consists mainly in the act of appropriation then carried on by the bodily vital system. Hence, dreams then usually bear the impress of the *lower* and more purely animal *senses*, for at such a time these lower sensuous elements are all that can excite dreams. The higher and least primitive forms are in general but imperfectly and rarely conscious in dreams, and are therefore unable to correct or drive away false and immoral ideas, a fact expressed in the saying that "conscience is asleep during dreaming." Plato observed long ago that "good men permit themselves to do in dreams and in dreams only, what bad men do when awake." Here also belongs the common expression, "I never even dreamt of such a thing." Consequently, dreams prove nothing for or against a man's moral character.

If we fall asleep with a heart oppressed by care and anxiety, we need not wonder that we are visited by perturbed and painful dreams, for that which is out of tune can produce no pleasurable emotions. If you go to bed with an overloaded stomach, or if you lie so that the blood is driven to the brain, if you experience any pressure or pain in any part of the body, these unpleasant corporeal feelings will awaken what is allied to them in the soul—disgusting and painful dreams are unavoidable—take nightmare for instance. Everywhere the law prevails, that the similar attracts and excites the similar.

Dreams, then, are nothing more than the same excitation of consciousness which occurs also during our waking hours, only with this important difference, that in the latter the excitation is *perfect* and *orderly*, in the former it is *partial*, and hence, *obscure, fragmentary, and confused*. Now if waking, with its clear notions, does not predict the future for us, how can dreaming, with its blunted and obscured fancies, do so?

That so long as the dream lasts we take our fancies for realities is quite natural. The realities which surround us are in fact blocked out, because the senses are closed, and as they no longer operate on external objects, any comparison between the external and the internal is impossible; and if, when awake, we frequently fancy falsely, as every one knows we do, without perceiving our error, how is it possible that our dreaming fancies should be recognised as erroneous? That which is only obscurely conscious cannot possibly make out its bearings by reference to the unconscious. It is only when the *fundamental* forms of our soul, when *intuitions* are clearly conscious, that the continued operation of the movable elements can be rightly directed, in such a manner that an *objectively* (really) correct consciousness is produced, i.e. that a *rational* psychical proof is possible [1]. But how could intuitions, which are derived from the primitive activities

[1] [So dass eine *objectiv* (sachgemäss) richtige Bewusstwerdung eintritt, d. i. eine *vernünftige* Seelenbethätigung möglich wird. The meaning is, as I understand it, that only when we are healthy and wide awake can we rationally prove to ourselves which of our fancies are true, which false, which have an objective correlative, and which have not.]

of the senses, be excited when the senses are in such repose that they are incapable of being affected by the external world[h]?

§ 77. *Consciousness of* Psychical Processes, *which depends on Special Concepts. Internal Senses, Internal Perception.*

Experience teaches universally that children do not at first perceive their own psychical acts, though nothing is nearer to them; indeed, there are grown-up people enough of whom the same may be asserted to a great extent. They have clear intuitions of what exists and goes on without them, but their own inner life and processes remain obscure to them, and in a great measure totally unknown.

There is, however, nothing in this fact of experience which ought to astonish us. No doubt all intuitions consist in *a union between powers and their corresponding stimulants*, that is, between the *subjective* and *the objective*, and one might suppose that the soul would from the first moment perceive the *subjective* (its own powers): but it will be proved presently that such a perception requires concepts which can only arise at a later period.

All souls, without exception, begin to develope by receiving *external impressions*, and so form sensations and intuitions of the objects of the external world. These give birth to *Concepts*, and that presupposes (as we saw in § 15) that the *internal movable elements* awaken, along with a present intuition, those elements resembling it which have been already acquired. Now since intuitions are intuitions only because the objective—the stimulants—occupy the larger share of consciousness, what must happen?

The movable elements are more abundantly shed over that objective element, it attracts them with overwhelming force,

---

[h] For further details as to sleep and dreams as well, see *Beneke's* "Lehrbuch der Psychologie," 3rd edit. § 312 sqq.; the subject is pursued at still greater length in *Dressler's* "Beiträge," (mentioned at p. 82) part ii. p. 232 sqq. An important notice on Dreams will be found at the end of § 78, below.

and consequently the *stimulant* side in these psychical forms is, and must be, more vividly conscious than the *power* side of it. From this it follows that *subjective* concepts, those which spring purely from the peculiar nature of these powers, cannot at first come into existence at all. It is only when, as development proceeds, we become, as it were, sated with stimulants, that these forms can be excited more strongly on their *power* side than on the other, and then only can that side be separately presented in consciousness.

Notwithstanding, as soon as objective concepts begin to be formed, consciousness is partially diverted towards the subjective side. Consider the following.

The concept, stone, for example, contains less objectivity than the intuition of an individual stone does: for the former merely contains the *similar* constituent parts in the intuitions of stones from which it was formed, and the like is true of the concepts, Man, Mountain, House, Field, Forest, &c., as contrasted with the intuitions of particular men, mountains, &c. In order to produce such concepts, the soul necessarily exhibits greater independence and activity than is required merely to form intuitions, and by producing them it gets continually nearer to a concept of the subject. That the difference between such concepts and intuitions is, at first, but little noticed is natural, since they are, as it were, concealed by the vivid consciousness of the words by which they are designated, and also because we are obliged to give the same names to intuitions and to their corresponding concepts (see § 16). The effect of these two circumstances is that concepts ripen into clearness slowly, and therefore we only arrive very gradually at a consciousness of the *parts* contained in our intuitions.

We rise most effectually above mere sense intuitions, and therefore above the purely objective, by means of *simple* concepts, which we gain gradually, i.e. by those which involve only one mark or attribute, e.g. round, smooth, pointed, long, thin, little, &c. The intuitions from which these are gathered, could never give rise to them at all if they were all present to consciousness in their *totality:* only a fraction of them must be present. Take, for instance, the concept *pointed.* The objects from the intuitions of which this was abstracted (see the note on p. 35) were and are much more than pointed, they had and have length, thickness, weight, colour, the material of which they consist is hard, or soft, &c. And as these qualities are contained in the things themselves, so such marks are likewise contained in our intuitions of them; and yet in order to yield us the concept "pointed," all those other marks must disappear from view! the movable elements which render the concept conscious must be concentrated solely on one, viz. 'pointed,' otherwise that simple concept could never be formed. Hence, we find that

In order to form concepts, our intuitions are not always reproduced side by side in their entirety, *but mere fragments and fractions of them are presented to consciousness.*

The concept 'Intuition' springs from a number of intuitions reproduced together and almost *undivided:* so also the concepts, 'Man,' 'House,' 'Tree,' &c., likewise: but those like 'over,' 'there,' 'out of,' 'from,' 'to,' 'by,' &c., since they are strictly simple concepts, can only have been produced by *single fragments* and *fractions* of intuitions. That this may and does happen is natural, since the movable elements ebb away from points just now excited in the same quantity in which they are diffused over other points, or it may be, over some single one. In such cases the intuitions are excited as regards a minimum of their contents (their powers and stimulants), and the question arises whether the *whole* stimulant may not remain unconscious, so that the relative powers, from having the whole of the movable elements concentrated on them, would alone be conscious, to the total exclusion from consciousness of the object. And this actually does occur in the formation of many concepts.

Take the concept '*to see.*' This indicates something exclusively sensible, but *what* it is that is seen, *what* the stimulants are, it does not indicate; it represents a mere elementary *act of the soul.* Nor is the case different with the concepts to hear, touch, taste, smell, feel. Here we find the intuitions of the visible, audible, &c., brought before consciousness only on the subjective (the power) side: the stimulants are at best but faintly indicated, and as a rule are completely excluded from consciousness. Since seeing, hearing, &c., are the first acts of a child's soul, it is not to be wondered at that the concepts of them arise very early, although at first they are somewhat obscure, being produced by intuitions as yet poor in traces (compare § 55). Moreover, seeing, hearing, tasting, smelling, &c., are acts which cannot so easily be confounded together, and hence the psychical fact which lies at the bottom of them cannot be well confounded either; each power will always easily proclaim its specific character. In a similar manner, all concepts of the subjective are produced, and they may gradually rise to a clearness as great as that possessed by intuitions of external objects, indeed to greater clearness, for the spring and source of consciousness lies in the powers rather than in the stimulants.

To instance one or two more examples, take the concepts, *to desire or repel.* It is not the stimulants, but the *powers* within us directed to them, that desire or repel. This subjective community of quality coalesces when such concepts are formed, as soon as ever different desires or repulsions are reproduced together, and the objective side becomes unconscious. The same takes place in the formation of the concepts *to feel* (feeling), *to judge* (judgment), *to infer* (inference), *to think* (thought), *to will* (will), &c. On a still higher level stand those concepts of the subjective which we call the clearness, vivacity, tenacity, obscurity, &c., of the soul's acts, for the production of them requires that the powers therein regarded should only come into consciousness partially, as to a single mark and characteristic.

Observe that (as was asserted in p. 149) there are actually in the soul traces which, to a certain extent, are again divested of their stimulants—for concepts representing the subjective are composed of such traces. Moreover, these concepts are formed precisely as those of external objects are (§ 15)—their gradation also is exactly similar (§ 16). For instance, as soon as the concepts Perception, Concept, Feeling, &c., are produced, the points, common to them all, may coalesce, and form the higher concept,

Psychical Form. The only thing peculiar to these concepts is, that they are harder to form than others, because, at first, the objective presses too strongly forward, and because our psychical processes are not so permanent and fixed as external objects affecting us are. They, therefore, presuppose a careful attention to what passes within us, and what occurs there is of itself more or less conscious; they presuppose that we take the trouble *to bring simultaneously before consciousness what is allied*—these general conditions for the formation of all concepts cannot be rigidly fulfilled in the present case, and that is the main reason why they are so difficult. But if we once succeed in our attempt, future success will be assured and easier, and then concepts of the subjective arise as surely and certainly as those derived from external objects.

We know, from § 17, the fact that, as well as the reason why, concepts are decidedly clearer notions than the intuitions which lie at the base of them, or than lower concepts. That which, *ipso facto*, involves consciousness (let us call such consciousness attributive, or adjectival), is strengthened and enlightened by the homogeneous concept added to it, exactly in proportion to the quantity of light possessed by that concept; and thus, for example, if I have the concept 'Recollection,' it will enable me clearly to recognise my particular acts of recollection, (which, by their own consciousness, I should distinguish from each other, or from similar acts, imperfectly or not at all,) the moment I excite that concept into consciousness along with those acts: which excitation, for the most part, occurs spontaneously in accordance with the law of the Mutual Attraction of Similars. It is thus that the judgments arise: "this internal process is a recollection," "this a feeling," "this a desire," "this an act of will," &c. Although we do not enunciate these judgments, we still make them, and generally with such rapidity, that there is no time to express them. In such cases, then, we have what may be called substantive (independently produced) consciousness (i.e. the concept) beside the adjectival consciousness (beside the concrete act); the latter kind is apprehended or apperceived by the former; it is, as it were, perceived through a magnifying glass, whence it follows that it becomes an *object* as regards the concept apprehending it. The latter is like an internal eye apprehending this *psychical* object; it is the percipient power of it, and hence we call such concepts *Internal Senses.*

This proves that, 1°. *the internal senses* (powers percipient of the mental and spiritual) *are nothing more than those concepts which relate to the qualities, forms, and relationships of the psychical, and by which we first properly apprehend and perceive the interior of our soul.*

2°. *It cannot be said that we have only one internal sense; on the contrary, they are as numerous as the concepts that we have acquired, in which the peculiarities of the psychical have been elaborated into any special form of consciousness; the old assumption that the internal sense is one and innate is false.*

Hence, what we call internal perception, or internal sense, is but the consequent of a special kind of consciousness, which has been formed in relation to our psychical acts, and out of them. If, after it has been formed, it remains unexcited, because too much of the concrete is excited, then the activities of our soul proceed unperceived by us, and this is especially the case when they are performed with great rapidity.

The above-mentioned concepts are called the consciousness of the acts of the soul, in order to distinguish it from the proper or adjectival consciousness implied by, or rather contained in, our concrete psychical acts. The note on the following § shews in what sense this may be called *Self-consciousness.*

It is, moreover, well known that even *external* perception is but imperfectly performed if the corresponding objective concepts are wanting. For example, a man may speak his mother tongue fluently, and with a tolerable freedom from faults, without having ever perceived that he is handling substantives, adjectives, verbs, numerals, pronouns, &c. So, also, many a one sings agreeably, and yet he has never noticed that the sounds of his voice proceed in progressions of whole tones, semi-tones, thirds, fifths, &c. Moreover, a physician usually sees in his patient something more, as well as something different, from what strikes a non-professional person: the former sees by the help of determinate concepts of diseases, and therefore more clearly than the latter, even though his eyes may be sharper than those of the doctor, &c. So long, then, as those concepts are unformed which, as it were, help us to see and hear, &c., what affects our original powers and merely produces intuitions, so long is consciousness deficient in that clearness which is required in order to discriminate the object of intuition, and hence, in such circumstances, perception and observation must remain imperfect.

The lower senses only imperfectly retain what they apprehend, and hence that there should in them be more feeling and less perception proper is quite in order; and this explains why we only imperfectly distinguish the finer qualities of what we taste, smell, or feel, and why we are almost totally unable to point them out by words; for words must be absent if the concepts are absent which they were formed to represent. Compare §§ 14 and 15, and p. 129 sqq.[1]

[1] Why is it that so many men are so wanting in knowledge of themselves? They have never learnt to carefully observe their internal constitution. Why do many declare that the new psychology teaches things which do not exist in the soul? Because they are wanting in those concepts which are called internal senses. The acquisition of them, no doubt, causes some trouble at first, but that trouble is abundantly repaid. Such concepts lead to a kind of knowledge which extends far beyond the truth and certainty of knowledge acquired through the senses. The senses merely perceive external things as they *seem* to be, and if we had other senses we should apprehend those things as possessing different qualities from those which we now apprehend in them. What things are *in themselves* no sense can reveal to us; for every sense stamps its own character on its stimulants, and thus it is natural that the products of external objects are, for the most part, totally different from their factors (see p. 104). In internal perception, however, what perceives (the concept) and what is perceived (the individual psychical act or process) are completely similar so far as their subjective constituents go: *the same* psychical fact which was already contained in the object to be perceived returns in the light shed by the concept, *only that it is then multiplied*. Notion and Being are here absolutely coincident; Being, the Existent, receives nothing which could produce that kind of alteration in it which is produced by the power on its stimulant. Hence, in all psychical products, the factors producing them are preserved as-

§ 78. *On the Ego.*

The treasures of a carefully-developed soul are prodigious. It not only possesses innumerable particular forms, but the changes that go on in it are infinitely numerous. Take the case of a man who is thoroughly acquainted with three, or even more, civilized languages, and who is, besides, a mathematician, a natural philosopher, or, say, only a botanist. He must know hundreds of thousands of words, which implies thousands of notions constituting the meaning of those terms. And yet not a sign of confusion in all this marvellous complexity, which exists without any local separation, without any local limitations. What is it that mainly creates and preserves this order? *The Law of the Mutual Attraction of Similars.* Abolish that law, or interfere with it, and immediate anarchy is the result. But of all that passes in the soul, or is formed in it, this common property may be affirmed:

The moment it arises it belongs **to this soul alone,** *whether it originates in the powers of sight, hearing, touch, taste, smell, or feeling* (vital powers); *for all our powers of sense, together with the products springing from them, form one intimately connected whole,* **they are the soul.**

Consequently, the fact that they all do belong to one and the same soul will gradually shape itself into a special consciousness, i.e. a concept will arise, *having for its content this one mark: the belonging of all spiritual forms and processes to one and the same soul.*

What is this concept called?

Before answering the question we must say a word or two about our perception of ourselves (our notion of self). In per-

---

changed, for even the stimulants continue to exist in the concepts, judgments, acts of will, &c., in exactly the same shape in which they were apprehended by the original powers. Consequently, the deliverances of self-consciousness furnish us with notions which are *fully* and *absolutely* true, and they are therefore the highest to which man can attain. Compare *Beneke's* work, "Die neue Psychologie," p. 54, sqq.

ceiving and representing ourselves, *four* kinds of things may be concerned, which ought not to be confounded together. We think either, 1°. of the whole man, consisting of body and soul, as when one says, I live, I dwell at Leipsic; or we think, 2°. exclusively of the soul, as when we say, I increase in knowledge, I am immortal; or we think, 3°. mainly of acquired permanent qualities, by which we are distinguished both from others, and from that which changes in ourselves, as when a man says, I am a musician, I am an astronomer; or we mean, 4°. merely those activities of the soul which are, *for the moment, strongest* in consciousness, as when we say, I am glad, I am angry.

In all these cases it is not a concept that is directly concerned, but an intuition, a perception; for when self is expressed, as it is in the above examples, it is not as a something universal and general, but as a something particular and concrete. Now it would sound odd if a man were always to use his own name when speaking of himself, e.g. Dressler exists, Dressler is a schoolmaster, Dressler is satisfied, &c. Civilized speech requires the pronoun 'I,' in such cases—I live at Bautzen, I am immortal—a word in itself indispensable, in order to distinguish the speaker from a Thou (a person *addressed*), and from a He (a person *not addressed*), in such a manner that the hearer may know what to understand. Here the pronoun 'I' is a substitute for the *name* of the speaker: it therefore marks a definite person, either completely or partially. Now children at first always use their own name, although they have heard that pronoun a thousand times in the mouths of their parents. How is this to be explained? Why do they always say: Charles wants his dinner, Mary wants to play, and not *I* want my dinner, *I* want to play? It cannot possibly arise from a defective vocabulary, it must have a deeper cause.

In early childhood the *concept 'I'* is obviously not present. Children's *perception* of self must be imperfect; for they do not yet know that they have got a soul, and it is only the most obtrusive internal processes that are presented to their consciousness. Being as yet completely the slaves of sensation, the only clear notion that they have of themselves is that of their bodies:

the inner selves (sit venia verbo!) are too unsteady as yet to become conscious, and exist, for the most part, in an obscure condition. In general, children regard themselves to-day as 'quite different from what they were yesterday, because to-day different regions of their soul are excited; and hence their emotions are different. It can hardly have struck them yet, that everything in them belongs to one subject, to one and the same person; but at length, towards the beginning of their third year, this unity is presented clearly to consciousness, and then they cease to talk about Charles, Mary, &c., and use the term '*I*.' They have at length discovered in themselves the Unity (not the identity) of *that which represents*, and *of the notion represented;* that is to say, the connexion of these two in one thing, and this fact they express by the concept '*I*,' which results from it.

This concept grows simply out of the notion of self: perception of self must precede it, and the quicker the latter is produced, the quicker does the *concept* "I" come into existence. Moreover, (as is equally clear,) the concept remains constantly like itself; though the notion of self necessarily changes as the soul unfolds. Although, however, both are indicated by one and the same word, we are bound to distinguish them carefully: for the notion of self is a rich concrete *intuition;* the Ego or '*I*' is a strictly simple abstract *concept*, which, being one of the highest we possess, regularly attends the perception of self.

Accordingly, the concept of the Ego or 'I' is characterized as *the fusion of the active notions in our notion of self in the single mark, that the representing and the represented belongs to one and the same being, constitutes one and the same person,—a unification which equally attaches to all other psychical acts, and which therefore is gradually raised into consciousness, so that the belonging of all conscious forms and processes to one and the same soul is stamped and expressed in the concept 'I.'* [m]

---

[m] Since both from this abstract, as well as from the concrete Ego, there is excluded all consciousness of notions produced by the external world (our consciousness of external nature), both bear the name of *self-consciousness*,

It hardly requires explanation now why this concept obtains such *strength*, and such *a readiness to start into consciousness*, that in those respects it transcends all other psychical forms. At every step in the development of the soul it is increased by one trace; since whatever passes in that soul proclaims itself as belonging to it.

Moreover, it is clear that it never can attain to any sufficient completeness in *the souls of brutes*; because their untenacious original powers are not capable of leading even to a clear notion of self (§ 11). And experience shews that complete idiots are unable to develope this extremely derivative and complex kind of consciousness, nor does the *word* 'I' ever supply the want of the missing concept.

Nor is it less clear how little the healthy human soul is destined to indulge its lowest propensities, since a child of two years old is able out of its as yet imperfect notion of self to abstract a concept which belongs to the highest region of psychical development.

When we awake from sleep, the concept of the Ego awakes simultaneously, and it in particular assists in producing the illusion of our having a completely general or universal consciousness (see § 71, at the end). In children it not unfrequently happens that in the morning, for some time after they get up, they do not know what they are about, for the concept *I* is still half asleep, because the senses also are not yet completely awake.

When we are deeply absorbed in contemplating an object, the exciting elements are withdrawn from this concept, because they are wholly concentrated on the form, by the help of which we are thinking the thing before

---

which, (in a wider sense,) is also the term used to express the consciousness *of* our *individual* psychical processes or internal perception; for this kind of consciousness also is opposed to that which we have of external things. See the preceding §.

One question more. Can selfishness be engendered by this abstract Ego? Never! Selfishness is engendered solely by our connecting our estimates of objects more with our *notion of ourselves* than with those which we make of the persons of others. If we co-ordinate our estimates of objects mainly with that group of notions which represents ourselves, we shall almost invariably seek them, and use them only so far as they may produce some advantage to ourselves, and that leads to selfishness, to self-seeking. But if, on the contrary, we co-ordinate them with those groups of notions by which we think of others, that association will lead us to kindliness for them, we shall apply the advantage to be found in valuable objects not to our own benefit, but to theirs. Of course that other or those others must be persons whom we regard as of value to us. How they become that has been sufficiently pointed out in § 57.

us, and then we forget ourselves, our ego: we do not notice that it is *we* who are thinking.

The consciousness of the Ego is notably absent in dreams, because there are by no means enough exciting elements present to arouse its multitudinous traces; and thus may be explained why we do not remember that we are a totally different person from that which the cunning jugglery of dreams represents us to be. In earlier days I have dreamt many a time with anguish that because of my ignorance I had been obliged to leave the University, return to school, and begin all over again. And yet it ought to have been easy to scare this trouble away, if I had only said: 'You are a director of a seminary, and your real concrete self is totally different from that of a senior boy at a school.' This judgment, however, did not present itself to my consciousness, because the true notion of myself remained unexcited; and it was necessarily unexcited, because the *concept "I"* continued to sleep. *Very* painful dreams not uncommonly cause such a disturbance that this concept must awake, and then we are glad to be freed from our imaginary torments by the complete awakening which is implied by it [a].

§ 79. *On Reason and Rationality, or Capacity for Reason.*

The external world contains nothing but *objects* and their *activities*. These produce effects on us as soon as we are born, and continue to do so as long as we live. Now if we had in our soul nothing but forms exactly corresponding to the things and effects thus produced, there would be nothing to astonish us in the phenomena of our psychical life. But we find within forms to which the external world offers but faint counterparts, and in some respects offers none whatever. To instance only a few: the external world (with the exception of men and brutes) has no intuitions, no concepts, no judgments, no inferences; no efforts like those of men, therefore no desires, no repugnancies, no will, no estimation of good and evil; no conscience, no morality, no religion,—in short, it has none of those higher objects which rest on man's supersensible ideas. Now what the external world does not possess, that it can never give

[a] Compare, on this and the preceding §, the essay, '*Ist Beneke Materialist?*' p. 20, sqq.

us; and if it be objected, that at any rate there are teachers capable of infusing all this into us; it may be answered that the remark is worthless: for teachers, when all is said and done, can give us nothing but words, (which differ in every language,) and sense-impressions like those produced by lifeless objects; and all these are far from being the forms which we possess, and what is more, *consciously* possess. Or are the words or other effects produced by a man, as soon as they have left him, *self-conscious* elements with which he transmits consciousness to us? If so, a forest must have consciousness when it re-echoes my name to me, and the snail must forthwith know what I mean when I tell it to get out of the way.

No! the self-conscious lives only in the souls of men, and cannot travel out of them. The external world excites us, but by elements which are in themselves spiritually and mentally dead, and it is impossible by them to vivify the dead. That this dead something creates life, *mental* life in us, is a consequence solely of the powers and laws innate in us, which, however, at our birth, are widely different from the products afterwards developed from them. How are these products brought into existence? The present treatise has hitherto striven thoroughly and systematically to answer this question, and, as we hope, not without success. If any one after mature consideration does not find our explanations satisfactory, we must leave him to his own devices.

Suffice it to say, that the original powers of our soul (this will have been made clear) are, at first, *sentient* only; but by excitation and education they become consciously *intuitive, attentive, understanding, judging, desiderative, averse, willing, feeling, &c.* They thus attain to forms of development which are *purely their own* work, and they thus raise themselves above all that is sensible and material. They win an independence and freedom, as against the external world, such, that the latter with its forces is compelled to submit to the prescripts of the soul, so far, that is, as the powers of man can control nature.

Everything which is thus formed *normally* in us, we call collectively by the title *Reason:* what deviates from it we call un-

reasonable, or *contrary to reason;* whilst the word 'irrational' indicates not something blamable, but mere *deficiency* in reason; for irrational things may be very valuable. It is only those higher products of our soul, however, which lie far removed from the region of sense, that we dignify by the name of rational, and hence Reason is nothing but

The sum total of our highest faultlessly *developed psychical forms in all their shapes: whether as notions, efforts, feelings, remembrances, attentions, fancies, æsthetic creations, moral and religious feelings, or actions, &c.*

Take the superstitious man, for example. He is justly stigmatized as 'unreasonable,' because he denies the truth of the higher concepts of cause and effect rigidly deduced from carefully observed connexions and reciprocal actions of things. In like manner he flies in the face of reason, who renders himself a slave to excess, especially to the baser pleasures; for those desires and aversions alone which *harmonize* with the *true* gradation of goods and evils, in other words, with their real value, deserve to be called *rational*. 'Morally good' is another name for the same thing.

Now it is self-evident that Reason, thus understood, cannot be any single, any *innate* power. So long as our original simple sensations have not been worked up into higher and more complex forms, have not been elaborated in accordance with the laws of the soul, so long must such Reason be totally absent; and even supposing such forms have been acquired in certain relations, still a man must be irrational in all others where such have not yet been obtained. For instance, a person may be very rational in Mathematics, and destitute of reason in Music, and he who has a good deal of reason in matters of Chemistry does not on that account have any in Philosophy, &c.

Hence, it follows further, that the Reason certainly cannot be met with *equally* in all men; it must differ in them according as a favourable education has produced these higher forms in one with more perfection than it has in another. Compare in this respect an educated German or Englishman with an Esquimaux or Hottentot chief who is reckoned among his countrymen as a man of superior knowledge: the difference between the two in this case is certainly obvious.

This difference may be produced by two totally different causes. It may be that the *innate tenacity of the original powers* in the German or Englishman is greater than in the Esquimaux or Hottentot; but it is also possible that the former may live under circumstances *more favourable to development* than the latter. Of course, the spontaneous activity of the soul must in itself produce higher forms out of lower ones, and yet the influences exercised by good teaching, by a suitable form of polity, by trade, and intercourse, &c., must greatly assist in producing these results. Why do we Germans possess all our numerous educational establishments, unless they promote the development of the soul? These institutions enable us to stand on the shoulders of all past ages. The Esquimaux, &c., if destitute of the tenacious original powers of the German, would not become, even in our schools and universities, a rational German or Englishman; for the same reason we see scholars in one and the same school, and of the same ages, attain to very different grades of mental development.

So we come round perpetually to the same proposition: that it is the innate *tenacity* and strength of the original powers on which alone depend, not merely the higher and highest Forms (the Reason), but also the *mass* or *degree* to which that development can be carried. In the soul, as elsewhere, nothing valuable can be made out of what is weak. Since, however, all healthy human souls, as compared with those of brutes, are endowed with *greater* tenacity and strength, we may, if we please, call that quality, *potential Reason*, or a *capacity* for reason, and hence it is clear that Reason is *innate* only so far as that tenacity exists. We must, therefore, carefully distinguish the developed reason—reason *proper*, from innate reason. The latter is only the germ, the disposition to become reasonable: it is identical with what we in a former passage called the *mental* or *spiritual* part of man's soul, which may be called its *natural rationality*. This *property*, however, of the original powers of man is found mainly in the higher senses, in those of *sight*, *hearing*, and *touch*, these being the chief sources of human reason *. (See § 8.)

Rationality or Reason, therefore, does not reside in a *special* power, as it were in a corner of the human soul, from which it forces its way, and gradually ennobles the remaining faculties; but those very powers which we call sensitive, i.e. receptive of external impressions (see § 5), are at once spiritual and rational, nor are there in the human soul any elementary powers whatever which are destitute of all rationality. Hence, an infant's very first act of sight, hearing, &c., is totally different from that of a brute, and (be it well observed) even such acts of sensation are very early manifested in children in a manner quite different from that which is observed in the case of the lower animals. As thirst is only the thirstiness of the palate and stomach, so mind is only the mentalness of our psychical powers; but with this important difference, that the thirst is transient, whereas this mental nature is permanent, and increases. Therefore, the mind and rationality of man is nothing apart from his soul, it is only a property of his original powers, which leads to consciousness and to products unlike any evolved in a brute. These products

* Why is it that persons born blind, whose most powerful and tenacious sense is closed, are not so backward in point of intellectual development as those who are born deaf, and are able to cultivate the sense of sight? Because the man born deaf cannot participate in the uncommon advantage offered by verbal speech, considered as the medium by which mutual mental instruction is communicated. He who can hear another speak is able to acquire the whole sum of mental treasures which thousands before and contemporaneously with him have gained. In like manner he is able—a matter of no less importance—to retain with far greater perfection (compare pp. 13 and 100) groups and series of psychical forms by connecting them with words and propositions, than if they were left to themselves, in which case they would soon fall asunder again. If the latter happens, it becomes impossible to raise those forms to any higher condition within by internal elaboration of them, and such, as a rule, is the case with those born deaf. The person born blind, moreover, can supply a good deal which the want of sight deprives him of, by means of the sense of touch, as well as by other senses: for though the mark of what is coloured is unknown to them, yet the real and objective part of things is not.

taken together constitute the mind in the narrow sense of that word, and hence, the developed reason, or reason *proper*. (Compare § 10 at the end, and the note in § 69 [p].)

§ 80. *Varied Combinations of the Qualities of the Psychical Powers. Temperaments.*

The innate qualities of the original powers of our soul we are already acquainted with (see §§ 5, 7, 8, and 14).

If we consider their mutual relations in general, we find that *tenacity* in all healthy souls is greater in the higher senses, lower in the lower (§ 8): *sensibility* is sometimes greater in one system of powers, sometimes in another (§ 5): and *quickness* seems to be in the highest degree peculiar to hearing (§ 14), that is, *speaking generally*. For on comparing individual men together we find these qualities very variously combined.

To take the power of *sight*, for instance, we may find them in one man,

a. in a *high* degree tenacious, sensitive, and vivacious as well; or while *very* tenacious, they may be but *moderately* sensitive and vivacious; or they may join a *high* degree of tenacity with only *small* sensitiveness and vivacity. Moreover, they may be

b. only *moderately* tenacious, and in a *high* degree sensitive and vivacious; or but *poorly* tenacious and highly sensitive and lively, or

c. they may be *moderately* tenacious, and *moderately* sensitive and lively; or they may have a *low* degree of tenacity combined with little sensibility and vivacity. There are many other combinations of the kind; since every degree of tenacity, from the highest to the lowest, may be supposed to be combined, and may really be found in combination with every degree of sensitiveness and liveliness.

---

[p] The subject which is merely sketched in this § will be found thoroughly discussed in an essay by *Dressler*, "*Ueber das Wesen und die Bildung der menschlichen Vernunft*," in *Diesterweg's* "Pädagogisches Jahrbuch auf 1864."

Equally different may be the combinations as respects hearing, touching, tasting, smelling, and the vital powers. When one reflects that in the above examples we have specified only *three* different degrees (high, moderate, and small), whereas, in fact, an endless number of degrees and gradations are to be found, it is easy to infer how infinitely various and infinitely numerous the combinations of these qualities of our powers may be. And in reality we do not find two men who are exactly alike in these respects.

We have already had occasion several times to point out the influence exercised by this kind of combination on the evolution of the human soul.

Thus we find generally, that a higher degree of *tenacity* produces greater strength and clearness in the psychical forms (§§ 7, 10, 53, 54, 55), more *sensitiveness* gives them greater richness, complexity, and delicacy (§§ 5, 10, 50); greater *vivacity* causes a quicker apprehension, elaboration, and consciousness of the impressions (§§ 14, 21). Consequently, where a man is endowed with these three qualities in a high degree, it naturally follows that very favourable relations are offered for the evolution of his soul. Possibly we might venture to call such a texture of soul 'a *choleric* temperament.'

It often happens that one quality so predominates over the rest as to prove anything but an advantage.

Thus we find men, for instance, who combine a low degree of *sensitiveness* and *vivacity* with a high degree of *tenacity*. It is natural that they should be wanting in those products which result from an equally high sensitiveness and vivacity. Such a man may indeed develope such forms as are produced in him into great clearness and strength, yet they can never attain to great variety, to great multiplicity and subtilty, nor can he apprehend them quickly, or elaborate them, or bring them rapidly into consciousness; for great tenacity joined to defective vivacity cause these psychical acts to be performed with too much slowness. This kind of disposition is commonly designated '*phlegm.*'

A totally different effect is produced when the vivacity of

a man's powers greatly predominates over their tenacity and sensitiveness. In such a case we find impressions quickly apprehended, elaborated, and rendered conscious: but the retention of them after they have ceased to operate, a firm and deeply rooted hold on them, great clearness and strength as well as the abundance, multiplicity, and delicacy of psychical forms, is absent. We find such men quickly take up any subject, they throw themselves into anything heartily, but they are not steadfast in their efforts, not deep in their feelings, and but superficial as to their knowledge. We may perhaps venture to place them in the class of '*sanguine*.'

It is different again when *sensitiveness* greatly prevails over the other qualities of our powers. In such a case, since the soul, from its want of tenacity, is unable to attain to strength and clearness, over-stimulation (compare § 36) must easily take place, and this being likewise defective in vivacity cannot soon pass away, but must be long permanent; and thus a foundation is laid for defective psychical forms of all kinds, such as fear, sensitiveness, selfishness, ill temper, &c. Possibly such a disposition is to be looked for in the '*melancholic*.'

The mode, therefore, in which these several qualities are combined at birth, exercises a most important influence on our psychical development, so important, that as these relations vary, so must *the whole developed condition* of the soul be different. Hence it is that no two men, even if their external conditions are *completely similar*, can possibly exhibit exactly the same results in their development (see the note on p. 30). Although directly after the birth of a child these different modes of combination are scarcely perceptible, still their constant and progressive influence confirms the old truth that 'great effects spring from little causes.'

The whole constitution of soul arising from the innate differences between the several qualities of the original powers and their combinations is called a man's Temperament.

If we are now convinced that the various degrees and modes in which these qualities may be combined are infinitely numerous, we may at once declare that the various 'temperaments' are equally numerous and complex, and that the old-fashioned attempt to divide all men in this respect into *four* classes (the *choleric*, *sanguine*, *melancholic*, and *phlegmatic*) cannot possibly lead to any valuable results: moreover, instead of deducing these temperaments from the soul itself, they erroneously attempted (as they frequently do now) to explain them from peculiar qualities of the blood and other fluids. It is true enough that the bodily constitution, as a whole, the different powers of which have, in different men, different degrees of tenacity, vivacity, and susceptibility, exercises no contemptible influence on temperament; but the psychical, after all, is what decides it; and as many a man possesses a dull body, but a quick and lively mind, so there are others whose body is strong enough, though their mind is weak, and so on.

It must be allowed, that this division into four classes, where nothing more than a rough outline is required, occasionally enables us to hit off the characteristics of individual men excellently well; but it is useless for scientific purposes, for there these special, not general, peculiarities are all-important, whereas, out of a thousand cases, you can scarcely find two that exactly resemble each other in point of temperament.

What, then, ought we properly to understand by 'Temperament,' and how many temperaments are there? The *natural* and *complete* similarity of all men, so often asserted to exist, is, accordingly, a palpable fiction. Even at their very birth there are no *two* human beings alike, whether in body or in mind; how can they, then, afterwards become so, when these innate dissimilarities are constantly multiplied in the course of evolution? To suppose that the souls of brutes and men are at first precisely similar in all respects, and that there is not so much as a difference *of degree* between them, is totally inadmissible. Even the noblest brutes are in psychical power essentially *inferior* to men. Compare p. 17.

§ 81. *Force and Matter; Soul and Body.*

Formerly, the following was the way in which people regarded Force and Matter (that out of which something is made, bodies). *Force* or power, it was said, *is that which lives and acts* in *matter*, for matter was looked upon as being *dead*, hence they said, Plants (for instance) have different powers, as a power of tanning or healing, &c.

The more modern view correctly declares, that *there is no such thing whatever as absolutely dead matter; that all bodies in God's world are life, and nothing but life, i.e. living power and living force, but it maintains that this vitality exists in different degrees.* Accordingly, a plant cannot be said *to possess* powers, it is power and force and nothing else—*a system of divers powers,* which appear to our senses as something long, broad, thick, heavy, coloured, &c., &c.; in short, appear as that which we call body, material, matter, or, if you please, substance. Hence we ought to say, 'Force is what acts in all *that occurs*'—in what happens or is done by things, be they material or spiritual; for only by such an expression is the essential activity of objects set in a true light. If force and matter were two distinct things, were they actually opposed to each other, it would follow that we must be able to separate, e.g. in plants their forces, or powers from the dead material. But cut a body into its smallest particles, divide it mechanically or chemically, as much as ever you desire, or are able, and you will never light upon a power without matter. Force and matter will always be found united; they are never separable except in thought, just because they are, in fact, one thing, i.e. force or power. What follows will serve to explain this.

Men and brutes require nourishment in order to exist. When they have taken food it is changed by chemical metamorphosis, so far as it is capable of being assimilated, into blood. The blood deposits its constituent parts over the body, and these parts are required by the body in different places where it has suffered loss and decay. Thus the organism is renewed daily, and obtains new powers by the nutriment which it takes in. If the material thus acquired was the opposite of force or power, whence did those powers come? Yes, it is said, it is exactly these forces which are appropriated; all else, both in men and brutes, is afterwards expelled. If so, forces must be liberated or extracted from materials or substances, a thing unheard-of in physiology or in chemistry. Matter and force, even in the sharpest chemical separation, remain one. What these Power-substances are in themselves, and how they may have originally come into existence, we do not know: all that we see is certain materials taken into the body, and bodily power as the result of doing so.

Nor does any separation we can effect shew us dead matter—matter deprived of its forces. In the dung, out of which 'Force' is grown in the fields for us, we see every day that chemical combinations which were no longer of use to the organism turn again into 'Force,' and they do so by entering into fresh combinations. Where, then, does this Force cease? Can we wonder that there are creatures which live on our excrement? that the wood-worm, the clothes-moth, consume what is apparently dead? Why even the seemingly dead metals, like iron, quicksilver, sulphur, when introduced into the organism, shew life and force; for they enter into combination with the elements of which our body consists, and then operate as curative or detrimental agents, according as the physician applies them.

We are forced back to the proposition, *that in God's world all is living force.* If the stone or the tiles on the roof were absolutely dead, they would be incapable of change. But bring them into contact with things for which their elements have a chemical affinity, and they will immediately exhibit an external change. Capacity for chemical combination appears, in such a case, to be universally possessed, such as may be conjectured to have operated at the very origin of the so-called dead natural bodies (earths, metals, &c.) But, in order to conceive how a plant could be formed, we shall at once find this universal capacity for chemical combination possessed by the original materials insufficient. For, as all things on the earth are compounds of the same fundamental elements (of which we already are acquainted with about seventy), the question arises, what determines their infinitely multifarious combinations, which are never casual, planless, but always consistent in this plant, just as in that. Who says to the elements here you must combine in this manner, there in that? The question recurs with redoubled force, when we consider how the bodies of brutes and men have been produced: they likewise consist of a combination of precisely identical elements. Obviously all these connexions require something beside the fundamental elements with their mere chemical action; something which compels them to produce bodies formed in this way or that: bodies, too, which invariably reproduce themselves in the same shape, so that the species and genera of things remain constantly what they were. These bodies also continue to live in the mode once adopted for a considerable period, though at last they fall to pieces; and the latter fact is incomprehensible, if we are to suppose that all is produced by chemical forces only; for the elements lose none of their peculiarities. Whence, then, this dissolution of the body which we term death? The dictum that 'it is a law that so it should be' explains nothing: what you here call a law must be based on something superadded to mere chemical action. These purely chemical processes are, in fact, not our friends merely, *they are also our bitterest enemies*, as the experience of every day proves. In a dead body the chemical combination of elements still continues—they are, indeed, paramount; yet the corpse does not by them acquire fresh life—it tumbles to bits. Chemical action, therefore, and the preservation of the vital force, are two distinct things. What is it, then, by which the bodies of creatures so infinitely various are formed and kept living for a definite time?

In plants this fundamental cause is usually called '*a Type*,' '*a Principle*,' &c.; for people are shy of talking about the soul of a plant, which would explain everything; but we shall hardly be able to escape from such an assumption. The concept 'Principle' is still less applicable to the bodies of brutes and men: the *primum agens*, in their case, must, at any rate, be called *soul*, or else we find ourselves in the region of contingency and chance. Souls evidently are what arrange the original materials, control them, and direct their operations, until they are again separated from those materials, whereupon the latter simply continue to exercise their chemical powers.

It is true that the concept 'Soul' involves the mark of sensation and voluntary movement, which is absent from plants, with a few exceptions, and therefore we are willing to dispense with that term as a name for their prime active principle, although we do not see why plants should not have souls. That which is contained in the seed of a plant as 'a developmental law' is not, at any rate, a *peculiar vital force*, like those which were formerly falsely assumed for every creature not absolutely dead; for all elements are, as such, living, though they live in different degrees; but it is a kind of soul, and where, consequently, this essence, this prime agent in uniting matter, is wanting, there we find no orderly organic development. On the other hand, where it causes the elements fit for a *pink* or for a *melon* to unite, there we find that in the one case a pink, in the other a melon, comes into existence. The ultimate cause in all this can only be the Creator.

From this mode of stating the matter, it follows that the laws according to which our body is developed can only be clearly learnt by studying the soul; and by way of entering a little further into the subject, we may make the following brief remarks.

1°. The soul requires for its evolution external elements, which produce an effect on its original power (senses): the soul tends towards these elements (stimulants), and appropriates them. These acts are preserved in the form of traces, which distinctly differ from each other according to the elements from which they arise.

The case is exactly similar with our body. None of its external or internal organs can grow or be preserved if food from without is denied it. Even as an embryo and fœtus it strives after this by growing out of and feeding on the blood derived from its mother's body. After birth, this effort is manifested as hunger. The body appropriates the food obtained in consequence of that feeling by digestion and assimilation, though, at the same time, fresh air, warmth, light, electricity, &c., nourish it; and thus its parts grow larger and stouter by new elements being added to the old, which continue to exist as traces, i.e. the acts by which the organs are formed become quiescent, and cease to be excited.

2°. In the soul, elements (original powers and stimulants), not yet firmly conjoined, flow, in the shape of movable elements, from one psychical form to another, and accumulate on the more fixed of them: by this process quiescent, and therefore unconscious, forms are roused into consciousness, painful forms are driven away by pleasant ones, and conversely, &c.

In the body we find exactly similar phenomena. Its fluid and movable particles (contents of cells, lymph, blood) spread on all sides, and are deposited on what is already consolidated, which acts likewise, widely different as they are from those just described, continue in the form of traces when they cease to be excited. The blood has a special organ, the heart, for distributing it about: a muscle well used is strengthened by these movable elements, an unused one gets weak; the stimulant of a sensitive nerve is propagated to a motor nerve (e.g. writhing in pain), and the whole nervous system may be got to sympathize with the diseased state of one or more nerves. It is, of course, well known that sickly and disorganized parts of the body may be restored to a healthy condition by this distribution of forces produced by exercise (e.g. walking); but it has not hitherto been explained by assuming that, in such a case, healthily acting elements are transferred to those which are morbid and unhinged, by which means the latter are restored to a sound condition. Yet what is called 'the healing power of nature' obviously consists in such a transference.

3°. In the soul, like attracts like, and fuses into one whole.

This law prevails in the body as well. The fresh material is so connected with the old that it assumes a similar character to the latter. Accordingly, the original formation of the body, such as occurs in the mother's womb, is as it were the prototype and original which will be copied all our life long. Fresh hair and nails are always like the old: lost tissue (skin, bone) is reproduced in such a way, that, at least, it, in the main, resembles the old: even deformities, provided they originated when the body did, continue themselves, e.g. six fingers instead of five, a crooked spine, and later growth and development does not transform them into something opposite to what they were first, and so on.

4°. The life and energies of the soul, as will be seen in the following paragraph, are propagated from within outwards by the perpetual formation of fresh original powers.

After what has been stated, it needs no detailed exposition to shew that the body does the same. It would be impossible for the materials received to be turned into new corporal powers, unless the chemical activity of the elements were forced by the body, so far as it at present exists, to form a substance resembling itself; whilst it produces the substance of a tree in the case of a tree. The soul it is that invariably conforms these substances to that total form which we call bodily organization. No doubt the original pattern of the body which the soul contains within itself may be distorted by violent external influences, and so the body may be abnormally formed, for the soul is not omnipotent.

We arrive, then, at this result. The old view which held that the body is dead matter, and nothing but matter, and that it stands in the strongest possible contrast with the soul, must be pronounced an error, because both body and soul are developed in accordance with similar *laws* [a]. In its connexion with the soul the body must rather be regarded as a system of living *forces*, a truth of *the highest importance in explaining the reciprocal action between the two.*

That such a reciprocal action takes place no one denies. Thus, for instance, after great mental exertion, we find our body tired, and, conversely, a violent strain on the latter fatigues the soul. Moreover, it is acknowledged that a contented, cheerful temper is conducive to health, as, on the other hand, that bodily sickness is detrimental to the well-being of the soul.

What an influence is exerted on all our bodily activities by mental excitement, e.g. joy, anger, desire for revenge, &c.! The pulse is quickened, respiration is shorter and more hurried, the

---

[a] On the wide difference between Force and Law, see the note on p. 52.

whole expression of the face, the whole attitude of the body, is changed. And, on the other side, what a commotion is produced in the soul by bodily excitement, e.g. by spirituous drinks. Have there not been many poets and composers who were only able to unchain their fancy by a bottle of wine, mainly because they gradually accustomed themselves to excitement produced by such means? Now the absolutely dead can neither excite nor be excited, and, consequently, in the reciprocal action of body and soul, *living force acts on living force*, and the whole of that process consists in nothing but the immediate transference of the movable elements from the one part to the other. Thus the excitement and liveliness of the body is of advantage to the soul, and, conversely, a powerfully excited soul must promote the activities of the body. The well-being of the body is extended to the soul directly it feels itself enlivened, and the same effect is produced on the body by the soul when *the latter* is in thorough good order. Any diminution of well-being is equally propagated from one to the other, whether it be the soul or the body that is directly disordered.

The examples already instanced at the end of § 39 shew that these mutual influences are not completely indeterminate and general in their mode of occurrence; they are, for the most part, subject to rule, and depend on fixed associations between bodily and psychical forms, established from the time of birth by the transferred elements which are passed from one to the other. *Indeed, from the very first, Body and Soul are mutually transferable*, since they mutually interpenetrate; consequently the soul does not dwell in the body, as a bird does in a cage, or a captive in a prison. But whenever the corporeal and the psychical are *often* mutually excited, this general and vague interconnection turns into a *special*, a *more intimate and intense* union. Such mutual excitation occurs, in particular, between those bodily muscular powers and those systems of psychical powers which are capable of influencing the muscles. For as the law of the formation of traces is equally valid both for soul and body, a portion of the exciting psychical element remains attached to the act excited as a connecting trace; and consequently where, at first, we found only a general and vague connection, there we afterwards find, so far as the joint excitation of the two extends, a more *intimate* union established.

The reason, then, why my fingers perform with such precision and readiness the different movements implied in writing, playing the piano, violin, or the muscles concerned in speaking, go through the complicated acts necessary to form vocal sounds, &c., is this. Between them and the forms of the soul *connecting traces* exist, by which the exciting elements produced by the soul receive their peculiar direction, owing to the fact that, in this case also, out of several points united, those are first excited which are most closely connected (compare p. 198). In exactly the same manner, associations formerly established explain the peculiarities which men exhibit, and why it is that many find their thoughts flow more freely and better when they are walking, another when standing, a third when sitting, a fourth when lying down; why many people always wake at a particular hour, or can only sleep soundly when all is still, while others, e.g. millers, enjoy the best of sleep in the midst of a considerable noise, &c.

But does not this mode of explanation throw Body and Soul, after all, into one and the same class? Certainly not. For although everything in God's world is *Force*, and hence ought to be called so, yet anybody can see at once that there is a great difference between the innumerable forces which exist on earth. According to the common and well-known division, they are distinguishable into the material and immaterial; and the former again into the organized and the unorganized. No one denies that the organized (men, brutes, and plants, so far as they are of a material nature) stand far higher in the scale of perfection than the unorganized (minerals). But immaterial or psychical forces are a still higher and nobler kind. As from the very first *every class* of these immaterial forces has, like the material and organized, its own definite form, so *every particular* power receives, in the course of development, its own peculiar form (the forms of notion, desire, concept, &c.); and these forms are more *exact, more delicate, and more complex* than the forms of organization exhibited by material things. To these immaterial forces belong the souls of brutes and of men. Now, if the possession of feeling and voluntary movement raises the lowest brute soul far above the forces of plants and those of the brute and human body, which of themselves never exhibit any feelings, what is to be said of the clearly conscious soul of man? Of all the mundane forces with which we are acquainted it stands highest in the scale of perfection.

That the souls of men are immediately connected with bodily forces and powers proves, unquestionably, that the psychical and the corporeal must have a certain affinity with each other; for how else could they possibly be connected? But besides those properties by which the forces of the soul are enabled to contract such a connexion with those of the body, the soul must possess other qualities which essentially difference it from the body. If this is true of the two kinds of forces in brutes, it is *à fortiori* true of those connected in man, and the question therefore may be asked: *in what does the fundamental distinction between the psychical and corporeal forces of man consist?*

The soul incessantly catches up external stimulants, and appropriates them: by this its original powers transform the innate *capacity* of becoming conscious into *actual* consciousness, and retain it even when, by the removal of the stimulant, it turns again from the excited to the unexcited condition, or to a trace. The body likewise daily appropriates nutritive elements from the external world, but its powers never become conscious by so doing.

All the powers of the soul developed by stimulants, and thus carried on towards perfection, follow their respective affinities and fuse into a whole, the effect of which is, that *more clearly conscious* forms are produced in proportion as the traces from which they result are more numerous; but however complex the resulting whole may be, however varied may be their association into groups and series, still they never produce *anything extended*. In doing all this the soul never swells or enlarges the head, however much it may have enlarged its acquisitions by study. In the body, also, the homogeneous powers derived from nutritive material increase, as long as the body is growing, and the forms thus produced increase, in respect of traces, just as the soul does; but in so doing the body becomes larger and larger, *it increases in extension locally, whereas, left to itself, it never can become conscious:* only so long as the soul lives in connexion with it, and is itself excited to consciousness, can the bodily forces be raised to consciousness by special excitation. Consider the stomach, which, when hungry, manifests itself to consciousness; the intestines, which, if violently excited, become painful; the muscles, which, after great exertion, become likewise conscious in a disagreeable manner. The indispensable condition, however, for this is that the nerves of sensation resident in those parts should be connected with the corporeal central organ—the brain, and that connexion must be continuous, and neither broken nor impeded by anything, and also that the soul be not in a state of syncope or profound sleep. Just as completely external elements, air, sound, odour, &c., become conscious, so the bodily powers become so when, and only when, they are appropriated by the psychical powers, and are *simultaneously excited along with them.* The relation in which the soul stands to the consciousness of the corporeal is that of an internal sense apprehending it, just as the internal senses, spoken of in § 77, were related to purely psychical objects. But if the soul has fled, no amount of excitement can produce consciousness in the body; its power of becoming *conscious along with the soul,* of concomitant consciousness, is lost. Accordingly, it is clear what constitutes the special distinction between the soul and the so-called material body.

In accordance with the law of the formation of traces the soul acquires **consciousness,** *and* **increases** *it by the mutual attraction of similars; but all the while it remains* **spaceless;** *whereas corporeal matter, according to the same law, gains only in* **local extension** *and* **fixity,** *and at last becomes* **rigid** *and unchangeable.* For details, see § 83.

On examining the development of consciousness in the soul in detail, it is found that it, too, does not attain to an *equally vivid* consciousness in all its powers (§§ 7, 10, and in other places): on the contrary, it exhibits gradations of clearness and distinctness, which qualities are less in proportion as the tenacity of its powers are smaller; and thus, at last, the soul, with its powers which are lowest in point of tenacity, interdigitates and mingles with those *bodily* powers which are highest in that respect; though psychical powers, however weak, are always superior to those of the body, however strong. There being, then, decidedly a distinct difference between soul and body, it is idle to talk of an identity between the two; but at the same time we have just as little right to assert a rigid opposition between them; both together, by their intimate union, form that being, Man, who, from the strength and tenacity of the original powers of his soul, stands highest among all the creatures of this earth.

We have already explained, in the note to § 46, and further illustrated in § 76, the fact that, as well as the reason why, those powers are called *vital powers* which together make up man's body. Besides these, however, there are also vital powers of a *purely psychical* nature, namely, those of the so-called 'common sense[1],' which is diffused over the whole of the exterior and interior of the body, and is not, like sight, &c., bound to particular bodily organs. They are open to the impressions which we receive from warmth or cold, from pressure, from the sultriness of the air, from tickling, &c. Of all psychical powers they come nearest to those of the body; and their *feelings* are so like those of the body, that we are often unable to accurately distinguish the two; and, in fact, we, for the most part, indicate both by the same words (pleasant, unpleasant, painful, oppressive, racking, irritating, and the like).

From this account of the matter it may be seen that the New Psychology does not leave the body aside as undeserving of attention, but takes a due account of it. Still, it is unable to attach that great importance to peculiarities of organization which are so much insisted on by physiologists, phrenologists, and especially by materialists; according to their view, the brain and nerves, their structure, their parts and functions, are of supreme importance in explaining the life of the soul. We acknowledge the value

---

[1] [See p. 32.]

of enquiries into our bodily constitution; they are of the highest importance to the physician; but psychology has hitherto gained next to nothing by all the discoveries of anatomy and physiology; nor will it gain much in time to come, for *self-consciousness* alone can explain mental facts. The body merely serves as a *force* to support the soul (§ 2), for the soul is its superior, and by its directing agency even the organization of the body is produced. Materialists would prefer to reverse this proposition, for they assert that the phenomena of the soul are merely 'so-called,' they are the effects of man's more delicate bodily organization, and a soul as an entity apart from the body has no existence. This the New Psychology can never concede, and all we have hitherto said shews why it cannot do so. Any corpse proves that the body alone neither *thinks* nor *feels* nor *wills*; and this is what might be expected, seeing that the spiritual and material, notwithstanding all their affinities, are, and ever remain decidedly distinct things.

That the brain is the chief and central organ for the support of our psychical activities no one will deny, nor need it be disputed that therefore something depends on the size of it, although experience shews that dwarfs, in spite of their small brain, are often mentally more clever than giants with their large ones. As to the phrenologists, they really ought to see into what palpable contradictions they fall with the strange mental powers which they invent, such as 'philoprogenitiveness,' 'love of unity,' 'combativeness,' 'secretiveness,' 'acquisitiveness,' 'love of praise,' &c. Our psychical forms may, without being changed, form part of groups and series of the most diverse kinds; and by so doing they become interwoven and crossed one with another, so as to form a kind of variegated web. From this it unquestionably follows that one and the same form may take part in philoprogenitiveness, in combativeness, acquisitiveness, &c.; for everything is capable of becoming a constituent part of that with which it fits, and by which it is required. It is hard to see how this is to lead to those particular elevations in the brain, and in the skull as well, which the phrenologists assume on behalf of the powers which they so illogically invent. We should sooner expect that the softer parts in the head, e.g. the eyes and ears, would be enlarged by constant exercise, and yet experience decidedly proves that they are not. It is not even true that the nerves of sight and hearing, though they are always employed when we see and hear, and are continuations of the brain, grow any larger when the psychical powers of seeing and hearing are strengthened by exercise. Naturally enough, therefore, we find no impression in the brain of that complicated tissue into which our psychical forms are woven.

§ 82. *Acquisition of Fresh Original Powers.*

"*The human soul constantly acquires fresh original powers, which are identical in nature with those which it had at first.*" This proposition expresses the fifth and last fundamental law of the soul's development (the fifth fundamental process). By this it is not implied that it is the last in point of importance; on the contrary, were it not for it, psychical development must soon come to a standstill, and this law therefore occupies almost the highest rank in importance. But as it would have been unintelligible without a previous knowledge of the other fundamental laws, we *discuss* it last, and moreover the order of these laws is, in itself, indifferent. Let us, then, carefully note the following facts.

Directly we apprehend or perceive anything, the original powers and their corresponding stimulants unite (§ 4).

Who has ever been in an exhibition of works of art or industry, in a gallery of pictures, or a museum of natural history, &c., and spent one or two hours in carefully examining the objects there, without feeling a considerable fatigue and relaxation in his visual powers? The same effect is produced on the auditory powers at a concert, if one listens to the music with close attention for several hours; the like is the case with the powers of taste and smell, when they are stimulated for a long time together; and he who has spent the day in chopping up wood, or wandered from village to village, from town to town, will not deny that his muscular powers flag considerably. In like manner we feel tired, even though the senses be unemployed, when we think of anything intently for long together, or keep our psychical forms awake and as it were in agitation by cares and anxieties, &c.

From this it is clear *that the available and unoccupied original powers decrease in proportion either as they unite with their corresponding stimulants, or are used up as movable elements.*

In both cases, of course, the soul has *gained*, and not *lost* in point of development; for in the former case new traces were formed, and in the latter the original powers are deposited on already existing traces (forms), which so far from harming, only strengthens them, and one might perhaps suppose that such an employment of these powers should produce a feeling of increased strength rather than one of fatigue. But the traces can only make their power felt while they are maintained in a state of excitation, and that implies the presence of movable elements which have not themselves the fixedness of the traces, but are able, from their movable nature, to impart to the latter a kind of impulse. This can be effected only by the free, void powers, and the general vague stimulants received into them; and consequently, on their withdrawal, the feeling of fatigue or lassitude must arise. We find the same relation subsisting between the solid and fluid parts of the body. The activity of the former is crippled if the latter are withdrawn from them. But after a sound sleep all the exhausted original powers are replaced; indeed, by the rest in which we indulge after exertion we feel refreshed, which, however, is less a proof of the acquisition of fresh original powers, than that many developed powers are under such conditions again released from their stimulants (see p. 76). Again,

I was obliged to apply my visual powers (original powers), because a number of minerals had been given me which I had to carefully observe in order to learn to distinguish one from the other. After some time I grew so tired that I was obliged to give over. But after a good night's rest I found it so easy to comprehend the whole matter that I soon mastered it.

On another occasion, I thought for a long time on a knotty point. In doing so, as we already know, original powers were consumed. I could not succeed in making the matter quite clear, but I managed to tire myself very thoroughly. In the morning I attacked it again, and, as compared with the preceding day, I handled it with far greater ease for a longer time, until at last I made it my own perfectly, and with full consciousness.

Lastly, any one who has taken part in pleasure-trips has experienced the following. If, for some time before, he had been leading a sedentary life, he found that he was really tired by the end of the first day's outing. If, however, the first exertion was not too great, and his feet were not blistered, he got on much better the second day, and so on.

It seems, then, that, *in the body as well as in the soul, the greatest number of original powers are formed exactly where the greatest number have been used up*. And it really is so: we shall presently see why. Fresh original powers are gained, if not exclusively, yet mainly during sleep. The essence of sleep does not consist in our being unconscious, but rather in an increased activity of the vital powers, by which the bodily forces used up during the day are replaced by new ones (§ 76). What these new powers are formed *out of*, if we did not already know it, we might learn from the well-known fact that inevitable death by starvation occurs if a man takes no food, and that insufficient forces are generated if a man does not eat enough, or the stomach digests badly. Hence, the body does not replace its exhausted powers purely from itself and from within *, but from the *external* materials or forces which it takes in and assimilates (§ 81).

Nor can the soul preserve itself and grow without nourishment taken in *from without*; because there is no such thing as a making something out of nothing in its case, any more than there is in that of the body: what kind of elements it requires for its preservation and sustenance we already know well enough. It is not indebted to the body for its continuance (on this point see § 83), still less for its evolution and increase, or for becoming richer, stronger, and more perfect: for all this it owes solely to those stimulants which it appropriates mainly through its visual, auditory, and tactual powers, and afterwards *internally elaborates*; and uniform experience proves, in particular, that deprivation of the impressions of light, sound, and touch, brings the life of the soul to a standstill, and prevents it from further

* This would be a reparation, a generation of something out of nothing, because the body can only give what it has, and it does not yet possess the forces which have to be repaired and supplied.

development. Now, if the soul had at starting far fewer powers than it possesses at a later period (and we have found this to be the case), the question whence those increased powers are derived hardly admits of any other answer than this: *they are engendered out of the stimulants which are received, and out of that portion of them which are appropriated with least firmness, after being subjected to the necessary transformation.* Hence, (this follows quite naturally,) **the sensible forms produced afresh** *every day* (the latest sensations and perceptions) *must be the special material whence new psychical powers are acquired.*

Now, as these freshly-generated original powers are subject to the law of diffusion, it is quite natural that immediately they are formed, and therefore during sleep, they should attach themselves mainly to those forms whose previous conscious activity has used up the largest number of old ones, and that consequently they should remain where they were produced only so long as they are not more powerfully attracted elsewhere. In the body we find the same to be the case. Forces generated in the intestines, the special centre of their formation, spread thence in all directions, but chiefly to those parts where there has been the greatest waste; so that, for instance, not the left but the right arm is considerably the stronger, if that is the one generally exercised. *These* forces, too, are distributed during sleep.

Thus the phenomena which we have mentioned may be accounted for.

It is quite consistent with what has been stated, that psychical original powers are scarcely ever produced in our waking condition, when the *largest* portion of our psychical forms are unconscious or asleep (see p. 193), but during the time when *all* conscious activity is suspended, and, therefore, only in sound sleep. For so long as the soul is consciously active, it requires the stimulants which it has received, and which remain movable, for the purpose of supporting consciousness. But it has already been shewn that when thus applied, all the stimulants are not *irrevocably* connected with the forms which they excite.

But if our fresh psychical original powers are produced in

the way described, does it not follow that the soul is a thing consisting of light, air, odour, &c.? By way of reply, I ask whether it follows that because we eat potatoes, &c., the body must needs be a thing composed of potatoes?

No doubt we are bound to assume that light, sound, &c., have affinities for the powers and forces of our soul, just as the materials of food have affinities for the powers and forces of our body. And why are we not to assume this? Is it not a fact that when the soul forms definite and precise feelings and perceptions, the external stimulant fuses into most intimate union with the original powers? Does anybody know what light, or sound, &c., are as to their *internal essence;* is not his knowledge of them limited merely to their external appearance? No doubt we are unable to say how it is that stimulants are converted into fresh original powers. Can anybody explain to me how it is that precisely the same external forces are converted in the pear-tree into pears, in the nut-tree into nuts, in the rose-bush into roses?

This is the mystery of the innermost process of life in all organized things.

Nevertheless, all evidence tends to shew that *the bodily powers also may contribute their share in the acquisition of new psychical powers.* For in the first place, the soul is perpetually abstracting something from the body, and in many conditions to such an extent that the latter visibly grows leaner, as in care, sorrow, anxiety, long-sustained severe thought[1]. The waking period is hence always the time when the body is the losing member, and this loss, by a natural law, necessarily leads to sleep (see § 76). Add to this, in the second place, that the acquisition of fresh mental powers occurs at the time when fresh powers are being acquired for the body, namely, during sleep, so that the one transformation proceeds hand in hand with the other; and thirdly, experience shews that in most diseases of the body, the original powers of the soul are more weakly formed than is the case in a state of health. Are we

[1] Children who are urged on to learn at too early an age, suffer thereby such serious bodily damage, that even death may be the consequence of it.

not justified, then, in inferring that the corporeal is a joint source of psychical forces? However, it is never more than a joint source of them: for unvarying experience proves that the strongest bodies, if tenanted from the first by a weak soul, never do strengthen the powers of that soul, and conversely, that a strong soul acquires strong powers, even though the body in which it lives be ever so weak.

Again, when, for instance, we examine a city, or any other complex object for the first time, we do not gain at the first glance anything like a perfect notion of it, not even when the object is presented to our eyes all at once; we are obliged first to examine it in detail: thus in a city we must observe its several towers, gates, lanes, houses, &c.; we must get a good daylight view of the trunk, branches, twigs, leaves, flower, fruit, &c., of a tree. It is only after these intuitions *of the several parts* have been obtained, and fused by the movable elements into a whole or group (§ 38), that we gain a perfect knowledge of an object. Compare also § 7. What is the inference to be drawn from this?

Our visual powers must have been formed in the soul each completely apart *from the other:* for if the power of sight were really *single*, there seems no reason why an object actually viewed at one glance should not be directly and immediately apprehended *in all and each of its parts.* It is of course true that we gain, even in a glance, a kind of total image of an object, and that image is clearer the more tenacious our powers are (§ 7), and more precise, individual, and exact, in proportion as they are more sensitive (§ 5): but such an effect is produced only in so far as we have already within something ready to be reproduced by this impression: a *complete and perfect* image it certainly is not. When, therefore, we find some men who are able to seize a highly complex object in a very brief time, they do so only because they already possess a larger quantity of notions corresponding to it, and because of the greater vivacity and quickness of their visual powers, by which their time is economized; but *particular* and repeated examination of the object, by which alone a *perfect* notion of the whole can be obtained, is as necessary in their case, as it is in that of those who require a longer time to apprehend it. Our visual power, then, works not as a mass, but invariably as special and individual, as it were point by point (drop by drop); and the smaller a child is, the narrower is its field of vision, and the longer is the time required by it to look over a whole; e.g. the letters in a word, which we seize in the twinkling of an eye, they are obliged to take up one after the other. Nor is the case different with the sense of hearing. In a piece of music in three or four parts, the ear only apprehends a few sounds definitely at the same time; and if a practised musician is able to do more than one who is no musician, he is indebted for that power solely to the numerous traces which simultaneously listen, and which he had to acquire one by one at some previous time: for these are able to operate more in a mass simply because they only require to be *reproduced*. The *elaboration* of the original powers, on the contrary, their union with stimulants, always takes place singly, one by one. From this we infer with justice that *the original powers are acquired by the human soul as they were at first*, singly, one by one.

But we must go a step further.

In § 24 we stated what the relation between stimulant and original powers was, and we then discovered that the former might be *too little*, *sufficient*, *very full*, or *too strong* (either suddenly or gradually too strong); all of which cases would occur, if, for instance, we were to light a room by degrees from an unsatisfactory twilight up to the most dazzling splendour, and we were to let all these light-stimulants in all their degrees successively affect our visual powers. A dim light would produce displeasure, because the stimulant would be too little for our powers; one, two, or three candles would suit them; ten, twenty, or thirty, would set them in full swing; a thousand, however, all concentrated and blazing together, would upset them: and this would not occur once or twice as a matter of chance, it would always regularly recur as often as we repeated the experiment. In the other senses, experience shews that the same thing occurs.—Hence it follows:

That our powers are from the very first exactly similar as respects their strength, i.e. *their capacity of apprehending and taking up a certain mass or amount of external stimulant*, (that is, be it well observed, the individual original powers of *one and the same system*).

It is true that in different men this power is also different (§ 80), so that one finds himself comfortable under a given stimulant which would be too much for another; but in the *same* man these powers are all alike, so far as they belong to the same system. If this were not so, if their strength were different, or if they formed a whole in which the individuality of each was obliterated, how would the phenomena above-mentioned be possible? how would it be possible that stimulants, in proportion to their strength, should produce effects so different (dislike, pain, pleasure, &c.)? Whilst a strong stimulant would always be weak when applied to a collective power or mass of powers, it might easily happen, with *unequally* strong individual powers, that a weaker stimulant came into contact with a weak power, a stronger stimulant with a stronger power, and the Mutual Attraction of Similars would certainly prove so favourable to this result, that stimulant and power could but rarely be at discord. But in that case how could there be such a thing as disgust or pain?

When we are unwell it often happens that we cannot bear the glare of ordinary daylight, or the ordinary sound of the voices of those around us. This fact harmonizes entirely with the account which we have given of our original powers: for we see from it that *in many cases of sickness* the fresh powers are *proportionably* depressed: as a consequence of the malady, those that are generated are weaker either *in all*, or only *in some systems*. It is noticeable that at such times the vital powers, which are the support of the mental, are below their ordinary strength.

If we now gather up all that we have said about the acquisition of fresh original powers, we arrive at the following results:—

1°. fresh original powers are acquired mainly during sleep.

2°. where most original powers have been used up, there most are generated.

3°. they are formed, by some kind of transmutation (which constitutes the most secret process of life in the soul as well as in all organized things,) from a portion of the stimulant taken up, and therefore

4°. the special centre for the formation of fresh original powers are the newly-produced sense-forms (§ 4), and in like manner

5°. the bodily forces contribute their share to the formation of fresh original powers,

6°. the original powers are formed in the soul, as at the first, singly, one by one, and

7°. all of them that belong to one and the same class, or one and the same system, are exactly similar as respects their strength (magnitude) and qualities. They deserve the name of "original powers" because, though of later growth, they do not differ either in essence or in operation from those really original and primitive powers of which the soul consists at birth.

Visual power, auditory power, &c., in the singular number, ought only to be employed when we speak of the power of sight, &c., *in abstracto*, and wish to express ourselves in the most general terms. In like manner, 'original power' in the singular is only allowable when we really mean some individual definite single power.

In the production of these fresh original powers it is very possible that forces may co-operate which are, at the time, completely unknown to us, because they lie too deep to have been brought to light by any observations on the soul that we may have been able to make up to that time.

§ 83. *Final and Necessary Separation of Soul from Body, Death: Continuance of the Soul after Death.*

If a trace is left by every thing that takes place in the soul with any approach to perfection, and if such a trace is always associated with those resembling it that have already been formed, *the soul must be continually increasing in internal strength up to the very moment of death.*

Is this borne out by experience? Apparently not, at least not always: for we find that not the mentally weak only, but not unfrequently mentally strong souls also fall, at an advanced age, into a condition of *Idiocy*. Now, although numbers may be instanced who, up to the last moment of advanced old age, shew no such symptoms, still that does not do away with the other and opposite fact. Thus much, however, is obvious at first sight, that this kind of Idiocy, which is completely different from the *congenital* form of it, must be based, not on some law of nature, but on something accidental and contingent, for otherwise it would constantly occur in all old people. At any rate, we must consider this as well as other phenomena of age somewhat more narrowly.

Any one who has been moderately attentive to what passes within him must admit that there are occasional periods in his life when mental activity is all but impossible. One's head seems at such times as void of thoughts as though it had come into existence but yesterday. After a busy day such moments are not uncommon. Strive as you will to reflect on an object, still all remains dark and unconscious. In many maladies this is so much the case, that the patient seems to do little more than vegetate.

But as soon as these conditions have passed away, the soul is again exactly *the same;* active, vigorous, strong as it was before. Hence that weakness, that impotence, can in no wise have affected the *interior*, the centre of the soul; it cannot have touched those forms (the so-called "inner substance of the soul") which make up its peculiar essence: for in that case, by what magic could it directly afterwards have become again exactly *the same* as it was *before* that weakness? We have already met with the true cause of such passing weaknesses in § 13, and discovered that it is to be found solely *in the deficiency of void unemployed original powers and general vague stimulants*, since they are the elements which excite our *unconscious* psychical forms *into consciousness.* For *without excitation the strongest and clearest psychical forms are, for us, as good as non-existent.* Consequently, a deficiency in the elements of consciousness must always produce *a stoppage in the current of our thoughts* (§ 76).

After a hard day's work there is directly a deficiency of void original powers, because almost all of them have been used up in forming traces, and the necessary result of this is that no general stimulants can any longer be taken up, for that is absent in which alone they can take up their residence. The same must be the case in many maladies, where either the formation of new powers is impeded, or some damage is done to the *connecting* traces. The latter is notably the case where, in some violent sickness, the whole memory (as people call it) appears to be so deranged, that the patient on recovering, has to learn to read, write, cipher, &c., over again. But as experience has always proved, they are all learnt with remarkable quickness, so that after a few weeks' work that is again produced, i.e. active, which before it took years to acquire. The malady, therefore, only affected what was constructed out of movable elements, namely the *associations* and *connexions* between the psychical forms, and not the forms themselves so connected. But how affected? Did it dissolve them? No! it merely, through weakness or impediment, so damaged them that the exciting movable elements which are directed by the connecting traces were unable any longer to find access to those forms directly after the illness. The moment this damage is repaired by fresh movable elements which revivify the dispositions favourable to such connexions, the forms themselves return in all their freshness back into consciousness. Hence there is nothing inexplicable in the above-mentioned attacks of idiocy, or in an incapacity for mental exertion: *it appears that they are only stoppages in the process by which our psychical forms* become conscious, *produced partly by a deficiency of movable elements, partly by damage done to the connecting traces.*

Now, if we should be able to shew that as we get older those elements must needs decrease, we should at once have an explanation of the idiocy which sometimes accompanies advanced age, and we should have proved that *it is no weakening of the interior substance of the soul, but merely a defective excitation of our psychical forms.*

If we observe a child, we find it almost entirely the slave of external stimulants. A fly on the wall destroys its attention, and a cart passing by the window attracts its eyes towards it. It resists impressions of pain just as little as it does those of pleasure, it is equally the captive of either.

A boy is already far less dependent on external stimulants. He can endure pain and abstain from pleasure, he can in general withdraw his attention at will from external things, and he begins to elaborate the knowledge he has already gained in a more independent manner.

A mature man occupies himself by preference with what he has already acquired, and is often only with difficulty open to the reception of new truths, especially when they run counter to his former notions: hence it is that among all classes of men who have attained this age, we so frequently find an attachment to the usual and beaten path. In old age this is very much more the case: and of many we say that they are dead to the world.

The following observations will reveal the cause of these phenomena.

When we meet agriculturalists, what is their favourite topic of conversation? Agriculture. Go into the company of teachers, and you will find that education is the staple of their talk. Go amongst physicians, theologians, botanists; listen to merchants, mechanics, soldiers, &c., and see whether their conversation does not mainly turn on their respective occupations. It is so, nor can it be otherwise; for that which is *strongest, that which is based on the largest number of traces* in our soul *must be the easiest to rise into consciousness.* And this is the case with all men as respects notions relating to their daily occupations: such are *nearest to consciousness* (see p. 207). Now since our psychical forms can only be made conscious by the addition of movable elements, we see *that these movable elements flow to or are attracted in the largest amount by those psychical forms which are strongest in the soul, or which rest on the largest number of traces.* Compare on this §§ 73—75.

This explains the phenomena instanced above.

In the child's soul, there *are* as yet no forms based on numerous traces, and hence the movable elements are not particularly attracted by any, *consequently their original powers are free and open to the influence and reception of external stimulants,* they abandon themselves to such. In the boy the strength of his psychical forms is already considerably greater, and therefore the movable elements are far more attracted to them, and to rendering them conscious, and are in the same proportion drawn away from external impressions. Briefly: *The more the psychical forms increase in the number of their traces* (*in strength*), *the more are the movable elements applied to rendering them conscious, and the more they are withdrawn from the reception of fresh impressions.*

Hence, the man of mature age is far more disposed to elaborate and use what he already knows, than to apply himself to acquire new information, or aptitudes; whilst the old man has almost entirely broken with the external world, he lives rather in the past than in the present. *Therefore, the strength of the internal substance of the soul, which increases as we grow older, ipso facto produces a decrease in the formation of* new *feelings and perceptions.*

But still more follows from it. We are aware not merely that the movable elements consist of void original powers and of internal stimulants, (either quite vague and general, or only loosely appropriated) (§ 30), but also that the former (the original powers) are formed by some mysterious transformation out of a portion of that *stimulant* which is taken up and still remains movable, that consequently the newly-produced feelings and perceptions (§ 82) must be regarded as the special centre and place where fresh original powers are formed. Now what must happen when the larger number of these original powers are no longer able to take up stimulants, in consequence of having been exhausted by bringing into consciousness those forms which are now more abundant in traces, and which therefore call for a larger amount of the movable elements?

It was proved in the last § that a total exclusion of external stimulants must produce a total cessation in the formation of fresh original powers; consequently, both sources of the movable elements must gradually dry up, in proportion as a larger number of original powers are applied to this purpose: external stimulants are taken up in *a decreasing amount*, and as a consequence, fresh original powers are only formed in *smaller numbers.*

But more than that. It is an almost universal fact that old people complain of the badness of their memory (§§ 7 and 75). They have a complete and clear recollection of what they saw and did thirty, forty, or fifty years ago, but what they saw and heard just now they often forget after the briefest interval. According to this, the original powers generated in old age are not only less numerous, but also *less tenacious.* Thus each circumstance helps the other: *external stimulants are taken up in continually decreasing numbers, and the body also which has become deadened and decayed is continually less able to assist in the formation of new psychical powers.* What other result then can follow, than that *the movable elements should constantly become less, and that one kind of them* (the original powers) *should become continually more and more imperfect?*

Now if the internal nature of our soul is excited and rendered conscious by these movable elements, ought we to wonder that when they decrease the current of thought is less rapid, less comprehensive, or that at last the most cultivated soul retains in conscious existence but a few scattered psychical forms*? *In this consists the Idiocy of age.*

It is, therefore, not in the least a consequence of any *decrease* in the strength *of the internal substance of the soul* (of its forms), but is rather an effect of its *continually increasing strength.*

Experience confirms this conclusion by numerous cases. Thus we are told of *Kant*, "that at the time of his greatest weakness, when he was unable to express himself intelligibly about the commonest things, he gave astonishingly correct and precise answers when questioned about matters of physical geography, natural history and chemistry, as well as about learned subjects in general."

Now, if the *internal substance of his soul* had been affected by

* Law: *a psychical form can only be conscious when and for so long as it is excited*, (see p. 190).

this weakness, how would such answers have been possible? Must not the more difficult have been destroyed before the easy? And yet we see that, notwithstanding his extreme weakness in other respects, it was exactly the most difficult that was manifested with its wonted strength and clearness, although he was unable to give any account of objects around him which he had only seen the minute before, &c. Is not this astounding? Not in the least: it only proves that the powers which were then generated in him were very weak, so weak, indeed, that impressions just made were either not retained by them at all, or only so feebly that he could not attain to a consciousness of them.

But few aged men retain their mental vigour till within a short period before death, because few enjoy such a happy constitution of body that it causes no essential diminution in the elements which excite the soul. In most men, when arrived at old age, there is a progressive decrease in the power of taking up light, sound, &c., because the organs of sensation get less and less able to perform their functions and to assist the soul in its.

We have, then, arrived at these conclusions:

1°. *that the soul constantly increases in internal strength up to the moment of death;*

2°. *that this very increase in strength produces a constant diminution in the movable elements* (original powers and stimulants), and that, consequently,

3°. *the* alternation *of consciousness* (not consciousness itself, § 71) *is more and more impeded, until at last*, when the formation of fresh psychical powers is brought to a stand-still by the same cause, *it stops altogether*, and the soul abandons the body in the society of which it is no longer able to increase its powers, and, consequently, is unable to make any progress. *This is that death which is necessitated by nature;* death from disease requires no explanation. In both cases, however, the man dies; not 'because life (a special vital force) leaves him,' but because the soul leaves the body, though in so doing the soul by no means ceases to live.

What reason, then, is there for holding the continued existence of the soul *after* death? *Its constant increase in strength up to the moment of death.*

The body grew, was consolidated in consequence of the increase in the number of its traces, but then it again became weak, and both processes took place gradually. It gradually increased, and as gradually decreased. Is not this last circumstance very strange? No; we are not astonished to find that, in accordance with the laws which constructed it, it grows less, and at last crumbles into dust. For as the increase of its powers, unlike that of the soul, implies increase in space, and since the limit of *external bulk* is reached, at the latest, at the age of twenty-five, a limit which it is impossible for it to transcend[1], it necessarily follows that, as it never ceases to grow, i.e. to form traces, it must increase in *solidity* (§ 81); since these traces, as they are accumulated, press more closely one on the other. This explanation is justified by the fact, that the desire for food and drink and digestion continue, though not with the same strength, as a rule, up to the most advanced period of life: this would not have been the case if the body, when formed, merely required to be *preserved*. The elements which vanish day by day might be replaced by a considerably less amount of food than we are compelled to take.

The necessary consequence, then, of all this is, that the organized parts of the body (the limbs), which are formed out of these traces, gradually grow harder and ossify, by which their *nutrition* (formation, acquisition of fresh movable powers) is gradu-

---

[1] As the size of the several members of the body, e.g. the eyes, ears, hands, fingers, &c., is fixed beforehand (predetermined) in that innate constitution with which we are created*—a limitation which can never be transcended—so for the body, as a whole, is determined beforehand what degree of extension it shall inevitably reach, and disease alone can cause any change in it.

* ["Wie im Angebornen vorherbestimmt (prädeterminirt) ist, welches Mass der Grösse die einzelnen Glieder des Leibes . . . . annehmen sollen." He means that, from the very first moment of our existence in the womb, the size, shape, number, &c., of our limbs is, in some way or other, fore-ordained. He holds a kind of physical predestination, only limited by disease, itself predestined].

ally diminished; because, though the soft appropriates and assimilates the fluid with ease, yet the hard, being dissimilar from the fluid, is constantly less capable of doing so. By this process of hardening it loses its power of retaining movable elements: the body becomes constantly poorer in fluid elements, and therefore lighter in weight. Hence, the formation of bodily traces and powers, *though it never quite ceases*, proceeds at a slower rate and less perfectly; and this is the reason why, in our later years, sleep diminishes more and more (see § 76), and simultaneously a decrease of appetite takes place. In particular it is the brain that shrivels up more and more, and loses its power of supporting the soul. The final result of this must be, to render the body a perfectly useless tool or minister for the soul, which can derive no more assistance from the constituents of it now that they have become so rude and coarse. It depends on the peculiar combination between the properties of its powers, or, in other words, on the temperament of the body (see § 80), whether this result follows at an earlier or later period (in extreme old age), though the temperament of the psychical powers must have an important influence on it as well. The separation, then, of the soul from the body is a necessary result, but it takes place only *because we are always growing*, i.e. are always forming fresh traces both in soul and in body. As the rising and setting of the sun is the result of one and the same law, the law that the earth revolves on its axis; as summer and winter are produced by the one immutable law that the earth revolves round the sun, so also the rise and decay of corporeal perfection depends on one and the self-same law, that of growth. Since this law incessantly operates in body and soul alike; since it never varies, never gives place to another; since, moreover, the chemical laws, to which matter is subject, remain invariably the same, it follows that their *results* must gradually become more and more different, and *chemical agency, which was at first our friend, must necessarily become more and more our enemy* (see p. 243). This agency continually renders the body more dry and brittle, less elastic, because continually poorer in fluid elements, and hence it must gradually become less vigorous, more weak and perishable, so that at last death must result on the side of the body (compare p. 267).

But the soul also grew, and became *continually stronger and stronger*, yet without in the least extending itself locally: what can dissolve and destroy it when it separates from the body? The separation and dissolution of *its own constituent parts* alone could prove its death and annihilation; its separation from the body does not kill it. Experience, of course, does not enable us to give a more precise account of the matter, and we freely allow that the immortality of the soul does not admit of being proved as the correctness of a sum in arithmetic does. For all that, however, we can never grant that we are justified in estimating the fate of the soul from that of the body, or of material forces in general, seeing that it really consists of totally different powers from theirs. At last the question comes to this, *whether God designs to preserve our soul or not?* But all the facts of experience cry aloud *that He does design it*. Even the one fact, that He elevates the soul over all present existences, not by making it grow weaker, but stronger, must convince every unprejudiced person that such is His intention. Or are we to say that the soul will perish because it is not *simple*, but infinitely complex? Every one who thinks with clearness must allow that it would be far easier to destroy the former than the latter, in case the Almighty designed to destroy it at all: human experience, at least, shews that while one arrow may be easily broken, a bundle of them may bid defiance to the greatest strength; and that a fibre of wood is destructible in a manner very different from that in which a stem consisting of millions of fibres is. No doubt the soul developes only in the society of a body destined to support it, and we have no knowledge of any soul capable, as God is, of existing without a body; and hence it might seem that on losing its body the soul must necessarily be dissolved. But the soul supports and bears the body much more than the body supports and bears the soul[7]; and as the body acts as a support to it, so,

---

[7] He who desires to live to a good old age must preserve his mental calmness; and he who dies, as people say, 'of a broken heart,' is one whose death

in many cases, it impedes and perturbs it to such an extent as to produce madness. May we not justly infer from this, that the soul will meet with a happier lot, as soon as it can get loose from its doubtful companion, 'the body?' At the same time, these disturbances in the body are never *disturbances* for the soul, for healthy psychical life returns in a moment, when the material cause of the disturbance is removed; and there are instances where madmen, after long years of derangement, have recovered their sound, clear consciousness a short time before their death. The inference from all this is, that it is completely inconceivable that the material body can cause the death of the soul; whether we regard merely the *loss* of the body, or any influence which it may be supposed to exercise on the soul during our last moments. Indeed, we have, in this respect, nothing to fear from the material. Is it possible that the unextended can be annihilated by the extended, at a moment when the former no longer possesses any powers capable of being affected by the latter? Is it not the *original powers* of the soul alone which are susceptible to sensible material impressions? And as the soul is still able to grow when the brain decreases with age, and loses in bulk and weight; since, moreover, as we saw at the end of § 75, the results of seeing and hearing still continue after eyes and ears have been destroyed; since, lastly, large portions of the brain have been found destroyed, without any sign during life of any impediment or disturbance in mental functions,—how can we regard the immortality of the soul as imperilled, when, in addition to these nobler parts, it loses in death those which are less noble? All that it requires for new life, i.e. new activity, is simply new sources of exciting and supporting elements, which the Creator will then give it, and then it becomes again the same soul that it was before, beautiful or ugly, good or bad, rich or poor, according to the development which it had attained to here below.

---

was caused by his soul. Terror and exaggerated joy, when they kill, kill always through the soul. "Sorrow and care make us old before our time." From examples like these, one may see clearly how greatly the body is dependent on the soul.

As to the circumstances under which this renewed life of soul will take place, we can, at best, form no more than gue and conjectures; but this much is beyond dispute, that devel ment and progress will be as little denied it there as here, that that progress can only tend to ennoble it. The acquisit of fresh, original powers will certainly then be effected bet and with greater ease, than in this world, since its future cumstances will, at any rate, furnish it with better materi than it could obtain here. Let us wait hopefully; we sh know all this by-and-by.

§ 84. *Recapitulation.*

I. The Original Powers of the Human Soul.

The human soul is distinguished from the body, and from other forces upon earth, by its *unextendedness* and *higher stren and tenacity*. On Force and Matter (§ 81).

Moreover, on this higher tenacity of the psychical pow depends the rise of *consciousness* (§ 71), and *the rationality* of t human soul (which, at a later period, leads to Reason), a spec *quality*, distinguishing it from all brute souls (§ 79), and a no less degree the perfection of its *Memory* (§ 75). Great *Vivacity* produces more perfect *Recollection*, whereas great *Sensibility* leads to greater power of *Imagination* (§ 75). T various modes in which the three different qualities of the orig nal powers are combined, produce general differences in men *developed* psychical character: on these combinations depen what is called *Temperament*, and as such combinations are in nitely various, so are men's temperaments endlessly divers What truth is there, then, in the old division of all temper ments into *four* classes? (§ 80.) If psychical forms are arous into consciousness merely by *void original powers*, the result *voluntary* consciousness (§ 72). What are *involuntary sugge tions?* (§ 74.)

II. Stimulants of the External World.

Those stimulants which are not permanently appropriated b the original powers, are, by some secret and mysterious tran formation, converted during sleep into fresh original power

The amount of freshly formed powers varies always in proportion to the amount of such stimulants appropriated, so that, if they are totally withheld or not taken up, there is a total cessation in the formation of fresh psychical powers (§§ 82 and 83). If any psychical form is excited into consciousness purely by *internal* or *external* stimulants, it is said to become conscious *involuntarily* (§ 72). Why is it that external stimulants are more certain to excite consciousness than is the case with the internal and void original powers? (§ 72). Memory, Recollection, and Imaginary Notions are more perfect in proportion as the stimulant producing the psychical form is more perfect and full (§ 75).

III. The Fundamental Laws Regulating the Development of the Soul.

1. The Law of the Appropriation of Stimulants.

It is thus expressed:

The Soul forms sensuous feelings and perceptions in consequence of the impressions or stimulants which it receives from without. With this is connected the universal law, *that whatever is produced in the soul with any approach to perfection continues to exist in it as a Trace.* These are the two laws, without which neither Memory, nor Recollection, nor Imagination (§ 75), nor increase in *strength* (§ 83), nor any permanence in the soul, would be possible (§§ 82 and 83), just as it would be impossible that the bodily forces should continue unless they appropriated external forces (food), and the latter were retained. The same laws prevail also in the body (§ 81).

2. The Law of the mutual Attraction of Similars.

It is thus expressed:

All products of a like kind attract each other, and as a consequence fuse into a whole.

By this, consciousness becomes constantly clearer and clearer (§ 71), all psychical forms grow stronger, and hence, more permanent and less easy to be lost (§ 75). Concepts engender constantly higher concepts, and we arrive at what we call *Reason* (§ 79): by this, in particular, the *subjectively* homogeneous (the merely similar powers) in the internal processes of the soul fus into special concepts, which (as "internal senses") cause interna perception (§ 77); by this, moreover, the concept of I, or the Ego which never leads to selfishness, arises out of the notion of sel (§ 78): in one word, this law collects and reduces to orde whatever enters the soul in obedience to the first law.

The same law plays a no less important part in the develop ment of the body (§ 81).

3°. The Law of the Disappearance of Stimulants. It is thus expressed:

A portion of the Stimulant which is (not firmly) appropriate perpetually disappears from the original powers.

It may be asked whether what disappears vanishes from the Soul. That which is actually taken up certainly does not do so: on the contrary, the stimulants which afterwards get loose from the traces, besides forming a portion of the movable element (§ 30), are also applied to the acquisition of fresh original powers (§ 82). Hence this law, so far as it causes stimulants to become movable, coincides with the next. In the body it prevails also (§ 81), only that then what vanishes is deposited in the external world.

4°. The Law of the Diffusion of the Movable Elements. It is thus expressed:

While we are awake the movable powers are perpetually transplanted from one psychical form to another; they are diffused (transferred) over them, and thus act as connecting elements.

Thus is produced the constant *alternation* of consciousness in the Soul (§ 71), which follows the *direction* in which the several psychical forms were previously connected most intimately with each other, and rendered one by the fixture of the movable elements (§ 73). Laws of Association (§ 74): thus also is produced Attention (§§ 71 and 73), and that defective consciousness of series and groups of forms during sleep, which we call 'dreaming' (§ 76); it is thus that those forms are connected together which constitute our notion (perception) of ourselves (§ 78); it is thus that groups and series of forms of the most extensive kind are formed, having for their objects our internal and external processes (§§ 77 and 79). As this law also prevails in bodily developments, it explains the reciprocal action of Soul and Body (§ 81), the body being not mere dead matter, but instinct with living forces in divers degrees.

5°. **The Law of the Acquisition of Fresh Original Powers.** It is thus expressed:

Soul and Body are continually forming fresh powers identical in nature with those which they originally possessed.

They are acquired mainly during sleep. For sleep essentially consists in the preponderance of the bodily powers of appropriation over mental developments, the latter being at that time deficient in the movable elements necessary to render them conscious (§ 76).

Where the largest number of original powers have been used up, there the largest number of fresh ones are formed both in soul and body.

The original powers of the Soul are produced by some mysterious transformation out of that portion of the stimulant received which remains unfixed and movable, just as the forces of the body are engendered out of the external materials (forces) prepared in the stomach and intestines; and hence the newly-produced sense-feelings and perceptions must be regarded as the pecial centre and focus where fresh psychical original powers are formed. Since during our waking hours stimulants are used for the purpose of supporting consciousness, it follows that they must be transformed into new powers, for the most part during sleep.—The powers of the body also contribute their share to the formation of fresh psychical powers.

The original powers of the soul are formed from the first *singly, one apart from the other*, and all that belong to one class (system) are, as regards their *magnitude* (strength) and *qualities, completely similar* one to another.

Since, however, in proportion as psychical forms become stronger, they attract a greater number of void original powers to enable them to become conscious, which causes a corresponding diminution in the number of external *stimulants* taken up; since, moreover, the forces of the body, as life proceeds, become continually more stiff, and prone to decay, and therefore constantly less able to contribute to the acquisition of fresh original powers, it follows that with increasing age the formation of them gradually diminishes, the fresh original powers become progressively less in number and weaker in force. This is the cause of that Idiocy which often accompanies old age[a], and of the final and necessary separation of soul and body (§§ 82 and 83). What reason is there to believe that the soul continues to exist after Death? (§ 83.)

The five laws above enunciated as the *Fundamental Laws* of the human soul (see the note on p. 52) lead to *derivative* and secondary laws, in so far as they operate afresh upon that which was produced in accordance with them. The new results produced from what was previously generated constantly assume new forms, and they are a necessary result of these laws of development. Take, for instance, the derivative law of the strengthening of consciousness depending on the fundamental law of the coalition of the homogeneous (p. 22); the derivative law of the formation of Feelings; of the connexion of forms by movable elements, &c. What is the difference between Force and Law? (see the note on p. 52). The fundamental laws of bodily development can only be clearly known and understood from an acquaintance with the laws of the soul (§ 81).

The remark made at the end of the third part (p. 179) is justified by the conclusions at which we have arrived here, viz. that the powers within us which think, judge, infer, fancy, will, feel, &c., are no others than those which at the very first, saw, heard, felt, &c., only that they are differently applied and modified, and the general result is, that *the developed human soul is a product of simple original powers, and of that which has affected them and been permanently retained by them.*

---

[a] There is *congenital* idiocy, as well as idiocy which is the *result of disease;* both are to be distinguished from that mentioned in the text, and depend on other causes. On congenital idiocy, see p. 70, and *Beneke's* Lehrbuch der Psychol., § 395 sqq.

PRINTED BY JAMES PARKER AND CO., CROWN-YARD, OXFORD.

CPSIA information can be obtained
at www.ICGtesting.com
Printed in the USA
LVHW030128210323
742063LV00002B/547

9 783382 126629